# THE BURNING OF THE ROSE

# THE BURNING of the ROSE

### Ruth Nichols

ST. MARTIN'S PRESS
NEW YORK

THE BURNING OF THE ROSE. Copyright © 1989 by Ruth Nichols. All rights reserved. Printed in the United States of America. No part of this book may be used or reproduced in any manner whatsoever without written permission except in the case of brief quotations embodied in critical articles or reviews. For information, address St. Martin's Press, 175 Fifth Avenue, New York, N.Y. 10010.

Design by Susan Hood

Library of Congress Cataloging-in-Publication Data

Nichols, Ruth.
    The burning of the rose / Ruth Nichols.
      p.    cm.
    ISBN 0-312-03299-4
    I. Title.
PR9199.3.N496B87   1989
813'.5—dc20                                               89-30429

First edition
1 3 5 7 9 10 8 6 4 2

# THE BURNING OF THE ROSE

# 1

To Monseigneur Jean d'Aubry,
comte de Saint-Aurèle

>From The New House
at Saint-Aurèle
in the duchy of Normandy
October 1461

My beloved lord,

Two days before I was murdered you laid on me a penance, to be fulfilled at your pleasure when I was well enough to bear it. Your Grace has a long memory; that night is now seven years ago. *The story as I lived it:* That is all you asked.

In that case I require you to keep these papers secret. And one other thing. Seven years has given me time to question, to assess, to understand. I will quote conversations as though I had overheard them. No word I write must pass to your friends or to your heirs. I know that you, sir, love truth even more than you love honor or kindness; and so I begin without fear.

My name is Claire Tarleton—or, in the Franco-Italian that comes most easily to the tongues of many of my friends, Claire

Tallon. I have kept enough English both to speak it and to answer naturally to the name. My father also is indifferently Walter Tarleton or Gautier Tallon. My mother calls him Walter. Absurd, but no more so than the mix of language and blood that has mingled English with Norman over a century of war. As for the surname with which I was originally born, let it lie buried with my real parents, in a plague-pit in London.

My foster parents, Elisabeth du Pléssis and Walter Tarleton, adopted me when I was two. By that time I suppose they must have guessed their union would be barren. I have always pitied, since they love each other, that lack of children of their own. I am an only child—shy; blunt and honest like my mother; slow to develop and, once I have seized a talent or a love, abnormally tenacious. I do not know whether I have brilliant gifts: any precocity, like any failure, was early overlaid by the care with which my parents trained me. They schooled me to earn my own living, as an artist's model and as a musician. I have worked since I was five. Not that my parents had need of money—Elisabeth after all possessed the estates in Normandy that ultimately drew us northward when war threatened Italy—but both my parents worship and enjoy work.

As to the modeling for painters, it was chaste and came early, at the suggestion of Walter's artist friends in Paris. I have dark hair, full dark lips, a sloping jaw, and the short straight nose required by the classic canons of proportion. My eyes are a luminous yellow-brown ringed with gray. I was ten years old, and Walter had received a respectful request across the supper table, when my father informed me I was pretty. He made it clear that this, like my gift with languages and my excellence at music, was an asset to be used—if possible, compounded, but only by honest means. My father is a merchant in his soul—what of his soul he can spare from his love of scholarship. He and Elisabeth agree excellently together. She taught me to be elegant; perhaps it will not surprise Your Grace that I was never allowed to be vain.

I am, then, not a noblewoman. I am the kind of musician—reserved, protected by her own servants, professionally exquisite—who entertains at the best of Your Grace's parties. A noblewoman must not be quite so skilled: too much skill implies a need to earn one's bread. My parents taught me also to be chaste, since they knew that, if the plague took them, I would be left alone, unless I happened to marry very young, which they rightly did not desire. The unchastity of artists' models is, wrongly, a byword; and they knew that for a young woman alone, the descent is easy. Gentlemen, unless cleverly handled, do not marry women of my birth. My father always hoped I would marry a painter or a goldsmith.

Of my babyhood with my real parents I have a few memories. Walter and Elisabeth, just arrived from France, risked plague in taking me. As it was my parents lay dead in the house and no one would come near us, and I had eaten no food for several days. Elisabeth says it was a month before she could coax a word from me, or discover whether I had learned to talk at all.

You have known Elisabeth, sir, since you were children together, and you will not imagine I am describing a saint. But a stoic practical charity is part of her nature, and my real father had been Walter's friend at the Sorbonne. He was a painter. I gather he had failed at Court, and the house from which my new foster parents took me was very poor.

An original darkness; and then light that explodes along three themes. Music and beauty and the pagan scholarship that has only in the past century (more, now Constantinople has fallen to the Turks) begun to reach us from the East: these formed the cradle into which I woke. Elisabeth nursed me with them, along with the pap of eggs and crumbled cheese, wine and honey with which she tried to tease my appetite—working against my inarticulate terror. My first baby words were polyglot, and I learned the argot of all such households, dropping from French to English to Italian as the rhythm of our thoughts carried us. It was Elisabeth who taught me texture, running my palms over the figured velvets she cut out for us both with her maids in her sewing room. It was she who taught me to cook—how to roast a joint and candy violets and make a potpourri of rosebuds and dried lavender. She taught me, also, how to fill the fireplaces in hot weather with baskets of irises and dried grass, and in winter with seasoned fruitwood; how to have the servants cover the scrubbed tiles with fresh herbs in season, so that every step crushed out their fragrance.

She nourished our bodies carefully. The doctors have at last discovered, of course, that the plague kills fewer among those who are well fed and well housed. She had a temper that could show itself in a brief, curbed but wounding sarcasm; but it was not temper that made her order whipped every servant who left the privy without washing his hands, with soap, at the pump in the inner court. I may as well remark, what Your Grace will remember, that she is very pretty, with a girl's freckled face and blonde hair streaked with white, and the schooled good nature of women who have a temper to control.

I think she tried, too, to give me color. I always had my paint pots and my stubs of graphite wrapped around with string, and played with them as children will, on sheets of rag paper or scraped-down parchment, the monks' farm records sometimes still faintly shining through the pictures I drew. She asked me to *think* what colors of cloth (always the best set out for my choosing and my handling) might suit my coloring and the purpose of the gown: Was it for a music lesson, for performance in public, for Mass, or for playing with my friends? (I had too few friends: I was intelligent and shy and highly trained, and occasionally across the table I would catch between my parents glances of hesitant, ambiguous inquiry.) Once for Christmas there were two tiny vials of gold and silver paint, each with its own camel-hair brush, small for my hand.

When we went to church she would linger beneath the windows, often watching as a glazier (the priests kept several on the payroll, for people were always breaking panes) glued into its place within the cames a new square of amber, emerald, crimson, or indigo. Sometimes at the sight of these colors she would cry silently, without ostentation, without explanation. I think the indigo meant something private to her: She kept a few shards of this color, salvaged from the church floor, propped where she could look at them.

She gave me much. Perhaps I am still trying in some ways to free myself from her. But I was different enough that I could afford to pay in absolute loyalty my debt to Elisabeth. And I was equally my father's child.

I will talk about Walter presently, but the thought of him somehow suggests the other conditions into which all those who now live were born, within which we will die: the plague and war.

I was born, like my parents and grandparents, into the knowledge that war was permanent. England and France had long since ceased to understand the nominal claim to a throne that had locked them into an embrace like a palsy, at intervals exhaustedly renewed. The kings who began it had died; and the grandchildren of their soldiers still crossed the Channel—the French to burn Dover, the English to win back Normandy by destroying it. Now each French and English family had its private grief to avenge, and upon the original causes were piled the habits of war. Burned villages were rebuilt, or—if the latest band of armed horsemen left the villagers no time—they and their beasts took shelter in underground tunnels, or in barges moored in the river. One chronicler pleaded that the farmer, without whom we all starve, might at least be let alone; but I have seen people die of hunger during the panics in Paris. Abbeys were fortified like castles, and soldiers manned their walls. Every man, even every priest could fight. People died young, as I suppose they always will.

The war began long before my birth. Long before it too, and marking me in ways I cannot trace because no doubt they seem natural, had come the visitation that killed half Europe in six months. There had been rumors, I gather, from India and China of some appalling sickness, but no one had thought it could cross distances so vast. When it did (carried how? by dirt? in the air we breathe?) people died, their armpits and groins distended with grape-colored swellings and their souls with a strange despair of God: some within three days, some between sleeping and waking, some doctors before the astonished eyes of their patients. "In case any member of the race of Adam shall survive," wrote one Irish monk, "I write this in record of our sufferings."

Cattle and sheep caught it too and rotted where they fell—I have heard, fifty thousand beasts dead in one single field. The woods reclaimed tilled land, and wolves, though they had grown bold and numerous, would not touch the infected carrion. "Plague and the English brought back the forests," they say in Normandy. And Petrarch cried out to us, his descendants: "O happy posterity, for whom our suffering shall be but a fable!"

I have survived the plague that killed my real parents: starved though I was I took no infection, so I do not think I shall die in a future epidemic. In the past several generations it has returned less frequently and has killed mainly the children.

Walter had told me that the Danse Macabre—the Dance of Death—only at this time began to be inscribed on the walls of churches. And funeral effigies too changed from a stone repose to a secret riot almost sensual.

I remember one such mockery—as if both the sculptor and the man who hired him had wished to vent their own anguish by tormenting with terror, by arousing every secret doubt in those who lived after. I was eight; we had gone, Walter and I, to see a friend, a stonecarver making a rood screen, at some church in Paris whose name I cannot remember. The table tomb attracted me first by its beauty. The girl's name had been Victoire. By rising on tiptoe I could see her: young lips, eyelids almond-smooth, her forehead clear as a child's beneath the stone reproduction of its beaded cap; and from her enameled sleeves, modestly rising to the second finger joint, her two hands spired in prayer.

I dropped to my knees, dirtying palms and velvet on the flagstones, to find the secret behind the grille. The sculptor had hidden it teasingly, a shadow within the bronze-wire rosettes that meshed the base of the tomb. The same girl degraded, naked, shrunken, worms carved over the hands that guarded her pubis below the sculpted ribs.

I had seen death before, stinking and blackened, nailed above the city gates; my father always ordered me not to look. My russet velvet filthied, I hugged my knees. "Walter, are graveworms a special kind?"

"They are earthworms, child, and their work is to return to Earth what belongs to her. The same soft pink things you knot around your fishhook: no worse. Stand up, your hands are filthy." He drew me out into the porch, scrubbing at my palms with his handkerchief. Finally he gave it up, and we sat there gazing out over the tombs. By the church wall grew a pear tree.

He was in his mid-forties then, and he had been a handsome man. I sensed the passion that existed between him and Elisabeth, and was to realize as I grew that the powerful body, the hunched shoulders, and graying hair still attracted many women. Both mouth and nose were sharp, his blue eyes hard, his bluff voice falsely tentative. Now he reached up and nimbly plucked down the lowest pear. "Look at this."

I did: a fragrant, freckled globe, swelling downward like my lute or like the line of a woman's hips. "*This* is dead flesh, Claire. All honest men and women pay their debts. God gives us a soul; Earth clothes that soul with flesh. When we die she takes that flesh and makes it into pear trees." He bit into the fruit—offered me a bite. Hesitantly but with trust I took one, my small white teeth leaving two precise arcs in the white flesh. Walter nodded as if to praise me. "And wheat to make our bread, and the salads you enjoy. Our flesh is part of the gift we leave. This is the Resurrection: you hold it now in your hand."

He finished the pear, tossed away the core, and led me back into the church to find Monsieur Gérontius. We were alone there—alone with the comfort of frankincense and the humid-haloed candles. In their chapels stood the saints—stoic, pitying, their painted eyes calling us to justice and self-knowledge. My father moved past those gleaming eyes raised to consider a horizon parallel to our own but invisible, and came to rest before a Virgin whose carved black hair coiled down to her hips over a robe painted with gold daisies.

"Christ withered a fig tree once, just by wishing it dead." My voice was unctuous: I was pious that year, but Elisabeth said it would not last.

Adult sarcasm gleamed down at me. "Time distorts legend, Claire. The Muslims tell many tales of Christ that we do not remember, and each begins with the words: 'Said Jesus, on whom be peace.'"

"The Musselmans who worship Mah"—an English word came back—"Mahound?"

"Ah!" His laughter was as quiet as his reply. "Whenever an Englishman does not understand a foreigner, that is to say frequently, he makes an insulting pun. God, you and I *are* English. Sometimes I almost forget it. In Constantinople, if you ever go there"—by the age of eighteen I knew for certain that I never will—"I have heard there stands a tomb. In it lie two friends, a Christian saint and a Muslim saint, who so loved each other they wished to rest together until God should come for both. Islam is wise in some ways, Claire. In a Christian country it is prudent never to say so." He crossed himself and, tipping a candle, used it to light another before the Virgin. "As for the fig tree, consider it a lie. I am convinced it was a pear tree, and he made it bloom."

* * *

War, when I was eleven, drove us down to Florence, city of bankers and Medici princes, and of the artists they patronized. My parents had sunk in rank when they chose the arts for their profession; but war and plague had changed the unchangeable—not least the subjection of the lower orders. The men who were to become my father's colleagues—intelligent, articulate, proud of their own worth, educated either in their fathers' shops or within the ideal of a rediscovered Rome—had risen from among the people: Pollaiuolo from his parents' poultry shop; Paolo Uccello from apprenticeship to his father, a barber; Andrea del Castagno from a farm outside the city. The nobles considered them common folk, just as my parents had sunk—Elisabeth from among the gentry, my father from the London merchant-bankers among whom he had been born—to be commoners as well.

The artists laughed at the pretensions of breeding and ignorance, especially when combined in the same man. They laughed—despite their lucrative devotion to religious art—at a superstitious Christian orthodoxy. They starved, and fell in love with women or with each other, or hired themselves out for hack work or walked miles in wooden clogs to see a finely carved Roman sarcophagus. They were no better, I suppose, than any other human community; but the idea of the nobility of genius touched even the mediocre among them with talents that were somehow a special gift upon us in that time.

I was a child and an observer, not the equal of these people. I have heard when they were fresh stories Time will make stale, no doubt. I remember, for instance, the Botticelli brothers, of whom the younger, Sandro, was handsome and a flirt, and who once walked the streets all night to prevent a hideous dream of matrimony from recurring. That unclerical priest Fra Filippo Lippi had already been tortured for forgery, and was in the process of seducing two sisters, both nuns, who remained in his house as his infatuated concubines. (I hear, by the way, that Cosimo de Medici has this year had Fra Lippo relieved of his vows. The relief must, I feel, have been general.)

I was to model for Luca della Robbia, whose passion for work was such that he would push his feet for warmth into a basket full of wood shavings rather than move from his drawing board of a cold night; and for Andrea del Castagno, whom necessity forced to do so many posters of hanged criminals (to be displayed as warnings in the churches) that he became known as Andrea of the Hanged Men. But a young model of my physical type had nothing personally to do with Donatello, who, refusing a summons from the Patriarch of Florence, had once ordered the messenger: "Tell him I am as much a patriarch in my work as he is in his."

The nobles admired and smiled—but at genius, not at this reasoned disobedience, nursed often in the same farmhouses that had bred the artists' brothers, the turbulent leaders of the working mob. A merchant might own works by della Robbia, Botticelli, Donatello, Piero della Francesca, and Paolo Uccello, all as investments to sell off in a bad year. Artists might argue the equality of genius with birth; but they were poor, and to coerce them there still existed money and inherited obedience.

They came and went in our house—sharing supper; borrowing money; talking with my father when he locked the door of the study; being treated for hunger in the kitchen and for knife wounds and broken noses in Elisabeth's stillroom; bending down, with a smile and a word for me, to stroke my cat Bianca; or sitting on stools reading, by the last light, volumes from among my parents' library of ninety-six. They were honorable about books, and never borrowed or stole what they were too poor to replace.

Everything was new then, or seemed so. Florence—the ancient Florentia—rose from its grid of Roman streets in the bowl of its olive-green and cypress hills, clouds soft above its pink and yellow stone. Toothed walls pierced by watchtowers belted the city, with its geometry of thick-walled, small-windowed houses. Ferrymen punting high-prowed, flat-bottomed boats carried people across the Arno, and below the four bridges naked fishermen dragged seine nets or dug for shellfish on the mud flats, wearing nothing except straw hats against the sun. Few villas had yet risen outside the city walls. Instead among the gray olives the towers of the ancient savage nobility spired in a strange and ominous isolation.

Scaffolding hazed the cupola of the Duomo, for Brunelleschi had died leaving it unfinished. A square crater smelling of earth occupied the site of the Palazzo Rucellai, and the Medici lived in the finished three-quarters of their palace while tilers and plasterers labored to finish the rest. The river wound rippling and stinking—mustard-yellow in the flood season or, on dull days, a flat beige bloomed with silver. Goldsmiths' shops, their tiers propped with timber, crowded the Ponte Vecchio, and feral cats in their thousands basked in alleyways beneath windows crossbarred with four hundred year old iron. Church façades went up in pink and green marble; the markets sold fresh-killed pork and vegetables and sweet pears; dung carts moved through the streets, carrying human excrement outside the city to manure the fields. Grilled gateways shut one out from gardens filled with roses, fountains, orange trees, and lilies with thick yellow pollen.

It was hot in summer—a wet heavy heat. In winter frost dulled the red tile roofs and stiffened the laundry that hung on lines among the house tops. Everything smelled of paint, of timber or turned earth; and marble blocks stacked for use still showed the delicate diagonal marks of the stone saw.

It was not a kind place, this Florence where the bells called us to the mild seasons: a spring of wild chamomile and orange blossom; a summer so hot the stones scalded the feet through shoe leather; an autumn of yellow leaves; a winter when floods drowned the destitute who slept beneath the bridges. Every man wore a sword. The artisans in the cloth factories had risen more than once, demanding higher wages and some power in the government of the city, and had been put down with branded foreheads, with lopped earlobes and amputated hands, with pincers that roasted the muscle as they tore it from the bone. Heretics died on the wheel as the executioner broke each bone, from finger joint to thigh bone to pelvis to skull, according to a gradation that prolonged torture and left them screaming for four days. Young men killed each other at eighteen years old for sport, their dust-grimed shirts dragged from their hose, fighting through the alleys of the city. The Signoria hanged traitors from the windows of their own houses. The cloth workers, balked of human victims, broke the spines of cats with iron bars, crammed the creatures into bags, and hanged them after a mock trial.

And in this Florence of russet and pink and yellow, of white skies and jade leaves, I learned the pride that made us citizens of a Republic equaled, we believed, only in one other span of human life: the climacteric of Athens when Sophocles was alive. (You have noticed we were not truly a republic? So had the subtle old man who counted the Medici gold and took care, like Augustus, not to call himself our prince.) We knew men would remember us simply for having been here. Sadder generations would look back on us with envy: we felt their longing.

That pride moved us to brutality, to the cruelest vulgarities of commerce, and to a voracious intellectual competence that partook, I now think, of a sort of collective childhood. Everywhere, for these intelligent self-educated men, discovery was a kind of omnivorous ecstasy. Colors had a vernal freshness, and lines the simplicity and accuracy of fine caricature. A supernormal energy haunted us, as though the whole community could call up the vitality that sometimes characterizes a child of genius, whose versatility promises more than any maturity can fulfill. "I will take what I must: behold me, I am good," he says, and sees himself flattered by the envy in his elders' eyes.

In our complacency we created—and knew it—a dream Florence. Perhaps with Time the pastels will degenerate to become, in the hands of future artists, cold or unnatural, and that simplification of the body which draws its power from ideal beauty will become mere prettiness. Perhaps it is harsh to say that I, even as a child—and a Northerner, though I had forgotten it—recognized in Florentine beauty a potential emptiness. But a visitation of collective genius is a privilege and a joy, even though one must glide kindly over the elements of that genius lest one see how much, perceived individually, was bad or borrowed or mercenary or vulgar.

Later perhaps, as the North adopts what Italy began, we may develop our own version of this art—harder, more appreciative of human idiosyncrasy; perhaps more truthful. "Hellenism and Italy," my father used to say. "A dangerous mixture, if done badly."

So I sat, a child curled at the feet of my parents and their friends, and listened to the music of Landini, of Binchois, of Dufay, played by artists whom I might, one day, by study equal. I listened to lyrics in which vernacular speech could be heard breaking free from the Latin that had bound it. My parents discussed Boccaccio's innovations and new theories of government and international commerce. I watched as the elder Botticelli traced in a single line the profile of the Virgin, her brow plucked high, a sapphire on her forehead—Greek in her proportions, but with her beauty blended by three thousand years of human mating into a type not yet born into the world when Athenian sculptors carved the Caryatids.

We took ancient ideals and applied them to a world with which the Ancients had not had to contend. The stability of our future, I now suspect, may depend on our understanding this—that an ideal archaism is a dangerous toy. For if all excellence was revealed to Greece and Rome—and I have met scholars who passionately believed this—then we risk forcing an archaic simplicity, miscalled purity, on religion and on law; and there lie many dangers.

But then I watched architects trace empty cities whose lines converged on a point theoretically infinite. Our friends divided the human body into units of proportion; pointed out, in the curve of a hip and leg, the plumb line of balance that conveyed the body's relationship to the Divine Harmony. The Pope reprimanded a scholar for maintaining that Plato was a saint.

The House of Medici under Cosimo—that lank old man whom I saw being carried in his litter through the streets—reached out across Europe to establish sixteen branches of its bank. The cloth workers banded into a mob again; people fought in the streets; and strangled figures, their hands bound, twisted from the streetcorner gallows, submissive to every wind.

Our house was made of burnt tile and yellow stone, and enclosed a courtyard where lemon trees grew in hooped wooden casks. There lay the stable (reached by an archway), the kitchen, the washhouse, and the servants' chambers. The privies were cleansed with earth twice a day, which rendered them surprisingly inoffensive. We bathed at the public bathhouses, or in copper tubs by the fire.

Of this house I remember chiefly the music room; Elisabeth's stillroom, whose contents she later transferred to our Norman house so as to produce a virtually identical place; and my own bedroom. Here a brass chandelier holding six candles offered light in addition to the fireplace, whose flames cast glistening shadows over a floor tiled in hexagons of blue and cream. My washstand, clothes press, and bench were of heavy dark wood, but red cushions gave the settle a bright delightful softness, and on the carved marble mantel stood my ornaments: a Roman perfume flask of fragile iridescent glass, my collection of stones and shells, my milk teeth in the box Walter had made for them, and a jar of dried herbs and flowers. The bed had tall slender brass posts and hangings of red cloth, and when it rained I closed shutters studded with ornamental nails.

In the music room the cushions were made of the same soft, brilliant cloth, this time in blue; a cupboard held hundreds of score sheets; and a carpet from Persia, worked in crimson and emerald, covered the table on which rested my instruments.

I have possessed most of these instruments all my life; I took them with me into that long exile during which Your Grace became not my lord but my friend. I do not need to touch them to open, in imagination, the cases with their taffeta linings. The lute; the small harp held on my knee; the psaltery—a panel of strings laid flat on the lap and plucked with a quill. The shawm, a flaring pipe; the crumhorn—a curved pipe, soft and low in pitch; the finger drum and the tambourine.

By the age of twelve I could, then, sing to my own accompaniment (Alessandra Torelli was my singing teacher) or accompany Elisabeth when we sang together. Her voice was soprano, mine a pure, strong alto, at times achieving the lower soprano range. I was too closely guarded a virgin to be allowed to sing in public; my parents rightly judged that the seduction of a twelve-year-old musician would amuse some of the courtiers who surrounded the Medici, and so I never appeared at their court in Florence. At most, for practice, I sang at my parents' parties; it was largely to myself, with Elisabeth softly timing me on the speckled pottery finger drum, that I sang:

*Ecco la primavera che il cor fa rallegrare:*
*tempe d'annamorare*
*e star' con lieta cera . . .*

Behold the spring that maketh the heart glad . . .

Or the lyrics of my forgotten home:

>Your eyen two will slay me suddenly:
>I may the beauty of them not sustain,
>So woundeth it throughout my hearte keen.
>
>And but your word will healen hastily
>My hearte's wounde, while that it is green.
>>Your eyen two will slay me suddenly:
>>I may the beauty of them not sustain.
>
>Upon my truth I say you faithfully
>That ye be of my life and death the queen:
>For with my death the truthe shall be seen.
>>Your eyen two will slay me suddenly:
>>I may the beauty of them not sustain,
>>So woundeth it throughout my hearte keen.

I must sound a docile child. I was. Gratitude is one of the strongest passions in my nature, and I knew I owed these parents everything. I should add that I was now fourteen: slender, with hands a little too large, and pretty breasts; not tall, nor likely to become so; and that my menses had not yet started. This lateness caused Elisabeth an inconspicuous, serene concern.

I think I did possess one active—that is, deliberate—virtue: I had from my childhood controlled my temper, not because I had been punished or trained, but out of consideration for those around me. I had known since I was about six that when I spoke in a certain way no one could move me and even my parents would obey me. I would, in a cold passion, have let myself be killed (I mean this literally) rather than be bullied or persuaded. That I seldom used this power was, from my childhood, a matter of conscious self-control that arose, I think, from a true gentleness in my character. Because I was so young, this self-restraint was little known; and my temper was not known at all until it lost me half my livelihood in Florence.

Chaperoned by a manservant and by my maid Caterina, I had been sitting to Jean-Marie Tavella, in his studio up one flight of stairs, for a *Salomé with the Head of John the Baptist*. Prop-heads made me shiver and I would not hold one, so Tavella let me pose without the prop, my hand hanging down where my fingers would twist into the hair.

Jean-Marie added to his mixed name some trace of German ancestry, and I still vividly remember his yellow bottle-brush hair with its white temples and the taut red skin of his face, lined with laughter and temper. He was intelligent and did not like me, for reasons I could not understand but that hurt me, being young; and as he painted he told me that Salomé had been young too, perhaps fourteen or even twelve. Judith, he said, he imagined as a woman of twenty-five or thirty, powerful and beautiful, who hacked off (I winced, stirred, was rebuked) Holofernes' head with her own hands. Salomé, in contrast (the intelligent blue eyes scanned me; a hand, with live rapid authority, mixed cerise with white lead on his palette) had been a virgin, obedient to her mother, if he was remembering the story correctly, he had not confessed or read his Bible in years; and when Herod granted her a boon for her dancing, she had obeyed her mother in demanding the Baptist's head. Salomé's sin was that she had killed in ignorance. This, said Jean-Marie Tavella, was why her face need show no passion; and indeed the less expression he had from me the more he seemed to like it.

This confused me, and he laughed. He was about thirty-six, and would no more have thought of touching me than any other man who had seen Walter use a dagger. In any case, I doubt he was tempted, because as we faced each other across Jean-Marie's dirty atelier there passed between us a trace of genuinely adult antagonism—dislike being, ultimately, as elemental a chemistry as love.

On the day he summoned me to see the finished work I was to receive my fee. My parents let me use this as pocket money, or deposit it in my small bank account. I spent it with the frugality of those who need nothing, or gave it to the poor.

My servants behind me, I folded back the dark-red veil I had worn in the streets over my gown of equally somber green velvet, and greeted Jean-Marie, my voice steady despite the heat in my forehead and the strange, stuffed headache with which I had awakened. "Come and look," said Jean-Marie; and, flicking back a square of stained sacking, revealed the completed painting.

I beheld myself, my face simplified to the exquisite vacuity that Florence has made the fashion (Florentines like Sandro Botticelli seem easily to mistake a perfect prettiness for beauty). This painting was softer, however, more hazy than Sandro's clear golds and ambers; and the innocent face seemed to float, wickedly indifferent, above the thing the fingers held.

And what the fingers held was no prop-head, no John the Baptist, but the severed head of Jean-Marie Tavella.

The thing, a charnel vulgarity with its rolled eyes and dragged-open jaw, stunned me silent. My most effective riposte—and ten years later I would not have hesitated to make it—would have been to laugh. I suspect no adult judge would have found the painting anything but ludicrous. But I was not adult, and skill has always intimidated me. The polish of it was formidable, Salomé's face melting like cloud into the shine of her pearls and satins and into the sunset-glow around her; and the head seemed real.

For a long time I stared at it, examining the shock of those two faces juxtaposed, absorbing the discovery that the painting for which I had posed had become—had, in Tavella's mind, always been—something different: a joke whose frankness and vulgarity rendered it, to a girl my age, still more elusive.

I cleared my throat, and said in a voice that frightened me: "Have I offended you, Signor Tavella?"

"No, Mistress Tarleton"—the title came in English, to my surprise—"you have not. By the way, here's your purse." He tossed the thing to me: Inside it I felt the few small, valuable coins that were all an artist could afford to pay.

"Let us go, Mistress Claire." Caterina laid a hand on my arm, and her voice conveyed a disapproval—not of me, but on my behalf—that at least told me I was not mad.

I tugged away from her, just unwell enough to be unwise; and feeling, also, the need of my integrity to identify the joke of which he had just made me the victim. "Why," I demanded, "have you depicted your own head, sir?"

"Call it a fancy, mistress." Tavella braced himself against the wall, arms crossed; he had not yet given me his full attention.

"I do not find it amusing," I said. Caterina pulled gently at my arm.

Tavella shrugged, casting me a glance that combined tolerance with a certain bored wariness. "Why?" he asked. "May I say it was not meant to amuse. It was meant—"

"To arouse the spectator's pity." I was shrewd enough to see I had found the nerve that would lead me inward. His face flushed scarlet.

"Pity." I said it again, my voice wobbling as Tavella raked a hand through his hair, moving with such violent suddenness that I knew I was facing, undefended, an adult anger. "Why do this to *me*, Signor Tavella?"

Marco stirred; Caterina plucked at my sleeve. Persistent as a drunkard, I shook myself away from her. Pretension; ludicrous falsity—the words became clear in the years to come. At that moment, however, nothing came but the recoil of my self-respect and my hard adolescent honesty: for truth had been somehow offended. "I have killed no one. I am innocent."

"Then you should not have sat for Salomé, who was guilty."

"And thus you invent my guilt. You will send me down the

centuries—as long as this canvas lasts"—humbly I shared Tavella's opinion of his own immortality—"nameless and defenseless, but guilty of your hurt. You have painted a lie. When a poet or a painter accuses us, what defense have we? Who is more wronged than Lesbia, because the whole world believed what Catullus said of her?"

"So now you are Lesbia's equal." With a laugh the active body rebounded from its pose of rest. "Let me tell you what you are, Claire, so you may make no mistake. You are a pretty child whom grown people use. What fame you have I gave you, and painters like me. Thank us for it before I send you home to be beaten into manners, for until you apologize you will not sit for me again. Each of us, Claire, will when he dies be forgotten utterly. In that you are no different from the hundreds of little Salomés and Madonnas who open their knees to the painter when he has finished depicting their faces. Five years will see you some man's breeder of children, so make no mistake: you have no distinction beyond what your parents and men like me have given you. We have made you, my dear: we have created you."

It was annihilation so conscienceless that only ten years would show me how much of what he said had been brutally and wantonly wrong. And against this attack I had no defense. My fingers felt for the coins he had given me. Neat as a pebble skimmer, I shot them at the face of Salomé, scoring through the paint to the sized canvas. Trembling and sweating in the appalled silence, I said to him, "Then get another model."

"Take her away." His voice was hoarse with violence controlled.

My servants hired a mule to take me home. There I burst into strange screaming sobs through which Elisabeth held me.

At last, mopping with the cold towel she gave me a face swollen into ugliness, I whispered, "I'm sorry."

"So am I," said Walter from the doorway. He had come from

the enamelist's, and a faint smell of chemicals hung about the brown, belted robe he wore. "Tell me, Claire."

I did, as clearly as I could. Elisabeth touched my forehead. "You're cooling. There's no fever, thank God. Poor child. I'll have Caterina heat bath water and fill your tub; then it's something to make you sleep. In sleep, you know, I believe we think things out. Claire, do you regret what you did today?"

I considered, then shook my head. "No. I was right, and I did what I wished to do."

The simplicity of it drew a dry glance from my parents. I looked up at Walter. "It will be all over the city by tomorrow, won't it, sir?"

"That you screamed like a harridan at one of the fraternity? Oh yes, in a town this size; and the artists are a town within the town."

"Will anyone employ me again?" I whispered.

"I don't know, Claire. Elisabeth, my dear—?" She moved away; the bed sank heavily as Walter seated himself beside me. His arms still akimbo, he offered no embrace of comfort, but his glance at me, though reserved, was not unfriendly. "Yes, you'll lose half your custom. And those who hate Signor Tavella will laugh and praise your spirit. Whether they will consider you worth the trouble, when they've finished laughing. . . ." He laid a palm over mine. "But we'll see. Why did you do this, Claire—to yourself, to all of us?"

At least I met his gaze. "I do not know, sir."

"So I feared," said Walter, and left me.

I paid for it, of course. Other pretty faces proved more docile. That there was worse to come did not shake the loyalty of our friends—above all of Walter's and my great friend Luca della Robbia.

I woke in the morning cool of skin and calm of manner, with a bleak, cold sensation of congestion—I could not say whether in body or in mind—that I concealed from Elisabeth. And it was at Master della Robbia's studio, within twenty-four hours of the episode Master Luca and his twelve assistants and his fourteen apprentices had discussed so amply that their discretion seemed almost natural, that I turned thief. I revered Master Luca; and my mind was severed from my hand when I picked up, and inconspicuously took away, a small chisel he had made himself, one he treasured and often used.

That night when I undressed for bed I found my shift soaked with blood. I sealed in a scream with my fingers and ran the other hand between my thighs, to find skin also slippery with blood.

I washed body and shift in cold water. I knew what it was, knew even where to find the soft cloth napkins Elisabeth had prepared. The pressure in my head was easing; I knew now why. In the clarity that came then, I dressed in my nightgown and in a robe of old dull velvet, and recovered from my day clothes Master Luca's stolen chisel. My parents would be reading in the solar, or perhaps in the music room Elisabeth would be softly tuning the lute.

I found them there, talking by firelight. At my appearance Elisabeth looked up. "Claire? Do you need something?"

"Sir. Madame." The polyglot formalities came naturally as I sank on one knee before their chairs. "Forgive me. I stole this from Master Luca della Robbia today."

"You *what?*" Walter lunged forward. The chisel, adroitly caught by Elisabeth, flipped from my hand as the first blow I had ever received hurled me back across the room. As I landed, sprawled on buttocks and aching elbows, an agony contracted within my abdomen. The strings of the psaltery shivered like spun silver.

In the silence I sat up, nursing my cheek where the bruise would come violet tomorrow, the other palm folded over my belly. Walter's temper was not quick, but he was advancing on me when the authority in Elisabeth's voice stopped him.

"Walter, wait! Claire, what is wrong inside you? What is hurting, can you tell me?"

"My courses. They have begun."

"Then what have I done?" Walter knelt, his hands cupped my face. "I swear I will never do that again. Forgive me. I have heard it is a hard time. . . . Here, perhaps your mother can help."

Gently he gathered me up and carried me to bed. The agony was now wringing tears from my closed eyes. When I lay on my own pillows Elisabeth said, "Walter, get hot water for me to wash my hands, then leave us. I must make certain there is no other harm."

"Yes, of course."

When he had obeyed her she washed and dried, and laid her rings in the pottery dish where I kept the beads of myrrh I used to clean my teeth. As her fingers gently examined my spread thighs, she said, "Dear, has there been nothing else? No blow to the womb, no man? Did Tavella strike you?"

"No, of course not. I'm glad I ruined his picture for him. Oh, Mother, I'm sorry."

She smiled a little grimly, drying her hands again. Her fingers felt for the opal among the clots of aromatic gum. "Now you're clean for your father; we'll tuck the blankets over you. I have something for the pain, and I'll find something else in the stillroom to make you sleep deeply. I don't believe you have anything but late courses, hard begun. The pain, you know, will grow less with use—and when, in time, you bear children."

I stirred. Her hand, smaller than my long, strong-fingered one, clasped it firmly. "Well, and that will be years hence, won't it? And then I'm afraid you must talk to Walter."

"Hello." His motion onto my bed this time was ginger, as if his weight might hurt me.

I gritted my teeth against the slight jolting. "Father, tell me how to earn your forgiveness."

Walter sighed. "Tomorrow you will see Master Luca in private, tell him what you did, and give him back the chisel. And your money for three months, from whatever source, will go to the alms box at Santa Ambrosia. I am sure your confessor will be gentle."

"Yes, of course."

"Claire, you are not a thief, but you have stolen something. I do not know why. Study to discover the reason if you can. It must not happen again; it must never happen again. You may gain the patronage, even the friendship of the nobles: you may marry a gentleman. If you were to marry a great artist like Master della Robbia, then you will have done more than well. You may, also, earn and keep the respect of artists like Elisabeth. But all this you will forfeit if anyone whispers the word *thief*." Wearily, my eyes dilated, I nodded, watching his face. He said, "Master Luca will not whisper that word. But no vice, Claire, not even lewdness, is more despised. That shows a lack of pity, I think: anyone who has been poor has known the urge to steal. But you have beauty, gifts, a tongue, and a temper. Remember and accept a hard thing: no one pities such a woman. You cannot defend yourself against a charge when your heart knows it is true."

"Yes, sir. I do not know. . . ." My exhausted consciousness touched that moment. "My hand just moved—by itself, it seemed."

"No. On behalf of some part of you. Here comes Elisabeth." He rose and kissed my forehead. "Forgive my seriousness. Here at least is what will make you sleep."

And, as Elisabeth tipped four green drops into a glass of wine, I drank thirstily of oblivion.

And so the great whitewashed atelier of Luca della Robbia— with its easels, its solid tables, its scaffolding, its skylights of clean glass; with its ovens, its chisels and molds, its pounds of clay swathed in damp cheesecloth, and its bins of stinking chemical color—was deserted when I knelt before him and held out the tool he had made to fit his own hand. "Master, I must ask you to forgive me a sin against friendship. I stole this from you yesterday."

Luca della Robbia was at that time aged between forty and fifty—I found it difficult to tell with men so handsome. Where my father, also attractive, was broad and solid, Master Luca's thin-boned face had kept an aquiline tension of bone and muscle. Black hair scarcely graying tumbled in curls over his forehead, which was grooved by a single horizontal line. His dark eyes were brilliant; his moustache and sleek beard gave him, not without his knowledge, a courtier's elegance; and the belt with which he contained the ankle-length robe proper to a Master was set with besels of green and white jade.

He accepted the chisel. His grasp was gentle; his hands conveyed and translated thought automatically, as do certain particularly expressive faces. Master Luca's face had delegated this expressiveness; and the brilliance that considered us was unreadable. He avoided the obvious questions. "Do you know why you took it, Claire?" He laid the chisel softly aside where I could see it.

I kept my head up. "No, Master."

Master Luca's eyes moved to my father's face. "Walter, how many friends has she now of her own age?"

A second's hesitation. "Since we came to Florence, Luca, none. She is shy."

Master Luca's index finger strayed up to press his lips, then fell. With sudden crispness he said, "Work a horse and break its back. Claire, my dear, for God's sake get up and give me my kiss."

As I scrambled up, stumbling a little with surprise, I glimpsed my father's crimson face. I bent to receive Master Luca's kiss on my cheek: one strong hand detained me, meticulously avoiding causing me discomfort, for the second it took him to assess my bruises. He glanced again at Walter. "My dear old friend, please sit down. I am sorry for your trouble. What penance have you laid on her for this?"

Walter told him.

Master Luca nodded. "Get rid of Alessandra Torelli. And throw out that damned psaltery."

"No!" It was my treasure, but my cry of alarm intercepted his rare, brilliant grin.

Walter said gently, "Alessandra needs the money, Luca, you know that."

Master Luca nodded. "Send her to me, she can tutor my niece. As a friend I ask you: reduce Claire's lessons with her to one a week. How often does Elisabeth practice with her?"

"Daily."

"Entreat Elisabeth in my name that from now on it be every second day. Claire, when is your next birthday?"

"In October, Maestro: in three weeks."

"Good. We will have a birthday party, at which you will be too busy to play or sing because you will be meeting my two nieces Francesca and Joanna, who have just arrived in the city and who would be glad of a friend. Do you go out much?"

"I—"

"No. Well, Tommasso, my son, is going to teach you to play *jeu de paume*, the silly game of batting a ball about with one's hands on a grass court. And my nephew Andrea"—I knew him; he later became partner in the studio, and was one of the kindest men I have ever met—"who will as a matter of course ask you to marry him (you will please me by refusing, at least until October) is going to teach you an even odder game, in which one hits with a stick a hard little ball." An expression of distaste crossed Master Luca's face. "I am told kings play it in Scotland."

From behind me I heard Walter's sudden relieved laugh. "And for the winter, Luca?"

"If I might make her a present of riding clothes—?"

"You may not. Elisabeth will help."

"But there is a little jennet in my stables, and I should be grateful if Claire would exercise her for me."

"I—" I began.

"That is for Claire to say," replied my father. After a moment he added softly, "You shame me, Luca. We do love her."

"I know." Nothing filled the pause until Master Luca tapped his temple, pantomiming memory. "Ah yes, your sitting tomorrow. You will come, Claire—no, no refusals—and sit to me in my private study for, let us say, the next two weeks." He had spared my bruised face the publicity of the studio. He rose. "Now come. My wife is preparing some spiced wine."

As we approached the far wall, the great medallions of color that had attracted my peripheral attention defined themselves and grew larger—grew, in one case, unbelievably large. "Vulgar, isn't it?" inquired Master Luca. "For the Palazzo Medici, when the builders catch up with me."

The della Robbia studio had begun that unique creation, which Luca's nephews and no doubt his great nephews will continue, of firing huge and brilliantly glazed maiolica medallions. The earliest of these, the size of large plates, had offered the buyer a novelty for his private devotions: typically, a Madonna in high relief against a blue ground, surrounded by cherubs and a molded border.

But the monster that now confronted me rose fifteen feet high. Against the famous cobalt background, yellow lions supported the crest of the Medici with its six balls, balls that have been variously and ribaldly interpreted; and around the edge, in a garland two feet thick, vine leaves twined with grapes, roses, apples, carnations, and pears, each as large as my forearm, and each rendered in a virulent version of its natural color.

Master Luca ran his fingers through his hair. "Subtlety of color," he admitted, "has not yet been achieved; but these damned glazes . . . one thing in the vat, another on the surface. And some of the most atrocious glazes change delightfully when fired—*if* one can persuade them to be consistent."

Walter whistled. "It looks like a monstrous platter."

"I know." Master Luca nodded somberly. "But no one since Antiquity has discovered how to fire in one piece and to transport, undamaged, ceramic pieces of this size. The *best* effects, I think, come with the blue and white alone. There elegance is possible. And this one"—we strolled on, past a row of commissioned pieces to a medallion about a yard across—"this one I shall keep."

He smiled at me. I had modeled it, a young Madonna with Saint Anne, eight months before. It was my own face that emerged in high relief, straight nose and gentle downcast eyes, to read the book held out to me by the Mother of the Virgin; the creamy glaze was only soft and subtle, not unnatural. Against the pure dark blue the only other elements of color were the eyes—of Saint Anne, of the attendant cherubs, and my own eyes transmuted to a dense and brilliant brown. I thought: Within her circle she goes on and on, but what am I, compared with her?

We turned away; and I did not sense—for no heart's yearning can ever let us sense—the friend who also stood there, invisible, still unmet, gazing at that same medallion and thinking of me, over a chasm deeper than eight years: over the chasm of death itself.

# 2

Both my parents had inherited money, which they have kept intact for me and which will make me, I suppose, eventually a fairly wealthy woman. Elisabeth's rents came from the Norman gentleman farmer whose only living child she had been (she had had a twin, a girl who died in strange circumstances at the age of sixteen; how I should have liked to meet this identical aunt!). The steward who had been her father's trusted employee still administered these estates, which I had never seen. He had known Elisabeth before her marriage to the elderly friend who had been her first husband (Walter was her second). As for Walter, his father had left him shares in the banking house of Tarleton-Fugger: he wrote often, about business and personal matters, to his elder brother in London.

I had, then, kin in London, but the long war between France and England—however ignored by merchants on both sides—had prevented our return, even had my parents wished to exchange Paris and Florence for the provincial Court of King Henry.

My father was no gentleman amateur; he was a competent translator, mathematician, enamelist, and goldsmith, and chose to work mainly among the smiths during these years—assisting, learning, and performing a few commissioned pieces.

Nevertheless he seemed to lack purpose, as I have heard men of his age (now about fifty) often do for a few years. It was while working among the Florentine artisans that he came to know Damianus Coster, the great goldsmith-printer from Mainz.

As for me, by the time I turned seventeen I had regained some of my popularity as a model. Our community was fertile of newer scandal, and what was my small notoriety when *both* Fra Lippo Lippi's sister-concubines had foresworn their illegitimate children by him, made contrition before the altar, returned to the vows as nuns from which Fra Lippo had distracted their attention, and then *re*absconded with him, along with their babies and *three more* of their sisters? This *ménage à six* (or, counting the babies, *ménage à neuf*) was currently convulsing Florence, either with rage or with delight, while the unrepentant household eluded all pursuit.

Fra Lippo was at this time, I think, the most admired male in Florence. What might his erotic exploits have been, wondered my father's friends aloud, had his parents *not* consecrated him to Holy Orders? We all liked Fra Lippo so much that one colleague of Walter's felt emboldened to say to a priestly patron: "Father, it takes thirty years to make a man like me, while to make a man like you takes only a little collar and a few seconds of nepotism."

On my next birthday—we did not know then that it would prove my last in Florence—I would be eighteen, and my time as a model was passing. Even as a child I had been too dark for the Florentine ideal, which is red-blonde and hazel-eyed; but my features, being childishly undefined, could still sustain that type of idealization. As a young woman I was still pretty but sinned by being not only dark, but increasingly individual. My face had thinned and had acquired that trace of austerity which Time can only intensify. I was becoming too different, and, like every child who has early received some public attention, I had cause to think early, too, about the passing of beauty and opportunity.

But I had begun to perform in public in duet with Elisabeth. Surrounded by our small suite of servants and always accompanied by Walter, we achieved a certain prestige, which I enjoyed with a fierceness that disturbed me.

On the day the earthquake struck us, it was May. Fruit blossom rustled, shook, and crumbled on the wind; clouds of untraceable scent would stop one, arrested with delight; and everywhere new leaves unfolded, crisp as taffeta. In a crackle-glazed vase, its mouth pinched into a clover shape, one purple and one yellow iris filled the music room with their surprisingly powerful perfume.

I had been working on a song accompanied by my own hands on the drum. It had not been going well. I frowned, paused, started again.

> *Ce mois de mai, ce mois de mai*
> *ce mois de mai ma verte cotte*
> *ce mois de mai ma verte cotte*
> *ce mois de mai je vestiray.*
> *De bon matin me leveray,*
> *ce joli, joli mois de mai—*

"It's hard, of course, with only the drum, but you're a quarter-tone flat. Please try again." Elisabeth softly struck the tuning fork. The patter of my fingers resumed on the stretched parchment.

> *De bon matin me leveray,*
> *ce joli, joli mois de mai;*
> *un saute, un saute en rue je feray—*

"Ladies, good morning." Walter came into the room, the skirt of his blue robe swinging, and strode across to the window.

From there he stood regarding us, a hand across his mouth, and in his eyes a reserved, almost apologetic laughter.

"Ah." Elisabeth set down the tuning fork. "You may as well stop, Claire. Your father has, so I guess, decided our fate for the next ten years. So it is to be the press after all, Walter."

"I beg your pardon, Madame?" I said.

She glanced at me. "Your father's long nights with Master Damianus Coster."

Walter, his arms folded, leaned on the windowsill. "Claire, I have not been as frank with you as with your mother, but the matter may not in any case involve you very deeply. I mean to set up as a printer. Italy has only one other, and Master Damianus has much to teach."

Elisabeth shrugged with tolerant irritation. "Why take the trouble, Walter? Everyone has books enough."

"Each one copied by hand, incorporating all the errors of the weary hand and weary mind of scribe after scribe. In our ancient texts we have thus compiled centuries of error. A printer who is also a scholar can find the best text of, say, a Roman author; he can restore it, purified and uniform, to the world."

"I agree," said Elisabeth, "but set against this the beauty of books made by hand. Each is unique; each has its individual being."

"They cost," said my father, "far more than a poor man can pay."

Frowning, my mother assented softly. "That is so."

"Think," demanded Walter, "what could be offered those now too poor to read: manuals of mathematics, architecture, carpentry, husbandry, foreign languages, perspective; the Bible also, that a man may know what he believes and why. A scholar-printer could *write* textbooks—could teach, as well as purifying the ancient manuscripts that have come down to us in such corrupted texts."

"And how glad will the Church be to see each man

pondering his faith?" When my mother spoke in this fashion—as scholar to equal scholar—I glimpsed the lover and colleague my father kept for himself alone. Bright-eyed I watched them, and was silent.

My father shook his head. "The Church teaches truth. Why should it hate a tool for the dissemination of truth?"

"For God's sake, Walter!"

A long silence.

At last my father said gently, "No, I am not simple-witted. All those who have power—Church and princes—will hate the removal of that power into the hands of the poor who can read. If removal it is—for as yet we do not know what the presses can do or can cause to be. It may be the poor would seek power without them; and it may be that knowledge leads, as I hope it does, only to innocent love. But, Elisabeth, it is happening already. I have bought not one press but two. I ordered the type from Damianus' partners in Mainz four weeks ago. We must find a shop with a forge. The type wears out quickly, and costs of paper are enormous. I have purchased the dies; we can recast worn type. And I have engaged two of Damianus' assistants, who can train others. Antimony—"

It was then, as I screamed, that the Roman perfume flask jiggled, considered, slid sideways, and crashed in shards to the floor. The mantelpiece itself, the floor beneath me were sliding from side to side; and from somewhere came a rumbling sound.

"*Get out!*" shouted Walter.

One of us on each arm, he lifted and dragged us down the stairs, shouting to the servants. From the street we watched the tremors subside. As the profound growling rumble died, Walter threw back his head and laughed. "Do you think," he asked Elisabeth, "that He wants me to settle for a single press? Or should I order, for perfect theological unity, a third?"

The lemons in the courtyard had begun to swell green among the leaves on an evening when I sat alone in the solar, my book laid aside for lack of light. My hair, newly washed and damp, lay combed on my shoulders; I wore a high-waisted gown of spring-green cloth, whose net of embroidered blossoms glittered metallically in the firelight. Frowning at the weight that dragged on my damp head, I glanced at the window. The sky above our house had faded from pink to turquoise; an early star had risen.

Outside I heard Caterina's step, and her voice, angry but soft; and another, replying, that made me recoil to the end of the cushioned bench. The door opened. Caterina said, "He has talked with your father, and Master Walter said he might come up to see you, but *I* think it most unbecoming." The door cracked shut behind my guest.

"You've grown . . ." The artist's eyes, their crow's-feet deepened, assessed me. ". . . only two inches. Salomé has another face now: I scrubbed you out. You didn't ruin it."

"I regret that; I tried. What other unfortunate—?"

"An imaginary unfortunate." Jean-Marie Tavella sat down at the end of my bench. In his hands, I noted, he carried a parcel.

I had not seen him for three years. In a city so small that entailed, on both sides, a persevering dislike. He had changed little: his hair whiter, his color still too high, seemingly sunburned even in winter; his small active body disdaining to acknowledge middle age. He was clean, I saw, and dressed in blue and red particolored hose beneath a short brown coat that covered the buttocks. At its square neck I glimpsed the gathered hem of a voile shirt. "I'm leaving Florence. Going to Rome, in fact. I shall not come back."

The replies that occurred to me were too childishly sarcastic to be worthwhile, so I said nothing.

He had not asked my permission to sit. He pushed the parcel toward me. "One hears of the oddest things; and I, as it happens, heard about your perfume flask. Will you open it?"

I enraged myself by repeating the little throat-clearing of

three years before. Lowering my shaking fingers, I said too quickly, "Of course."

I fumbled at the paper. Thank God my hands steadied by the time the contents of the parcel made me gasp. Jean-Marie had moved gently with a taper to the fire, and now I had candlelight in which to study the treasure I lifted from its box.

A Roman bowl of millefiori glass. I had seen fragments of such things among the debris, the twisted aquamarine lumps of an ancient glass factory. Such bowls, I remembered Walter's saying, had been made from glass rods—ring within ring of yellow, orange, viridian, scarlet, and indigo, each stick brittle as candy. The glassmakers had sliced these rods, layered the wafers like cut pastry in a mold, and remelted them to produce objects like the ancient fragile thing that lay in my cupped palms, glowing like the thousand flowers of its name.

I glanced at Jean-Marie, struck with the compassion of one artist for another. "You cannot afford this!"

He shrugged. "It came to me from a friend, who was present at the opening of the tomb from which this bowl and other treasures were recovered. Yes, it comes from a tomb. Please don't let that make you sad."

I had never heard him speak gently before. I said softly, "Tell me."

"It is a true story. You may have heard—no?—well, they have discovered a street of Roman tombs beneath the Church of San Giovanni in Laterano. Her name was Fannia Redempta; and as they lifted the lid of her stone coffin, for an instant my friend saw her. Her father, a consul-designate, had laid her to rest in a purple robe and a golden veil. For just an instant my friend looked through Time and saw her, a shadow within that purple and gold; and then she crumbled into dust."

"Poor Fannia Redempta." My voice was light, my eyes full of tears. "Always—or do I mistake you? in which case it is, no doubt, my fault as usual—you have some point for me. Womanhood is cruel, beauty evanescent."

"Congratulations," said Jean-Marie. "You have just, unfortunately, discovered most of philosophy, and most of poetry too. What more can they hold for so forward a scholar? No—" At my motion of questioning, of thanks. "I am quite as disagreeable as you think me, Mistress Tarleton; but I wanted, and I cannot explain it, to confide Fannia Redempta to the single other mind that would never forget her. You said I could not afford this gift. I should like a payment."

I stared, damp hair masking my shoulders, at the bowl, then set it delicately aside. "One within my means?"

"Perfectly. Your father is downstairs, and Caterina, almost certainly, at the keyhole. I should like to kiss you."

I considered him. He had given what he chose to give; his manner made clear there would be no more; and it was some moments since I had identified one element of my dislike. "I will never see you again?"

A grin of simple fellowship suddenly, charmingly changed his face. "You will never see me again."

"Then yes."

He came to me with rapid efficiency and took me around the waist; the strength of his arm surprised me. With gentle authority he cupped my chin. The kiss that followed was hard, exploratory, and long. Then suddenly, both arms around me, he bent his head down to my breasts, crushed and kissed them both, and sealed my cry of shock with his mouth.

When he had finished he let me go and rose. It pleased me to see that he was breathing hard, his color higher even than usual. "Thank you. Good-bye, Mistress Tarleton."

I sat for an hour alone, with the millefiori bowl in my hands. Once Caterina looked in, then went away, closing the door more softly than last time.

Did all men kiss like that? I wondered. If so, I decided after some consideration that I wanted it to happen again. Then suddenly I found myself crying—the bowl laid meticulously in a place of honor, my palms shielding my face—at the thought of Fannia Redempta, forever vanished, forever silent about that ancient world on which she had closed her eyes: Fannia Redempta crumbling into dust.

Jean-Marie Tavella had been, I believe, my only enemy in Florence. Beyond that he had not mattered to me, the destruction of my career as a model having been (I had the justice to recognize even then) due largely to my own fault and to Time. But with his departure much began to change, for Italy was no longer safe from war.

By 1452, the year I was eighteen, we knew that the Turkish Sultan Mehmet intended to attack and take Constantinople. I never saw these enemies who had us all, now, restive and quarrelsome with fear. My enemies? I was a Christian, but there opposed Italy now, pressing northward, an attacker Walter had taught me to consider human like myself. This Faith—made invincible by a fervor that should have pertained to our own truth—despised us as idolators and weaklings; and Islam possessed a skill and a collective power that seemed to destroy every nation on which it turned. In a Constantinople long stripped of its gold and its statues, where Roman *fora* had reverted to field grass, the last Emperor, Constantine Palaeologus, faced the certainty that his appeals to the papacy had failed. No help would come. He chained the harbor shut and waited.

Weeks passed before we knew the Sultan had dragged his ships on rollers overland to reinforce the hundreds of thousands of troops attacking the walls. "If Constantinople falls," said Walter, "and, due to the treachery of Catholic Christendom, it will, the Sultan will turn next on Hungary—or on Venice. Let him once take Venice and he has a hold in Italy. And from Italy he can look north to Germany and France."

A chill iced my skin. The Turks are torturers, worse even than those among us who practice judicial torture: They do it, so rumor says, to terrify the conquered. For this purpose torture is, I suppose, one of the most effective tools of state. The greatest weapons are the simplest. Human terror of pain destroys the intellectual faculties and appalls the soul with despair. Nothing more effectively removes us from opposition. This the Turks know and deliberately use; though I do not suppose they produce more than the usual number of monsters who enjoy it.

They also exploit slaves. For me, as a virgin, there would be, if not rape, then medical examination, followed by sale to a brothel, which would kill me with use; or, if I was lucky, to a private buyer. If Walter and Elisabeth survived I would never know what had become of them.

These prospects caused me only a cold resolution. Death seems natural to the young, but they find waiting hard. It might be months before I knew whether, and how, I must die.

One February night, when wet clots of snow fell blurring out of the darkness to dissolve on the windowpanes, Walter sat down beside me where Jean-Marie had perched, the parcel in his hands. The gift my father brought he delivered lightly, with a calm for which, when he held up the chain with its pendant, I felt grateful. "Claire, you will never have to use this, but ease my heart by wearing it. Something strapped to the wrist would hinder a musician, but this, worn around your neck, would lie within reach of your right hand. Elisabeth has one too." I slipped it over my head. From a chain of strong silver links there hung between my breasts a dagger in a leather sheath.

I interlaced my fingers. "I have heard that to cut the wrist tendons one must slash an inch deep. A musician's hands are strong, Walter, but I do not think I can do that."

"There is a simpler way. Tonight let Elisabeth mark on your breast with ink the place you must stab to pierce your heart. Renew the mark every time you bathe. I will teach you the angle, Claire, and how hard to drive the knife, holding the hilt with both hands." His hands sketched the motion, then dropped, as if ashamed of frightening me. "The one time that matters will seem like any other practice time: the same angle, the same force of thrust. And remember, His Holiness has promised that laymen and also women may perform the Sacraments in emergency; so that even if you find yourself alone you need not die unshriven."

The dagger hung between my breasts, warm from my skin, on the night we dined with Luca della Robbia and learned that Constantinople had fallen. I remember the grave, still faces around the table. Into the silence Master Luca said, "And the emperor?"

Andrea, still panting from the run that had brought him late to supper, reached up and dragged off his cap. He crossed himself; dazedly we did the same. "Dead, his body mutilated beyond certain recognition. He rode into the fighting when he saw the day was lost. The old men had remembered an ancient gate, the Kerkoporta, long bricked up. They opened it to attack the enemy's flank. The Turks discovered the opening."

"Sit down to supper," said his aunt gently. Andrea laid his cap on the sideboard and obeyed her.

Master Luca said, "Hungary? Or Venice?"

"Will he be ready," wondered Walter, "to mount another campaign so soon?"

"Why not? This has cost him almost nothing: What are three hundred thousand troops to such a Prince? And he has gained Constantinople. And the momentum of fear."

"Will you fight?"

Master Luca shrugged. "If I must. And you?"

"I think," said my father, "it is time to go."

Late that night my parents talked, sitting side by side on their bed. "Paris again?" said Elisabeth.

"I suppose so. There is no hurry—a fleet cannot move fast.

We will have time to load everything—the library, the furniture, the presses."

"That means we must travel slowly."

Walter nodded. "With a company of archers—in convoy, probably, with other travelers. The roads will be full this summer and autumn."

Elisabeth stirred and then spoke sharply, as if she had suddenly resolved some doubt. "Walter, let us go to Saint-Aurèle. My father's house there has a big shop on the ground floor. We could build a forge. You could reassemble the presses."

"In *Saint-Aurèle*? How many times have the English taken it since the war began?"

My mother smiled faintly. "Four. And lost it. Walter, you know *that* war is ending. Even the last military governor, Sir Edward Palmer, hated it so much he did everything possible to repair the houses and the walls. They liked him—so my steward writes."

He grinned. "A governor had best retreat through a friendly mob."

"He knew that too, of course. Well, he is gone now. The Duke of York recalled him and gave up the town when King Henry went mad. You know England is settling for civil war; they must, with the nobles fighting to possess an insane king."

"—Who, if he cannot govern, can still beget another king."

"And set his name, poor soul, to other men's proclamations. England can no longer afford war with France. We should be safer in Normandy now, than here."

"And your friend?" said Walter softly.

She shrugged, her face serene. "My lord the Count ransomed himself out of English hands with some help from his sister Madame Agnès, who sold, I hear, the plate from Sainte-Bertrande. He returned home a year ago. Even in prison, my steward says, he approved Sir Edward Palmer's restorations and confirmed the appointment of his Master of Works."

Walter smiled, but spoke about something else. "Why, Elisabeth?"

"I do not know. I need to go home. The farms, of course, I have not seen them for years, and it is disgraceful to lay such a burden on Mercier—not that I suspect his honesty." She laid her hand over his. "Later, perhaps, we can go to Rouen or Paris—somewhere you can make your name. But for now, Walter, I have a hunger to go home. I never said farewell: I was young and bitter and married to an old friend of my father; all I wanted was to escape. Perhaps the time has come to say a true farewell. Just for a year, while you try the presses and train your people, assemble a list and begin your translations. Then we can decide."

"Well, I made the last two decisions. I would rather know how a press works when I present myself in Rouen. A year, then, at home . . ." His emphasis demonstrated gently, without sarcasm, that it was her birthplace, not his. He added, his cool eyes level on her face: ". . . to meet whatever awaits us there."

# 3

Those who are infatuated with Florence may think I must have been sad to leave it. Indeed I cried at leaving Master Luca. But at eighteen I had begun to be restless, even for the northern port where Elisabeth wished to settle her affairs. There I might find traces of kindred I thought of as my own, and I could look across the Channel to England. Something unfinished troubled me there; and the sea will always draw people like me, who seek within experience for the source from which it comes.

In any case the humidity of war panic, with its tendency to distort all judgment, had grown so oppressive in Florence that to leave it behind, as day followed day, was a relief almost physical. I do not recall that I looked back at the city where I had spent seven years. The North reclaimed me, with its cold, its pines, its sea. This seemed natural.

We traveled in a convoy of about forty people, living in the dozen canvas-covered wagons (three of them ours) that contained our movables. All the men rode armed; in addition we hired a company with crossbows and short-swords. At night we drew the wagons into a circle around a central fire, and sentries rode out to take their stations in the dark.

No one marks the borders in those regions, perhaps because centuries of fighting have left everyone uncertain where the borders are. I remember I was sitting, full of a savory supper, arms folded around my knees, my brown cloth traveling gown and hooded cloak in billows around me. In our wagon Elisabeth, who had excused me from this chore, had begun to unfold the mattresses. Evening tasks were underway. Washed clothing hung from makeshift lines; children had been bathed and combed. Beside me by the bonfire Walter sat, leather squeaking in his hands as he mended a piece of harness. To the sounds of leather were added the occasional spitting of the fire and the soft jingle of ring-mail from under his clothes. Somewhere farther off a mother was playing a palm-patting, hand-clapping game with a sleepy child. To my left a man was washing, crouched naked in the darkness by a wagon wheel: the night outside the ring was dangerous, and the unfastidious did not always choose to seek it. Firelight-shimmer obscured the soft August stars.

Behind us lay the wagons, whose tarred canvas sheltered my bedroom furniture—the hangings folded in their boxes, with a square of soap made in Elisabeth's stillroom tucked among the folds to discourage moths. The cushions, the plate, the books locked each with its own clasp; the lutes, each wound for soft traveling in an old velvet gown; the dismantled presses. And the close alcove where the three of us would sleep tonight, where morning light would glitter in prickles through the canvas, and the night would be aromatic with the smell of pine.

I was, I remember, in the act of wondering whether the pine trees whose scent mingled exquisitely with those of wood-smoke and crushed grass were Italian or (already) French, when three men rode carefully into the periphery of our light: one leader, two behind. Walter sprang to his feet, his sword out. I tensed with fear for him—an arrow could have taken him out of the dark—then remembered he wore shirt-of-mail beneath his coat. A voice from the darkness called with strained clarity, "Peace be on all here."

"Friend, state your business," replied Walter. Behind him the naked man had quietly resumed his sword and a minimum decency of clothing. Other men had begun to move toward us with equally quiet purpose.

"I am Johannes Meister, a courier riding between Paris and Rome. I have two guards; we carry no money beyond the cost of our food and lodging. Nothing but dispatches. May we sleep by your fire tonight?"

"What house employs you?" called Walter.

"Fugger, out of Augsburg."

"I am Walter Tarleton: Tarleton-Fugger of London. Robert is my brother."

"Christ," murmured the rider, and, dismounting, led his horse forward and took Walter's outstretched hand. His guards followed gingerly, while our men watched to see they had told the truth about their numbers. "How strange to meet you on the road, sir. I know your brother's name, of course; I have not met him."

"Not so strange to meet us—not with the Turk behind us. Come, sit down. Marco, see to their horses, please. Have you eaten?"

"Not since breakfast. I'm famished," admitted Johannes Meister.

"I think our stew pot can fill three more bowls. Sit down and tell us all your news."

When bowls and spoons occupied our guests the whole circle relaxed, and several people drew nearer to listen. "What of the Turkish fleet?" someone asked. Couriers heard more even than their masters confided to them, and no one since the messengers of Imperial Rome had moved faster—and on these same roads, it occurred to me, where roads had not sunk to cart tracks.

Herr Meister grinned. "The ladies of Venice can sleep in their own beds this winter. Rumor goes he will move overland into Hungary."

"And Constantinople?" I ventured. Already I had heard the first of the songs, by the composer Guillaume Dufay:

*Omnes amici eius spreverunt eam:*
*non est qui consoletur eam ex omnibus caris eius—*

All her friends forsook her.
No single one of all her lovers consoles her—

The courier shrugged. "What is there to say, Mistress? Sancta Sophia will become a mosque. The Sultan saved the priests who crept out from behind the altar to embrace his knees. Them indeed he saved, and no one else. The city had little gold to yield him, but its location will make it a valuable gain. As for the rest, old people tortured for sport, virgin girls raped and sold, boys torn apart between their captors, since the Turk reserves them too for rape. Byzantine scholars will enrich our universities. My master, Karl Gottfried Fugger, has authorized me to ransom two men whose names I carry, and one woman if she is not dead."

The sorrow in our silence was so familiar a burden I scarcely weighed it. "And France?" said Walter.

"France is not a kingdom but a cluster of duchies, several of which owe allegiance to England. I wish King Charles well of them. Keep clear of Bordeaux; his troops are fighting the last of the English there. The French will win, and then, I think, England must look to her mad king."

"Then at last it may be ending," murmured Walter.

Johannes Meister set down his bowl and, extracting a handkerchief, used it neatly as a napkin. He refolded it and felt for his pocket. "You, sir, travel to the coast?"

"To the Norman coast, to Saint-Aurèle."

Meister laughed. "Then forget your English brother. The Count means to hang anyone not found loyal."

"My wife is French, my own loyalties flexible within the limits of honor."

"Well spoken. Be flexible, sir, toward Paris: The Count cherishes a strange conviction that the capital of France lies there, not in London. However, on the coast you will, I think, still find English raiders for some time. When a war lasts one hundred and twenty years, people begin to forget—first why it started, then why they fight it, and then at last they forget to fight it at all. This war will die of boredom, but slowly and viciously. His Grace the Count means to have peace in his own lands. He does not dislike the English—he rules too many crossbred men with crossbred loyalties. But," said Johannes Meister, "I should advise you to take care."

There came a day when the patois of the borderlands yielded to French, which I found I spoke as easily as though I had never left it; and I was no longer in doubt. Other travelers on the road brought us word that King Charles's troops had beaten the Bordellais. Crossbows loaded, we proceeded around the disturbance, circumspectly north.

In a deeply rutted lane where yellow leaves already shook down through the soft violet of evening, I watched my father go down to bathe in the river. The cold brown stream tempted me, and the men and women bathing in the half-light observed the courtesy of a mutual self-absorption.

I watched Walter strip: studied the hard buttocks and thick shoulders, the graying mat of hair at his chest, the dark weight of the genitals. I knew what a man would do with me when Nature drove me to that strange act. But what a *strange* act, I reflected, trying to imagine what pleasure it could possibly give me to be opened and occupied by the distended rod of flesh that, in the visual promiscuity of the camp, I had come to find so unbeautiful. True, a man's body seen from behind—the beauty of function in shoulders, back, and buttocks—moved me with a powerful longing. I turned to Elisabeth. "I'd rather bathe in the wagon."

She laughed up at me from where she knelt by the cooking fire; she had seen the direction of my gaze. "Good, because I have your water hot. Wash your hair tonight."

"I will." And because I trusted her absolutely, I blurted, "Elisabeth, what makes us enjoy it? Does the virgin-blood hurt?"

"Not at all. I know you fear childbirth, but I will help you there, and your husband too: a baby should be born into its father's hands." From a box she unfolded towels. Walter had submerged and was swimming. We paused, arrested absurdly with a towel between us, and my stepmother said softly, "What makes us enjoy it? It is hard to explain beforehand. God made us love their beauty, and the act brings one so close . . . so near to him. And the thrusting of his effort, and his joy—how hard they work for it, Claire. One feels, I think, a human delight in giving so great a service. And the act is a pleasure that can be learned." (Of more specific pleasures I had long known in solitude.) "Unlike the animals, we have to learn, so gentleness and love both help. And when they are clean," she added, "they *smell* so good, Claire!"

I laughed and, balancing my pails of hot water, climbed into the wagon.

In the space now cleared of its mattresses I spread the bath cloth and sopped a sponge. The ball of black soap smelled of roses. I loved the laboriousness of this task, its care and neatness, and the sharp herbal fragrance of the rosemary wash I combed at last through my wet hair. I coiled it in a towel, pulled on my gown and laced my blue leather shoes, and, climbing down the wagon steps, presented Elisabeth with the empty pails.

"Now," she said, "go fill them for me."

I nodded happily. Dusk had deepened to a jeweled brilliance; smells of summer mingled with the delicate acid scent of the first turning leaves. My skin felt like supple velvet; it delighted me to be alive.

I met Walter coming up from the stream. He had dressed; a towel hung across his shoulders. "Here, let me take those," he said. "Hello, what's this?"

"A puffball, I think," I replied, peering through the dusk at the pale dome his foot had stumbled on. "Or a strange rock. Kick it: puffballs send up such clouds of dust."

"Just a moment." Walter laid down the pails and knelt, searching with his hands. "It is a skull."

"Oh," I whispered.

My father grunted, lifting it free. "He's got earth in his eyes, poor old fellow. I wonder if he died shriven."

"Who was he, do you think?" It did not even stare at us, the anonymous rind, the astounding transformation of a living person into a thing. I could not even imagine the soft shining of eyes within its sockets.

Walter shrugged. "An English longbowman. A beggar who died of cold. A girl who crept into the hedge to bear her baby. Let's lay it back to rest." His thumb traced a cross on the forehead; and as his hands scooped a hollow for it in the ground, I heard him murmur the words of Virgil: "What part of the earth is not full of our calamities?"

And so, pondering rumors of the first peace since our great-grandfathers' time (*signed*, swore someone who claimed to have seen it: *signed* between France and England), we came down into Normandy: Normandy of the wind and sea, of orchard trees now tattered yellow; of monolithic burial chambers shattered open to the sun, and of castle and abbey walls rising from a profound and brilliant green. Sea mist pearled my skin. My father told me of the bells sailors heard ringing from a lost town beneath the sea, and of the phantom dog that prowls by the side, at night, of those who are soon to die, and of ghost armies heard but not seen on the Roman road; and the green changed to an autumn haze of gold, of violet and orange.

We passed the cream-colored clifflike walls of the Abbey of Sainte-Bertrande, where the Count's sister, Agnès d'Aubry, ruled as Abbess. I looked at them with the watchful blankness of foreknowledge, but it remained unconscious: such powers conceal themselves until it is too late.

Under an oyster-colored sky we came to Elisabeth's manor of La Pipardière. The house stood in the cup of wooded hills. Trees crowded up to the key-shaped wall that surrounded it, leaving one small gateway that could be guarded. Within this ring of masonry (I was to be glad, years later on a night of murder, that the house had impressed me enough to be remembered) lay a thatched manor of rose-red brick and warped timber, moldering into a moat serenely clotted with oak leaves and water lilies.

The steward, Blaise Mercier, kissed Elisabeth and presented me to his grown son, his daughter-in-law and two grandchildren, Suzanne and Isabelle. During the next day Elisabeth, her scrutiny disguised by a charming flow of talk, went over the farm accounts and those of the three other holdings; Walter talked to the little girls about Florence; and I, courteous and shy, explored the place.

By early evening of our second day the sky had turned blue. As I passed him, carrying a grimy Bible on whose flyleaves my step-great-grandfather had painted some watercolor sketches I wanted to examine, Monsieur Mercier said to me, "Mademoiselle Claire, I have not happened to see your mother in the past hour. If you should run across her, would you tell her from me that the house you desire in Saint-Aurèle was vacated by its tenants, who left it in good condition, at the end of their lease? Since then it has stood empty except for a resident watchman. As I knew about the presses, I took the liberty of having the partitions removed from the ground floor, which leaves a large single room. I could not install a forge, as I had no specific instructions."

"Thank you very much for your care, monsieur. I'll find my mother."

"Oh no, just if you should happen to meet her. . . . Otherwise I shall certainly see her at supper."

I found her on the upper floor, standing, her cloak about her shoulders, in the middle of an empty room. Sensing I had intruded, though on what I did not know, I hesitated, silent. The room was big, with latticed windows and the combination I was to see over and over in Normandy, of a ceiling heavy with black timbers and walls of polished, almost greasy-looking gray stone. No furniture: nothing, apparently, to engage my mother's interest. I remember only a fireplace, blackened with ancient soot; and that, in a cold house, the temperature yet seemed to me abnormally cold—a chill that, when I ventured across the threshold, surprised me by beginning at the sill, neat as a knife edge.

She turned and saw me. "Yes, it *is* cold, isn't it? Always. This was my sister Catherine's room. Will you get your cloak and go with me? I feel lonely on this day. I must go to church and pray for her."

And so we made our way along a track worn a thousand years deep in the pebbly soil, past fields where black-and-white cattle browsed among the stones, to where the church raised its roof—a note of sea-blue unexpected as a jewel—and its spire against the deep green of the hills. Both roof and spire, I surmised, were newer than the buttressed walls, whose simplicity gave the church a resemblance to the neighboring farmhouses.

"I was baptized here," said Elisabeth. "We both were."

We opened the old wood door, and dipped and signed ourselves in holy water that looked, I thought, suspiciously brackish. There were no pews, only a smell of cold and of old worship. Before the Virgin who was the church's only adornment someone had placed a brown pottery vase filled with oak leaves. Elisabeth sank to her knees; I, lingering at a distance, gazed at the Madonna.

Some local carver had made her, I guessed, a hundred years ago, and her robes had split a little to reveal the pale satin grain of the wood. Her gown, painted blue, fell straight to her feet; a veil covered her yellow braids; and her broad white face, with its shallow planes and small red mouth, was more primitive than her beautiful hands. These were ringless, and her gaze followed them downward to the tiny haloed Christ child—not quite a baby, but a staggering toddler—tugging at her skirts to hold himself upright.

At last Elisabeth rose, and, her face closed against me, moved past me out the door. Outside the threshold I caught her arm. "Elisabeth."

"Yes?"

"Sit here." I guided her to a stone bench beside the wall. With obvious impatience she obeyed me and said again, "Yes?"

"Tell me how Catherine died. Tell me now. It is time."

"Ah God." It was a sound of assent. Her hands, the marriage finger circled by Walter's broad gold band, sealed her mouth, then fell. "Of course, the house will come to you."

"I do not think of such things."

"No, of course not, but you have the right to know. I wish you had never thought to ask." She folded her hands and seemed to gather her body, still gazing straight ahead. "I will not describe her to you—either her looks, which were not quite like mine, or her wit, or her loving kindness. How can we re-create a person who was unique in all Creation? Never mind, old age has made me garrulous."

"You are forty-two," I said steadily, "and you are not old."

Elisabeth nodded as though she had not heard me. "The house has no history, you must understand, nothing at all. My great-great-grandfather raised it. Aside from the usual sieges and famines, *nothing has ever happened there*. There are no traditions."

"Traditions?" My voice was careful.

She nodded. "Of anything malign." My skin tightened over the muscle. "My room lay down the corridor. Both of us liked our solitude, so we did not share a bed, as sisters often do. I wish now I *had* slept in one bed with her. Perhaps I could have fought what she could not fight."

I was now certain I knew, and wished I had not asked. "A man?"

With a curious desperation Elisabeth shook her head. "No, no. On the night my sister died it was about an hour past midnight. All of us had gone to bed at sunset, by the custom my father set. I was reading by candlelight in my room when I heard my sister scream. I raced down the corridor and threw open her door. She lay in her bed open-eyed, and dead, and receding through the far door"—I remembered now I had seen a second door, closed, in the wall beyond the fireplace—"I saw something so appalling I must never describe it."

"But what *was* it?"

"I cannot say."

"Elisabeth, please, I beg you."

"No. Never ask me again, Claire. *I must not say.*"

"Why? For her?"

"I simply know I must not."

There was a long silence. At last I said, "Is our family cursed, then?"

"I do not believe so. Nothing similar has ever been seen in the house again. I asked Mercier, and I would know if he was lying."

I nodded. Then I said with sudden authority, "Elisabeth, put the room back into use. Not as a bedroom: as a clothes pantry, a stillroom, anything, but use it again."

"Yes, you may be right."

"Since then has there been anything—any dream, any sign—to tell you your sister still existed?"

"Nothing. Whatever took her from us that night seemed to annihilate her. I have no feel of her; I have never received a sign. It is as though"—Elisabeth hesitated—"whatever came to her concerned her alone, for a reason I will never understand. Do not seek an answer, Claire; you will find none. Of that one thing I am certain."

A cowbell sounded; the cattle in the field opposite lowed; some heaved themselves up out of the stream; and the whole herd filed down the track into the dusk, the bell jangling remotely. The smell of dung intensified the sweetness of grass and of the distant forest with its moss and rotten logs. All around us lay a luminous peace, blue and green both exquisitely deepened by the day's final light. Within ten minutes the light would visibly recede, the colors sink to gray.

"Claire," said Elisabeth, "do you believe the Church tells us truth when it says the blessed souls still live?"

I gazed into the fading sweetness. "I do not know. I think of death as a blow; something that hurts and is swiftly over. I have no feel of what comes after."

Elisabeth's hands twisted. "Never to wake—never to know if we *shall* wake."

I took her hand. In a landscape whose beauty seemed like goodness rendered into color, scent, and sound, we sat in a profound silence.

---

When we rode past the Abbey of Sainte-Bertrande, ruled as her own fief by the sister of Jean d'Aubry de Saint-Aurèle, I had failed to draw the logical conclusion—that we had now passed the borders of the comté. My parents, preoccupied for their own reasons, also neglected to mark by any comment our entry into the territory of our new lord.

And Elisabeth's first liege lord, I remembered: for much of

the year her family had lived in the town, which had since Roman times been a considerable port. She had played as a child with Jean d'Aubry, his elder sister Agnès, and his younger sister Marie. She had danced with him when both were young, in the years before his father died and bequeathed him the seigneurie. When she spoke of him it had always been with courtesy and serene goodwill; but they maintained, so far as I knew, no correspondence, and it struck me suddenly how seldom she spoke of him at all.

I glanced at my stepmother's pretty freckled profile. At the moment she was laughing over something Walter had said; I glimpsed her excellent teeth. I mentally thanked God I had inherited them, before I remembered.

The end of a journey always involves us in some disappointment; and I felt the sorrow of ending—or the dread of beginning—bring to my eyes tears of a shallow anger as our cavalcade halted on a wooded hill to gaze down on Saint-Aurèle. Here I would live for at least the next year. Suddenly I minded that I was going to nothing and no one I knew.

The day was cool. The sea lay before us, a plane of brilliant blue. The blaze at the horizon might have been the far white line of England, or might have been the cloud that was beginning to blend upward into streaks of rose. At this moment the sea had the subtlety of a great jewel: sapphire in the depths, decreasing to turquoise and emerald until it washed aquamarine over the beaches that had crumbled from the chalk cliffs. In their clean brilliance (Walter had told me one could find embedded in them the shells of creatures that had lived before the Flood) the line of these cliffs, stretching for miles on either side of us, looked curiously artificial, for the turf that carpeted them was still brilliantly green, laid down on their whiteness as neatly as velvet.

Turning my attention to the town, I could see the great scoop of the bay with its wharves, its floating docks, its fishing smacks and clinker-built caravels, the packed roofs of its taverns and warehouses—and its ruins. I noted the mended lengths of city wall, here gray and small-textured, there patched with bigger stones; noted the little river that entered the town, its course blocked against enemies by a spiked grille driven deep into its bed; noted the hopelessness of this precaution—for yards beyond that point the wall crumbled off into dense green forest. Forest blocked my vision to the right; girdling the town from the point where we stood lay its rich autumn fields.

I glanced again at the wall. It would serve, if the forest could to some extent defend the town where the wall had broken, but from the sea there could be no defense. All the roofs, I saw, were tiled, either with slate or with weathered grains of red-brown on many gabled roofs. I saw the single city gate, and to its left the steep red roofs, the walls and plump solid cylinders of the castle. One gray street plunged down (the whole town fell toward the harbor) past a square: I glimpsed its rectangle, surrounded by the timbered fronts of houses. There, I guessed, would be the smithies, bathhouses, shops, and—yes, a church tower.

First, then, and farthest from me, the scoop of the harbor. From it the town seemed to rise in three divisions. To my left a section dominated by the castle and the square; in the center a section that seemed all roofs, no doubt threaded by alleys invisible from our hill. To the far right, beyond the river and its modest humped bridge, another, more thinly peopled street plunged down to a seawall. But this section dissolved landward into meadow and into the thick forest; at the seamost end, in an emerald desolation on the cliffs, stood a partly destroyed church.

"God, how much they've burnt," said Walter quietly.

Elisabeth nodded. And then, my perception refocused as if by his command, I saw how much of it lay in ruins: how many of the houses were roofless shells, how many beggars' shacks had sprung up to fill holes where even the earth had been burned black. I noted a whole section of rubble to the left of the square and saw the torn-open roof of the distant church. "'The English brought back the forests,'" quoted my stepmother softly.

Walter laid his hand over hers. "I am sorry."

She shrugged. "So were the people of Dover last time we sacked it."

"You said," I interrupted, "that monsieur le comte has appointed a Master of Works?"

"Sir Edward Palmer appointed him," replied Walter, "and monsieur le comte, apparently liking his choice, confirmed it."

"I hope he's an able man. He has much to do."

"And perhaps," said Walter, "with the peace signed, time in which to do it. Poor things, they must have broken their hearts over it. No wonder the Count means to have peace in which to rebuild. By the way, Claire, do you see that field below the damaged church? Elisabeth tells me it conceals the Roman town."

She nodded. "We used to dig there as children and find shards of pottery and bits of glazed mosaic."

"Then I shall dig there." Roman antiquities fascinated me far more than did the Greek statues with their shallow idealization and empty eyes. "And you say there was no real man called Saint Aurèle?"

My stepmother shook her head. "There was, as you know, a Roman emperor Marcus Aurelius. My father believed that Saint-Aurèle is a corruption of his name christianized over the centuries. People pray to Saint-Aurèle here, and the priests accept it."

Walter grinned. "How can they not, as they accept the rites of Saint Jean-Baptiste? Rites, Claire, that involve women leaping naked over bonfires among the Standing Stones. Caesar says the Gauls did that to make the women fertile; but the Church is a capacious vessel. Priests do not mind local usage; that is, if they can read and are not heretical—"

"How hard it is to be *sure* on that point," interjected Elisabeth earnestly. "Walter, do you remember the Bishop of Durham who, when struggling to decipher the word *aenigmate* in Saint Paul, exclaimed—"

Laughing, we all three chanted a family joke: *"By the Mass, this was no courteous man that wrote that word!"*

Wiping his eyes, Walter resumed. *"If* they can read, and are not heretical, then they think mainly of their rents, their bellies, and their concubines."

"I should like to see the Rites of Saint John," I said. "Elisabeth, did you ever go?"

She tossed back her head, and a smile—secret, wicked, and delightful—made Walter glance at her in tolerant boredom. "Oh, no. Girls of decent family never visited the Standing Stones at night. Not on that night, Claire."

"But if some gentleman went with me . . ."

"There *are* no gentlemen on Saint John's Night. We shall see, but probably no."

"I am *quite sure* I should come to no harm," I said, wishing I sounded sincere.

Both my parents laughed. So did I, for all at once Saint-Aurèle held something for me alone, something of my own for which I had come: a determination to evade them on the Feast of Saint John and to see the women leap naked over the bonfires among the Standing Stones.

"Come, let us go down," said Walter. The sun had faded; below us crocus-yellow lights came pricking out of the dusk. Soon I would be asleep in the bed of friends, for a family was waiting to welcome us with supper and with news. The faint, sour sadness of journey's end vanished, and in comradeship we rode down into Saint-Aurèle.

# 4

The noise of hammering had at first echoed maddeningly through the torn-open shell of the Church of La Vièrge-aux-dames. But habit had now made it, to the ears of those who worked there, almost inaudible, and the smell of new timber pleasantly countered the fire-stench that still lingered. A group of English had been trapped here and had fired the place before they died, putting a barrier of flame between themselves and the Frenchmen who must reach them. The smoke had killed them; the heat had brought down the roof; and what of humanity could be salvaged, after days while the beams cooled, had been interred, with prayer.

Now the cracked but scoured-clean tiles communicated no trace of such commotion. Richard Linacre de Verneuil, Master of Works, decided the old tiling could not be saved; decided on diamonds of black and white marble. He must commission them from the quarry. Fortunately the Count's allotment for the repair of La-Vièrge-aux-dames would more than cover it. He glanced upward, where carpenters, aloft against the cool September sky, had completed the new rafters.

"We must roof it quickly if we mean to work all winter," remarked his brother Thomas.

Richard nodded. "I expect the roof to be closed by late

October. And no, we will not stop for winter. Where we cannot work out of doors there is plenty to do inside. I will not let this church go unsalvaged."

"Why? Because it was the pagan temple?"

"To Diana of the Fishermen, yes. Our oldest building, save for the foundation of the public bathhouse, and . . ." He gestured landward, downhill, to the meadow where forest swallowed a great half-moon depression.

"And the old arena."

"Where, so Placidius Gallus tells us, in A.D. 175 there occurred a riot so murderous between our people and those of the next town that the Emperor closed the arena for a year."

"Someone must have placed a rotten bet," remarked Thomas Linacre. "That would explain the name, perhaps."

"The Ladies' Virgin?" His brother smiled. "Perhaps; all my researches have, I admit, discovered no other explanation. Perhaps, truly read, our church should be called The Lady's Virgin."

"And that would please you."

"That," replied his brother, "would mean we have worshipped for at least sixteen hundred years in this place: which would, I think, please both Ladies, whether on Olympus or in Paradise." They were speaking softly and stood far from the workmen, in the sunlight by the porch door. Even so Richard, checking, cast a glance out over the others. Then, in answer to his brother's eyes, he shrugged. "All the Bishop asks is prudence."

Thomas—younger by seven years; as tall as his brother at five feet eleven inches; in ten years, no doubt, to be a handsome, burly man where now he was a boy of extraordinary beauty—looked away, to the road that spent itself against the seawall. He was bad at lying even to the Bishop and did not enjoy it.

Everything in Saint-Aurèle that was not the green of forest or the red of tile was white or gray or brown. The chalk cliffs had crumbled to make the sand that the tide exposed, and human feet had grooved white paths in the turf. But one could not build in chalk, so house stones came from one quarry that sent gray blocks, or from a more distant one, whose revenues went into the strongbox of the Abbess of Sainte-Bertrande, that supplied blocks of a pale gentle brown. Five hundred years ago the masons had built La Vièrge-aux-dames in the shape of a cross out of this brown stone. Where nave met transept they had raised a squat tower, whose fabric Richard Linacre had recently passed as sound despite the fire. A porch, untouched by the fire and still roofed with the original flaking slate, admitted people from the road; but the church itself, like the temple before it, faced out to sea.

From the harbor below Julius Caesar had launched ships toward Britain, after sacrificing a white goat to the Lady who, governing the moon, governed also the tides. The descendants of his mariners still prayed to the descendant of the Lady, and prayed for the same things: winters without storms, good catch, tides that would carry them to the icy fertile waters of Le Bras d'Or, to the rock inlets of the New-Found Land; prayed for currents to carry them home again, and for salvation should they die so far from her protection, so many thousand miles from home.

"I wonder how long before erosion reaches the church," said Richard.

Thomas glanced at him sharply. "My God, I hadn't thought of that."

His brother shrugged. "How much has gone since Caesar's time? Do we know? It just falls into the water." Fell straight down, both remembered, from the knife-edge five hundred yards away; fell down two hundred feet of green-streaked ancient lime to crumble into the sand of the narrow, perfect beach, or to drop off, as did the harbor, into deep green water.

"But now look at this." They had been speaking French. Now Richard dropped into the English they both kept fluent for private communication. From the shadows by the wall he drew into the light of the porch a round object, apparently heavy, wrapped in cloth.

Thomas dropped beside him, his gentle, high-colored face kindly with interest. He wore hose and a short, warm coat, and resembled his brother in the contrast of dark hair with light eyes. But Thomas's hair curled as richly as an Italian's; his eyes were blue-gray; and the fresh healthy lips were fuller and wider than his brother's. "What is it?"

"I think, the head of Diana, on whom Caesar's eyes have rested."

The fine brown wool of Richard's robe, worn over his day clothes and belted with worked leather, swirled over the broken tiles as the brothers knelt side by side. The long, clever, dirty fingers (being Master of Works had rendered Richard not only an adept sheriff and accountant but also carpenter, roofer, tiler, sculptor, whatever the need for extra hands demanded) gently folded back the cloth.

From it emerged the white oval of a face, its curled hair delicately crannied with age, its nose springing straight from the forehead, its mouth full and small below the perfectly indented upper lip. Between the lids Thomas could still discern the ghosts of pigmented pupils. "She was *painted*," he whispered.

Richard nodded. "They did paint their statues. Many ancient writers say so. What a brilliant show they must have made. But I dare not paint her when I set her up again in her right place, on the body of our broken Madonna."

"*What?*"

"Father Paul would bless her. We could repaint the old robes and drape her head with a veil, then say she is some ancient Madonna newly recovered."

"With the chisel marks of a Hellenic sculptor still on her? You dare not."

Richard settled on his haunches, the stone head balancing his weight. Unlike his hands, which had to be scoured every evening, his hair was clean. It waved back from a center parting, almost cloudy with the sea wind, and lighter in color than his brother's. His eyebrows were straight and thick, and long black lashes shaded eyes of a cool gray-green. Soldiering had taken him from the Sorbonne at the age of fifteen, and had left him with scars on ribs and left forearm; to his father's relief (their mother was then dead), boredom and smallpox had ended soldiering, leaving him marked only by two pits in the angle of his jaw. After that had come the Jagiellonian University at Kraków, fluency in Polish and in German, and a return to work for which his education had, by the accident of its variety, fitted him. He had never, thought Thomas, lost condition, and the hands and arms that lightly hefted twenty pounds of marble did so without effort.

Richard sighed. "No, I dare not. But when this work is done"—he gestured out toward Saint-Aurèle—"all of it, which I have sworn to do, I will build our family chapel here, and she shall be our Madonna. I'll carve her body with my own hands."

"When you have time." When, as Thomas spoke it, meant never.

Sudden motion in the street attracted him. "Look: five horses coming to that empty house by the seawall, and the women riding astride." That meant they were not ladies of the Court, who rode sidesaddle.

The party dismounted. Some commotion ensued, figures pointing and summoning, until a servant led the horses away. "Two women, both pretty. Good God!" said Thomas, as the younger of the two threw back her hood.

His brother glanced at him. "You know all the news, you idle taker of His Grace's money. Who is she?"

"You *know* I'm off to the Sorbonne next year. I'm only trying to help you, and you can take your salary and. . . ." The girl, waving and laughing, ran down to the seawall. Thomas choked.

Richard grinned. "—While *I*, industrious soul, thatch roofs all day long. So who's the beauty?"

"Almost certainly the printer's daughter. I *told* you, damn you—"

"About the daughter?"

"About the printer, only you were wondering how to rehouse the poor around the marketplace. His equipment comes from Mainz. He was the second printer in Italy. Now that he's left, I suppose they have only one."

Richard frowned. "A press? My God, they have not one in Paris, not yet!"

"But this man, if he's good, could send his books as far as Paris. Let me see, there's one at Mainz, one at Augsburg, one at Florence. . . . Soon, they say, many towns will have them."

"What an unfortunate honor to come to us after so much trouble."

"Why? Do you think the Count will dislike it?"

"I do not know," murmured Richard. "It could be turned to the good. I hope he expects a visit from the Count: he will receive one soon." He rose, dusting off the robe that established him at sight as master in his profession. "As your elder brother—come along—I'm going to present you to your beauty."

"*Thank* you."

"My hands are dirty, though."

"Spit on them."

Richard cast one calculating, ultimately negative glance at the font; then, with regret, spat on his hands and dried them with his handkerchief. "How dirty am I?"

"You sound as though you bathed every six months instead of twice a day. You look dirty enough to establish your hard work, and therefore your character. Come *on*, she may turn back. I'm going to marry her."

"No you're not," said his brother, with tolerance.


But I did not turn back. I was still wondering if it was England, and behind me all but the servants had vanished into the

64

house. I had glanced uphill at the church, then dismissed it to turn back to the smoking green and blue of the sea. Above me gulls wheeled and mewed, and the wind was cold.

As I fumbled to draw up my hood, a voice said, "Good morning, Mistress."

The lilt came easily, and the accent, so I knew at second-hand, was London. The hood forgotten, I turned. Two men—both by my standards tall, both handsome—had joined me. I saw Marco stir warily. "How did you know I spoke English, sir?"

"I am Richard Linacre, Master of Works, and this, Mistress . . . ?"

"Claire Tarleton."

"—Mistress Tarleton, is Thomas, my brother."

"Good day." The brother, fresh-colored and sweet-faced, shook my hand. "We came down from the church to greet you, Mistress Tarleton. We had heard the printer was an Englishman."

"I see. From the church?"

"I am conducting the repairs there," replied Richard Linacre. The name, I noticed, worked in either language. He had given it, and my own name, the hard English consonants and crisp vowels both would bear. "So we shall, at least on some days, be neighbors. Welcome to Saint-Aurèle. I hope to meet your father."

My parents had obviously been called out of the house. Now both stood waiting. I led my guests toward the presences that had, with firm friendliness and without a word, commanded me to do precisely that. "Sir, Madame, I should like to present His Grace's Master of Works, Richard Linacre, and Master Thomas Linacre, his brother."

Walter, smiling, held out his hand; Richard took it. I noticed that despite the sea wind his lips were unchapped and wholesome and that his teeth, when he smiled, were even. His cheekbones were thin and high, his long nose sharp, his chin strong and slightly cleft. An intolerant face, quick to anger and laughter. At the square neck of his gown I glimpsed the band of a shirt of fine voile. "I should not take your hand, sir—I've been working all morning."

"I do not doubt you have. We have heard of you, sir, as far as Italy. My wife, Madame Elisabeth."

Richard bowed and, when she held out her hand, took it with comical reluctance. "Heard of me? How odd."

"Not at all. My steward has written how well His Grace approves your work." Elisabeth's voice was warmly kind.

"You know His Grace, Madame?"

"Since I was a girl here."

"Of course," began Richard, "now I remember—"

He stopped. Elisabeth filled a pause that proved a fraction too long. "Yes, I believe I knew your father; he was Judge Matthew Linacre, was he not? And other old friends here, thank God, have not forgotten me."

"Yes, of course," said Richard. "The Count will visit you, sir. He will want to decide for himself whether the gift you bring us is dangerous."

"Thank you," replied Walter. "For the warning" remained unspoken.

A thought occurred to me. "Master Linacre, have you discovered any Roman antiquities in the course of your excavations?"

He grinned and, to my pleasure, blushed brick-red. "What do you want, Mistress? The wharf Caesar built in the harbor? The cleanly but disreputable lower levels of the bathhouse? The villa I think the landfall buried?" He gestured to the steep hill on which the church stood, and I saw that, despite the regrowth of turf and trees, its side had a lumpy, unnatural contour. "Or"—Thomas and Richard exchanged smiles—"the overgrown arena?"

"Do you mean," demanded Walter, "the arena where, according to Placidius Gallus—?"

"The same, sir."

"You must take me to see it when I have dealt with this business of the forge."

"B-but"—I was stammering in my eagerness—"will you please take *me* to see it *now?*"

Richard's glance intercepted Thomas's voluble pleasure. "If your father permits."

"Where would you take her?" inquired Elisabeth.

"Not far. Down to the bottom of the meadow, and have her back to you, madame, in an hour. Sir, I've cleared the fighting place and had the turf torn from rows of seats." My father moaned with longing. "I'm hoping to find the works below, where they caged the beasts. Mistress Claire can see it and tell you whether she thinks it worth your while. I won't let her climb into any of the underground works; they are certainly unsafe."

"Mistress Claire possesses a Roman millefiori bowl that she carried from Florence on her lap. Sir," said Walter gently, "you are gentlemen, you and your brother. Keep to your hour. She may go with you if she wishes."


In spite of my shyness I felt at ease with them as, my cloak torn out behind me in billows by the wind, we walked together down the steep gray street—Thomas on my right hand, Richard on my left. I glanced up at them. "How tall you are!"

Thomas grinned. "I'll pass six-foot-two, like my father. But Richard is quite an old man, twenty-six, and unlikely to grow any further. I am nineteen, and—"

"And means to propose marriage to you, Mistress Tarleton," Richard cut across him. He laughed at his brother's indignant glare. "Thomas, hit me when we get home. How unkind of me."

"Mistress Tarleton," Thomas assured me earnestly, "I do *not* mean to propose marriage to you."

"Thank you," I replied, bemused.

"Shall we turn off across the field?" inquired Richard. "It will not prove easy going, I'm afraid."

I looked at the expanse of turf and yellow wild grass. "Rather than cut across from the street? I don't mind."

"I hope we don't sully your clothes, then. Take my hand." His strong fingers lifted me impersonally over the ridge of rubble that separated road from wasteland. I noticed then that he, like Thomas, wore a sword.

"I wish I had brothers," I said, liking them.

Thomas smiled down at me. "Have you none, then?"

"No, nor sisters either. I'm a foster child, and my parents have no other."

"Of English parentage," said Richard, "or do you know?"

"Of English parentage, yes. Have you sisters and brothers?" I tried to distribute my attention courteously between them as we labored over ground that, being lumpy, was indeed hard walking.

"We have two sisters, both married and settled, one at Rouen, one at Dieppe," replied Thomas. "Our mother died when we were children; our father died of the smallpox six years ago."

"I'm sorry. Did you take the sickness?"

"No." Thomas shrugged. "Perhaps God will spare me. Richard's had it."

"Yes, I see," I said, then blushed, for I had noticed the two deep scar-pits beneath his jaw.

"That's all right," he said gently. "The doctor in our company proved good. He gave me something to drink, wrapped me in blankets till I sweated, and laid me by the fire. I sweated it out and escaped alive."

"I'm glad, of course. When I was about five my mother took a knife she had passed through fire, nicked my arm, and rubbed into my cut the pus from a cowpox sore. I was sick for two weeks after, but she says my skin will stay clear as a farm girl's.

She says that's how farm girls escape it, by catching the cowpox instead."

"So that's true, is it? I shall remember."

"You said 'the doctor in our company.'"

"I was soldiering, Mistress Claire."

"Why?" I asked baldly.

Richard came to a halt and looked down at me, his hands on his hips. "Because I thought that to fight would prove more exciting than studying law at the Sorbonne. But the day I saw a friend lose his right hand to a gangrenous wound, I thought: 'If I lose my fingers I will never be able to sculpt, or to write a letter, or'"—he hesitated, but only for a second—"'or feel the touch of a woman's skin; and if this evil frivolity costs me my hand *for no good cause*, then it is sin, and God will require it of me.' And then I got smallpox, and smallpox helped."

"Why is the ground so lumpy?" I demanded.

"We think the Roman town lies buried all around here," answered Thomas, his face reflecting in its quick compassion how fleetingly his brother had angered him. "Whereas our town rises from the harbor and to the right—the new square—we believe the ancient town rose from the harbor and to the left, toward the Temple of Diana." He gestured toward La Vièrge-aux-dames, its squat homely shape pointing seaward from the summit of its crumbled hill.

We had come many hundred yards south, down steadily declining ground. I wondered over what buried houses, over what *fora* I might be walking. "Master Richard, do you investigate these things as the Count's servant? And with his money? Will he be angry?"

Richard shook his head. "What I find will interest him. You will discover him to be a learned man. I hope he and your father like each other. No, I use my own money for this, my own time and my own men. Most of the turf Thomas and I cut away ourselves, by torchlight."

And so, in the shadow of the brown and orange trees, we

came to it: a great stepped cup in the turf. Saplings had rooted themselves in the green-velvet tiers, their roots grappling the hidden marble. But the bared tiers were white as bones in the earth, and at the bottom I could see the ancient arena floor.

The two men helped me down; the benches, I found, could also serve as steps. At last we stood where the beasts had fought and gazed up at what Richard had freed from the earth: the huge rings of seats that vanished, behind me, into earth again.

Richard pointed to a row of sculptured chairs, their every surface patterned with Latin letters. "Those were for the notables: magistrates and so forth. Will it please you to sit down?"

I sat down. All around me the haunted air rang soundlessly with the will and energy of minds long dead. My two new friends, laughing, bowed. I inclined my head. "Thank you, Master Linacre. You will not believe me, but no one has ever given me a greater gift."

"There will be more. Shall I call you when I find something?"

"Unless you want me to pester you like a child."

Thomas frowned. "We must go, Mistress Claire."

"And," said Richard, glancing at the ring that rose above us, "there's no way but the climb. Listen, Mistress Claire. Stand up on your chair, so." I obeyed, smiling expectantly, as docile as a younger sister. "Now"—they jumped up beside me—"take her elbow, Thomas. Stiffen your arms and lift your feet clear— that's good. We'll lift you up tier by tier."

And so, carried like a parcel, I arrived laughing at the higher ground level. As we set off homeward I said, "Master Thomas, your brother has a history; he has had smallpox and gone for a soldier and given up the law. What have *you* done?"

"Gone to school with the monks here—and to the Sorbonne next year; we intend to give the law a second chance with us. And last year I visited our cousins in London. You remind me of one of them, our cousin Alison." Richard groaned. The sound, I thought, comic as it was, covered some actual irritation.

"In London?" I exclaimed. "But the war?"

Thomas shrugged. "The blockades never worked, Mistress, even when people cared. And I can turn English if I please, enough to take passage from either side without questions."

We found Walter alert outside the door of our new home. In answer to his raised eyebrows, I said, "Sir, it is worth your trouble."

"Then thank you for taking her."

"We enjoyed it, sir," replied Richard. "We should like to be her friends, and yours."

"And so you are from this moment." Elisabeth had come out. "Master Linacre, if you work at La Vièrge-aux-dames, surely you must want a hot supper nearby. You could come to us, and Master Thomas with you."

"I should like that, Mistress Tarleton, but I could not present myself to you at the end of a day's work, not without washing."

"Then make use of our Turkish bath. I mean to have one built."

"Come to us again soon," said Walter. "And tell me, if you can, the name of a master builder who can make me two forges to my own specifications."

Elisabeth had never, as a child, lived in the house we were now to inhabit. Her father had rented it out, which explained the solidly built shop, whose commerce weighed down a flagged floor laid on Norman stone, with no cellar to undermine it. The floor could, in fact, take almost any weight, to Walter's delight. But the windows were inadequate, and as fires burned to warm us, we let in the October winds. Local masons, glad of the work and curious about us in a friendly way, crumbled away the margins of the windows, to enlarge them along the whole front that faced the street. The forges now waited, still reeking of chemicals and of the first experimental fires; and as Walter's choice of local workers swirled quarreling and debating around them, the great black frames of the presses began to rise.

In gray wool and furs, a shawl over my hair, I began to enter in our ledger deliveries of binding string; of ink powders; of metal bars; of hides, stiff and live-smelling; of Italian paper and wood for wedges. I would move about, ignoring fragments of Walter's conversation. "You see, it is perfectly simple. We set up the sheet—you'll note the type goes in reverse—which takes a single man about two days. Then we roll out the jellied ink onto a roller, and ink the type two or three times. Then on the inked type we lay the paper page, then a protecting screen, and then we *press*." A squeak, a squeal, a thud. "The same page, as many times as you want."

"And then"—the voice was Thomas Linacre's—"your compositor sets up another page?"

"Yes, we set up another and move on, and so we gradually compile our edition. And the sheets, of course, hang until the ink is dry."

Such fragments would cut across a workman's gently flirtatious "Good day, Mistress" and masculine signals most of which no doubt I missed. They liked me and knew they could not touch me; in return I treated them with a friendliness my mother had warned me never to make too warm. "It would not be truly kind, Claire, for they are not your equals. I know you would never play on the longings of those who cannot have you." Elisabeth tucked a last puff of hair under my headdress, which made me, I thought with pride, look plain as a novice. "You may work in the shop, if you like, part of the time. Someone needs to oversee the drying sheets and to keep track of stores." (This I could do ruthlessly.) "Eventually we will come to binding, and to making translations and even woodcuts of our own. Thank God for the trained people we brought with us; and Walter says some of the merchants' sons are promising, and their fathers willing to tolerate us."

"Thank God for Thomas Linacre," I said.

"Ah, don't trust to him."

"Why not? He's charming."

"Charming and good. And he will *be* charming and good at the university next year, and wherever his brother's business takes him. Steady effort bores him, Claire. I think Richard can hold him to a task; and it is for Richard that he will work—while he stays."

She had known our new house long ago, but had lived at her father's home in the town. We passed that site, walking through mud in our outdoor pattens, on our first trip to the market. And at the hole we discovered, its stones cracked and its beams crumbled into charcoal, Elisabeth laid her head against my shoulder and cried with a quick, soft, public violence.

I was shielding her, folding my cloak about her against the compassionate stares of passersby, when a voice I knew said, "Elisabeth. I will build you a better." She tried, with dignity, to shake herself free of his arm, but Richard's grasp sustained her as I brought her home.

Our house was drab and cold compared to Italy: a hollow rectangle of gray stone, steeply roofed with slate. I disliked its colors but found its plan familiar. The front wing, to which new windows would give light, faced the street—and the windiest height in Saint-Aurèle. A round tunnel defended by a grille let into the courtyard where the well and the pump stood. At the back lay the stables and the servants' rooms. The right-hand wing was given over to domestic work: roasting, baking, brewing, sewing; and to Elisabeth's stillroom. Here also lay the hot little wood-paneled chamber where demented enthusiasts of the Turkish bath threw water over scalding stones, then sweated in the steam, after which a servant sluiced them with buckets of cold water.

The fireplaces required repairing: we would need them all. The left-hand side of the square contained our living quarters, guest chambers, and the music room. With my own hands I washed walls and floors made of stone so cold I sometimes shouted curses at it. I knew I must not so waste a musician's hands, or a singer's voice either; for already several of the richer merchants had inquired whether Elisabeth and I would sing at private parties, and for what fee—a large one, for our pride. Our prestige was beginning: my prettiness, conserved like the sheets of calf and the fine Italian paper, had caused talk; and Elisabeth warned me I must break no more nails in scrubbing floors.

I was ready to stop, to resume practice, to talk with a little court of merchants and merchants' sons and lords' sons whose fathers disapproved of me; to discuss with Elisabeth what of Italian fashion we could adapt into the thick patterned velvets and furs we must wear—whether the French train would not hinder a musician, and whether the *henin* (the pointed head-dress draped with gauze) could not be replaced by a cap of embroidered lace. We must learn to be warm and teach Saint-Aurèle to be elegant. In the sewing room we pinned tissue-paper patterns over velvets in whose brocading the fingers sank like moss; cut orange satin whose roses were woven of real gold, of which even a single wiry thread must not fall uncollected to the floor; and decided, with regret, on warm shoes.

Farmers had sown the winter wheat. Rusty leaves blew tattered in the woods, and herdsmen had shaken down acorns for their foraging swine by the time I first had leisure to seek, exhausted, the calm of Elisabeth's stillroom.

All that was best in my home she seemed able to concentrate here, like the roses she distilled into thin syrup, to be used impartially for perfume or for cooking. From this room came the almonds pounded with honey that we shaped into tiny fruits. Here pickled pears, each jar adorned with a green cross in wheels of lime, lay cool on the shelves. From here came the rosehips and shriveled lemons that would keep our teeth solid in our gums over the winter, and the decoction of cedar bark used against scurvy by the tribes of Le Bras d'Or. Vinegar to wash dirty wounds, eye-bright against pinkeye, gentian for a woman's ailments, and cotton-root bark to induce menstruation. Lavender buds, mustards compounded with white wine, borage for a tea that cleared the mind.

At last, after six weeks of work, house and shop were prepared: the walls resealed against winter around their new windows; firewood laid in. I was bathing in my copper tub, and lay naked, gazing with dreamy resignation at the beams from which my chandelier now hung and at the walls of stone so old they seemed polished. My red cushions on the settle caught my eye. Suddenly I longed with a single pang for Florence and Master Luca.

But the slender brass bedposts shone and rose to a canopy of red cloth delicately draped. I would sleep tonight on clean linen. My millefiori bowl lay on the mantelpiece, and beside it an onion to absorb odors and a lemon to scent the air.

In such rooms, I thought, the painters . . . The painters for whom I would never model again. I caught, in the merciful rose shadows of the bronze mirror, a steep-jawed, full-mouthed face, its eyes distended: a haggard prettiness, stopped short in a pose almost of arrogance.

The water swished. I moved—reached for a hot towel. My borage tea sat ready on the hob. I lifted the cup, saluted no one, and murmured the old saying: "I, borage, bring always courage."

Drowsily I drank. In such rooms the painters depict the Virgin startled at her prayers, and she turns in a swirl of velvet to find—what? What is the Angel of the Annunciation? A glow of light, pulsating, not the fire; a mist of silver, and within the silver light a face—a man's face, merciless, beautiful.

Wind shook the shutters. As I laid down my cup I checked, as well as I could with blurring eyes, that I had bolted out the wind and, beyond it, the sea. Would I ever grow used to wind and sea? The sibilance that was no human voice; the long hushing of the breakers below; the gulls whose screams, with the smell of fish, were inescapable.

Some people live out their lives here, I thought, pulling off the towel and groping for something velvet, something warm. Cold and work had brought back the hungry sleep of my childhood. I fell forward, hands and tangled hair sprawled over the pillow. Lived out their lives here. . . . Where would I live mine? The year would prove longer than a year: Walter's zeal had already made that clear to me. Would I ever leave here? And if so, where would I go? To Florence, where more beautiful children modeled now for the Madonna? To London, made more dangerous by civil war?

I stirred, half sleeping. And in my sleep a body—hard and warm in its authority—laid on me a hand that could have enfolded both my palms. A man's lips crushed me gently, with expert gradation, and his sweet saliva sought my tongue. My belly pulsed, and drew out, to my sleepy gasping, a pang of pleasure pure as a violet springing from the earth; and I slept.

# 5

In October the fog came in. Sea and sky vanished in a wet, swirling haze; La Vièrge-aux-dames became a shadow; and, in a shop haunted by the surf and the crying of the gulls, we went about our work by torchlight. Each time someone opened the door—and our work was beginning to attract the idle and the interested—more fog came in. It dimmed vision like a delicate smoke and lent haloes to the torches.

Walter set up a fence around the margins of the room to keep out the idlers. The more intelligent he invited inside to see the workings of the press, but he refused to let our cook pass around any hot spiced wine, even on the coldest mornings. "We are not a tavern," he remarked to one curious farmer. "Monsieur Hériot across the way will gladly entertain you." There was a constant milling of watchers even so, and some of them, especially the educated merchants, began to become our friends.

One press we kept occupied with small books—breviaries and ancient authors, books so small they could slip into a pocket. In the back of the shop our cobblers, their apprenticeships bought up from their masters, would soon begin the work of binding. These little books we hoped to sell cheaply and in quantity. My father had now become a master of men, a payer of wages—to printers, compositors, and binders; but before the shop could earn we must build up a stock. There seemed no lack of money for food, for wages, and for new clothes. Walter guessed the shop might yield some profit within a year, as word of our work spread through the district. Already one or two scholars had come to see us from Rouen. I was glad my parents' affluence had at least rendered immediate profit unimportant.

On the second press Walter had begun the great Bible that has since established his fame. It would take, he guessed, three years to produce, and would be illustrated with woodcuts he himself had made. Now his drawing pad often occupied him as we sat in the solar at night, and in October I saw come off the press the first sheets, a grid of delicate lines impressed into the thick rag paper; each page ornamented with an initial capital in red ink, its type imitating the gothic penstrokes of the scribes.

The fog and the cold had induced in me a lonely, not unpleasant emptiness. With chilled fingers I went about my work: bathing with bath cloth and sponge in the morning before I went down, dressed in gray or brown wool, to help in the shop; glad when the noon meal freed me to wash off ink and dust in the tub my maid would have waiting for me, and to change into more elegant clothes for music practice. Occasionally marketing or visits interrupted this serene monotony. On the evenings, rare as yet, when Elisabeth and I had sung before some merchant's feast, a second tub would be allowed me, and then sleep so avid it gave even to my unconscious hours a quality of work.

On October the eighth—I remember the date because it was the day on which this story truly began—I woke to find the sky blue and the ocean green, rolling in breakers crisp as frost onto the sand below the seawall. The air was cold, but the sunshine delighted me, and as I dressed (stockings, chemise, undergown, and brown robe lined with fur) I hummed a nonsense rhyme in the English Walter had kept accurate for me, the English to which my friendship with the Linacres was now giving an unforced suppleness.

> Martin said to his man: "Fie, man, fie!"
> Martin said to his man: "Who's the fool now?"
> Martin said to his man: "Fill up a cup in either hand:
>   Thou hast well drunken, man:
> *Who's the fool now?"*

I whistled the last line as I wound a dark red shawl over my hair, and grinned as I mentally saluted Jean-Marie Tavella. What, I wondered, had become of him?

"Claire!" called a voice from below.

I leaned out the window two stories over the street, to see Thomas Linacre, warmly dressed in robe and hooded cloak, waving at me. "Good day, Thomas!"

"Will you walk with me on one of our last fine mornings?"

"Only if Father will let me," I said, hating the childish prohibition.

"Oh, surely he will. Meet me at the bottom of the spiral stair."

I did, cloak around my shoulders, whirling and tumbling down the stairs that coiled around their central post. On the ground floor I met Walter, dressed for work. In the shop beyond him compositors were already setting up the third double-leaf of Genesis. "Where are you going so early?" inquired my father.

"With me, sir, I hope." Thomas appeared, so wholesome and glowing that both Walter and I laughed at the sight of him. I do not think he knew why, though he smiled back. He was the handsomest boy I had ever seen, and—though he lacked his brother's wit—his intelligence, humility, and gentleness made him liked by everyone. "Will you let me take her to walk on the beach for an hour? I promise you the tide's full out."

"What, the path down from the seawall?"

"Yes, she's never seen it." I knew that a chalk path cut down the steep slope below La Vièrge-aux-dames and that it would lead us to the beach below the cliffs.

Walter frowned. "It's a dangerous place. The drop-off is very steep and lies near in."

"I know, sir, but there's no danger at low tide. God knows we have few local marvels, but she may have no chance to see this one, such as it is, again this side of spring."

"All right, but don't ravish her," said my father.

I laughed as Thomas blushed crimson. "Sir, I have no intention—"

"One never does: these things just come over one. Marco!"

"Sir?" Marco, in his shirtsleeves, came out from the shop. He had become our best compositor.

"Forgive me for interrupting you, but Master Linacre wishes to take Mistress Claire down to the cliffs. Will you accompany them at a distance?"

"I'm sorry, Marco," I said.

He grinned, pulling down his sleeves; he had been watching over me since I was eleven. "Let me get my cloak, sir, and a mug of something hot from the kitchen. I may as well drink while I skim stones at the water." Walter nodded; Marco passed Thomas, giving him a wink of fellow feeling.

Walter turned to Thomas. "Please understand. If you want to talk he'll keep well clear of you. But she must not get the name in the town of walking alone with men."

"Of course, sir." I could see Thomas's disappointment.

So we tumbled hand in hand down the groove in the withered turf, laughing at the momentum we could not stop. When we halted La Vièrge-aux-dames was invisible two hundred feet above us—and in it, I supposed, Richard and his workmen, if this was one of his days away from rebuilding the devastation near the square. I liked Thomas the better, but Richard also came to us with a cautious yet persistent frequency, and I treated him with the respect due to his advanced age. Everyone, I knew, expected me to fall in love with Thomas. Since I found him delightful, I was content to let them think it. As we slithered stumbling to a halt, his hand supporting me, I reflected that Jean-Marie Tavella had moved me more. I would no more think of desiring Thomas than I would of desiring Richard his brother.

"Oh, how beautiful," I whispered.

"Very. But never come here alone. Your father's right, it's dangerous. Come, let's walk."

Behind us, Marco had found a fallen slab and was both skimming stones and sipping at his tankard. I reminded myself to leave him some small present for his kindness. He resented neither his interrupted work nor the certainty that we did not want him. I had seen a good pocketknife at the swordsmith's in the marketplace; I must buy it for him.

The pale packed sand smelled of salt and weed, and stretched before us in a ribbon unmarked by footsteps. *We* marked it, feeling like the mariners who adventured far from Normandy to fish off the great island called Le Bras d'Or—setting our soles carefully to make a trail of perfect prints. A few seabirds sailed over us, and high above their wings rose the chalk cliff, its striations green with algae and stained by the occasional spill of rusted iron in the rock. Waves curled, hissed and broke, as clear as aquamarine. Yes, it was dangerous here at high tide: the cliff-foot was slimed with weed like emerald hair, and thirty feet out I could see the blue of deep water.

When we tired of walking we sat down, side by side on two of the boulders that had fallen from above—another reason for caution, I reflected, glancing upward. Today I could see no line of white on the horizon. "I cannot see England," I said.

Thomas smiled, looking out to sea. "You cannot in any case. A hundred miles away lies the Isle of Wight. You should know the Channel is only narrow enough at Calais, and then only on clear days."

I glanced at him and picked up, as if nothing had intervened, the thread of our first conversation. "Am I so like your cousin Alison?"

This time the smile was real, the blush less fierce. "No, not very; but you remind me of her." A short hesitation; then he said abruptly, "I wanted to marry Alison."

I could not tell what he required of me, but I knew I must not joke, so I said gently, "And will you?"

Thomas gathered a handful of sand. "Not unless I turn Englishman."

A pause. "And had you other cousins in London?"

Thomas nodded. "There was also her brother James, with whom I became intimate." Suddenly he added, "Claire, have you ever felt that you belonged in some other place?"

"Yes, often. Always."

"Where?"

"I cannot remember."

"Richard says everyone feels like that. He thinks it is our memory of Paradise."

After another silence I said, "And Paradise lies across the water?"

"I do not know." He leaned forward. His gentle, ruddy face and dark lashes moved me (I thought with a small private shock) as the manhood of her son, understood for the first time, must hurt a mother. "I only know that I belong somewhere, and that place is not Saint-Aurèle; yet I have always lived here."

"Are they your people, then?" I demanded, gazing out over the water.

His hands found a stone, and in it the whorl of an ancient snail shell. "They are not Richard's people, I can tell you. He hates them; he is French." After a long silence he said, "I do not hate them. My flesh is of their substance and I do not find it any less a man's. We gave them their kings; we are theirs, as they are ours. Why Paris? Why *not* London?"

We ought, boy and girl, to have played at our approach to

one another. I have known some couples whom the sight of sea and clouds seemed to move to erotic play, just as others (to me, incredibly) claim to find desire stimulated by the ice-blue light of the full moon. And there are others whom moon, sky, ocean call to truth.

We had descended to it instantly, without preliminaries. I recognized and understood this as the only way to honor the beauty that surrounded us. Therefore I sought within myself for an answer. Perhaps, also, neolithic stones, their granite hallowed with a will that leapt clear of Time, called to me beneath the surface of consciousness even then. For there issued from me, in answer to Thomas's question, a conviction that did not merely echo the passion of my father—the first of the authentic voices Normandy was to demand from me.

"Why Paris?" Thomas had said. "Why not London?"

"Because," I replied, "we have fought for five generations and no one has won. First, as I understand my history, the Vikings conquered Normandy; then Normandy grew so strong a kingdom that she conquered England. And so the English kings, being Norman-descended, have the rapacious impudence to claim the whole of France."

"The blood is mingled," Thomas objected. "Blood calls to blood."

"Then every son of Adam is your brother and you may claim the right to rule him, and every daughter of Eve is Adam's chattel and you may claim the right to rape her." I could not keep out of my voice a sarcasm far more bitter, but no less in dignity than his glance of open, comradely surprise.

"Go on." He had the gentleness of someone who perceives, startled, a serious opponent.

"I dare not, or I may rave." For the anger, which to my astonishment I seemed to have been meditating for a long time, sprang now fully formed to my tongue. "The blood was always mingled, Thomas. I was born in London."

"I have kindred there," he reminded me softly.

I cast him a glance of aloof suspicion. His color heightened, but he did not look away. I said, "Blood will seem to be a worthy argument only as long as men enjoy shedding it; as long as they find peace a puzzle too complex for their rages and stupid lusts; as long as chivalry calls destruction noble, instead of the hard necessity it is. Men *enjoy* killing, burning, raping, wasting fields so the enemy's children will starve. They enjoy playing little gods to the helpless who cannot escape them. Peace demands from us the labor of goodness, war allows us the relief of sin. Normandy is the most ancient road to Paris. A King of England twists the Salic Law to invent a claim to the French Crown, and his people follow him for the enjoyment of cruelty and theft."

"Or out of loyalty, or in fear of punishment," said Thomas.

I was shaking, and pulled my cloak around me. "Punishment is a terrible thing. Disobedience to the king may be sin, and bewilders the mind. Where the king orders, I understand the common man may fear to die in sin for disobeying him. Thomas, my father will not choose, and nor will I, though both of us are Englishborn. I take it that you, born here, are English in your heart?"

I see them in memory: boy and girl trapped in that pitiless perfection of white and blue and green, which can be loved only in truth. I had not known my heart carried such a burden; nor had I meant to force truth so far.

Thomas stirred, turning to me the beautiful, immature face with its elements of goodness: the firm lips, the eyes that opposed me, since I had demanded opposition. Perhaps we were shaking, though we did not know it, with the nearness of man to woman. I saw a shudder ripple through his body. He said, "Some of us want England for our overlord. I have thought seriously how I will fight when the next war comes."

"You will fight your brother," I said.

Thomas's eyes closed, then opened, staring at the sea. "How then," he said, "shall we find our way?"

I cannot explain my divination, only that I made it. "Thomas," I said softly. *"What have you done?"*

His profile with its slightly snub nose did not turn to me. "A thing of which I am ashamed."

"Did Alison know?"

He shook his head. "No. A year ago a courier suddenly died, and they needed someone quickly. I was taking ship home, to a town still in English hands. It seemed a little thing, a favor; even, perhaps, a test of myself, of what I believed. Of," he corrected himself, the tears held in hard control, "of what I loved. Then His Grace ransomed himself and returned to Saint-Aurèle, and a favor to my cousin James became. . . ."

*Treason.* The word hung between us, breathed, not spoken—the word for which rulers invent punishments to send the soul to God in despair of God. Turquoise, chalk, and emerald enclosed us, and beheld the young flesh that must bear an adult penalty; for to experiment with disloyalty—even to make a wrong choice—is to forfeit pity.

He had not spoken the word; technically I did not know. Now he stirred, his face rosy with the wind, his eyes honest but—I saw with a despair that made me feel ten years older than he—too self-absorbed to have earned my trust: already impulsively given, already betrayed. "Claire, I did not knowingly bring you here for this." I nodded, my cloak swathed round me like the statue of a girl I was to see years later in a place to which no dream of mine, that day, could have convinced me I would go; and said nothing. To his credit his eyes stayed steady on my own. "I suppose I have been brimming with this selfish need, and to a pretty woman, a stranger . . . strangers seem outside the reach of our hurt, and we long for them to judge us good. I gave you means to judge me. What you have found, I must bear."

I shrugged. "I came here to walk with you, Thomas; it seems I depart your accomplice. Have your loyalties changed?"

"No." His lips thinned in a smile more adult than his gaiety.

"I have come to understand a thing about myself: I am loyal to what I love. I love Richard, and will not defend what he hates. He is more intelligent than I, as you may have noticed. He says England's cause in France is lost and that we owe a loyalty to the achieved fact. A year ago I loved Alison: I suppose James knew it. James made use of me, and that is my fault, as it is my fault I laid this burden on you." He turned on me a grave gentle look. "I forced this knowledge on you, Claire. You are not my accomplice. The town will never know my affairs. His Grace does not; the English burned the records when they left. You and I talked here"—he gestured to the green water, beneath which the fossil shell had sunk to be rolled from wave to wave—"we talked about the renovation of the church."

I nodded and rose. "We must go. Thomas, I give you my oath I will not tell what little I know. Stand up, Marco is waving to us." I did not ask: *Have you told Richard this secret?* I could not bear the answer.

He stood and, looking down at me, said, "I am sorry, Claire. Please forgive me and be my friend." The voice in its dignity was a man's voice, not a child's, and pleaded for nothing.

"I forgive you," I said. "And I am your friend. Care for yourself, Thomas, because we care for you."

We turned back in the estrangement that, for me at least, had suddenly succeeded my furious anger, an anger that must compose itself before we reached Marco. At my father's door I wished Thomas good morning. He bowed; and as I shut the door on him I had to stand for a moment gripping the newel post, because I was shaking and could not stop.

But it was Richard, not Thomas, who was present in the shop on the afternoon a voice said from the doorway, "Master Tarleton. I have not precisely seen your star in the East, but I hope you can endure one more curious visitor."

"My lord." My eyes met Richard's, both of us acknowledging

that Walter had spoken *before* he turned and set eyes for the first time on Jean d'Aubry de Saint-Aurèle.

The man who strolled forward from the doorway, so that workers and onlookers bowed before him, wore a sleek beard in the French style, and his dark blond hair was not yet gray. A narrow, clever face; cold eyes; a lined forehead, a fan of fine creases at the corner of either eye; a mouth pursed now against (I suspected) laughter that came easily and warmly. He wore a belted robe and carried gloves that he slapped softly from hand to hand. "Welcome to Saint-Aurèle. Tell me, how does the press work?"

"Oh, very simply, sir. The Chinese had it before us. Here—Christophe, please—is a panel of our type."

"But it goes backward."

"Only like a mirror, that it may better reflect the truth. Watch." And as the press labored we watched them, all of us silent before the easy, intelligent questions and the calm replies.

"May I hold one of the dry sheets?" inquired the Count. "Thank you." He scanned the thick page, the sixth of Genesis. "I find it surprisingly good, though not so beautiful as the handwriting of a scribe, which contains the soul of the man. Do you not think *our* books"—a courteous hesitation—"will now rather increase in value? Excuse me, but I doubt any patron would prefer these to a copy specially created. Why should any library admit them, or any collector value them? They are made by a machine, and every copy is alike. I have in my own library a Book of Hours painted a hundred years ago by the brothers Jean and Lucien Vianney, who took fourteen years to make it. I must show you the picture that illustrates Christ's Passion in the Garden of Gethsemane. It is painted all in shades of dark, and the only light comes from the gold of the stars." He set the page delicately down. "What printer can compete with that?"

"None, sir. But we cannot all wait fourteen years, nor can we all pay the hundreds of florins that sustained the brothers Vianney. A poor man will never see, will never touch such a book. I print for the poor, or for men and women of moderate means. I do not see why writers, whether ancient or modern, who wrote for all men should be read only by a few. I print so that the intelligent artisan can make himself a learned man."

"And thus gain power?"

"And thus gain wisdom, which is power."

The Count's own entourage fell back as he circled the press, still softly slapping the gloves from palm to palm. "I remember when I was a child—too small, they said, to learn Latin—how I hungered for it: hungered. *When you are older*, they said. *When you are older.*" He halted and smiled at my father—a smile that held a curious shyness. "No, it is *not* right that the artisan should never see or touch a book. It is not fair. Master Tarleton, the quiet you find here is the only peace we have known since I was born. It is fragile in our hands. Do not help to break it."

"I think, sir," said my father gently, "that if we fill men's minds with the wisdom and the goodness of the best intellects ever known to us, then surely men will grow in goodness. The presses will print political tracts, as you fear, and humble people will read them and be moved to think. But this press will print the best books I can discover. May not thought teach men to be better, as well as worse?"

There was a long silence. At last the Count said, "What price do you put on your Bible when it is done?"

I knew the price, and almost leapt to prompt my father: *Give it to him as a gift.* But Walter was quicker, and wiser. "Whatever price Your Grace may choose to set."

"It will be a high one: some songs from the two ladies of whom I hear so much"—he bowed to me; I curtsied deeply—"and a few dinners, with good arguments."

Walter smiled. "My lord, let me present my daughter Claire."

My new liege lord gazed down at me, measuring, without

discourtesy, my lack of resemblance to my father. He would have spoken to me, but a woman had come softly down the stair. Jean d'Aubry saw Elisabeth, and forgot me.

She had not waited until he summoned her, and in choosing to be public she had, I thought afterward, done wisely. "My dear lord," she said, and sank into a profound Court curtsy.

He moved quickly forward to raise her, and all at once a rustle of normal motion and of voices could be heard throughout the room. "Elisabeth! Did you think you could surprise me? I have known for weeks." Stooping, he kissed her with brisk gentleness on either cheek and, taking her hand, led her forward to Walter. The two men confronted each other.

Jean d'Aubry laid Elisabeth's hand in Walter's outstretched palm, and I saw the two hands, those of wife and husband, fold together in a quick pressure of reassurance. From Walter's composure I knew suddenly what message had been conveyed, and out of what memory. All my life, I thought, he has known my mother had a lover. And Saint-Aurèle knows too, and has talked of it for weeks.

I stared at them where they stood enclosed in the private rhythms of their maturity: of the time before I was born when they had endured and survived adventures of which I did not know. A respect that was near to love brought tears to my eyes.

A hand fell gently on my shoulder and pressed it briefly, without intrusion. Richard Linacre, alone in all the room, had not forgotten me.

"You must come to my house," said Jean d'Aubry. "I must hear your daughter sing."

"If you will honor me, sir," said Richard's voice beside me, "will you come to my house instead—Verneuil?"

"I should like that," said Elisabeth; and so it was agreed.

The year's first snow had turned to sleet as I sat on the green cloth cushions of the window seat at Verneuil. I wore dark orange velvet with a necklace of amber, and my hair, which custom allowed a virgin to wear unbound, flowed brushed and shining down to my hips. I knew from the men's eyes that I was beautiful.

Thus recessed from the room, I had a few moments, while servants laid the trestle table with its fine linen cloth, to study my surroundings. The ceiling was heavy with dark beams, but from it hung a chandelier of intricate brass horns, and the candlelight lent angled shadows to the light of the fire. Richard had just cast into the flames a few grains of frankincense.

On the scrubbed tiles beneath my feet lay mats, woven that morning, that gave off a fragrance of fresh straw. This took the chill off the flags, and tapestries warmed the walls. Richard's grandfather had commissioned them, he said, eighty years before, and their scenes of battle—of Trojan towers and descending goddesses, of chariots and women carried captive—had had time to mellow into a pastel gentleness of blue and rose and green.

I glanced at the spitting dark behind the panes. "Is that your garden? I can't see a thing."

Richard joined me, robed in brown velvet, with clean cambric at his throat and wrists. I glanced up at his face, which I found sharply handsome, its lines too full of a potentially wounding sarcasm. He settled close. I caught the good sent of his flesh, and reflected that even in the dark my senses could have told a man's skin from a woman's (and one man's skin from another's. I have never believed Boccaccio's idiot story about a woman deceived into intercourse with an ambitious lover merely because the room was dark and she *thought* he was her husband). "Yes, that's our garden. Some good fruit trees, bare now; roses with which our gardener has endless trouble; the boathouse and the river."

That farthest blackness was, perhaps, running water. "You have a boathouse?"

"Yes, the small stone building: you cannot make it out now.

And a little dock beside it. Thomas and I liked to go fishing on the Cerne when we were boys. The name, by the way, traces to the Gaulish god Cernunnos."

"And your parents are dead, and your sisters gone?"

He nodded. "The house seems a little empty without them. I miss Alice and Jeanne. Still, both have children and they bring them here sometimes, and I suppose someday one of us will marry. Come, they're calling us to supper." As I followed him I wondered, from his reserve toward me, whether there was something about me he disliked.

We moved to the table. Every guest washed his hands in the presence of the others, since each pair would dip their spoons into a shared bowl. When we had handed our towels to the servants we sat down: the Count at the table's head in the single great chair; Richard on a stool at its foot; the rest of us on benches along the side.

The meal proved simple and well cooked: soup; a salad made of pickled vegetables; bread, stuffed capons, a ham studded with cloves; red wine; at last an apple tart, almonds fried in honey, and the dry apple brandy for which the region is famous. I ate frugally, for I knew that I, not Elisabeth, would be asked to sing.

Of course I had not questioned Walter. He gave no sign of having noticed my attention. But I felt shy of the Count this evening, even fearful; and if my puzzlement issued in any clear emotion it was pity for my father, and anger at Jean d'Aubry and at Elisabeth.

Nothing in Walter's manner invited my pity. To the extent that I could penetrate the privacy he shared with Elisabeth, I thought his manner to her had gained in tenderness. They seemed at one this evening—Elisabeth in her blue gown with pearls at her ears; my father solid, calm, and witty. Every man present wore the long belted robe of ceremony; his was dark green, and—the only note of the unusual, as printers, like musicians, prefer to keep their hands unencumbered—he had chosen to wear on his ring finger a Roman intaglio emerald reset for him by a Florentine goldsmith.

Therefore I crumbled my bread and caught only snatches of conversation, interrupted by the scrutiny of Richard Linacre from across the table. I looked back at him and did not smile, judging that my smile would seem what it was, false. For an instant he studied me, frowning, his eyes frankly somber. Then we looked away, and I recalled, with a pang, his *"Of course, now I remember. . . ."* Remembered what? And from what source?

"King Henry is a good man, they say, more monk than prince," remarked my father.

His Grace shrugged, the dark red velvet creasing across his shoulders. "I have limited patience with unworldly fools. Yes, he did recover from the first spell of madness, and he may recover again. I hear Queen Margaret is now with child. He comes near her so seldom that he was heard to confess"—a smile, gentle yet scornful, as he swirled the wine in his cup; his hands were never sufficiently still—"that it must have been begotten by the Holy Ghost."

"Poor man," murmured Walter.

"Poor Queen Margaret," said Elisabeth a little sharply. She reached for an almond. "And to whom, excepting the Holy Ghost, does rumor ascribe the child?"

"To the Duke of Somerset." At Walter's groan the Count held up his hand. "Never mind. It may prove his only achievement before his rival the Duke of York takes the throne. In any case *someone* must rule, and Queen Margaret is a warlike princess."

"How old now?" said Elisabeth. "She was fifteen, I remember, when the French sold her to England."

"Yes, as the price of peace, and she got for her dowry the ravaging of the Loire Valley by an English army. Forgive me, Master Tarleton." Walter's gesture excused him. "That would make her twenty-three and pregnant after eight years' waiting. But she has become loyal to England, to her husband, and to her husband's cause, which she thinks Somerset can save."

"The Duke of York is an able man," remarked Walter.

"Most able. He paid the rebels at Bordeaux."

I did not look at Thomas, and felt, not saw, his stillness. Then he glanced at me and said with a smile, "Shall I tune your lute? We, like His Grace, also exact our price."

"Yes, please, I should like that." It gave him an excuse to rise, which he did with a grace that elicited perfunctory smiles of dismissal. He moved to the sideboard where the instrument lay in its case, and sat down with it on a stool.

"What are the symptoms of the malady?" asked Walter. "Have you, sir, heard anything new?"

Jean d'Aubry shrugged. "It seems to be some strange affliction of sorrow. He sits for days without speaking. Sometimes he weeps."

"Poor soul. I have heard that when he saw the body of a man quartered for treason he said, 'Take it away. I would not that any Christian man be so tormented for my sake.'"

"Then he may discipline those of his nobles who still covet France. I agree: the virtues wanted in a prince are precisely those he does not possess, while his real virtues must deepen his misery."

A silence fell. Richard broke it. "Master Tarleton, I saw a most wonderful thing when I was last at Paris, a medallion by Luca della Robbia. I believe you know him?"

To my delight Walter threw back his head and laughed. "Oh yes, I know him. I hope you meet him someday. I have never seen a kinder heart married to a shrewder cunning. And if you *do* meet him, I warn you do not underestimate him."

"I wish I had plans to travel in Italy, but work will keep me here."

"Stay," said the Count. "I need you."

"Your Grace, I will. Underestimate him, Master Tarleton? How?"

"By forgetting that, beneath his boasting and his airs, he sees everything and understands the human heart. I love him, I confess. He will let you think him a boaster—a handsome man who is not *quite* a courtier. That is how you could underestimate him."

"The lute is tuned," reported Thomas, softly breaking into our conversation. "Claire, will you sing for us?"

"Gladly." As he handed me the instrument, its glossy wood light as blown glass, we exchanged a smile that was tender if not gay.

I sat down on the cushioned stool he brought me and threw back my cuffs to reveal their brocaded lining. "Your Grace, may I sing in English?"

"Whatever you wish."

Sleet hissed against the panes. I glanced at the darkness and said, "This is a spring song, sung only because I *wish* it were spring." They laughed, and settled more easily to listen.

I swept the strings and began the ancient words:

> Lenten is come with love to town,
> With blossoms and with birdës round,
>   And all bliss bringeth:
> Daisies in the dales,
> Notes sweet of nightingales
>   That blithe song singeth.

They were watching me. I returned their gaze, proud of my grace, proud of the pleasure I could give. In the fire- and candlelight they presented a tableau of courteous attention. Velvets in brown and green and burgundy absorbed the subtle light, which shone on pearls and silver and on the Roman emerald. Experience had molded each face, until each uniquely embodied a quality all shared: intelligent goodness. The kindness in the room was almost palpable.

I was to remember that for many years; and to remember also something I could only understand in retrospect: that I too, in flowering, partook of some quality beyond myself and in that moment possessed its power. That thing is holy: people call it youth, and it is not the greatest of the holy things. But I shall never cease to be grateful for the night I felt that power rest on me.

> The throstle-cock he threateth O:
> Buried is all the winter's woe
>    When woodruff springeth.
> These fowlës singen very well
> To cry out all their bliss and weal,
>    That all the wood ringeth.

# 6

We did not go to Verneuil again before spring. Richard, and Thomas as his foreman, had as much work to do all over town as the weather would permit. I saw less of Thomas now, but not so little as to arouse my parents' questions. When we did meet I found him friendly, reserved, and quiet. To Thomas I remained, in my thoughts and also when anyone spoke of him, warmly loyal. He carried with him no air of danger; his quiet seemed designed, with a lonely desperation he never forced on me, to baffle danger; and I hid even from myself that my liking for him now contained an element of disappointment.

Considering the winter that descended on us by late November, it does not surprise me that Saint-Aurèle contracted, for me, to the opacity of fog beyond the seawall; to the ribbed, clay-colored sea; to a few warm houses; to the Roman excavations of which rumors continued to come to us from La Vièrge-aux-dames; and to the shop. The wind never stopped. I learned to swathe my throat and ears, and to endure the gloves I had refused to wear in Italy, so much did I hate any hampering of my hands. Well, I thought, we could look forward toward Christmas, and then the long arctic endurance until spring.

On clear days the sails on the water had grown fewer. All the ships that would return from the far Atlantic fishing grounds had done so, and unloaded the salt fish half the town would eat all winter—the cod that was the wealth of Saint-Aurèle. For those ships that would not return there were Masses of intercession and wreaths cast on the water.

I had ceased to be an artists' model, but in this place my musical skills were loved with a hungry delight, and I had become in my way a greater personage than I could ever have been in Florence. I had also begun truly to interest myself in the press. Meanwhile the thought of spring set me to devouring the preserved fruits and vegetables Elisabeth had so carefully laid in.

We served, now, the Count and some landowners and intelligent merchants around Saint-Aurèle; and Rouen, the greatest city between us and Paris, had begun to hear of us. None of us was quick to make friends—friendship in all three of us grew slowly, though deeply; but we *had* become close to the family Lalemont, one of the wealthiest in Saint-Aurèle.

Gérard Lalemont, a dark lively little man in his forties, imported English wool, and exported, past whatever blockades happened to be in effect, the finished Flemish cloth. His wife Béatrice seemed, through a marriage that had begun when she was thirteen, to have acquired her husband's vivacity and intelligent charm—even his size: she was a little bustling woman with straw-blond hair and a broken nose. They had two pretty rosy daughters, aged fourteen and sixteen. These girls, Jacquette and Antoine, I found delightful. Both were already buxom and promised to grow taller than either tiny parent. Gérard had wearied of ribald doubts, freely expressed by friends, as to what giant had engendered them.

"I begot them myself, in the usual manner," I once heard him say. "And quite enjoyed it, as I recall."

"No descents of Jove, alas, for me," remarked Béatrice gaily, picking up her sewing silks. "No bulls, no swans, no showers of gold. . . ."

Gérard considered. "I might," he said at length, "manage the bull. As to the *swan* . . ."

"How about the shower of gold?" demanded Jacquette from her corner.

"Absolutely not," replied her diminutive but imperious parent.

It was at the house of the Lalemonts one evening in late November that I suffered a shock which afterward made me feel ashamed of my naïveté. The party that night included my family, Richard Linacre (Thomas, he said, was ill in bed), other acquaintances, and a family who had recently moved out of Saint-Aurèle to their newly inherited estate fifteen miles away. These guests were therefore staying in the house, which fortunately was large, since they brought with them their little daughter, a smaller son, and a baby four months old. I think I will not name them, even to Your Grace. The lady I will call Marianne.

Every district has its local beauties. She must have known that even after three children (and I judged her to be no more than twenty-four) she was one, but her manner gave no sign of it. Where children and husband did not preoccupy her I found her to be that genuine rarity, a piece of likable perfection. She was the kind of beauty *women* like. I remember she was tall, a flaw many slender beauties have (well, sir, I tried to be charitable!).

How can one describe extreme prettiness? It ceases to have individuality the moment one's pen touches the page—because, I suppose, beauties by definition conform to some type we admire. It is hard to describe a human being, whom in this case I barely knew, and at the same time to describe exquisite conformity to a type. An oval face, a full mouth, gray eyes with pale lashes, skin that escaped all the flaws that should have accompanied her red hair. Above all, a look of sweet temper that lacked nothing of intelligence—a combination of graces I have found very rare. She must, I think, have been proud of her hair, since she let it fall to her waist in a flow like apricot-colored silk, covered only by a nominal veil. Her breasts were full considering her slenderness, and I remember thinking that she must be nursing the baby herself, a thing certain careful mothers do despite the fashion.

"She had no choice," remarked Béatrice, whose love for her friend seemed compatible with a frank and innocent malice. "The wet nurse died and they could not find another. She says she does not mind it, except when he bites, and she pulls it away from him to teach him. *Men.*" Béatrice laughed. I did too, and saw Richard glance at me from across the room. "One knows a man-child straight away: they bite what they'll squeeze later on, and so begin as they mean to continue. Look, the nurse is bringing the baby to her."

We had scarcely heard the child's crying above the babble of adult voices, for Saint-Aurèle passed the winter chiefly in arguing. Marianne moved to take her son from the nurse. I watched a conference, which I saw Richard ignore, as he was deep in conversation with Walter. Then, when she asked him, my father pulled a chair to the fire. Marianne thanked him; she could not have lifted it—the thing must have weighed as much as a bishop's throne. She sat down with the baby in her arms, and, shielded by the chairback, opened her bodice and put the child to her breast.

A common sight, and people treated it as they ordinarily do. The suckling child was in himself delightful, and everyone, man and woman, enjoys a naked breast. So everyone looked, of course. Walter remarked gently, "He's a lucky boy," and drew a flashing laugh from the mother. Then our party went on around the quiet little scene.

"And I'll tell you something else." Béatrice was whispering, and glanced at me mischievously as she accepted from a servant a jug of hippocras. "Hand me those goblets, please, Claire, one by one. No, none for her or the baby will sleep drunk, poor little boy."

"*Tell* me the something else," I said, picking up a pewter goblet. We stood sheltered by the buffet, out of hearing.

She poured the hot wine; its steam of sugar and cinnamon made me press my upper lip against a sneeze. "She had to wait, because the first one was a girl; but then came the son, who is already, thank God, his father's image. During the six months her husband spent in Flanders she took Richard Linacre as her lover. Or he took her. The latter, I should think."

I did sneeze—thank God, not into the hippocras. "Oh, poor dear, how *shaming*," murmured Béatrice, mopping the wine spills with a napkin. "There, they've stopped looking. How appalling when one cannot help it."

"It was the cinnamon," I said, glad of the excuse to hide my crimson face. As Béatrice talked, which she seldom ceased to do, I gazed at Richard, to whom Walter was now making typesetting gestures. He stood looking down at my father, his elbow on the windowsill, goblet in his hand; then he spoke, his teeth lightly clenched upon the laughter he was restraining.

It struck me that where Thomas gave an impression of gentleness, the impression Richard made was one of clarity. From the clean dark hair to the long nose and strong chin—from the thickly lashed gray eyes to the good teeth and powerful, gesturing hands—the effect was one of intolerant intelligence. I had never seen Richad truculent, or indeed anything other than courteous. What temper required—I now thought suddenly—such restraint? And what happens when the restraint breaks?

Naturally he had felt so long a regard. The cold gaze considered me, asking again the question I had not deciphered. He glanced away.

I thought, I have no right to be as shaken as a child. Every man has mistresses. And I said, "I don't believe it. Who told you?"

Béatrice dismissed the servant with the now-loaded tray.

Then she picked up her own goblet and described with it a discreet gesture. "She did."

As December deepened, my shyness of Richard kept me away from La Vièrge-aux-dames. Apart from other considerations, I remembered Walter's curses upon women and idlers under the feet of busy men. The church had now been roofed over, and I caught a delightful smell of new timber the few times I looked in the door. However, the town continued to worship at Saint-Damien on the square, and at La Viérge-aux-dames the stonemasons now began the work of dislodging the ruined flags.

Work around the square now preoccupied both brothers. Ruins had been cleared from the burned sites, and half-built foundations covered for the winter. I continued to see Richard about once a week when he accepted Elisabeth's invitation and came, scrubbed and pleasant from the Turkish bath, to our supper table.

I had, I told myself, no just reason to change my manner to him, and I believed I had not done so. If he detected a change he asked no questions: I took my part in our supper conversations, and he answered me as usual, never by his manner trespassing into the family circle or beyond the boundaries set for a guest.

I was used to the idea that women must be virgins, while men need not. The danger of children pragmatically explained it; yet the information Béatrice had given me caused me a recoil I could not adequately understand. I was, if not guileful, at least clever enough not to *intensify* my apparent liking for him on this account. But from December on, I privately dismissed him; and from his coolness, assumed he had done the same with me. Had it been Thomas, I might have asked why. With Richard I refrained. The difference in age was too large to make me feel his equal, and though I had passed nineteen I did not possess the knack of a presumptuous honesty with men. I did not flirt; my character left me no alternatives but bluntness or silence. Richard watched me across my parents' table, answered my questions courteously, even fully, and gave me no help.

"Look, the first snow!" exclaimed Elisabeth. We had finished a leisurely meal in the solar (my parents often preferred to set up a trestle here, in this room we used for all purposes, rather than dining with the household at the table in the kitchen). Richard was our only guest that night.

He smiled as the big, loose flakes drifted against the panes. "One never loses the first delight, and every year one forgets how sick we'll be of it by March. I wonder if it will hold for snowballs."

"Oh, surely. Wet snow packs the best." Elisabeth offered him hot wine; he nodded assent and thanks.

"You saw His Grace today?" said Walter.

"Yes, our fortnightly meeting."

"What about the poor around the square? Where are they to go?"

"That was the problem we discussed. Into the almshouse, I'm afraid, till spring. They hate it as much as I should in their place. The problem is to rehouse them decently at a rent they can pay, in buildings that will not sink to slums in fifty years. Not on the square, but west of it, in the burned ground. I should like to build some kind of communal house to be paid at a shared rent, perhaps with the town itself as landlord."

Walter nodded. "And how are you liking the Marcus Aurelius I lent you?"

"The manuscript? I like it, and hope you set it up in print. The sections are so condensed that I make slow progress with it, though. Do you consider the text genuine?"

"Yes, though of course the original has vanished. Even so, I think we have here a good example of transmission through the centuries. The book is too elliptical, and the situations too obscure, to be anything other than a genuine private diary. No forger would take the risk of such vagueness."

"In that case I think it, except perhaps for the letters of Pliny, the most remarkable private document that has survived from the ancient world. It seems like one half of a conversation, of which the other half has perished"—he glanced again at the indigo dark—"perished so long ago."

When it seemed no one would break the silence, Elisabeth said, "Tell me, Master Linacre, is there a crypt beneath the church?"

"Certainly not a full one. The building rests on smoothed bedrock. When we have stripped the old tiles off the flags I may find some clue whether there is a forgotten partial crypt or an ossuarium. Why do you ask, Elisabeth?"

"I was hoping," said my stepmother steadily, "for news of the Roman town."

"Ah." He set his wineglass down and surprised me by a faint, twinkling smile. "I do have hopes of examining the hillside. Placidius Gallus mentions some villas below the old temple."

"For me to see," I added, because I had been silent too long.

Richard nodded. "I keep my promises. For you to see by spring, I hope."

"But," said Elisabeth, "if the foundation is so simple, it cannot give you access to the hill."

"I might, however, slice into the slope from the outside. The so-called landslide interests me. The hill is too low to sustain a spring slump or a significant avalanche—not one large enough to entomb ruins. In any case the debris appears not to have fallen off, but to have been *added on*. When I have time, I want to find out why someone would *add* to a thinly turfed chalk hill."

Elisabeth nodded—I thought, with a curious constraint; but said no more.

Until that evening. The trestle had gone; so, I thought unkindly, had Richard; and at the table my father sat drawing one of those (to me) repellently simplified scenes suitable for cutting in reverse into a pearwood block. I disliked the crudity of woodcuts. The design must be elementary enough to reproduce by carving. I glimpsed, upside down, an Expulsion from the Garden of Eden. I sat in my chair mending a chemise that I must, I decided, soon throw away.

All at once Elisabeth laid down her sewing. I glanced up at her in the bright light: Walter had a terror of blindness, and our consumption of candles was enormous. "Claire, has Richard Linacre mentioned any passageway between the walls?"

"Of La Vièrge-aux-dames?" I frowned, and noticed suddenly that my manner to her since our arrival in Saint-Aurèle had become the courtesy of woman to woman. "No, not at all. Why?"

"Because I remember hearing of such a thing when I was a little girl."

"I'll ask him."

"No, please not." The authority in her voice irritated me; but I forgave her as she sighed with weariness and folded her work. "I should hate to think he knew I had discussed him, even in so small a matter. I shall go to bed." She stood up, and said softly to Walter: "And take a sleeping dram, I think."

I was awake, reading and boiling water for mint tea at my own fire, when two soft, solid raps sounded on my door. "Yes?" I called quietly. It must have been one o'clock.

"Claire," said my father's voice. "Come out to me."

Never in my life had he summoned me like this. I spilled hot water, cursed, found slippers and warm robe. I opened the door. "Sir?"

He stood in the corridor at the head of the stairs, a fur-lined robe thrown on over his naked skin. I saw he wore his bedroom slippers. "Come down to my office, please."

Wrapping my robe about me, I followed him through the dark and sleeping house. In the shop the embers smoldered coral, and the watchman snored. My father's gesture forbade me to wake him. "In here," he whispered, and, leading me into his office, turned the key in the lock.

I had gone tense. Walter seated himself in his chair, and by the glow of the banked fire I saw him gesture me to the only other chair the room contained. "Sir, what is wrong? Have I offended you in some way?"

"No, of course not." A tinder box struck light; a flame leapt up between us and illumined the desk, the benches, the clutter on the floor. "She is fast asleep and will not wake, but I wanted to be sure. Claire, there are certain things I think you have the right to know."

"I agree, sir."

"Do you?" His voice was cold. "What then have you heard?"

I twined my hands in the warm velvet of my robe. "That some in this town have secrets."

"What a false reply from an honest woman."

"I cannot break an oath, sir."

"An oath?" His palm rasped the bristles he would shave in four more hours. "No, that is sin. Claire, I wanted to explain why you *must* not let slip to Richard Linacre that Elisabeth has asked about a passageway within La Vièrge-aux-dames."

"Why not, sir?"

"Because one exists. It opens from the clerestory, cuts down through the thickness of the wall, and then through bedrock to a hidden opening at a cove half a mile away. How Richard has failed to detect a hollowness in the walls I cannot guess. Granted, memory of the passage has been lost; the church is old. But Elisabeth's uncle, who was priest there fifty years ago, rediscovered it, and asked his brother—Elisabeth's father—to work with a small team to clear it out. They did, working only at night, and kept the matter secret. With the war in its second decade, they thought an escape might be needed from the church."

"So," I said slowly, "Saint-Aurèle is not aware—"

"That the English could enter it by an unknown back door? No. But the English are aware."

"How?"

"Because your mother told them."

After a long silence, I said, "Is she still an English spy?"

Walter sighed. "For two years, during her marriage to Marc-Antoine du Pléssis and their residence in London, she passed information to the Privy Council. Her husband did not know. He was one of the best men who ever befriended me—I was his friend before I was Elisabeth's. When we married, she confessed this matter to me on her knees."

I thought of Elisabeth—her warmth, her sarcasm, her kindness. "For two years before I was born—before you took her back to Paris?"

Walter nodded. "Yes. And she wants now to deserve forgiveness—to find the passage and have it obliterated. She dares not approach Richard Linacre; nor can I, without admitting to knowledge dangerous in an Englishman. Claire, it was long ago. She has stopped."

"Why did she start, sir?" My voice sounded pleading. In my disappointment in her I felt five years old.

This time the silence lasted very long. Then, with all the gentleness he could, Walter said, "Because she had borne the Count's child, and he would not marry her."

I steepled my hands against my face. It was once the Saracen fashion to slit the tear ducts of a girl-child so that tears could stream down her face without unseemly grimacing. To my astonishment I felt water flowing from my eyes as if I had turned Saracen, and could weep without a contortion or a sound.

Walter pulled up a stool and sat beside me. He pulled down one of my hands and held it firmly. "Claire, do not dare condemn her. She loved him so much—since she was fifteen—that, if she could have had him, I have always known that I. . . ." I nodded, understanding. He went on, "But the father would not let them. She was a playmate and friend, but not his equal; and the sister, Madame Agnès, opposed it strongly. He gave way and married his cousin. As you know, she died, and they raised no living children. No, do not curse him. He has had twenty years to wonder what he lost."

Softly he released my hand and left me. From the other side of the room he said, "My dear, are you a virgin?"

I raised my head. "As of this night, sir, yes."

"If ever you are not, for God's sake come to me: I would not cease to be your friend. Elisabeth was your age when His Grace begot her child. But it was her father's friend who gave that child a name."

"Have I, then, what? A sister or a brother?"

"Neither: the little boy died at six months old."

"Poor Elisabeth," I whispered.

Walter shrugged. "Can you understand that her suffering felt like hate? She had no means of healing—his shame made him cold. Claire, we never waste revenge on those we genuinely despise; and I have come to doubt that hate exists as a separate passion. The whole world will tell you hate exists: every war springs from it, they will say. But tell them this when I am dead: *Men do not hate; they only love.*"

The tears had congested my head, and I felt at the back of my throat an ominous rawness. "Was he worth it, sir?"

"Selfish boys are never worth the suffering they cause. But in a sense, I think, he has come to be worth it, yes."

I stood up. "I must go to bed."

"I'll give you my arm up the stairs. Claire, I'm sorry, but you risked blundering into more than you knew." He came to me and laid his hand on my shoulder. "Two things. *When* Richard Linacre discovers the passage, we will urge him to have it blocked, and thus it can be rendered null with no harm done to Saint-Aurèle. Perhaps I was wrong to let her come here, but one longs for so many years for the resolution that might heal."

"Has it happened, sir?"

"I think it has begun. I did not expect to find him formidable, or capable of helping her. He is both." I nodded. "Be discreet and we can survive here without scandal; undo the harm, or some of it; and leave. *I* owe that to Saint-Aurèle. You owe it only by association with us, and I am sorry. The second thing: Jean d'Aubry is now your lord. Do not insult him with childish anger. He longs, rightly, for this war to end. Let us do what we can to help."

In my own room I stripped and, despite the cold air, washed away the sense of dirt with which the interview had left me. Then I lay down, and had no time to feel surprise before I fell into a rigid sleep.

I woke on December seventeenth to the news that Gérard Lalemont had invited us to pass Christmas Day with his family and a party of friends. And I woke with a headache so savage, breathing so stopped, and a throat so sore, that Elisabeth found my tears of wretchedness natural.

For three days I lay in bed, sponge-bathed with warm water by a mother to whom I clung like a child, crying out my love for her. Elisabeth, startled, embraced me and laid her wrist against my forehead, checking for fever. When the sweat of sickness made me hate the feel of my hair, she and the maid gently washed and combed it. A cloth over my head, I obediently breathed steam; sipped honey to make speech possible; smiled at Walter's jokes; and slept and slept.

By the fifth day I was well enough to sit up in bed, my hair combed over my shoulders, wearing Florentine lace and smelling perceptibly, I fear, not only of medicine but of the lavender with which I had insisted on splashing myself because it cleared my head. Nevertheless Thomas Linacre, ushered in by Elisabeth, found me able to wish him a merry Christmas.

"*Not* so merry, it seems," replied Thomas. He grinned at my stepmother. "May I sit down on the bed? These presents, I swear, nearly break my back."

"No wonder, considering the size of that one. Yes, sit beside her. I'll leave you."

Thomas settled near me. "This one comes from Richard." I took, with a surprise I could not conceal, a long parcel wrapped in cloth-of-gold. Inside it I found an exquisite bone flute whose texture and luster made it a pleasure to touch. Softly I sounded it, and unfolded the note he had wrapped around it.

> Dear Claire,
>
> I made this myself. It has a true pitch as far as I can tell. I cannot sing—Nature does not, in every case, transform boy soprano into baritone—but I love music, and I love to look at you. Stay here to give us joy.
>
> Richard

I looked at Thomas and exclaimed, "I did not know he liked me!"

"Didn't you? He's a very cautious man. He has spoken of you."

"And said what?"

"I refuse," said Thomas, "to tell," and received a blow on the arm that he parried, laughing. For a second we hand wrestled, and enjoyed the losing and the winning equally. Then he said, "Now open mine. I will not lie and claim I made it; I bought it last time I was in Paris."

I unwrapped, this time from cloth-of-silver with red velvet ribbons, a leather case. It folded out into a chessboard, and as Thomas set the pieces in order I cried out with delight. The sculptor had obviously copied each piece from some living face. In each brilliantly painted king, each queen, each peasant-pawn there confronted me a minute individual, as though the pictures in the Count's Book of Hours had been transformed into three dimensions. "It will be like playing with dolls," I said.

Thomas was stern. "It will be a battle of the intellect. Are you well enough to play? Say, best of three?"

"Elisabeth won't let me, you'll be here all day."

"Best of one, then," suggested Thomas.

I rang for hot lemonade for two; Elisabeth, delivering it, exclaimed over the chessboard; and I settled down to win, to Thomas's savage murmurs of "Bitch. Doxy. Hussy. Damn you, how do you play when you're *well?*"

"For blood. Bring me that book, Thomas, and that inlaid box."

He obeyed. The book was one I treasured, a manuscript breviary with blue and gold capitals. I wrote in it: *For Thomas*, and gave it to him, saying "I do not know if you are devout. If not, forgive the choice. Luca della Robbia gave this to me when I was twelve years old. I have nothing better."

He blushed scarlet, his handsome face unguarded with surprise. "Then I cannot take it."

"You must, it bears your name. And to Richard, this." I opened the box and took out a Roman asper stamped with the regnal year and titles of Septimius Severus. The ancient copper still smelled as sharp as though new-minted, and left its metal-scent on my fingers. I folded it into a square of paper on which I wrote:

Dear Richard,

Thank you for your kindness: the pitch is true, and you shall hear me play it when I am well. Please find a Roman villa for me, and sit there with me and tell me why people long for places they have never seen, and people they cannot remember.

Claire

\* \* \*

Our Christmas proved delightful. To me, moving in green velvet through the fragile haze of well-being that succeeds sickness, it remains in memory as a glow of candle flames, of polished woods, of food to which I paid little attention, and of walls thickly hung with carpets too precious to tread on. A group of about thirty people had assembled to watch the snow and wait for midnight. The Linacres were there, and all our other friends from Saint-Aurèle (Marianne had left, with her family, to celebrate at home).

Through the laughter and well-being we listened as the clock ticked toward midnight. It stood, cumbersome and gaudy, on a side table, its copper body shaped like a tower enameled blue and red; inside it, gears turned, attached to golden balls. At last it rang. Amid the kisses Thomas said softly, "This is the moment, people say, when the oxen kneel in their stables in honor of the Child."

"Who has seen them?" demanded Richard.

"Plenty of people. I talked with a shepherd once and he had seen them."

"Then," said his brother gently, "you met a drunken shepherd."

Applause called me to the lute. I knew I could sing tonight, but only once; and I had chosen well. Over the group of friends a silence fell as I began. The English words, in this often-invaded port, would offer them no trouble.

> Sinners be glad and penance do,
>     And thank your Maker heartfully:
> For He that ye might not come to
>     To you is come full humbly,
>     Your soulës with His blood to buy
> And loose you of the Fiend's arrest—

And only of His own mercy:
*Pro nobis Puer natus est.*

Now I noticed that in the doorway, shy behind the crowd, there had appeared a little girl. She was about nine years old, and prettily dressed for the festival in a robe of pastel pink and blue. Her hair, dark blonde, fell down her breast; her skin was fresh as a ripe pear, and her blue-gray eyes smiled at me with a delight so gentle that I smiled back, and sang to her alone. She stood half-hidden in the doorway, one little fist clenched as she leaned against the frame.

Now spring up flowers from the root—
   Revert you upward naturally,
In honor of the blessed fruit
   That rose up from the Rose Mary.
   Lay out your leavës lustily—
From death take life now at the lest,
   In worship of that Prince worthy
*Qui nobis Puer natus est.*

The silence was a tribute so unexpected it brought tears to my eyes. When I had controlled them and smiled at the applause I glanced again at the doorway. My guest had gone.

Now others would sing. As music sheets were sorted—as Walter, Thomas, and Elisabeth exchanged instruments and pages with all the efficiency of an ensemble—something moved me toward Gérard Lalemont where he sat at the end of the room, his arm around a sleeping daughter. As I did so I passed Richard Linacre. He sat forward on his stool, a wineglass in his hands—a familiar stance, though I knew he drank little.

"Gérard, who was the little girl I saw standing in the doorway?"

"Little girl? We have none in the house. Was it Jacquette?"

"No, certainly not. A little blonde in pink and blue. I thought her charming, and would like to kiss her good night and wish her a merry Christmas. She seemed shy."

Very gently Gérard disengaged himself from the sleeping Antoine. "Claire, come with me into the next room."

The next room was not lit, though a borrowed glow softened the stylized agony of a crucifix on the wall. Gérard said softly, "I am glad she came. I saw her myself twenty years ago, and my mother before that. She is a little aunt of mine who died when she was eleven. Her name was Suzanne."

He lifted my hand, kissed it, and was gone. I do not know how long I stood alone in the dark, but the next companion of whom I became aware was Richard Linacre. "Claire, did you see the child standing in the doorway? No one else did; I have asked."

"Yes, I saw her." I wish my voice had not shaken. "Gérard says she was an aunt of his who died many years ago."

"How pleasant that she comes back from time to time. Did you know," he asked gently, "that you possess the other sight?"

"No. It has not happened before."

"It may never happen again. I'll tell you a thing that even Thomas would laugh at, because Thomas has not seen him. Occasionally in La Vièrge-aux-dames an old priest stands with his hands tucked into his sleeves, watching our work. He seems an ordinary old man. Once I heard him make a whistling sound. I have inquired: No one else sees or hears him. I should doubt my eyes, but Father Paul says the last incumbent also saw such an apparition."

From the other room rose the weaving harmony of a round:

*Salve lux fidelium*
*fulgens in aurora*

*quo est super lilium (li, li, lilium)*
   *pulcha et decora.*

"Come back among us," said Richard. "And be glad. Why hide in darkness when our music and candlelight have power to draw her from wherever she has gone?"

He held out his hand—a gesture as ceremonious as though he meant to lead me to a dance. But before I took it I turned to the crucifix and crossed myself in thanks for the grace that had so delicately visited us.

# 7

Between Christmas and spring there extended a sort of busy wasteland. I did not mind, though in my first winter on the coast my mood had closed to me not only the sea but the town. When I glanced up from work I saw only gray sky. Sometimes the snow thawed to a rain or a cold sleet, but on the pleasantest days I would open my shutters and scrape fresh snow from the sill to cleanse my mouth in the mornings. On these days roof-tiles worked a fretted pattern in the snow, or vanished beneath white blankets layered with skins of ice; and ice glistened opalescent in the ruts on the road.

Because of my music I must save my hands from certain kinds of work, but I did accounting in the shop—Richard had praised my arithmetic, and I *did* value his praise for this; not a sou of His Grace's money went unaccounted for by his Master of Works—and help was always needed in stillroom or in sewing room. I could have had friends too, but I preferred to maintain my façade of shyness with the well-to-do young merchants who were beginning to court me.

Walter smiled on them with glacial courtesy and said to me one day, "I suppose you *must* marry, but if you choose someone in Saint-Aurèle, since Gérard Lalemont is spoken for" ("Loudly," murmured Elisabeth), "marry Richard or Thomas Linacre: Richard, for preference."

"But I don't much like him," I wailed, too tired for once to detect the joke.

"Then," said Elisabeth gently, "wait until you find someone you love."

And Thomas said, one day, "*Talk* to them! What a dull little dog they'll think you."

"Virgins," I replied, "are *supposed* to be dull dogs."

"No, they're not. They are supposed," said Thomas severely, "to flirt."

"Why? I never flirt with you."

"No, you don't." The thought seemed to surprise him, but he concluded generously, "And yet I like you anyway."

My parents went once or twice to the castle, to dine with His Grace in the suite of private apartments I had never seen. From these visits they returned cheerful and composed. As far as I knew Elisabeth had never received Jean d'Aubry in private, and he seemed careful not to seek her. All Saint-Aurèle would have known had he frequented Walter because of Walter's wife, but the conduct of all three remained meticulous. And if Saint-Aurèle remembered—as the elders certainly did—the ancient bearing of a child, it kept its collective tongue with a prudence more than Norman. None among my men-friends mentioned what, if anything, their parents had said; no one old enough to remember took me aside for a vicious act of "honesty"; no voice cried an epithet in the marketplace. Elisabeth was a daughter of the town, too old of course for citizens as young as Thomas to remember (and Richard? I thought. Did she remember Richard at four years old? Did he remember her?). The town received her, glad of her return but not surprised, and in the silence that closed around us I began to suspect a collective judgment—not against Elisabeth, but for her.

And their lord? They loved him because he too was theirs;

because he had watched over them as best he could even from an English prison; because he had levied no tax to buy his freedom. But perhaps, I thought, someone had pitied the girl who bore his child; perhaps that pity was remembered.

I had not yet been inside the castle. Whatever reconciliation moved those I loved was hidden from me. Their discretion seemed almost atonement enough for two selves, two decades, two entanglements. What risks, I thought, however small, had Walter once feared he ran in bringing his wife to confront her lover? If it came to such primitive affirmations he would fight for her, and Jean d'Aubry knew it.

But as the winter passed I became conscious that I now feared no disunion between my parents. They would not separate. That must, I thought, have answered a question for Walter. With a sort of dreary shock I recognized that it did not relieve the fear in which *I* lived.

His Grace paid us only one more visit that season, in February. Then, as his small retinue leaned joking on the barrier, he stripped to shirt and hose and learned to work the press. After an hour Walter grinned at him and said, "Your Grace makes an excellent workman."

Grimed with sweat and ink, and laughing, the Count wiped his palms on his thighs. "Then please give me a letter of reference. Perhaps Sir Edward Palmer will accept it next time he invades."

Hands on hips, Walter shrugged. "But the civil war in England, sir . . .?"

"Ah yes, the red rose and the white." The choosing of these famous emblems had marked, or so legend already insisted, the formal emergence of York and the royal House of Lancaster as enemies. "A war that will, of course, descend upon their children. Don't trust to that, Master Tarleton. They'll make mischief here until they lose the habit of it, if they ever do. France is a better prize than Scotland or Ireland, which merely threaten their back doors. What has Scotland to give them except security on their border? And Ireland will swallow as many soldiers and as much money as they can throw into the bog. But France offers much—not least a diversion from failure at home. I'll keep men under arms and watch the coast as long as I live."

"How many months," murmured Walter, "before you are proven right? The Duke of York, do you think? What has he to spare of money *or* men?"

"I do not know. I do know he has paid agents in Bordeaux. A provident man looks to the future."

"When he is king," said Walter.

The Count shrugged. "He or his son. Of England, Master Tarleton, of England. We here mean to refuse your national embrace."

"You may, sir, with my goodwill."

"I know." This affirmation, so casually delivered, silenced, I noticed, the faces around the barrier.

I was trying, in vain, to imagine the Count either unkind or young. He must have seen my eyes, for he turned to me. Still gazing at me, he held out his hand; someone put into it a towel sopped in hot water and vinegar. Mopping his neck, he said, "Mistress Claire? Of what are you thinking?" And his eyes said: *What do you know? And how much?*

I curtsied. "I was thinking, sir, of England." It was true, and the only near-truth I could find, but it deepened the silence.

Now he made a business of pulling down his sleeves and, fastening buttons, came to me. "And thinking," he said gently, "that war makes enemies of friends?"

"If you ascribe to me such wisdom, sir."

"I do. Some of us live on this border because we were born to the duty of doing so. I am one; in Elisabeth you might perhaps find another. In your father, who loves learning above all things, you may recognize that strength not be destroyed by the world the rest of us make. But you must carry everyone's parcels, must you not?"

The shrewd eyes studied me. Unavoidably we stood isolated—a target for gossip that might at least, I thought, divert talk from Elisabeth.

The pang of a new responsibility returned me with a shock to the sense of his words. "I do not think myself ill used, sir." Like him I spoke softly, direct to the understanding in his eyes.

I do not know how it would have gone had we been alone. As it was, he opened his arms for his short-coat, which someone slipped on for him; and drawing away from me, he said, "How could you be, when I know that you are loved?"

Elisabeth and I sat in the gray light from the window. Between us we held the ends of the same half-made skirt, into whose green velvet we were setting a delicate chain-stitch of gold thread. Elisabeth looked up at me and said, "Claire, what is wrong?"

I had been wondering what, in France, could be the penalty for an Englishwoman accessory to treason. The penalties for women were differently savage, I knew. If they took my right hand I had just decided to use the dagger as Walter had taught me, and to die with my body whole. I had achieved this decision when Elisabeth's question cut across my thoughts.

I raised my head, assembling these several reflections. If I were English, then I was an enemy; and the penalty for that, beyond killing, I did not know. If the Count judged me to be French by fosterage, then the secret Thomas had half-confided could bring me under a different law: the law for treason.

Of which my stepmother was guilty without, if I believed Walter, any ambiguity at all. My oath to Thomas lay in me like a dead child; and admission, to anyone including Elisabeth herself, of what I knew about her would involve me in a double complicity, and therefore—if it were revealed—in an apparent double willingness to be party to treason, here where my birth made me suspect already.

I folded my work, my hands shaking, and demanded, "What are you made of: ice? Do you think I do not know?"

Her soft brow creased. She spoke without sarcasm. "Know about what, precisely?"

"About the baby."

"So Walter has told you."

"Yes."

Elisabeth laid aside her work and sat confronting me. On her knees her hands lay loosely open. "And do you despise me for it, Claire?"

"I? What right have *I* to—" I controlled myself; thought rapidly. "No."

"Do you despise him?"

The silence lasted longer. At last I said, "Not for begetting it, if he had had the manhood to be kind." She tried to speak—obeyed my interruption. "But if a man had so renounced *me*," I said, "I would have killed him."

"God help us, Claire!" Her small hands gripped my shoulders. "I will decide who is wronged here! Have I brought you up to be a son, and my champion?"

Frantic-eyed, we stared at each other. Then Elisabeth moaned: "*Oh!*"; stood up; sat down. "Oh, oh."

At last I said, "Mother, why must I *be* so much?"

And then I was into the safety of tears: the deep screaming sobs I had not heard since the day of my first menses, and I was on my knees and in her arms, velvet crushed between us.

"Hush, hush, we will make it right. Shsh." Making baby-sounds, she rocked me to and fro. I felt her gesture someone away from the door and hoped it had not been Walter; for the terror of losing my right hand had begun to pour out of me in unintelligible babble. Elisabeth rocked me. "Cut what off, my darling?"

"My hand, my hand!"

"No, no. We'll take care of you, Father and I. You've done nothing wrong: why should anyone hurt you?" This brought such a scream of despair that she pressed me into the comfort of her breasts. Again I felt her gesture someone away and heard the door shut on us with a soft click.

When I finally lay exhausted among the ruined velvet and the rushes, she went to the door, gave a quick order, and returned with basin and towel. Then she was beside me on the dried, sweet-smelling grass that covered the floor. "Sit up, dear, and wash your face."

"I wanted to make you feel *better*," I wailed, half-laughing now at the childish sound. "I wanted to *help* you."

"Grown-up people can help themselves, Claire. There, that's a little better. I think, you know, we should discuss Jean d'Aubry, and a certain cold taskmaster who looks like myself in the mirror." She set the basin aside, slopping as her hands trembled, and said softly, "I have been a harsh teacher, have I not?"

"I thank you for it all—"

"No." Her hand stilled mine. "Claire, listen, I must say it while I can. I know I am cold. I *do* love you, enjoy you, respect you. I would fill you with my warmth if"—she stumbled and looked away—"if someone would fill me."

"But my father—"

"I love your father more than any other man on earth. Did you think I would leave him for my lord?"

"Never really, no."

She nodded and said rapidly, as if her opening to me were something vanishing before our eyes, "My father, you know, let me learn only stillroom skills. That and childbirth, he said, were all a woman need know. Oh, Claire, how I longed for learning." I took her hands. Elisabeth said, "And it was his mother who—"

"Whose mother, Madame?"

"Madame Alice, His Grace's mother. It was she who took me in to be tutored with Agnès and Marie and Jean, to be taught by scholars from Paris. Taught Latin, mathematics, astronomy, music. . . . And I vowed that no daughter of mine should grow up ignorant. I suppose I fed you in memory of my own hunger. I am sorry."

"Mother: am I genuinely gifted, do you think, in any way?" Her pretty freckled face looked startled. "But, Claire, do you not see? We taught you so much, *and you could do it all.*"

I found I could breathe again. "And must I continue? *Can* I continue? If I do . . ." Softly I spoke the secret I had not known I feared. "I think that I will break."

She did not let me dwell on the fear. "You will *not* break. We have asked too much. You are going to rest"—at my expression—"oh, rest *working* if you must, until you decide what you like to do, what you enjoy: what you want. Do you want," she said softly, "to marry, Claire?"

"Not yet, madame."

"Do you want to leave us, Walter and me?"

"Not yet; but it will come."

"I know."

"Oh, thank you." I sank against her. Through the fragrant fullness of her breast I could feel her heart beating.

At last she stirred. "Come, we must clean this up." I nodded, and moved with her to erase the traces of violent activity from the room. Seconding each other, we cleaned the flagstones, straightened stools, folded ruined cloth, and carefully scuffed the rushes. "I must have Margot sweep these out tomorrow," murmured Elisabeth. "Come, sit with me on the bench. Are you hungry?"

"Yes," I said, surprised at the discovery.

"Good." She settled her blue skirts elegantly, and sat, her hand still holding mine, gazing into the fire.

I said, "Mother, do you still love His Grace?"

The eyes she turned to me were reserved and gentle and shockingly full of pain. "Love him? Of course. Claire, for your own peace forget the nonsense that says we cannot have two loves."

"But you hated him!" Again my voice sounded younger than I had intended.

Elisabeth shrugged. "I came here to finish that, and—and to do another thing. One treasures one's hate—counting it, renewing it, explained it to oneself—for ten years; perhaps twelve. At fifteen one finds one cannot remember how many coins there were, or why they were important. At eighteen years my hands opened, and the coins spilled on the floor. And when I met him I only felt the love I feel for everyone who remembers my youth. It comes to be important, Claire, that another human being was with us in our past; not what he did there. In some way I am not sure is good, I think we all belong to the world of our youth—a memory that grows lonelier as other generations succeed us. I loved Jean when I was fourteen; and I have come all this distance only to find what I should never had denied, that I love him still."

"You are friends, then?" I said.

"I think we are friends, yes. And," she said softly, "and the desire."

For that admission I knew no help but silence. I hope we had been safely settled in it for several moments before an alto voice said behind us, "Elisabeth, your husband—whether wisely or not—told me I might come up. In my presumption I thought I perhaps could help."

Tiredly Elisabeth rose and said without spite, "But then, when did you lack presumption?"

She now stood facing our visitor. I, gaping, my hand clenched on the back of the settle, saw standing in the doorway a woman of unusual beauty. Her brows were arched and thick, and the full lips and great gray eyes so amazed me by their intensity that I took a moment to notice the white veil that concealed her hair and fell down over the finely woven stuff of her gray gown. The crucifix that hung from her belt was silver.

"Agnès," said Elisabeth, "allow me to present my daughter

Claire. Claire, make your duty to Mère Agnès d'Aubry, Abbess of Sainte-Bertrande."

I came around the settle and sank into a shallow Court curtsy: it seemed the best choice to a woman who was both an abbess and, by marriage, a countess. "Reverend Mother."

"Please rise, Mistress Claire. Excuse the clothing, I did not come to cast a religious gloom. I raised three children, you know, before I took Orders, but one does not"—she indicated the white and gray—"lay all this aside so as not to be noticed when one comes to market. I wish one could. My guards and two Sisters are downstairs, being respectfully instructed in the workings of the press. Elisabeth, may I sit down, or shall I ask your forgiveness standing?"

At last Elisabeth said, "And you chose for the child, as well as for me."

"I wish," said Agnès d'Aubry, "the young were kinder. When we grow up we understand at last that others too have feelings and are real. I betrayed both the child and you." She sank, with a strong, trained grace, to one knee. "For that I am deeply sorry."

"Then rise, Agnès." The taller body uncoiled, moving still with a practice that spoke of dancing lessons at Court, and the two women folded softly together, shoulder upon shoulder.

"So sorry," whispered Agnès, her brilliant eyes filled with tears.

It was Elisabeth who straightened first. "Come sit down and tell me about Marie."

Marie's sister shrugged and smiled. "What shall I tell you? She lived thirty-seven years and left two children, Charles and Aliénor. I gather you may meet them later on."

"Claire," said my mother, "wash yourself, please, and then bring us some wine. Bring it yourself."

I nodded. As I curtsied and turned to the door I heard Agnès say, "I thought thirty-seven years too small a portion of Eternity, but fifty, I now find, looks little more. And I love her still. Jean has made a marriage for Aliénor, to be celebrated here in, I think, August."

"And your House?"

"Thirty nuns, all widows who have left the world—if one leaves the world by entering a nursing Order with a hospital, soldiers, tenants, servants, pilgrims, the occasional criminal injudiciously sheltered for the night, and ten rather elderly novices. We *all* have children, my dear, we are the scandal of scandals: in *my* convent the nuns have sixty-seven children among them. We give parties for the grandchildren."

I closed the door upon them.

But winter had not yet finished with us. That night I slept profoundly and was allowed, by Elisabeth's orders, to sleep far into the next day. Of the noise that crackled around me, smashing panes and sending slates sliding off roofs like lethal dominoes, I remember nothing—as if I had died, and the worst storm of the century had occurred in a world I no longer inhabited. Rain poured from the steep-gabled roofs; drowned pigs and geese lay in the gutters. Wind hurled fishing boats against the jetties, leaving several smashed, and one beached on its own wharf. Perhaps my sleep was deeper than natural— was actually a kind of faint. Otherwise the roar of wind and sea must have wakened me.

I woke feeling drugged, very hungry, and trying to remember something. As my maid filled the bath I roused enough to listen about the storm. "A ship broke up on the rocks outside the harbor sometime last night. All day, since the wind died, His Grace has had men out diving for survivors. I hear there are very few, but many dead bodies washed up or dragged in, and smashed timber everywhere."

So, in a bubble of comfort within the busy, grieving town, I bathed and ate the meal Lise brought me. When I had dressed she said, "Most of the ladies have sent their apologies for tonight." We were to have had a small party, but I could imagine what twenty minutes on muleback would do to their velvets. "Apparently, however, several of the gentlemen still mean to come to talk about the rescue."

"Will His Grace be here?"

"No, he has too much to do. But Monsieur Lalemont will be here, and Messieurs Richard and Thomas Linacre."

Only by late afternoon, when I ventured out well wrapped, had the rain sunk to a drizzle. The sky had cleared to a gray-pearl color; each wave thundered onto the beach, broke and foamed away as the next comber rose behind it. The air held an icy freshness. As I enjoyed it I thought with a pang of the dead from Southampton who lay on the flags of Saint-Damien, and I remembered it was the first of March.

"Good evening, Claire." Thomas, cloaked and hooded, stood behind me. "I came up early; I couldn't stand it in the town any longer."

"What—?" I began.

He shook the question away and leaned on the seawall. "Pity Richard, not me. He also means to come tonight—he wants to see your father. He's been diving for the dead all day. When I left him, Béatrice was feeding him a huge hot meal. He's exhausted. I begged him not to come."

"I think he'll need the cheer, if we can provide any. I'll play his—" I avoided the appalling error of "bone flute," and stammered, "T-that is, I think Elisabeth and I might make some music."

Thomas glanced down at the beach and, slipping an arm around my shoulder, gently and powerfully turned me away from the seawall. "Let's go in. Make music, you said?"

"Is there something down on the beach? Has something come ashore?"

I twisted against his arm, which would not yield. "Yes. No, Claire."

But I too was strong, and he had not expected *my* thumbs on the nerves that would make him release me. I whirled—to catch a far glimpse of a doll, her arms outcast, hair streaming as her head lolled submissively to the waves. Then Thomas lifted and carried me away.

That night we did not make music. Dressed in brown cloth—I despised the advertisement of black mourning—I listened as the men spoke of salvage, of former wrecks, of the dangers of the rocks. Elisabeth, in black, contented herself with supplying hot spiced wine. Music would have insulted the sorrow of the day's work both Richard and Gérard had done.

Richard, his clever face haggard, had changed into clean clothes. Leaning forward, his knuckles locked between his knees, he ignored me. At one point, to gesture more easily, he slid off his signet ring and laid it beside him on the table. I glanced at it: a flat square-cut ruby with a flaw across it, the flaw creating a streak that had stamped, before I was born, the letters of Richard's father the judge. Caught up as he was in a trance of distress, I thought he had hardly felt himself lay the ring aside.

For the first time since I had known him he was drinking too much, of alcohol made more potent by heat and spices. His voice husky with exhaustion, he said, "They think the main-mast broke: half of it washed ashore while I was at supper. *Broke*, just like that." His hands twisted, then splayed too widely: his glass wine tumbler spun and fell crashing into shards. The ring slithered and fell too; I cried out as hot liquid scalded my thighs through my dress.

"Oh, good God, Claire, forgive me. Here, let me help." Among our fumblings and protestations my fingers, nimble from the lute strings, pocketed his ring. It vanished from the floor, and in his concern with the expensive glass he had broken he did not even think of it.

Glass had been collected, wine sopped, and I was rising to

change my gown when Richard said, "Elisabeth, I think I must ask the use of one of your beds. I *wish*," he explained with an almost steady earnestness, "I could invite you to join me there, but I *think* . . ." He steepled his hands across his face, and in this posture pitched forward into Gérard's and my father's arms.

"Be still, he's breathing," said Walter. "He's strong and young, but he's had a swim today. And I hope he sleeps all tomorrow. We can care for him here, Thomas, and you'll lie in his bed if you like."

"I won't leave him."

"No difficulty there," said Walter cheerfully. "Take his feet—no, Gérard, you've exhausted yourself enough today. Elisabeth, lift his hands into his lap. Here, I'll take his shoulders. There's a guest room up one flight of stairs."

I followed them, carrying the candles from the solar. The flames cast a cold slanted light as they laid Richard on the bed, and unlaced short-coat and shirt to feel his heart. Satisfied, my father stood up. "He's fainted. It will shade off into sleep— probably has already done so."

Elisabeth had opened the chest at the bed's foot; now she was shaking out blankets. The small group circulated, putting warming touches to a room that felt perfect but unused. Richard lay still. A long body, supple and hard; a lightness of build that surprised me now, remembering his strength. I felt for him the superstitious tenderness one experiences toward unconscious human beings. His face, withdrawn into deep unconsciousness, looked austere and young.

"Ladies, go away: we must strip him for the night." Walter pushed us out. In the corridor Elisabeth hugged me and sent me to my bed.

Alone before my fire, I examined Richard's ring. It lay in my palm, heavy, still warm with his life. And I had stolen it. Why, since I did not mean to keep it?

"Thank God I do not steal to *keep*," I murmured. Where then could I detect my reason? The opportunity had roused in me an unpleasant childish cunning: I remembered that. And to palm it successfully had been a trick as simple as a child's, and had given a strange satisfaction. But beneath these pantomimes I could reach no emotion that might explain what my hands had done. I squeezed out two exhausted, inauthentic tears, then put the ring thoughtfully aside. I would return it to him, with an explanation, as soon as he was well. That the explanation would be a lie I took for granted. It did not cross my mind to tell Richard the truth, or to ask for his understanding or his help.

*The last time I stole, my bleeding first began. What transformation hangs over us now?*

And as I lay in bed I thought of the two men several walls away, naked, breathing evenly, curled together for comfort in the dark. How many times had Richard risked his life today? It had not occurred to him to tell me.

I turned my head on the pillow. Once, from a state I thought was consciousness, I uncoiled myself gasping from hair that was not soaking, was not drowned. And as I sank deeper my own voice kept dinning in my mind:

*What are you made of: ice? Do you think I do not know?*


Richard slept for two days. On the morning of the third he woke, ate an enormous breakfast, and insisted on shaving himself, but allowed Walter and Walter's manservant to bathe him. After an hour's trial of walking he was ready to meet and thank his hostess. Elisabeth embraced him, as I marveled how far downward one had to bend to a man in order to reach his cheek. "Thomas will call for you at the end of the day. Do you remember what you said to me before you fainted?"

Richard grinned. "Tell me, in the hope the hideous memory can be disproven."

"You invited me to inexpressible—and, as it turned out, unexpressed—delights in that bed upstairs."

Richard kissed her hand, one eye on Walter. "And I repeat the invitation. The least word from you—"

"Young lecher, you'll have supper here, and Thomas can collect you," said my father. "Yes, I know, you're aching to see the work at La Vièrge-aux-dames."

"I'll come up later to see how you go on," I said.

It sounded impertinent, and I expected him to shrug it away. Instead, to my surprise, he gave me a sharp look and said, "Claire, I should like you to do that. Remember, please."

About four o'clock of a clean, clear March day I crossed the road and climbed the hillock to the church porch. The boards nailed across the windows had held fast. I hoped the fragile glass, like half-spun spiders' webs within the lead cames, had survived the storm.

I entered the nave. The peace of an old church, despite its temporary disuse, reached and calmed me. From habit I crossed myself, though no Host stood reserved on the altar—nor would till the Bishop reconsecrated what had become, in part, a new structure.

The reason for reconsecration rose above me in an ordered web of roof and crossbeams, adding a perfume of new golden oak to the ancient incense of stone. The fire-stench had gone. Torches, lamps, and candles, clustered by the half-dozen on man-high stands, cast a delicate artificial light, making darker the structure of glass shapes—aquamarine, honey, garnet, and indigo—that the glazier knelt on his scaffolding the glue into the leads. From the sanctuary a brilliant diamonding of white and black had begun to progress, a little preceded, I saw, by the bed of sifted beach sand that would cushion the tiles from the flags of the foundation.

And above me on either side, the clerestories. As I moved softly forward toward the distant figures of Richard and his workmen, I marked the height and make of each: the long running balcony that ran parallel to the nave on either side, its function to provide access to the deeply pierced supplementary windows. I passed, near the door, the two stairways that led up, each to a balcony so narrow that one man could—I suddenly understood—defend it alone against attack.

An entrance well chosen, then, but where? To judge by the depth of the boarded clerestory windows, each the shape of a shallow bishop's miter, the walls must be ten feet thick and could easily accommodate a passage. A plunge into the walls—from what place?—then down. . . . Neither clerestory appeared to have been damaged in the fire. Each ended, I saw, in a rounded balcony that looked down into the transept.

I walked forward. Richard saw me and beckoned. An opening near the end of the clerestory, then, so that one man could if necessary defend others from a single line of attack, the other being closed behind him. An opening where? In the walls? In the floor?

"Good afternoon, Richard." I stopped a little distance from him and smiled at the foreman, whom I knew. "Excuse me, but may I speak to you about a private matter?"

"Of course. Just a moment, Michel."

"Take your time, sir." The foreman, squatting, was measuring a surface that to me appeared perfectly level.

"I had not expected the sand," I said as Richard came to me, his Master's gown covering his day clothes. He looked rested and a little quizzical. "It's for cushioning, is it not?"

He nodded. "A little abrasive, but we must, alas, use what our land produces. I had it sieved and pulverized. It may settle unevenly and prove a bad choice, but I hope it will allow the skin of tiles to move slightly over the floor. Stones swell and shrink a little, you know, depending on the weather. Cement them together and they risk buckling like a crust."

"Stones *swell*?" I demanded.

He grinned. "Only a very little. What was your private matter?"

I felt in the soft leather of my hanging pocket. "This." I handed him his ring. "I suppose it got knocked to the side. I found it near the wall, and kept it for you."

"Thank you very much; I had missed it." He took it, still gazing at me with a strange seriousness, and slipped it onto his middle finger. "It was my father's; I should hate to lose it. Claire—"

I had turned to go. "Yes?"

"Claire, have you heard of the Rites of Saint John?"

"The ancient Midsummer Feast?" I turned slowly back to him.

"So the pagans called it, and it has some features of the May feast called Beltane. We, of course, celebrate it like the Christians we are."

"In precisely the same ways they did?"

"Not quite," he said. "There is, I think, no animal sacrifice, and no rumor of human sacrifice either, or the authorities . . . there, I've frightened you. I didn't mean to. In fact, it is a night of adventure, of dancing and whatever else one chooses, in the woods. If Thomas and I *both* swore service as your bodyguards, would you like to come with us this year?"

"*Would* I!" I exclaimed. "I'd decided to go alone."

"Past Walter's watchman?"

"Walter's watchman won't be there: he'll be in the woods, dancing and doing," I said impudently, "whatever else he chooses."

"So Walter will be guarding his own door," remarked Richard. "What about Elisabeth?"

"She went there herself as a girl. You could get around her."

"I shall. And around your father. Leave it to me."

"I will. Thank you, Richard! Tell me, would it be dangerous without two friends?"

He shrugged. "Let's just say no woman should trust to luck.

We'll come for you in force that night. Don't worry, I won't forget."

I retreated, and as I glanced back, waving happily, I saw him draw off the signet ring and flip it once into the air, then catch and hold it, as if in thought.

# 8

*Lenten is come with love to town.* . . . Now, as green rose in the turf—as sticky patterned buds turned from bronze to copper-green—as clouds grew soft and blew away, I could sing that song with truth. And my singing about the house dropped from language to language, seeking, in Italian and plattdeutsch and dog-Latin, words for the primal joy that had visited us hundreds of springs before.

*Iam liquescit et decrescit*
*grando, nix et cetera:*
*bruma fugit, et iam sugit*
*ver aestatis ubera.*
*Illi mens est misera*
*qui nec vivit, nec lascivit*
*sub aestatis dextera!*

Now spring sucks at the breasts of summer.
That man is a wretch who does not live and lust
    under the reign of summer!

How did green flow into the turf, working secretly while I slept one single night? I do not know; but one morning I woke

137

to birdsong and a softness in the air from which I knew this year would not retreat. Crocuses showed hard buds, then cups of saffron and purple; ferns uncurled almost as I watched; bees began to waver above the lemon-scented irises. For a few days bluebells made a haze of color around the roots of the trees. The green around us grew cloudy with apple blossom; chestnut leaves unfurled; and among cushions of moss I could find the lily-of-the-valley I used to perfume my chamber.

I was gathering the milky bells, each astonishingly fragrant, at the edge of the woods one day when I straightenened and glanced past the cup of the arena—most of its benches still carpeted with turf—toward La Vièrge-aux-dames. At the base of the hill I saw a cutting, square and dark. Richard Linacre had begun to tunnel into the slope.

I decided to ask him about it on the next evening he spent alone with us. We were seeing, I felt, too much of the Master of Works. With or without Thomas, he came to us about twice a week, and with courteous pleasantness accepted the bath and meal Elisabeth had offered him. Our house became the place he went after a day spent tiling the floor with his workmen in La Vièrge-aux-dames, or doing whatever else the burned carvings and devastated chapels required. Our family circle, small at its core, had ever since my childhood involved an outer ring of friends who seemed part family. Richard persisted like one of these, without ever seeming to persist; and he paid for his supper with a wit, intelligence, and lightness that my parents enjoyed. Often there, but never for too long, he maintained his distance from us. *I love to look at you*, he had written to me. But he did not, during these evenings, do more than courteously include me in the conversation. And if he watched Elisabeth, she sustained it with calm.

"Richard, have you decided?" I said to him one evening when the windows lay open to the hushing of the surf and to a long twilight. "About the foundation of the church?" *And about the walls*, I thought, but dared not say it.

"That it does not go deep enough to give me access to the hill?" I nodded. "Yes. I've decided instead to examine the pile of rubble."

"Pile?" Elisabeth chose a blue skein from among her sewing silks.

Richard nodded. "As far as I can tell, the rubble of a Roman villa. I intend to remove most of it in order to reach the hillside."

"Remove it?" I said. "But why? Is it just the ruin of a house?"

"A ruin deliberately preserved, I suspect, to cover an entranceway into the hill. We've found the planks of an old tunnel through."

"A concealed entrance," said Elisabeth. "To what?"

Richard smiled. "That you will see when I am sure. Please don't come near the excavation till then. I want to surprise you, and also I cannot guarantee its safety. And I think His Grace has the right to see it first. By the way, sir, your steward gave me these on the way up. From London, I think." From inside the breast of his robe he took a packet of letters.

Walter's sketching had already drawn him, courtesy notwithstanding, to the table. He leaned across a sketch of the Sacrifice of Isaac. "Ah yes, from my brother. Thank you."

"Did you write to him also from Florence, sir?"

*Write to him,* I noted: not *Did he write to you.* Richard's tone neither threatened nor pretended warmth. It hung there among us in the dense blue twilight like the interrogation it suddenly was.

Walter handed Elisabeth a taper. Silently she lit it from the fire, and the flame bobbed through the blue as he touched it to the branch of candles that illuminated his work. That done, he gazed at Richard. "Yes, about our home and about Florentine affairs. And yes, I wrote what the city said about the affairs of the Medici and other public matters."

"It is a common practice."

"Without such private correspondents as myself, and without

the bankers' couriers, news would travel much more slowly. Yes, I wrote about Florence. And yes, perhaps Robert found parts of what I said to be of interest to his patron, the Duke of York; I write to my brother, but I cannot govern the use he chooses to make of what I say. And yes, I write to him from Saint-Aurèle."

Richard's tone was gentle. "What have you found to tell him, sir?"

"I am sure," said Walter, picking up his string-wrapped pencil, "that His Grace's secretary could inform you."

With a soft movement Elisabeth set aside her work. I found I was trembling—uncertain, from the cues my parents' stillness refused to give me, whether this half-friend had turned our enemy. "His Grace's secretary," said Richard, "is Monsieur Sidonie, an old friend of my father and a good man. I doubt, sir, that His Grace intercepts your correspondence."

"I am glad you doubt it," said my father. I shrank back into the silence. Walter's graphite added a stroke to the Sacrifice of Isaac.

Richard leaned forward in the pose I had come to recognize. His fingers, loosely linked, appeared free from tension. "Thank you for the meal, Elisabeth. I will not come again if you prefer."

"We enjoy your company, Richard," said my stepmother, "and we have nothing to be ashamed of." From the controlled tremor in her voice I knew the lie sprang from the rashness of sincerity. "You know, I have seen a good deal of the world. I ought, perhaps, to wish for Florence or Paris, but I find that I do not. My husband has been good enough to limit himself to this place for my sake. I do not know what loyalty binds us to the square mile of earth where we were born; but that place is somehow the fabric of our bones."

"This is a fishing port."

"This is an ancient and honorable town, part of the nation of Normandy to which I owe allegiance," replied my stepmother.

*The nation of Normandy.* Walter had not moved. Richard said, and his voice was no longer that of an interrogator, "Elisabeth, we must choose."

"We are seafarers. We choose the sea."

Richard stirred with a controlled impatience. "Normandy is, and will always be, the corridor across which England marches on her way to Paris. *And we must choose Paris.* War comes from London; from Paris, I know, comes nothing but taxation and bad government. Let us accept the accomplished fact and have peace at last. England's conquests here are over. When she turns, as turn she will, it must be upon other nations."

He rose, a tall shadow in the semidark, and moved to the window. There he stood facing us, arms akimbo. Suddenly I became aware that the gentleness of his voice and manner was calculated—not to persuade us, but to control, to diminish, a passion that threatened to shake him bodily. "Walter, I hunger for peace. I long for peace in which to rebuild this town. I have made war, and it cannot equal the fascination of a peace in which to make something good. I do not know how many years I shall live, but soon or late we must mark our plot of ground and say: *Here I will live and create something for others who come after.* Elisabeth, forgive me, I must leave."

He gave us, struck silent with surprise, no chance to see him to the door, so we remained arrested by the fire. After a moment Walter's pencil again swept evenly across the paper. A little later Elisabeth rose and left us without a word.

My father and I sat on in the candlelight. I do not know what instinct moved me to dare the question I then asked. "Father, did you mean it when you said you wanted me to marry him?"

A sweep of the pencil. "Yes."

*Since you asked,* said the silence. Through my astonishment I managed at last: "Why?"

With a sigh and a rasping of his chin my father set aside his drawing. He had never taken the Roman emerald from his hand; the fingers, tapered and strong, were artist's fingers, at odds with the big slouched body and shrewd eyes. His voice was at its gruffest. "Since you ask, several reasons. Thomas has not, I hope, beguiled you?"

"No. He has never tried."

"No, he would not: he is a good boy. But Richard is a man."

"Is he our enemy?"

"Oh yes, I think so," said my father absently.

"Then why does he come here?"

"To enjoy us. To watch. And to watch you."

"Why do you want me to marry him? He hasn't asked me."

"And God knows a father's liking will probably suffice to drive you away from him. Claire, he is afraid for Saint-Aurèle, for this place he loves and for those whom the English have not killed of the friends among whom he was born. That makes us his enemies, potentially, until our loyalty is proven. Would you trust us, in his place?"

"No," I said, and added softly, "I fear we are not worth trusting."

"Nonsense. And I don't *want* you to marry him, I merely ask you to accept him as a friend—not to close him out. He is wealthy, well educated, with an excellent mind, and he likes to work. He loves, and has thought about what he loves. And there are other things, which prudence not shame forbids me to describe to a virgin daughter, but which you should consider. I think he could satisfy you there."

"So Marianne could tell me."

I was ashamed the instant the childish sarcasm was uttered. I winced as Walter's pencil, aimed precisely past my shoulder, shot into the fire, where it flared in a puff of yellow flame. "Oh, for God's sake, Claire!" Pushing the papers away, he came to sit beside me, and said, "Learn to distinguish what is important from what is not."

"I'm sorry, sir."

His arm came round my shoulder; the other sprawled along the settle's back. "Marianne was his mistress, the whole town knows it. Be glad of it, and never take a virgin man into your bed." He held up a finger in mock sternness. "Remember this, or I'll have to repeat it on your wedding night."

"Then find me a bridegroom who cannot be shocked."

He grinned. "I have, but he hasn't asked you, and you don't like him. How much more can a father do?"

I laughed and sat sheltered against him for a while, and was for that night comparatively at peace.

When I went out to the market with Elisabeth that spring, with Marco walking behind us, we would wear our pattens—high shoes to raise us above the muck—and light cloaks lined with taffeta. Both of us carried baskets, and through the narrow streets, so floored and walled with stone that horse hooves appalled the ears with their clatter, we would pass the tiled, thatched, or slate-roofed houses of Saint-Aurèle. On the spine of one roof, thatched thick as hair and gray with the fifty years since the straw was fresh, a row of daffodils had rooted. The English had left both thatch and daffodils unburned.

The houses were steep-roofed and, Walter said, not so tall as in London, where stories often overhung each other to five or six tiers above the street. But the houses of Saint-Aurèle stood two or three stories high, the ground floor often being made of stone, while above it the grid and crosses of half-timber showed pale brown against weathered plaster. If the building was a shop the shutters opened on little panes where lay displayed thread or lace, a single fine dagger, cones of sugar and vials of spices, or a pair of the excellent shoes made in the town.

On our way to the square we would skirt the harbor. Here lay fishing boats painted blue or red, and the deep-bellied clinker-built ships that every spring sailed west to the fishing banks. This area stank of hemp and hard billets of salted cod, and of yellow-green weed that smelled like medicine. In a clear sunset the water reflected the line of narrow houses; on windy days it fretted like an old silver mirror.

I can analyze sights and sounds, but in this and every other harbor I have ever seen there was an attraction beyond analysis. One could sense it in the men, fishermen and sailors, for whom this place merely served a function. They never forgot the sea, never turned their eyes from it for long. And in their self-containment I sensed the watchfulness, almost the repose of a shared arcanum: the magic of a perpetual setting out.

On the docks we bought fish and shellfish, but for vegetables, flowers, and fruits in season we went to the marketplace.

Here Saint-Damien stood, its door nested within twelve carven lintels. Opposite the church a new structure on an old foundation sustained the steady traffic of the bathhouse. Around the square lay the better shops—the spicer, the butcher, a tailor, and two smithies that smelled of hot metal, their sheltered dark too humid to enter on a summer day. Here too stood the armorer's house, whose advertisement was a steel cuirass damascened with patterns of gold, and the shop where one bought pewter spoons and platters, crockery painted with flowers, and copper puncheons. There too one could find the joiner who made tables out of planks, high narrow beds, and clothes presses of caramel-colored wood; and also the public stable, with its fragrance of straw and its sweet reek of straw dung.

In the square on market day flowers lay to freshen in the fountain, and we could buy asparagus, cabbages, apples, lettuces, and pears. Crocks of apple brandy stood for sale in a shady stall. And all around us moved the people: the men in their close-fitting robes, the women dressed in gown, white coif, and shawl—dark faces with strong features, though occasionally one saw the gray eyes and silver-blond hair that reminded one the Danes had come here.

On the way home we would cross a low hump-backed

bridge with a white keystone. Here lay the Cerne, its banks bitten from the chalk—banks over which it flooded in spring spate or in a summer thunderstorm. Then it ran six feet deep, and dangerously; but now the water, in which chestnut trees cast the shadow of their spiked flowers, ran smooth as green shot silk.

Elisabeth said: "Look, there is Verneuil, the Linacres' house."

I looked upstream through the trees, but could distinguish little. "The wall is very high," I said.

Elisabeth nodded. "It runs all around the orchards and garden. But there, I think you can make out the boathouse."

I could—a red tiled roof shielded by the fifteen-foot wall; and a pale strip that might have been a small wooden dock running close to the shore. Then, our baskets heavy with purchases, we turned down the street that led to the seawall.

After dark on an evening in May we saw torches moving in the field below La Vièrge-aux-dames. The Count, I gathered, had come with a small retinue to inspect Richard's opening in the hill. But why after dark? I wondered. And why had Richard built, around the opening, a stout wooden porch and a door with a lock?

He waited until night, too, to show my parents what he had discovered, and then they walked with him across the field. For an hour I fretted, explicitly excluded. My parents returned smiling, and Richard said to me, "And now, Claire, it is time to keep my promise."

I pulled on my cloak and followed him, alone in the darkness whispering of ocean. A subtle lawlessness hung about the night, shared between Richard and me. My companion—dressed in short-coat, hose and cloak, without his robe—remained the Master of Works and, by his manner, my host.

We came to the hill. To my surprise two guards stood watch outside the torchlit porch fitted with such incongruous neatness into the slope. A door smelling of new wood was unlocked. Richard gestured me through.

He had fitted the door so close I did not appreciate at once that we were also passing a second door with a Roman lintel. Once—behind me, where now torchlight shimmered against the stars—there had opened room after room of a vanished house. Time had demolished it and buried its maker in oblivion. But I stepped into a folly he had conceived and decorated. That master of a villa in the Gaulish provinces had chosen, for coolness or perhaps only for the novelty, to excavate a banquet room into the hill.

Candles in sconces mellowed the lines of walls and floor, but they plunged away from me crisp and straight in the chalk. The maker had left four pillars carved from the fabric of the hill, and had painted them that warm ox-blood red the Romans loved, with a band of black at top and bottom. I moved forward. Richard said, "Examine as you please. The ceiling is safe."

I turned from the flow of color—pink, blue, and fawn, eggshell, ox-blood, and gold—to confront the reason for the room's preservation. "An ossuarium," I said.

Richard shut the door. At my glance he said, "Look at the cracks around the edges, and how the candles are blowing: we'll have air enough. Yes, an ossuarium. Remember what I told you—that they did have a burial ground above here for the first hundred years of the church."

"But the turf is only four feet deep!"

"Precisely, which is why the cemetery now lies inland. And when they made that decision, they removed the old burials and put them here."

Along all one wall and part of another they confronted me: human bones stacked floor to ceiling. There was no flesh, no stink, only a wall; and into the dog-paw pattern of nested thigh bones someone had inserted a cross of skulls. Along the wall other skull domes gleamed in rows. Some alchemy of air or candlelight had turned each bone a rich, polished brown.

"How alike they look," I said, gazing at the skulls. Richard stood still, watching me.

I circled slowly to face the ancient life the priests had, for their own convenience, elected to preserve. Some artist had used, like Richard himself a thousand years later, the materials the region offered. The mosaic floor beneath my feet was made of sea pebbles selected in three shades of delicate natural color: against a white background the maker had traced squares, mazes, scallops, and flowers in fawn and gray. And the ceiling showed a similar elegance. Against the whitewash I saw garlands of faded gold.

"May I sit?" said Richard. I saw someone had set a bench and two stools in the center of the room.

"Oh yes, of course."

He took a stool. "I guess he worked in fresco on the walls—which I understand to mean that he drew directly with the brush onto a wet surface. Look at the quick, sketchlike quality of the paintings."

"They aren't very good," I admitted.

His smile shared my own delight. "What can one expect," he inquired, "in the provinces?"

No, they were not very good, but they filled the walls with a glow of blue and rose touched with flesh tones or with orange. Naked women predominated, their rich flesh escaping from their draperies: Venus lounging on a shell, her plump coarse face identical with that of Europa, riding the Bull in another panel, or with Isis restoring Io to human form. The male nudes were darker, their bodies shining with oil: Theseus extending his hand to be kissed by a child he had rescued; Pan watching the approach to his bed of a shy girl. And everywhere, sketched greenery: laurel trees, pine branches, palms; a hare eating grapes; the ibex and the crane; lattices and columns receding in false perspective.

"It's charming," I said. And indeed I had intended to be charmed, to be moved by the nearness of the ancient people. But my voice echoed beneath the roof, and behind me the skulls traced their cross. I turned to the wall of bones, hating the priests who had seen this room only as a crypt already excavated.

Richard said, "It's gone wrong, hasn't it. I'm sorry."

"So am I; so sorry to disappoint you. The bones," I said with precision as I took another stool, "the bones distress me."

"How like Elisabeth you sound."

"Do I?" I made a wry face.

He nodded. "Do you know how closely your voice resembles Walter's when he talks to you, and Elisabeth's when you come under her influence? You have a gift of mimicry."

"Which makes me no one in myself." *I will not cry*, I thought, and forced my face to stillness.

"I did not say you were no one in yourself." His presence in the soft light was brilliantly concentrated—a heat of vitality and controlled intelligence.

I said, "I did not come here to be baited, Richard."

"I did not bring you here to bait you. Something has gone wrong. Let us repair it if we can."

"Much has gone wrong here."

"Would it help," he said gently, "to tell me what?"

The impulse to do so—to give my family, in a rush of selfish indiscretion, into the power of a man I did not trust—almost brought the tears. I mastered them, with a pang of self-dislike so savage I did not fear their return. And what in me did not cease to calculate recognized that I now needed to excuse—no lie about a visionary dream (yes, I had considered it), and no openness either: my distress would excuse, I suspected, almost any aberration. "Richard, I have a foolish fear."

"Tell it to me."

Knowing I was abusing his gentleness, I forced myself

forward. "In your examining of La Vièrge-aux-dames, have you tested for any hollowness in the walls?"

"Yes, as part of the structural repairs."

"Did you find any?"

"None at all."

"It occurs to me, with so old a building, that you ought to take care. It lies near the coast. If a hidden entranceway existed, it could prove a danger. I have heard of such things."

"So have I." The gray-green eyes were cool. "Thank you, Claire, I'll consider your suggestion. What angers you here—the bones?"

I looked again at the glowing walls, their life mocked by the charnel arrogance behind him. "We, of course, are the saved. All who have not heard the name of Christ are damned. I believe Dante says the virtuous pagans live in a kind of Limbo, where they enjoy natural happiness but cannot see the face of God."

"And you hate us for our arrogance."

I gazed at him, hands twined in my cloak. He started up to come to me, then thought better of it without trying to disguise his hesitation. From the distance he had taken up he said, "Islam and Isarel will not convert to our Faith because they rightly judge us cruelly exclusive, as well as wrong. Any institution is fallible, Claire, and the Church from its foundation—and its foundation was not Christ, but Saint Paul—is an institution. Live within it, therefore: we must live somewhere. No descent of God exhausts or empties the divine, nor can we understand what is infinite. Therefore we cannot presume to exclude. Do not believe in exclusion. Who knows how many worlds exist in which to meet the renewal we name Redemption? Do you believe God damns for the reasons we do—pleasure in cruelty, revenge, or lust of the loins turned into doctrine?"

"'Behold I make all things new,'" I quoted softly, and stood up.

Richard rose with me. "How old are you, Claire? Twenty?"

"Not yet."

"Where did you learn," he asked, "to be so bitter?"

I shrugged. "A hundred years ago half Europe died within six months. What was it like, I wonder, to survive such a visitation? *For God so loved the world* that I was born to war and memories of plague. So were you."

"It is possible to be happy, Claire. Do not confuse your own imaginings with understanding of their pain. That is fantasy, not wisdom. Those whom the plague bereaved long ago joined those whom it destroyed, in nothingness or in understanding."

"They have their peace, then." He stood gazing down at me; his face in its stern alertness was both gentle and warm, yet did not spare me the focus of his full attention. My voice shook; distressed, I felt rush from me, as on the beach that day with Thomas, a passion I had not known I felt. "And we have the Danse Macabre painted on the graveyard walls. What convinces you, Richard, that this is a redeemed world? Have you seen a single thing made better because Redemption came?" Behind us the skulls shone in the candlelight.

He glanced over his shoulder at them and smiled. "No, Claire; not one single thing."

I stared at him, but he seemed not to be baiting me. At last I sighed. "You are older than I. I do not," I said wearily, "understand you."

"I am not so much older, you know." We had reached the door; the gold and pastels lay behind us. Richard leaned against the frame, gazing down at me, in his face pure friendship. "No one has heard us here. This is matter for burning. You will not repeat it."

"No, I will not. Richard, I apologize. I *did* come intending to enjoy."

"Never mind," he said; and, taking my arm, led me out into the dark.

\* \* \*

When he had seen me home and our house was only a shape beside the seawall, he walked back across the field, spoke a password, and was again let into the Roman room. To the guard he said, "Come help me move the barrier."

"Yes, sir." Together they pushed aside the smaller shelf of bones that obscured half the back wall—a pile that, though I had not noticed it, rested on a low trolley. Behind it blocks of chalk had been cut away to tear a doorway in the wall—a door of which the Roman banqueters had never dreamed.

"How did you find it, sir?" inquired the man, who belonged to His Grace's garrison at the castle.

"The wall rang differently here," said Richard. He stepped, using only the candlelight, into the tunnel that ran behind the ossuary. It smelled of rock and damp. "Thank God there are no bats. Their droppings are so dangerous." The guard nodded, following. Richard glanced upward to the shaft in the ceiling of the tunnel with its old wooden ladder. "Rubble from the roof has choked it permanently there. The fire did us that good, at all events. Have the masons finished?"

"Yes. The blocking wall is five feet thick, but the cement will take some time to dry."

"That doesn't matter. Between our new barrier and the rubble in the upper shaft, no English party will ever use this tunnel."

"What has His Grace ordered, sir? Shall we seal in the ossuary?"

Richard shook his head. "I see no need. We'll restore the wall—it was a pity to ruin the murals—and hide the cemented cut with bones. And then, behind a door selectively unlocked, our Roman chamber can remain to please the antiquaries. I would hate to seal it again in darkness."

"As for myself," remarked the guard, "I won't come here again once I've the choice. I don't like the bones."

Richard grinned. "They are its guardians."

Leaving the torchlight soft behind him, he walked alone down to the seawall. Above him shone cool white stars; below, the sea was only sound. He stood there for a long time, gazing at our house and searching for my window.

# 9

"Elisabeth," I said to her on the afternoon of July twenty-fourth, "I am going with the revelers tonight."

She regarded me, her chin cradled in her hand; the short, tended nails shone with the oil she had rubbed into them that morning. "I know."

"How?" I said, without surprise.

"My dear child, you have several virtues, but you are neither shrewd nor a deceiver."

"About whom," I inquired, "am I failing to be shrewd?"

"About the Master of Works. And about Thomas too."

"Is this a warning?"

Elisabeth's hand briefly shielded her face. At last she said, "Yes. Don't grow too intimate with Thomas."

"And whom," I persisted, "am I failing to deceive?" This time she did not answer at all, so I said, "What does Walter think, Mother?"

"That this feast is, at its best, a kind of Masque of Fools. Its worst your friends will take care you never see. Richard caught him the other night and told him the same stories *I* used to disarm *my* mother."

"And Walter," said my father from the solar doorway, "like your mother no doubt, my dear, was not deceived."

"Sir, would you prefer I not go?"

Walter gave a faint shrug. "I'll give you nothing to defy, Claire, and what fears I have for you won't move me to lock you in your room. I gather there is dancing; watch it and come home. Richard says the feast need be no more than that. But if anyone harms you, or if impulse moves you to do something you regret, remember to tell us, not conceal it."

"Wear blue," said Elisabeth.

"You know I've no blue gown, you say it makes me look sallow."

"Green then. And a light cloak with a hood, and sturdy shoes. Remember you'll be walking."

But Elisabeth did not appear to greet my escorts when they knocked on our door. Dressed in green cloth, my hair brushed in a shining fall concealed by a gray cloak, I followed Walter down the spiral stair. Beyond us lay the shop, deserted except for one resentful watchman. Those of our men who were not natives had scented a promising native custom and vanished after supper.

"Sir." Richard, as the senior, shook Walter's hand. Like Thomas he wore practical clothes—a gray coat with black embroidery around its square throat. His belt carried short-sword and dagger. "We should like to take Claire to the dancing at the Standing Stones."

"I hope you enjoy it. I wish I could go," admitted my father.

"With Elisabeth?" exclaimed Thomas, ignoring my venomous glance. "Why not?" In the ten months I had known him he had grown, and now stood an inch taller than Richard. His face had hardened, but it kept a boy's clear rosy coloring.

Walter grinned. "I'll not spoil sport, *or* come back to find my metal bars and Florentine paper stolen. Perhaps another time. Richard, I take it these revels involve drinking?"

"A good deal, sir." Richard's voice was calm. "But not by me."

"Well, take care of her."

"We will. Good night."

Both Richard and Thomas held out their hands. Before I slipped into the protection I leaned up to kiss my father. "Thank you, sir. We'll be back by dawn."

When we closed the door he had already turned away. I opened my mouth to speak to Thomas, when Elisabeth's whisper interrupted me. "Claire!"

We glanced up. I saw her against the golden window only a few feet above. "Catch!" she called.

I did: a dark red rose, its stem showing pale oval scars where she had peeled away the thorns. She shut the casement; I tucked the rose between my breasts.

We went quietly, away from the seawall toward the field. Above us the moon hung mottled like Roman glass, its unfinished edge—it was three days from the full—fading into indigo. All around us lay rich blue shadow. Now I noticed not one couple but several leaning lazily on the seawall. As we watched, one pair straggled away hand in hand and followed us—self-complete, not seeking us; silent as grazing deer.

There were to be others—men and women together. Some faces I was to recognize, though none intimately. No one wore a mask, though cloaks were common, and I saw no man without a dagger. All kept to themselves, practicing the courtesy of averted eyes. Everywhere the blurred subtlety of blue and black was stippled with the pallor of stars, of blossom, of human skin. Around me flowed air as tepid as sun-warmed water—a flood of ultramarine, of cobalt and indigo; and I moved as I had moved once or twice in dreams, when I walked naked through a world kinder than our own, where no one would hurt me.

"Where are we going?" I said softly.

Richard replied, "To the Ring. There's a path."

Ahead of us as we labored over the buried Roman town the forest rose in a black, rustling wall. But before we came to it we paused to look down into the arena. Orange flames cast a glow upward from its floor, transforming it into a cup of light.

Around a bonfire lit where once men had fought the beasts, several people were sitting quietly.

"God damn them," said Richard.

Thomas laid a hand on his arm. "Let them be. What do you think they can do, burn it?"

We passed under the trees and, with soft quarrels and soft directions, found the path. Above me shadows surged in the breeze, then stilled, then rustled again to reveal white stars. I craned to look, and the stars seemed to twinkle in the wind, shimmering with an orange and blue so subtle the eye could barely detect it. But we were now deep in the woods, and nothing moved me to say aloud that I had noticed the stars have different colors.

All at once ahead of us a woman stepped onto the path. She was naked and paid us no heed, but paced forward on her bare feet. She had dragged her loosened hair forward over her breasts; from the rear we could see only the undulation of her haunches and the dappling of starlight on shoulders and strongly furrowed spine.

Thomas's hand closed hard on my forearm. I smothered a cry. The woman heard and looked back at us, her eyes in shadow. Then she was gone into the woods, no more strange on this night than if we had startled a doe grazing in the rain.

"Excuse me," said Thomas. "I'll be right back." With deft silence he too plunged into the bushes, and I remained standing alone with Richard.

"*May she suck him dry,*" murmured Thomas's brother. After a moment he said, "Claire, this was not a plan."

"To leave me alone with you?" I do not suppose my surprise flattered him. His reassurance had just revealed to me that men might make such plans. "Elisabeth told me today I am not shrewd."

"Did she?" He laughed softly and drew me forward with a comforting pressure on my arm. "Our Thomas may or may not reappear. May she be Circe and turn him into a pig. Come along. The Standing Stones still stand—one can depend on *them*, at least."

"Don't worry," I said naïvely, "I'm not afraid."

"Good girl."

We found the dancers in the clearing that had, for generations beyond remembering, sheltered the Rites of Saint John. A bonfire burned in its center. Over and around it a line of couples wove and swayed and leapt, while others clapped the rhythm, their backs against trees whose bark the firelight transmuted to molten bronze. Farther still, in the margin between light and shadow, others lingered. I saw and waved at Marco; he covered his face and found business elsewhere.

Richard and I joined the watchers; and there, ensorceled, I dreamed away an hour. Women plunged themselves waist-deep into a tub of water and, thus protected, with their thighs and their knotted skirts soaking, leapt the bonfire, screaming with delight as they cleared the flames.

> *Hélas madame*
>   *celle que j'aime tant*
> *permettez que*
>   *sois votr' humble servant.*
> *Votr' humble servant*
>   *seray à toujours,*
> *et tant que je vivray*
>   *autre n'aimeray que vous.*

"*Hé-las ma-dame,*" I hummed, clapping. The slap of palm on palm overwhelmed the rhythm of the tabor. The light, cherry-red and gold, sleeked the curved pipe of the crumhorn and shone in the flaring bell of the shawm. These three and a tambourine made up the consort, as the musicians flowed from bourée to saltarello to the pulsing primitivism of an estampie.

At one point a flask was offered me. "Pass it by," ordered Richard's voice. I knew the dangers of a common cup and shook my head, smiling. Richard had been sitting a little behind me, leaning on one arm. "If you're thirsty, drink this." He took a small flask from his belt.

I tasted it. "It's lemonade!"

"Thirst-quenching," said Richard, grinning without sympathy.

*Allégez-moi, douce petite brunette,*
  *dessous la boudinette:*
*Allégez-moi de toutes mes douleurs* . . .

Soothe me, my brown-haired darling,
  just below the navel:
Ease me of all my pain . . .

The instruments slowed. The voices, momentarily sad, sang with them the strangely melancholy tune. Then the tambourine quickened, and the drum, emerged with its player from the darkness, beat our melancholy by sheer tempo into insistence, and the dancing began again.

I leaned back, encountered the warmth of Richard's shoulder, and without discourtesy moved away. Around us the Standing Stones rose in a circle, their abraded shapes only bulks against the stars. Once, perhaps, lintels as massive as houses had roofed the ring, but the centuries had broken it open, and now only the doorposts of the ancient circle stood—powerful guardians. "Where are the priests?" I whispered to Richard.

"Praying for our souls, Claire; but not here."

I sipped the lemonade and wiped the flask lip with my handkerchief before I handed it to him. He took it with a word of thanks, and drank. I clasped my knees, feeling with my mind for the magic within the stones. In thought I traveled among granite crystals, encountering the will that still impregnated them, waiting with patience for the blood and semen that alone could hallow this place as it deserved.

A ring was forming around the fire; people fumbling and laughing, arms spread, hands on shoulders. I moved, my limbs supple as though I had drunk a good deal. "Claire!" said Richard's warning voice behind me. But I had joined the circle and was whirling, the fire spitting and spinning in lights of yellow and orange and rose. And something within me that knew neither English nor French nor plattdeutsch nor Italian began to speak, a whisper unremarked by anyone but the watcher who had risen to his knees.

The circle snapped stragglingly apart. Weaving, the soft syllables pouring from my lips, I danced forward to the fire and cast Elisabeth's rose into it to burn.

I felt a blow. It was Richard's arms locked around me, lifting me and hurling me bodily down in the shadow outside the ring.

We lay side by side on the grass, panting; and his voice whispered, *"Be still.* Amen-Ra, and you named him, is not the god of this place. Thank God it was only a rose you burned."

"It should," I explained with clarity, "have been a living heart."

"You are all too apt to this. I was wrong to bring you." With angry tenderness he leaned over me, his arm pinning me, his side hot and solid against my thigh; and his face changed. "Oh, God," he said. "This will be quick. Lie still."

I was too relaxed to be startled; and of shock, I learned that night, I am not capable. Therefore I watched with compassion as he endured, with courtesy and brevity, what he could not prevent. With his right arm he held me down; his leg lay heavy over mine; and I studied his closed eyes as ecstasy forced him profoundly inward, to confront that sensual absolute in which the ancients rightly saw God manifest. He shuddered, groaned softly, and rested for a moment against my shoulder. Then he rolled away from me, his hand over his eyes. "Claire, I am deeply sorry."

"You couldn't help it," I said. At that he groaned again with shame, and lay still.

We rested for a long time. I turned on my belly and watched our companions. Two had stripped, their flesh golden in the light. Now the man straddled the woman, and I watched with instinctive sympathy the act Richard had spared me. They lay gently together, lost in one another, the woman almost covered by the bulk of her lover's body; and his ecstasy overtook him with a shuddering as decent, as natural, as seemly as the coupling of two animals.

Other couples were stripping. Richard said, "Claire, I promised your father you would not see this. We must go."

Chilled, not touching each other, we found the path. We were deep into the blackness of the trees when Richard stopped, evidently searching by sound, and spoke to me for the first time in half an hour. "Do you hear it?"

"The stream?" I did: a chattering of water some distance to our left.

"Yes. Claire, I need to wash. To say it grossly, I smell of it, and I cannot for shame take you back to your parents until I am clean. Will you trust me enough to come with me off the path toward the water? All you need do is sit at the foot of a tree and guard my clothes where I can find you. What is your patron saint?"

It should have been Santa Clara, but I prayed, when I prayed, to the Mother. "Mary the Virgin," I replied.

"Then I swear by Her that I will not hurt you. Come with me."

"If your oath is not good enough," I said, "there is little I can do." He took my hand; I followed him.

So I sat, his clothes piled still warm beside me, by a tree root while Richard, a pale shadow, slid into the water. "How is the bottom?" I asked.

"Smooth boulders," said his voice very near, "not welcoming, but nothing to cut the feet. It's about three feet deep, and very cool. Do you want to come in?"

"Yes," I said without hesitation.

Soon I found myself naked in the dark. Richard said, "Here—take my hand." I found it, grasped it, and was handed strongly down into the stream. "Have you got your footing?"

"Yes. Thank you."

His hand let go. I submerged, laughing as the water lapped my breasts, then my shoulders and the sweating face I was glad to wash. For a while I paddled, then said, "How shall we dry?"

"Have you a clean handkerchief?"

"Yes."

"So have I. I suppose they'll have to do."

The water had chilled all ardor from me. Suddenly I felt a hungry fatigue and the beginnings of a headache. Richard, moving beside me in the dark, said, "Have you a comb?"

"No."

"Use mine." A carved bone comb found my hand.

Our damp skin drying beneath our clothes, we came in sight at last of my father's house. No light was burning; I knew I would find the door unlocked as Elisabeth had promised. Outside the doorway Richard put his hand on my shoulder. "Claire, if I came here—say, in a week—would you receive me as a friend?"

"Of course. Nothing has changed."

"I'm surprised you think so, and very sorry I abused your trust. Excuse Thomas, and forgive me." He lifted my hand and kissed it with dry, unlingering touch.

"Good night," I said, and eased the door open.

In the upper hallway I paused outside my parents' door. After a moment's thought I knocked lightly twice. "Elisabeth. Walter. I am home."

Walter's voice said softly, "Go to bed."

* * *

Richard waited out the week. Then, with some constraint, he came to us, because to stay away would have involved both of us in suspicion. Thomas, when we were alone together, kissed me and said, laughing, "Well, now you know I am no chaste man. I'm sorry, Claire."

I accepted his apology. The Master of Works reduced the number of his visits gradually and with calculation; my parents made no comment. And Saint John's Night vanished like the ashes that lay unvisited among the Standing Stones.

# 10

July came in with a lazy stagnation that gave one the illusion, disproven for me nineteen times before, that summer would never end. White sails worked off the coast; the blossoms had fallen, and green apples were swelling on the boughs. A shipload of oranges arrived from Africa: the fruit sold for high prices, and we devoured it thirstily. A hot wind fretted at us all, and troubled my sleep.

In the print shop it was always hot, and I worked a little less there, dressed in pale linen gowns that showed, at armpits and elbows, the delicate if sweat-soaked suggestion of a fine voile shift. A scholar from the Sorbonne arrived, stayed two days, and left carting our entire edition of Suetonius' *Lives of the Twelve Caesars*, in the smaller size. Gérard and Béatrice had gone to their farm, and Thomas to Paris to seek lodgings for the autumn term. His Grace also was absent, having joined the Court, as custom required him to do for two months in every year. As a parting present he had sent my father a cask of dry white wine, and to chill it a huge pottery amphora of last winter's snow. But all of us would be present in Saint-Aurèle for the wedding of His Grace's niece Aliénor, late in August.

"I should like a holiday," I said to Walter one evening. "Couldn't we go somewhere?"

"The seaside is right below us. Go sit on the beach." The string-wrapped graphite stub paused, this time from sketching a Susannah, and pointed downward. "Claire, we have been here less than a year. I have founded a good little firm, but I cannot leave it under another year's time. I'm sorry."

"I have to go to La Pipardière next week," offered Elisabeth, "to see Blaise Mercier and to check the accounts. Would you like to come with me?"

But that place would be even quieter than Saint-Aurèle, and I thought of the room where an abnormal cold began at the threshold. I could be cool *there*, I thought with a shiver of irony. "Thank you, madame, no."

Elisabeth frowned with concern. "Endure it, dear, the cool will come. We have the town's own Saint's day to look forward to, and after that the wedding."

"Shall we sing there?"

"As hired musicians? Good God, no, His Grace would not so insult me. We are to be guests and sit on the dais, though not at the high table. I think, Walter, that next summer we should take Claire to Paris."

"Next summer," replied my father, "I'll gladly consider it."

But Elisabeth had already departed for La Pipardière when Saint-Aurèle celebrated the feast day of its Saint. On that day all the shops would close, and crowds in their best clothing would follow in procession the bust of a bearded emperor who looked, so my father said, suspiciously like Marcus Aurelius. One hundred years earlier a Roman burial had indeed been found in the corner of a field—a cinerary urn, the ancient glass still revealing ash, bone fragments, and a perfume flask half-melted by the funeral pyre. In a dream Saint-Aurèle had laid his claim to these relics, and over them, reinterred, had risen a stone cross. The procession would circle the cross, bless it, and return to Saint-Damien to hear again the legend of the Stoic Saint converted to Christianity, and therefore poisoned by his pagan brother. After that the town would go on holiday, dancing and feasting on trestles set up in the streets.

My bleeding had begun: I told Walter it was my time, and I thought I might stay home. He peered at me. "Are you sure? The house will be combed bare of servants, there'll be no one but the watchman to care for you."

"I know all Mother's remedies, sir, and all I need is rest."

When the house went quiet I did rest for a while, cherishing the rather pleasant ache in my belly with its sensation of release. I dozed, and woke aware that, across a field buzzing with insects, La Vièrge-aux-dames must also be standing deserted.

Quickly I got up and bathed in cool water from the basin, and pulled on a clean chemise, a gown of pale green linen, and soft shoes. Then I mounted the hillside through the sun-hot, fragrant grass. A green-white butterfly fled before me, and from the beach two hundred feet below the sea whispered, a profound and radiant blue. From the town came the tolling of a bell. The Roman bust had left the church; the procession had begun to move.

The soft scraping of the church door as I opened it echoed down the nave and sussurated beneath the beams, announcing an emptiness that offered the sound no challenge. I crossed myself and plunged up the stair that led to the left-hand clerestory.

I fled to the end of the balcony. From here the oak beams, still pleasantly redolent, interlaced their shadows thirty feet above, and a long fall below me I could see the black and white diamonding of the tiles, its color now advanced halfway down the nave.

I felt the walls: nothing but brown blocks closely fitted. Then, my palms already grimed, I dropped to my knees, searching by touch for any unevenness, any crack. A bolted ring? A crowbar somewhere, laid ready to pry up a flag? It seemed possible; who would pay attention to a discarded piece of iron?

How can one describe a contradiction? For I had felt him come—had even, in some depth, expected it; and something in me remained unsurprised even through the atrocious shock as Richard Linacre's voice said, "You've chosen the wrong side."

I knelt there, frozen in a posture no lie would explain, and watched him mount the last stair. He was lightly dressed in a linen coat and a white shirt open at the throat; I noticed he was armed. He said, "It's on the other side, in fact, and they scarcely troubled to disguise it: a ring fitted into a stone at the very end—easy, I admit, to overlook in the shadow."

Softly I cleared my throat. I said, "How did you find it?"

"From below. It passes the wall of the ossuarium. I checked it in both directions—where it rises in the church and where it runs down to the coast. Rubble from the fire has blocked it here. His Grace's orders and my workmen have blocked the rest."

I cannot explain my truthfulness, except to say that, in so compromising a place, I suddenly found I was empty of all lies. No possibility of invention existed. I crouched on the floor of the clerestory, staring up at him. "So you already knew when you showed me the Roman room."

"I did." He had come closer; his sword hilt scraped softly against the flags. "But you, Claire, on that night knew something only my masons sworn to silence could have known. Who told you? Elisabeth?"

He did not need to come any nearer: his relaxed pose, as well as the wall at my back, sufficiently demonstrated my helplessness. I thought: He will throw me over the balcony: no one will know it was not an accident.

Calm and relief flooded through me with this thought. I said, "Why Elisabeth?"

"Because, Claire, my father told me certain things when I was ten years old: things of which oral memory needed to remain in the town when he was dead; things His Grace refused to hear. And one of them came from Paris, from a co-ambassador of Marc-Antoine du Pléssis, your stepmother's first husband. It concerned her years in London, and spoke of information given to the Privy Council." He was smiling; and indeed the relief, if not genial, had charged both of us with energy. "Did you know of this, Claire?"

I nodded. "My father has told me."

"Then Walter is implicated too. What a pity; otherwise I find him a delightful man."

"Richard, my parents came here to repair the damage. If you know the story, then you know—you must know—Elisabeth's reason for anger against His Grace." He nodded. I rushed on, astonished at the clarity of the last words I might ever utter. "She wanted to find the tunnel and have it blocked. The war has ended. Surely it represents a small threat: none now, you say."

"There is no threat, Claire, except from traitors."

"What can they tell?" I demanded. "That this is a port the English have often used? They have more maps of it than you do. There is nothing new to reveal."

"That may or may not be, when the Duke of York is king. Then the state of our walls might interest him; how many men we have under arms; how much food, and hidden where. There *are* things to tell, Claire: the new things I will build, and war revived under a king who requires new information. And you are your mother's pupil."

Slowly I rose; he rose with me. I edged back from the balcony: it seemed safer, if abject, to flatten my back against the wall. "I am indeed my mother's pupil: in music, in stillroom skills, in languages, in the cutting-out of cloth. All you have enjoyed in me, she gave."

"And more, I fear." He came to me and closed his hands softly around my throat. "What are your loyalties, Claire?"

His hands eased upward to my chin. How easy, I thought, to

snap the vertebrae, to crush the larynx, to press the carotids so that death came in an instant. It came to me with clarity that I had never hoped to live long, and that in this moment I felt neither regret nor fear nor a desire to say good-bye. I thought of the blood, hot and clean-smelling as vegetable sap, that flowed at that moment from my womb. I thought of my children, and felt myself begin to weep.

He was shaking me; perhaps he did not mean to pound my head against the wall. *"Tell me!"*

"My loyalties? I do not know them." The shaking had made me bite my tongue.

Richard flung me back against the balcony. I went, obedient as a rag-doll. What rage, what fear in him had waited so long, and being tempted could endure no longer? He came toward me again; I slid through his arms onto the floor and lay there being shaken, my shoulders pounded against the stones. At last I screamed, *"I have no loyalties."*

By now I lay beneath him, my hair dusty from the flags, my gown tangled about me. I could hear his breathing, could smell the sweet health of his breath. We lay body upon body; and I too wanted what he then did: bent and crushed my mouth with his own—a kiss that deliberately bruised, that taunted my shut teeth with his tongue.

I had never before experienced a kiss so adult, so advanced in skills I had not learned. I considered it passively, watching him open-eyed. His cheeks, shaven that morning, were still rough enough to bruise me, and from his skin came an odor so clean, so strangely innocent of anger, so redolent of protection that it made me, oddly, long to doze off to sleep.

All at once he drew away, his face suddenly somber and quiet. "Get up, Claire."

Uncomprehending, I struggled up from the flags. He gripped me by the arm, and angry again (but less angry, I thought, this time) hustled me without gentleness along the balcony and down the stairs. *"Get out,"* he said, and, flinging the door open, thrust me outside.

A pale white sun dazzled me. Bees hovered above the clover, and around me breathed a landscape mellow as baked bread. Where could I go, my hair tangled, my gown dirtied from the floor? I must pray my father's watchman had not seen me. Knowing only that I must get away—from the eyes behind my father's windows, from Richard's proximity—I plunged down the slope, running.

I heard the church door open, and Richard's voice call, "Claire!"

He was following me, racing over the tussocks that hid the dead town; but I knew myself to be strong and fast, and I ran this time in fear for my life. We plunged down the pastureland toward the arena. He was closing on me, but since that first cry he had not called my name.

He caught me, as I had known he would, at the lip of the arena, and with a wrestler's ease took me over with him into the shelter of the dip. There he lay on me again, and his weight this time elicited such frantic screaming that he gagged me with his hand and, when I bit it, with cloth torn from his coat. Talking softly, he held me close. "Be quiet. I'll take the gag out if you can be still. Claire, you *must* be quiet."

But I could not; and he finally stopped my mouth by crushing my face against his shoulder. "Claire, I have been so afraid: first Thomas, and now you, and I did like you so." With astonishment, my own sobs whimpering in my throat, I saw that he too was weeping.

He controlled it and gently removed the gag. For a long time we lay side by side. At last he said in a normal voice, "When does the town come back from the procession?"

I tried my voice, and found it worked approximately well. "Not till dark. But my own people, I do not know."

"Then we must wash you or we cannot keep this secret. Our stream lies a few hundred feet away. Come with me."

He lifted me and gently supported me into the green dark of the forest. The stream shone earth-brown over its cobbled bed. I washed my face and mouth, and my enemy again produced his bone comb and softly untangled my hair. "I will walk you to the head of the street. I can go no farther with you."

"I can slip in unseen and burn the dress." My hair combed, my eyes puffed with crying, I looked at him. "Do you distrust me, Richard?"

"Yes, Claire, I do."

"We are enemies, then."

"I think we cannot be friends. I am sorry."

I said softly, "So am I."

At the head of the street I did not bid him good-bye, but turned from him and walked away, aware that he stood as he had promised, watching to see me safely home.

August was half over and the wedding ten days away—His Grace returned, and Thomas due—when Elisabeth said to me, "Claire, do you happen to know why Richard no longer comes to see us?"

"We quarreled," I replied, and would say no more, not even when I saw the glance that passed between Elisabeth and Walter.

# 11

August. Those crabapple trees that stood on the sunniest slopes had ripened their rose-red fruits, and housewives had begun to glean them to lie pickled—pink-fleshed and tasting of cinnamon—beside the Christmas ham. The green still hung heavily, but here and there one could no longer ignore a note of yellow. In gardens the purple and gold of autumn flowers had begun to replace the summer colors, and marigolds with maroon-velvet hearts now exuded, when I pressed them, their delicate, bitter scent.

No rain had fallen for weeks. The farmers watched anxiously, while the heat lay on the skin with a weight one could feel. The salt blue, lulled also by a heat as savage in its way as the February storm, could not irrigate the fields. The streams exposed dry pebbles to the sun.

In spite of the torrid weather, the wedding of Mademoiselle Aliénor to the bridegroom her father and uncle had chosen for her would go forward on August thirtieth. On the previous day His Grace would ride to meet the bridal party at the gates (they lodged now outside the town), and during the wedding feast roasts from his pantry would grill over makeshift hearths in the streets. His servants would tumble baskets full of loaves onto the trestles, and sweetmeats twisted in gold foil would be thrown to the crowds, cheerful with goodwill and boredom. The fountain in the square had, by some meddling with its works, been induced to run red wine. I myself would never touch wine from such a source, but no one got sick from it that I heard of.

Gérard and Béatrice were still absent at their farm, but they had ordered their steward to provide a buffet and to open the house to invited friends, since their windows overlooked the route the procession would take. The twenty-ninth proved clear and hot. In the afternoon—wearing day clothes and feeling no appetite for the display of chilled wine, fruit salad, and pickled eggs on the table behind us—I with my family joined a small group at the windows. Down in the street stood crowds beaten into silence by the heat.

Thomas Linacre came to lean beside me on the windowsill. I smiled at him, as I could never help doing. "Good day, Claire. Richard apologizes—work will keep him away." I restrained a shrug. As I had hoped, apparently Richard had told Thomas nothing of our quarrel. "I've got good lodgings on the Left Bank, where I can keep two servants and watch all the riots." (Your Grace will remember the Sorbonne is famous for its mob fights between students and the Watch, or even between students and the faculty.) "I like your hair caught up from your neck like that and twined in a veil. I shall miss you."

"And I you," I said, realizing with a pang how much of warmth my life would lose when Thomas discovered the larger world that might never again, I thought, find a use for me.

"Where," he continued, "do you intend to stand in the chapel? There are no pews, of course, only velvet cushions stuffed with straw. Damnably hard, too."

"We are not going to the wedding," I replied calmly, "only to the banquet afterward."

I saw him crimson with understanding. "Oh." Pride would not let me tell him of the short conference His Grace, on his last visit, had held with Walter and Elisabeth—a conference whose subject I had guessed from the Count's look of brisk, gentle regret and from my parents' courtesy.

"I'm afraid," said Elisabeth's voice at our shoulders, "that my presence has involved my family in embarrassment, Thomas. I am sorry for Claire's sake, but His Grace and I thought it best."

"Of course, madame." The blood still showed, betraying, beneath his skin. He turned away. "Look! Here come the outriders."

And I, fighting tears, thought: I know now why Richard befriended us: to protect you from our influence, or at least to put himself in a position to judge that influence. Perhaps he even intended, if necessary, to attract me away from you—for your sake, Thomas, not for mine.

The first outriders bore the Count's colors, pale violet and pale yellow, on pennons fixed to the ends of their lances. Even at a walking pace their horses' hooves battered and split the silence of the stone street. Then came the Count, his reins made of gilt and scalloped leather, and beside him his brother-in-law Martin de Brissac, husband of the dead Marie. I noted him: a handsome man with full lips and heavy eyes. The castle must do without a hostess tonight; although her nuns had sewn the wedding gown—since Aliénor was a favorite with them—the Rule of her House forbade Mère Agnès to attend.

The bridegroom was not handsome, and ten years senior to his fifteen-year-old bride. He rode beside her in white and silver, a lanky man with yellow hair, a narrow, intelligent, sarcastic face, and the calculated awkwardness that marks the temperamental disputant and practical joker. I thought he looked kind. As I watched, he bent to speak to Aliénor. Evidently it was a joke, for she laughed up at him.

I had never seen her before, and I envied her as every girl in the crowd envies the princess at its center. Her grown, white silk embroidered with golden iris flowers, lay spread by the yard over her sidesaddle and saddlecloth. She had thrown back her veil to reveal a face saved from winsomeness only by its intelligence. She must have been shorter even than myself—a tiny creature with brown curls, a straight nose and dimples, and eyes of that sparkling dense brown sometimes described as black. She surveyed us with a friendly lack of shyness, waving now and then with a gold glove she held in her hand.

"She'll rule him in a year," murmured Thomas.

"She might rule another man, but not that one," said Elisabeth, smiling. "I hope he makes her happy."

That night I slept naked, my window open on the small walled garden in which stood our apple tree, our rosebushes, and our walnut tree. I had looped up my plaited hair; the sheet stuck to my skin.

I lay awake for hours, increasingly enraged and frightened at the exhausted state in which I must face the wedding banquet and, probably, my first meeting with Richard Linacre since he had broken with us—an insult for which Walter had required of me woundingly little explanation. But the night seemed even longer than my waiting: seemed to have stopped, as though I had, hot and open-eyed, drifted into a temporal twilight where the rules were changed.

Accordingly, still awake but clothed in the green gown I had burned to hide the dirt from the floor of La Vièrge-aux-dames, I found myself standing on the hard-packed, soaking sand below our house. Above me fled the fast-moving clouds of February's storm, but the cold did not shock me or stir the plait pinned to my head. Indeed, I do not remember any sound either, though the waves lifted themselves in clay-opaque combers—lifted and fell and foamed away.

In the surf before me lay the tumbled doll: the dead woman Thomas and Walter had gone, those months ago, to lift gently from the beach once they had committed me to my mother's care. I thought: You lie dead in the churchyard, and we do not know your name. Yet here, a revenant—our work of charity returned to nothingness—she tossed, her arms spread, her head lolling, twined by the soaked hair.

The danger of her drove me nearer. The arms stirred; the head lifted—not with the tide, but with a return to the dead tissues of a will that sought to move them. I fought to wake as the dead woman dragged herself, lurching, to raise her head and stare at me. *She is dead but cannot die,* I thought, seeing the green-white of the face, the serenity of features already subtly caught between beauty and decomposition.

She had swayed to her knees, and I saw that she was naked. All the while I knew she was dead, pulled from outside herself by a will not her own. Articulated like a marionette, she stood and stumbled toward me, arms outspread. And her face was that of my dead, forgotten mother.

I fought myself clear of the bed on which I woke—tumbled naked onto the floor, screaming without (so I thought) making a sound. Apparently I had been too far away from myself to hear my own voice, for at that moment the door opened and Lise, my maid, exclaimed, "Mademoiselle, what is it? Mademoiselle, what has happened?"

"A nightmare," I murmured.

She was holding me, her arms warm on my bare shoulders, whispering comfort, when she said, "Oh God, here comes your father. Cover yourself." She flung a night robe around me. I turned away to tie it as Walter entered the room.

"Lise, thank you, go." She nodded and, with a last glance at me, curtsied and went. "Claire, what's this noise?"

"I beg your pardon, sir. A nightmare. Did I wake Elisabeth?"

"For a wonder, no. Tell me." He sat beside me on the bed.

I said, "I want not to remember."

"Tell me. You must."

"Father, I saw her. My real mother, the one who died."

"Ah." He laid his hand over mine, stilling me with its warmth and firmness. "Did she speak to you?"

"No. It was not a vision." I forced myself to describe it, and at last said what I had never in my life before felt moved to say. "Sir, what was her name?"

"Anne Carver, and she is at peace. This was not she, Claire, though it wore her face. Do not fear for her. She is neither in torment, nor does she seek you." I nodded. "Your father was David Carver, a Court painter and miniaturist. Both died of the plague in the house from which we took you. The one servant had fled. You had been starving for several days. I remember Elisabeth held you constantly. You just threw up the milk we gave you and made no sound."

I had to go vomit at the window. Walter came to steady me, and when it was over, brought me a goblet of water to rinse my mouth. Then he guided me, shaking, back to the bed.

I said, "Sir, what is my real name?"

"Claire—my child, my dear child—I do not know."

"Then I am no one."

"You are Claire. You are what you have become."

"I died in that house. I too died there."

"That is manifestly false. Oh Christ. Lise!" His call was soft, and brought her at once. "Care for her." My maid nodded, her kind, clear-skinned face white with concern. "Claire, I am going to put some of Elisabeth's elixir into milk for you. If you can hold it down, it will purchase you six hours of sleep. Otherwise you cannot go to the wedding banquet."

I nodded, slumped in Lise's arms. "I want to go," I said with exhausted insistence.

"*I* want you to forget this dream. I'd knock you on the head with the Holy Maul rather than see you lie awake." The reference was an unfortunate one: the Holy Maul is a hammer that hangs behind certain church doors and, with the priest's blessing, ends old lives when Nature has proven cruel. "Damn," said Walter. "Wait for me."

The milk came, warmed (I suspected) over the print-shop fire, and I succeeded in keeping it down. As I slipped into the voluptuous mercy of unconsciousness I whispered, "Father, I am sorry I cause you so much trouble. Do you know . . ." I felt for his hand, grasped his thumb, and contented myself with that. "I have made myself up, like a story. *Claire was pretty; she had long brown hair; she spoke five languages, played a dozen instruments, and was all her parents wished; but she made no marriage."*

I saw his face contract with pain. Gently he said, "The time for that will come. Richard finds you beautiful and good. It seems I know that better than you do, perhaps better than he does. He will learn."

"I should like for him to kiss me," I whispered, loose as a drunkard. "He kissed me once."

"Did he?"

"Yes. He said . . . he said Elisabeth had trained me to spy for you."

"So that's it. Well, I think I should talk with your Richard sometime."

Slipping deeper, I had lost interest in his expression. *"Please* talk to him," I said with the earnestness of a dreamer. "Tell him I will be lonely here when Thomas goes."

"Poor child." They were the last words of his I remembered before, still grasping his hand, I slid down into a garden party where lights shone elusive as stars among the branches of apricot trees; and I in a red velvet gown sat on the grass greeting friend after friend, though in my waking life I had never met even one of those loving presences.

I had had the six hours' sleep—and a meal, since I disliked eating in public—by the time Elisabeth came to plait my hair for the banquet. It was to fall, interlaced with gold, in a single braid down to my hips. My gown, delicate yellow silk embroidered with golden daisies, swirled belted from a waistline just below my breasts.

Elisabeth wore pink almost invisibly striped with silver, and from a wicker headdress with two modest horns (she and I continued to dislike the French train, or the extreme eccentricities of the *henin*) there flowed a short, elegant veil. She frowned at me with concern, but did not remark on my looks: I could see her own thoughts busied her sufficiently.

"Is the wedding done?" I asked.

"I believe they are in the chapel now. There's plenty of time, we were bidden for eight o'clock."

My father joined us, robed to the feet in raw silk dyed dark brown. We mounted our mules, and with Walter walking beside us and our guards before and behind, joined the crowd moving slowly toward the castle.

It rose before us against the lapis glow of twilight. Its windows glowed with the flames of a thousand pounds of beeswax candles—squares of saffron in the walls and cylinders that rose into the dusk. To me it was all an assemblage of gigantic shapes: the court through which we passed, huge enough to drill a troop of cavalry; the lobby with stairs of green marble, and an arched gallery in the Florentine fashion. The fabric of the building was old. The major chambers still followed the old-fashioned pattern: the Hall itself, and a guardroom we passed, its walls hung with shields and crossed pikes, above them a forest of antlers that recalled a hundred years of hunting. This was, I reminded myself, even now a living fortress, and only secondarily a home. The lobby had been renovated, and I heard His Grace had transformed his own suite with the help of artisans borrowed from the Pope.

In the Hall a great T-shape of tables lay covered with white cloths and silver. A servant directed us to our places at a short side table on the dais; we would be sitting at right angles to the bridal party, and raised above the guests who now, a quiet crowd, were likewise finding their places.

All rose as the bridal party entered. At this, her first appearance in public as a married woman, Aliénor was greeted by our applause and curtsied to us, smiling. Then we sat down, and an excellent consort began to play—resigned, until the dancing, to being ignored.

They announced each course with trumpets, which I nervously loathed, as I pitied the peacock roasted and then set with the green-gold shimmer of its quills outspread. Against all etiquette Thomas waved to me from the table opposite. His Grace and we had bowed from the waist when he caught sight of us. I saw Aliénor ask a question: saw him lean to answer it, and beyond her the arrogant slovenly face of her father, Martin de Brissac, beneath its red velvet bonnet.

The major-domo had set Richard Linacre, in brown raw silk belted with gilt leather, to Elisabeth's left, which appeared to disturb neither of them. I wondered what excuse, if any, he had made to her for his defection.

The courses passed me: the spinach tarts, the capons in white broth with almonds, the salad of lettuce and purslane, the salad of sugared lemons, the marzipan follies, and the fresh strawberry pie. I ate little, and was glad when rosewater and towels were brought to wash our hands and servants cleared the trestles away to make a dance floor, leaving only the dais tables where we sat.

With the meal at its height the musicians had retired for beer. Now, restored, they tuned their instruments while a double line formed for the first slow Court dance. At its head moved the newly married couple: the bridegroom in white, Aliénor (who came up only to his breastbone) in orange cloth-of-gold that trembled from apricot to a sheen of metallic light when she moved. Both looked happy. The husband pranced a little, kissed her hand, and then, by demand, her lips, and schooled his comedian's body to dignity as the dance began. They were to be bedded quietly, without any of the gross jokes or display of the virgin-blood that must have made so many bridal couples wretched under the old customs. In any case Aliénor looked, as a bride should, eager for the trial before her, and from his tender grace I could tell her husband was proud of her.

"By the way," said Walter beside me, "I hear the gardens have been opened to the guests. If you do not feel well enough to dance, Claire, you could wander there for a while."

"Thank you, sir; I think I will." At the high table people were stretching, joking rising to join the dancers. Only a few—Richard and Elisabeth among them—lingered over wine.

Only a few days ago, I thought, I would not have dared approach him. No single motive moved me toward him where he sat beside my stepmother, but rather a confusion of aggressive anger and of longing for the friendship he had thrown away—as he had thrown me away. I leaned down between them. Though I spoke to Elisabeth, I saw Richard start and blush. I said in a voice of normal clarity, "Madame, I slept poorly last night, I feel a little dizzy." I turned to Richard and added, "I am going into the gardens. If you wish to speak to a friend, you will find me there."

The publicity of it was in itself a rebuke, and I saw with angry pleasure several people turn to look. *I am not afraid of you*, said my eyes to him; and, seeing in them that message or another, he stammered: "I—"

"Do you want to go home, Claire?" said Elisabeth quietly.

"Not yet," I replied, and left them.

The private garden proved empty. I ventured down the shallow steps, suddenly intimidated by the humid, rustling dark. Behind me lay an open door, deserted apartments, and the distant sounds of music. I could smell no flowers—the heat had killed most of them, and the grass beneath my feet prickled like straw. Along the paths they had set wax torches: yard-high candles on sticks thrust into the turf. They would burn for hours, and their light just sufficed to dazzle out the stars and to crowd with shadows the trees about me.

I had been wrong: here there was no refreshment for the mind. Drawing on some underground cistern not yet depleted, a fountain hammered out of silver-gilt spat lazy streams from a circle of metal balls. The edifice shone coolly in the torchlight, and a rustling swept the trees. I hoped Richard would not come. Exhaustion had begun to drum behind my eyes, and I did not now feel able to deal with him.

"I am here," said his voice behind me. I stepped back from him; he did not move. "Why did you call me?"

"To offer you," I said, "the friendship I see now you do not want. To talk, perhaps, about loyalty. To put it simply, I have realized I am loyal to my friends, and to what I believe to be good."

It sounded stilted, childish; and in the moment of speaking it I realized the whole encounter was a failure, and that my defiance of him in light and safety did not translate into dignity. I said, and heard again the mannerism I hated, that exhausted clearing of the throat. "I am sorry, Richard, and tired. I find now I want only to be alone here. Please go away."

He came forward again and sat down, his hands folded, on the rim of the fountain. "When you have told me, Claire, why you stole my ring."

I heard myself moan softly, *"Oh,"* and recoiled into the dark beyond the fountain.

He rose, the intelligent face in shadow. "I thought I had remembered rightly. Claire, had you stolen anything before that?"

I had sealed my hands across my mouth; my eyes, dilated in the hot gray shadow of the candles, stared at him, appalled. He continued to move forward, in his face a new, startled interest. "Claire, I knew nothing, I only guessed. What is it? Can I help?"

*Remember and accept a hard thing,* whispered my father's voice in memory. *No one pities such a woman.* Richard moved and I moved with him, backing, circling the fountain toward the door where my safety waited. Richard said, "Stop it! *Stand still,* Claire."

His voice was harsh, though not, I know now, with anger. Its tone did stop me, trembling. He stood staring down at me. I do not know how I appeared to him; but in my mind there gazed at him a little wasted haggard woman, timid and ugly. Around us a moist hot breeze stirred; leaves scraped and pattered into silence. Richard said, "I asked why you took my ring."

Why does no one come? I thought. "I do not know." Each syllable had a desperate falsity.

"What use had you for my ring?" wondered Richard. "Do you dislike me, Claire?" A possibility struck him; he dismissed it as crisply as though he had spoken it, and concluded aloud: "No, you have money enough. Do you—?"

And so it confronted me, patent in his sudden stillness, in his eyes: the self-flattering guess.

My voice trembled downward to calm. "Do I desire you? No. Why did you beat me, Richard, that day you found me in La Vièrge-aux-dames?"

Blood flooded into his face; and suddenly all my hurt pride sprang to divination. "So that is it," I whispered. "How much it must cost you, Richard, to be gentle."

"Claire, stop."

But I could not. I was too young, too modest to have dreamed of serving a man lasciviously; but now for the first time that possibility whispered along my nerves.

"Sometimes," I said, "*I* would like to crush things—to tear and hurt. I would like to crush and tear myself."

"Why?" he demanded softly.

I shook the question off. "Why did you beat me in La Vièrge-aux-dames? Because that day at least you could invent a reason? And when you can find no reason, Richard, what is it you want?"

"Claire—"

"Why did you beat me? Because in your bed I would be willing to serve you with my suffering?" Lascivious, abject, it came.

Richard's hands were shaking. "Claire, do not tempt me; for temptresses we kill, and tempted I may break."

One instant more we hovered, confronting each other; then Richard came for me with a purpose frighteningly void of rage. I ran, my heart beating so appallingly it shook my body and sussurated in my ears. Up the staircase I plunged and through a door and up another twisting staircase, at whose top a pikeman stopped me, against the barrier of whose body and weapon I sobbed unintelligible explanations.

"What is this?" Crisp against the dark of the intervening chamber, a door opened and the Count appeared. He still wore the dark red costume of the feast and carried a bundle of papers in his hand. "Claire? These are my private rooms. . . . Oh, I see. Let her through."

The pike dropped. Sobered by shock, I found myself shaking within his arm. "You found the back stairs. Are you ill?"

"No, sir, not ill."

"A man is with me. I'll send him away. Come into my study and compose yourself."

I achieved some self-control as he led me into the warm and brilliant little room. Softly he dismissed a man who had obviously ridden hard, and whom he knew by name. Then he turned to me. In the clever face his eyes were gray-ringed with exhaustion. "Business, I'm afraid, from Bordeaux; it could not wait. I'll go back to the dancing presently. What is the matter, Claire? Can I help?"

"Please, sir, may I sit awhile?" Without his leave I sank onto a cushioned stool.

"Of course. Shall I call for wine?"

I shook my head and bowed my face into my hands.

Around me glowed a room as perfect as the Roman banquet hall: a jewel of Italy, from the marquetry of the desk with its delicately contrasted woods, to the gold foil hammered onto the ceiling. His workmen had starred the rose-pink walls with comets, each trailing a beard of golden hair; and on the table by the door lay a fragment of Greek marble—the head of a boy, the lips still smiling, the ghost of pigment touching the eyes with life.

"Can you tell me?" In spite of his weariness he had focused, for me, both his attention and his gentleness.

I could not tell the truth, so I found, as had become my habit, the nearest and the truest lie. "Last night I dreamed of my true mother."

"But she died in England," said Jean d'Aubry.

Softly I described the dream.

When I had finished, he said, "Walter told you, and told you truly I think, that this was not her soul. Rather it is some fear of yours that takes this shape and thus informs you it will not be thrust off. Do you remember nothing of the time before you were two years old?"

"Nothing, sir. That is—" A shadow importuned me and faded. "No, nothing."

The Count frowned. "You know, I do not believe small children understand and observe nothing of the life around them. It is my private belief that all our memories lie hidden in us somewhere, immortal as we are immortal. If memory belongs to the soul, then it cannot perish, though it may become unmanifest. The woman was some memory of your own. Some memory is seeking you."

"*Your Grace!*"

The suddenness of it made me start. I had barely time to identify the voice of Martin de Brissac when it seemed the door was kicked open, and Thomas Linacre, held between two guards, was thrust into the room. Behind him came Jean d'Aubry's brother-in-law, the father of the bride Aliénor. "I've arrested your messenger and also a man he brushed against in passing: Simon Guerre, a guest of yours." The deep, scornful voice was calm.

"I know him." The Count had risen.

"Then hang and gut him, because a letter passed from the messenger to him to Thomas Linacre. It is in code, but when we decipher it I suspect it will prove a loss to Richard Duke of York and to his purchased rebels at Bordeaux. They're dancing, there's been no commotion: no one knows of this. I glanced at the letter, I admit, but you'll find it on his person, where it properly belongs."

Thomas knelt where they had thrown him. I saw now that they had tied his hands behind his back. The Count said, "Thomas, do you admit you accepted this letter?"

The desperate eyes took in my presence but did not seek to understand it. Martin de Brissac kicked him, and when the Count's gesture restrained him, pulled him up again by the shoulder. Thomas raised his head. "Your Grace, I admit it."

From the next room the sounds of a fight, as soft as they were intense, had escaped us for a moment. Suddenly understanding, the Count sprang to the door. "Let him in!" he shouted; and Richard Linacre—still on his feet, his coat torn—also was thrust into the room.

"Sir, I must know what concerns my brother. Why have you arrested him?" His eyes too registered my presence and dwelt on me with a startled, cold attention.

"You shall know." The Count had seated himself, only to rise again at the sound of voices. "Oh God, what now? *Let them in*," he called. As Walter and Elisabeth entered, Martin de Brissac, laughing, slumped back against the wall.

"Claire," said Elisabeth, "the servants said you had gone from the garden up this stair. What—" She looked around, was silent.

"Close off every room in this suite," said the Count, "and search the men for weapons."

"And the women, my lord?" asked the man who was obeying.

"You may except them for the moment. I have a dagger; so does Martin, and there are now"—a glance, a signal of assent—"fifteen pikemen outside this door, and ten more at the foot of the stairs. Therefore," said His Grace Jean d'Aubry, comte de Saint-Aurèle, "therefore let us converse."

\* \* \*

"Thomas."

Martin de Brissac had straightened. I was still too weak to rise; but in the room, where candles shimmered under the golden roof, every other man and woman stood in stark formality. "Thomas, I ask not did you receive this letter, but did you accept it?" It lay now on the Count's desk, its uninscribed folds tied with a twist of string.

Thomas's face was crimson, his eyes bright and level. "I accepted it, my lord."

"Do you hate me, then?"

"My lord, I honor you, and I love—I loved—my English kin."

Jean d'Aubry nodded. "I have known for a year that, on your return from London, you served as a courier through Sir Edward Palmer to the English partisans at Bordeaux. Is this true?"

Thomas's eyes closed once, then opened. "It is true. Have mercy, sir, if you can find cause for mercy."

"Your Grace has cause already." It was—shaken, dangerous—the voice of Richard Linacre. "Or does my lord not recall the secret my father spared him: that Your Grace is not impeccable, since your own mistress betrayed this town twenty years ago and has gone on betraying it for twenty years?"

Elisabeth gave a cry. The Count sprang up, but I was before him. "And *you!*" They turned to me, staring.

"Sir," I exclaimed, "I break an oath to tell you that last autumn Thomas Linacre admitted to me he possessed a secret which, fully disclosed, would implicate me in treason. And in July Richard Linacre admitted to me, also by implication, that he knew this and had concealed Thomas's actions." From that instant, as I had intended, no one thought or spoke of Elisabeth.

"The law does not deal in implication," replied the Count.

Richard Linacre said softly, "Claire, I am going to kill you."

Moving quietly, Martin de Brissac stood away from the wall. Jean d'Aubry moved toward us and leaned (I thought, because he could not stand unaided) against the edge of the desk. Gently he said, "Elisabeth, on your knees. Confess."

With absolute dignity my stepmother sank to her knees. "I confess that, in my grief at Your Grace's rejection and at the death of our son, I confided to the English Privy Council the existence of a passageway from La Vièrge-aux-dames to the coast, together with several other matters that have since become publicly known, of which I will furnish Your Grace a list. I came here to undo the harm if that were possible. I entreat your mercy."

"Walter?"

The Count's gaze moved to my father, who also knelt. "I confess that I knew of my wife's treason to the country in which she was born, and that I have shielded her: not out of evil will toward Your Grace, but out of natural loyalty. I too desired to undo the harm and to protect our daughter. I entreat your mercy."

"Richard?"

There was a long hesitation; then Richard in his torn coat dropped to his knees. "Sir, as your Master of Works I have loved your honor, as I love this town. Every gift I possessed—of intellect, of bodily strength, of money—I have given to rebuild what surely I would not betray. I knew of Thomas's treason because he told me. I shielded him out of love, expecting that the university and all a young man's pursuits would change him from a childish, weak disloyalty. I entreat Your Grace's justice for my brother and on the service I have done."

I had sunk back on my stool. Shadows slid and shone under the gold-foil ceiling. Something cracked; rooms away a man coughed. No one moved.

At last Jean d'Aubry said, "Here is my judgment. Elisabeth, know that your treason has been rendered null: The passage was found and blocked five months ago. I believe you have not repeated a guilt that was, as everyone here knows, my own deep guilt as well. I beg your forgiveness. You may go.

"Walter, why should I punish you for being born an Englishman? You have brought us learning. If learning can create a better world, stay and create it here. You are not guilty for protecting two you loved. You may go." My father bowed his head.

The Count looked at me. "Claire, you have broken an oath to your friend, and you took that oath unwisely. You have slandered others by a vicious use of implication. But you are young and sick, and unfit to hear my judgment now. Walter, take her home and care for her. She may go.

"Thomas, for your father's and your brother's service I will not confiscate your lands. You will remain a gentleman of Saint-Aurèle and will go to the Sorbornne, though under guard. This once I will pity your youth. However, I will place you under oath never to traffic with the English again. Meanwhile you will be stripped and flogged, then held in prison at my pleasure." Thomas swayed a little, and steadied, his eyes dry.

"Richard Linacre." The Count turned to the man who knelt straight-backed before him. "I thank you for your service. For that and for your father's loyalty I will confiscate neither rents nor lands. I strip you of your post of Master of Works, for your concealment of treason renders you unworthy of my public trust. I am sorry. And because you watched your brother's treason, you will watch his punishment."

As they dragged me from the room I called, *"Thomas!"*

Still kneeling, he glanced quickly around and smiled. "It is all right, Claire," he said.


Their guards thrust them down below the sounds of music, to a cellar where torches burned and Thomas, stripped to the waist, stood passive as they as they tied around him a belt to prevent the kidneys from rupturing. Then they spread-eagled him to four steel rings. His eyes were fierce with terror, his lips bitten bloody, but he did not look at his brother as two guards held Richard, with two more stationed to catch him if he should fight.

No one fought. Used on the human body, on shoulders and back, the whip brought at first a stinging shock. Richard saw his brother brace himself against the wall to meet it, and saw how the red scars curled around Thomas's sides, shocking muscles he had no way to brace.

The blows wrapped round his body and grew harder. With each impact Thomas shuddered, eyes and lips shut. Richard felt, imagination quickening to the beloved flesh, the pain of the weals, attacking the sturdy muscles of the back, tormenting the undefended sides. He saw when the weals broke open and tore away blood and skin so that the torturer had to sop the thing in water. Then he saw the work resume.

Now every blow both pounded and tore away, striking on the naked muscle. Thomas began to scream, screams controlled as best he could. Richard, weeping, did not move. And at some point Thomas passed all self-control, and wept and sobbed as a child will sob at blows from the giants that surround it.

He was still conscious when they let him down and carried him, face toward the ground, to a cell with a clean pallet and a torch. Richard said to the jailer, "At least bring me warm water to wash him and a clean towel and bandages."

"I will, and leave you the light." He saw pity in the man's eyes. "I never heard he was condemned to worse than he has received already."

And so Richard was able to wash him gently, using endearments drawn from their boyhood, comfort remembered from their parents so long dead. And when he had finished he held his brother through Thomas's screaming sobs. And his eyes, staring past his brother's shoulder, saw only a woman running down a field: a woman, the vessel shaped for the pouring of his love, his seed, his rage. All that was in him, known and unknown, reached out for her to pour himself into her, the vessel made to draw man's mind as she drew his loins, from birth to a mutual awakening. The woman fled before him, her hair a shining tangle, the power in her fear saying: *Follow me*. He would hurl her with him down the lip of the chasm: down onto the ancient benches covered with centuries of moss, where body could crush body and blend with the fragrance of her hair; and so, sucking at her breast, he would sleep perhaps in peace.

Next day they gave him a meal—a good one, served hot. He coaxed Thomas, if not to chew, to drink a bowl of soup. Thomas had neither slept nor spoken. As Richard held the bowl gently to his brother's mouth, he glanced upward. A distant rustling sound filled the air. After weeks of parching it had begun to rain.

In the evening they forced him out. He embraced his brother and whispered a few words of reassurance, but though Thomas held him hard, he still would not speak. Richard left him. No one impeded him as he walked out into the courtyard. Above him the castle, whose banquet had ended twenty hours ago, stood silent as a cliff, and the streets through which he walked were black dark and streaming with rain.

The year had begun with extremes, which the events of that night were to continue; and so it did not surprise him when the rain turned to a flood, blinding him, destroying the thick torn silk of his robe, and pouring down the streets in freshets that soaked him to the calves. It chattered on the slates, pounding through air so humid it fell through its own mist, and rain and fog combined together.

The Cerne had overflowed its banks.

Richard was shivering, yet he felt hot. *Not good,* he thought, trying to wipe his face dry. The day he had lost, he had lost forever; and the night when he had climbed castle hill to the wedding blended, with a smoothness so unnatural it jarred the mind, into this night when he walked trembling through a town with all its shutters closed.

In the rustling, glittering dark he met no one; no lights shone behind windows. It was late, then: midnight? He bore toward the sleeping house of Verneuil, and his objects were precisely three: dry clothes, a short-sword, and a key.

The rain had cooled the air enough that I dragged on a linen nightgown. All around me the house lay restlessly asleep. *Oath-breaker,* the Count had said. *A vicious use of implication.*

So, with a publicity that shatters our world, the least thing we are can be made to seem the truest. But, beyond the profound shame the young feel when they are publicly rebuked, I knew I must watch with Thomas. *Flogged.* I will go on my knees to him, I thought. I remembered the diamond-pattern advancing with such confidence down the nave of La Vièrge-aux-dames. Richard, then, had known best from the beginning: I was none of the good I felt within me. I had heaved up tears as agonizing as vomit, and now, sitting dry-eyed on my bed, I stared into my first adult grief—a love betrayed before it is recognized, which must be borne, above all, without tears.

*His Grace spoke of a judgment when I am well.* How many years will it take me, I thought, to heal Richard and his brother? If they will not speak to me I will follow them: haunting them, serving them. . . .

And the new, adult voice replied, *No. You will endure the penance required of all betrayers: to bear for years, in silence, the turning away of those you love.* And through the coolness of the voice there came no merciful divination of the punishment Your Grace did ultimately exact. It lies before you, sir: It is the writing of this story.

A pebble clacked against my window—then, discreetly, another. I plunged to look down on the dark garden. Richard's voice called softly, "Claire!"

I think I whispered, "Thank God." I do not remember how I found my slippers, or how I pattered through corridors and stillroom to unlatch the sidedoor. I slid out into the darkness to him. Like me he stood soaking in the rain; I could not see his face. I said one word: "Thomas?"

He must have had ready what he needed. He gagged and whirled me in one motion to tie my arms behind my back, then flung around me a black cloak to hide the paleness of my face and gown. Then he lifted me, with a cruel indifference to my cracking arms.

I did not fight. I knew my reparation for Thomas, for himself, would now be complete. From the darkness in which Richard had swathed me, as he moved easily through the rain, I judged it just, and began to prepare myself for death.

I know now that he simply walked up the street. He could have faded into the field had the rain and dark offered him any danger. Fifteen minutes walk to—where would he kill me? Probably for security, I thought, at Verneuil. Across the bridge, then, and five minutes' walk more.

I could have died better, I thought, had it come quickly. Twenty minutes was too long to throttle fear. I tried to pray, and instead found myself letting my head fall into the hollow of his shoulder, where beneath my cheek his heart beat evenly and fast. I could feel him pace his breathing like the athlete he was, and only two layers of soaked cloth separated my skin from his. I thought, *Now I will always be a virgin.* The pang of that lost hope went deeper than the prayers which slipped away from my memory. I tried to understand *never:* soon I would not be. But neither my emotions nor my soul moved to the words.

I was as soaked as Richard by the time, the hump of the bridge identified and passed, I heard him softly open a door that seemed to be unlocked. He laid me down with some care and peeled back the sodden cloak, which he crumpled and cast into a corner. My nightgown can have been little less than transparent, but from that moment until our last together he observed a strange decency and did not study my body.

I was sitting, still tied and propped against a wall, on a narrow boardwalk that echoed. A sheet of sliding light filled most of the room—water that collected what iridescence the rain diffused through the darkness. By it I could see my companion's face. "Do not cry out," he said. The pale waterlight slid on a sword-blade, directed not at my heart but poised by its own weight on the skin above the right carotid artery. One slice sideways and I would die quickly—too quickly, I hoped, to see the terrible flow of arterial blood.

"I'll be quiet." I spoke softly. He kept the blade poised to cut. "I am to die," I said.

He nodded. "The rain is ceasing; in half an hour it will be dawn."

"Richard, the sword, not the river."

"A sword," replied his voice, "leaves blood."

I saw a deep shudder take him; peered through the dimness to see the sweat I could hardly distinguish from rain, and said with the artlessness of discovery, "Richard, you are sick!"

"No." He wiped his eyes with his left hand; the right, holding the sword, conveyed no tremor. "Claire, I wish I could shrive you, but I cannot. Can you remember a prayer?"

"I'll try," I said. O God, I thought, wherever death may send me, help me to experience completely these moments: they are the last. Soon or late we all stand before you. We have no right to be surprised. I had hoped to bring you more than I have become.

"A prayer," said Richard, his teeth closed and chattering. He wiped his eyes again with a soaked sleeve.

I was too innocent to calculate. What I said then I plucked directly from some element in his stillness. I said, "Richard, if I lie with you, may I live?"

A rictus almost of weeping crossed his face and was controlled. "No, Claire. Can you remember *Nunc dimittis?*"

"No," I whispered.

"Then speak it after me." And so I followed his prompting, while green light shivered on the sword. "*Nunc dimittis servum tuum, Domine, secundum verbum tuum, in pace. . . .*" The cadence of the Latin had soothed me all my childhood. "Lord, now let thy servant depart in peace, according to thy Word, for mine eyes have seen thy salvation which thou hast declared before the face of all peoples—to be a light to lighten the Gentiles, and to be the glory of thy people Israel."

And when my voice stumbled into silence his went on, offering me the Response: "*Salva nos, Domine* . . . Save us, O Lord, by dusk and by dawn, that we may wake with Christ, and that we may lie down to rest in peace. Amen."

"Amen," I whispered. "Richard, I cannot bear it, do it now."

The sword slid with a faint clatter onto the boards. He gathered me, lifting and crushing me for silence in the embrace he had used once before, my face against his shoulder. He could not, I clearly knew, stop shuddering now—deep cold tremors in the body's core; but the implications of his shaking belonged to a world I now must leave.

I heard the rushing of water. The Cerne ran turgid with mud, easily deep enough to drown a bound woman. Above me I saw the first yellow of dawn, and higher, the Morning Star. Richard kissed my brow. I heard him whisper, "May God receive you."

The stars shattered. Water engulfed me, choking, and as I thrashed it carried me into the dark—down to the Atlantic, to wash from wave to wave like the dead girl from Southhampton. After that I calmed and watched water swirl in patterns across the lenses of my eyes. I felt sleepy and cold. A long time passed in a lassitude that enclosed me like black glass.

"Over here!" The voice did not concern me; nor the standing bulk of a man, his body braced against the current as a barrier to intercept mine. "A woman. Thank God I saw something pale when she went under the bridge." Another man, equally strong, handed him out; they turned me over and made me vomit water; and I fainted.

When I woke I was lying naked but dry, my body spooled in a clean, soft blanket. I half-opened my eyes. By the fire three voices, those of two men and a woman, were talking quietly.

"I tell you," said one man, "someone had tied her wrists."

And the other man's voice intervened, "*No one tied her wrists. There: see the cords burn.*" All three looked at the wet rope sizzling on the fire. The same voice said, "We have rescued a suicide, not cheated a murderer. If she lives I will go to His Grace the Count. He may know who she is, or whom to ask. We have saved a life—that is all we know. The man who tied her must not come looking here."


"What have I done?" inquired Richard Linacre in a normal tone to the ebbing dark.

He moved; was stopped by a shuddering so savage he at last identified it. The rush of liquid from his skin was not rain, but sweat; and the pain in his joints informed him that the Sweat would desiccate him by quarts until—in three days, in five—it killed him.

"Claire," he whispered; and staggered; and lay unable to move—unable to remember what it was he must do, until his servants found him unconscious in the dawn-dazzled rain.


This time when I woke I wore a nightgown of clean wool, and felt warm. Above me there smiled the pretty face of a fisherman's wife. I smiled back. She said, "My lady has a visitor."

The man who now moved forward into the light had been

sitting on a stool and had, I guessed, been waiting for some time. "Claire, good day." Gently Jean d'Aubry, comte de Saint-Aurèle, settled onto the bed beside me. "You are alive and will mend. Forgive me: I must ask you to tell me who threw you into the river."

I fought for presence of mind and could find only an instinct of denial. "Your Grace, in the sin of my despair at your anger I threw myself in, hoping to drown."

"Although Walter tells me you can swim? Odd." He lifted one of my hands where it lay on the blanket. A rope-burn had scored the inner wrist, lashing it with a pink scar. I saw it with no emotion; and the Count said only, "Your father and mother know you are alive. The rest of the town believe an assortment of rumors. Thomas Linacre has gone to Paris under guard. Richard lies sick, but I think he will recover."

"The sweating sickness, sir?"

He nodded. "So I believe."

I turned my head on the pillow, already exhausted. "I knew."

For a moment he sat considering me. Then he said, "Claire, I am not sending you back to Saint-Aurèle. I think you need a holiday from us all and a place in which to grow well again. I have a sister gifted to heal both body and mind. I am sending you to be her guest at Sainte-Bertrande."

To the surprise of his household, Richard did not die. When he could take broth he did so with eyes closed, and dismissed as dream or quickly forgot that the spoon was held, some days, by Jean d'Aubry, who spoke softly to his servants.

Six weeks passed before, thirty pounds lighter, he could sit up to read a letter in Thomas's young, strong, sloping hand.

My beloved brother:

It grieved me profoundly to leave you ill, but His Grace gave me no choice. The death of Claire has strangely appalled the town; but I will not speak to you of such sorrow now. Since His Grace has sent me good news of you, it is a relief to write from my Paris lodgings, where I mean to become a better lawyer even than Father was. If the Count will not reinstate you, come to me here as soon as you can. Meanwhile he has assured me he will not touch our property.

Richard, this past year has been unwholesome in Saint-Aurèle. Come away from it as soon as you can.

Thomas

He practiced walking for a week, and made his plans in secret. All was done, his baggage rolls packed, when he sat at his desk to write a letter his steward must deliver.

Sir, I depart without seeing you, though I understand you nursed me in my illness. I thank you for Thomas's life and for our patrimony. Barthélémy Cottard will account, with records, for all the money you entrusted to me when I was Master of Works. I think you will find everything correctly ordered.

I have a sin to expiate, and do not know when or whether I will return. My steward, however, can probably find me: I will write to him. Remember, sir, that not only its lord has loved this town. I too was born here; I too have loved it in my measure. I tried to serve it—I now think, beyond my strength. About Claire I am more than sorry.

# 12

The recovery from a long illness can entirely engross the mind. He did not think about his healing: his healing thought for him—dictating certain hungers; bringing on an abrupt sleep in the protected camp he had chosen. He was too sick to sense behind him minds frantic to find him, to question him, to exact justice, and, in more than one case, to make atonement. Under the utmost exhaustion, indeed, clairvoyance overcame him, and he talked with his dead father one evening as he sat beside the campfire he had built. The answers came—silent, sensible, redolent of a love he recognized—into his mind; but afterward he could not remember this conversation. And once too, in this state, a girl's voice sang, apparently from the forest that surrounded him:

> *Salve lux fidelium*
> *fulgens in aurora*
> *quo est super lilium (li, li, lilium)*
> *pulchra et decora.*

When she ceased he hugged his knees and cried. But no one came to comfort him; and the forest was untenanted.

He had chosen well—a gully with a small cave at his back,

protected from rain and, except by one approach, from intruders. His bow brought him small game, and he could retrieve the arrows. He knew which herbs to eat, and hunger led him. Autumn was ripening wild fruit in the hedges; this too he ate, sparely but hungrily.

The emaciation of sickness began slowly to fine upward to a thin but normal weight. He washed his clothes in the stream that ran nearby; bathed cold; learned, lacking a servant, to keep his linen neat. Every morning he shaved with a razor he kept sharp, and soap he still had in adequate supply. The days he passed hunting, foraging, sleeping, or sitting, and the nights in gazing at the stars. If only, he thought, one could pluck them down with one's hands like flowers, or grasp them to lift oneself into Paradise. He believed in Paradise. Since his infancy he had remembered it more clearly than the world in which he found himself.

In his saddlebags lay letters of draft on several Italian bankers. When he chose to move, he need not go poor.

A man in sin must preserve himself, if only to give his life as God requires it of him. *A life for a life*, he thought, and also: *Thou shalt do no murder*. The question of salvation did not trouble him: the myths of damnation he had dismissed on the day when, a boy of fifteen, he had seen a criminal broken on the wheel, and perceived that man alone makes Hell in a self-idolatry of despair. That the Church asserted otherwise did not move him: he knew men had created high civilizations before a church existed, and his soul informed him of his kinship with these ancient men, and of their equal salvation. Nor did he feel an imprudent need to speak these things, except once to Claire.

Claire. Her name contracted his belly in a pang so intimate it made him shudder. Desire had gone; shocked into stasis on the night when, dreaming with sickness, he had let himself enact a perversity of the kind that only sometimes entered his sleep—penetrations so self-debasing that their excitement withered in the first shock of waking. Always he had dismissed such things with a shrug, understanding that dreams enact what the soul does not choose.

If I had raped her as I really meant to do, he thought, perhaps I could have healed it. Then I could have begged her forgiveness—could have courted her, could have married her. Then the soft hair would have lain on my pillow; the breasts, gentle to my kneading, have grown heavy with my child.

Staring dry-eyed into the fire, he thought, Was I so unjust as to bring her a rage she could not possibly have earned? Did I hate her—and for what?

Granted, she was a child and Thomas's equal—destined for the younger brother, not the elder. He had seen pictures that were like her; for Florence had taken her youth and made it into jeweler's work—a freshness enhanced by human arts beyond his competence. Had he coveted her out of a sense of his own smallness?

*Am I so embittered a man?*

He had thrown pinecones on the fire, and flame had entered them: each incandesced with petals of coral-colored light. *Claire, this understanding is too small a gift to offer you, but I have nothing else. Claire, forgive me.*

When he had healed he bore slowly south for Italy. Fortunately he met no bandits, for he carried a good purse, and weakness and indifference would have made him easy to kill. In Ferrara he got a good horse, more money, a plain gown, and the straw hat of a pilgrim. There was no need to provoke theft by any show of wealth. He had studied Italian from books, and found that book-fluency turned quickly supple for an unoccupied mind.

Northward lay confession, justice, and execution for murder, as well as his betrayed friendship for Walter and Elisabeth. Perhaps, when his mind had cleared, he would elect his liege-lord's justice as the best atonement he could make. Fear did not stop him: rather a wish to choose that justice with clarity, and the demand of his own soul for time in which to rest. He could feel his body healing cell by cell; the healing of the mind is hard and long.

The pilgrim's hat suggested that he go from shrine to shrine. It gave him a series of objects, companions on the road, hostels in which to sleep, and an approximate route. Because of the pilgrim companies, he was robbed fewer times than he expected; but on the road to Mantua he had to fight, took a blade through the shoulder, and passed half a year peacefully performing carpentry for the monastery that cured him. From there for the first time he wrote to his steward, but did not wait for a reply; and when a second letter from Thomas reached them there, he had gone.

Still he moved, searching now for traces of the Romans—finding them in the mosaic floor from which, with payment and apologies, he had to tear away the vines; in the blackened coins they gave him in change at a smithy; in a stadium left unfinished, its starting markers forever waiting for the moment of their use; in the massive collapsed vault of a burial chamber long since emptied. From an expensively dressed artist named Jean-Marie Tavella, looking sleek as he painted the refectory of an abbey, he heard, during an afternoon's acquaintance, the story of a woman named Fannia Redempta.

No word came southward. He had avoided returning to the places where he might find letters. And as winter passed into spring and into another summer, guilt changed in his mind—polished, altered like a jewel of glass rolled by the tide. What evil had he seen in her—a child whom memory distorted to seem younger and younger? What self of his own, forced on her unrecognized, had turned her loyalty to Elisabeth into betrayal of himself? His own concealment, which he did not regret, had destroyed his future. On one occasion clearly he remembered Claire's laughter, and a ringless hand with polished nails that swept with competence across the strings of a lute, as she threw back her embroidered cuff with a gesture of coquetry. But her face had vanished, to be recovered only sometimes in dreams. I am forgetting her, he thought, and God has not yet required my life of me.

A second summer came; and with it, unavoidable, a letter from his steward.

> My lord Count speaks of you and desires most urgently to talk with you, or that you should write. Thomas is well. Walter Tarleton has become famous for the great Bible, though I have heard they have one press in Paris now. Madame Elisabeth goes on as before, though very thin. Béatrice and Gérard Lalemont send their love, and want you to know Jacquette has married: the Cottard boy, younger son of the man who carries on your work.

He did not reply. He wandered the roads of Italy, seeking, if he sought any companion, the past in which he sensed a thread of clarity. The ancient men he loved had found their ways through a world as complex as his, a world that killed the single human being who was loved, if at all, by a god unmanifest. Others had endured and had found rest and with it, perhaps, understanding. They meant more to him than the northern border he had guarded, for it lived now in a fragile new security, reprieved by civil war in England and by the madness of England's king.

That year, on the planet the Ancients had known to be a globe, there was more than civil war to bewilder the intellect. In May the Duke of York won the Battle of Saint Albans, and a Venetian navigator six years Richard's junior explored the coast of Africa. Fra Angelico died at Rome and, at Florence, Lorenzo Ghiberti, of whom he had heard Claire speak. The Turks took Greece, and Hungary fought back. At Mainz

Johann Gutenberg issued his Vulgate Bible—two volumes compared with Walter's single one. From the north came rumors of robbery and homicide at the University of Paris; an exquisite poem, *Le petit testament*, was ascribed to the murderer, François Villon. Richard hoped, with resignation, that Thomas had not met him; and as he knelt in church after church, questioned his own soul whether he prayed to any God, or whether the cathedrals had risen upon some fantasy of love and human significance.

By Florence, in the second September after his departure from Saint-Aurèle, he was fully healed and had acquired a servant, to whom he spoke courteously and seldom. Freshly shaven and dressed in a thin dark crimson robe with sword and dagger, he went, by permission, to the atelier of a man for whom he had once expressed admiration.

Beneath the skylights, open to the hot autumn air, he heard at first only a noise daunting enough without the considerable echo. On the walls of Luca della Robbia's studio there glowed the moons of color too good for buyers, reserved to remind Master Luca of his genius. A group of frightened apprentices stood in a huddle, led by half a dozen less frightened partners and senior assistants. On the floor lay one of those wonders of which Richard had heard: a medallion twenty feet across. Molded into it he saw a coat-of-arms, its shapes of violet and turquoise and lemon-yellow rendered unidentifiable by the crack that had destroyed it, and now pocked further by the artillery of pots, crocks, and drinking mugs thrown at it by a man wearing doublet and hose—a man whose dark hair had acquired strands of silver.

The cursing, diminuendo, had lost conviction when Master Luca turned and froze, his rage altering to annoyance of a different quality. He came forward holding out his hand; his person smelled of chemical glazes. "Master Richard Linacre?" *Master*: the word came, to Richard's surprise, in English. "This is your hour, now I recall it. I am sorry, you find us in some distress. Andrea, clean it up, all of it. We recast from the mold tomorrow."

"I've come at a bad time, sir," said Richard.

Master Luca shrugged. "You are most welcome. We are not always so angry, so unsuccessful or"—he glanced with regret at his shirt—"so dirty, but the work, you understand. . . ."

"Of course. How are such things made? It fascinates me."

"I'd be pleased to show you. If you'll only give me a moment to supervise the cleaning, perhaps we could share a cup of wine. I need one. In the meanwhile, please inspect us as you choose."

And so he wandered examining the plaques, loving their elegant pastel brilliance. A strange sensation irritated him. For a moment he wondered if it was sickness, then recognized with a shock that he felt happy. He moved on, and came, as his destiny required, to the cream and cobalt of the *Virgin with Saint Anne*.

She was different—the contours as young, even, as his memory now made them; and surely her eyes had not been so dark? But he knew her. He felt a touch on his shoulder and looked down, only an inch, into the eyes of Luca della Robbia. "Something troubles you, Master Linacre?"

For two years he had never spoken her name. "Something troubles me," he said. *Hearts break if we cannot speak.* "I think I know your model. Is it not Claire Tarleton?"

"Yes, it is Claire."

"Did you know," said Richard softly, "she is dead?"

"Dead?" Luca della Robbia gave him a long stare. Then he said, "Master Linacre, you will come for that cup of wine in my office. Now."

He poured wine, but only for his guest. When he had seen Richard settled in a chair, he gazed at him from across the littered desk. "Drink that," he said gently, "and drink it all."

Puzzled, Richard obeyed, and showed the empty cup.

Master Luca said, "Walter Tarleton and I never ceased to write. He has talked of you, as it happens, and his words were kind." *I have a friend deeply troubled,* Walter had written. *He may come to you; be good to him.*

Richard said, "I did once know Walter Tarleton. I cannot imagine why he should speak of me. I did not earn his kindness."

"That may be. Listen. It seems you believe what the whole town says of Claire, that she attempted suicide when she betrayed—" Richard's eyes widened into a sudden brilliance of astonishment, of warning. With inexorable gentleness Master Luca went on, "—When she betrayed your brother Thomas. No. Claire is whole and sane, and has for two years lived under the protection of Mère Agnès d'Aubry at the Abbey of Sainte-Bertrande."

Through a crumbling shock that gave him the sensation of dropping through the floor, Richard said, "Living how? What does she do there? Has she taken the vows?"

"She has not. I gather that she was at first very ill in mind. Walter now thinks she is healing slowly. Because she wants to be of use to them, she has chosen to work as sempstress to the nuns."

"Doing what?" persisted Richard, and controlled a shrillness that seemed to cause his host more interest than surprise. "A sempstress?"

Master Luca nodded and poured more wine. "Hemming sheets, making garments, mending things."

"But she is a lutenist!"

His host gestured with a full goblet. "Drink it—and, if I may advise you, then go to a tavern and drink a great deal more. She is a musician still. The Reverend Mother, when her patient began to heal—before that, I gather, Claire would have destroyed the things she loved—has had her instruments brought out to her one by one. They rest, so I hear, in a cabinet Walter built for them, in the little house behind the abbey where she lives."

"Lives? Lives alone?"

"By no means—that would be neither decent nor wise. She has a small common room where she works, and one bedroom for herself, one for a maid, and one for a manservant who does the heavier work."

A miracle makes a silent clangor as though we lived within a bell; and he must disguise from this kind man the joy that cried *She is alive—alive—alive—alive*. Richard shook away the dizziness. "And Walter and Elisabeth, do they know, do they see her?"

"They come to visit often, and she loves them still. But you see," Master Luca said softly, "she has defeated them. I guessed she would. And she has punished them. They created not a girl but a masterpiece; and now they have a childless anonymity who works as sempstress to the nuns. I pity them. They never meant her evil, though they did it; and she loved them when she chose death instead of life."

"It was not all their fault." A ringing had started inside his head.

"No. There was something in England, I fancy. One may feast and still die of hunger, Master Linacre. One needs only to believe absolutely in the reality of starvation." Luca della Robbia rose. "I know more about you than perhaps you suppose, and guess things I will not force on you. Please stay here. I must go back to the studio; but I have a couch here, and wine. Perhaps you need them both." A hand lay, quickly and with calculated firmness, on Richard's shoulder. "I will be within call."

He had been gone five minutes before Richard stirred to thank him. And as he sank back on the couch, forgetting even the wine and his intention to drink it all, a pattern of

indigo lights shimmered before his eyes, and the silent bell clamored:
*She is alive.*
Alive.
Alive.
Alive.

# 13

*The cream-colored clifflike walls of Sainte-Bertrande,* I had thought on the day I first saw them. And indeed, wherever one went in the vast compound the walls enclosed us, a massif that seemed as natural as the hills behind the abbey; as the stream that ran through the grounds, closed from attack by a grille of spikes driven ten feet into its bed; as the forest that flowed, unimpeded by curtain walls and towers manned by the abbess's soldiers, up to my cottage door. For in this serene back quarter of the compound they had left a deliberate quiet. Here I could see only meadow, the cool shallow river, and trees fading to rust and orange—and, many hundred yards away, the two other cottages reserved for those who needed rest.

For rest and healing were the work of the thirty literate, mature, and wealthy nuns. A wall of peach-colored stone, pierced by two arches, closed my sanctuary off from the cattle, horses, children, servants, pilgrims, and men-at-arms who populated the immense forecourt. There, though the place now formed my village and my amusement, no quiet could be found. Sentries walked the walls, and the guards could look both down at us and out, toward the companies of brigands or English against which the abbey had in the past defended itself. As one approached the even more heavily fortified rectangle that sheltered the sisters, their church, and their servants, one passed the hospital; the hostel with its kitchen and chapel; the stables and the public latrines, whose manure went to dung the fields of farmers who paid rent to the abbey and who had a right to the shelter of its walls.

Perhaps I should not have called it a forecourt, for it was not paved. Everywhere grew meadow grass kept cropped by the grazing beasts, and paths, worn by use, meandered to the nuns' burial ground; to the menservants' dormitory; to the bakehouse, the washhouse, and the ovens. One Sister skilled at gardening had filled a triangular patch with flowers, which now glowed, as they had two autumns ago, in red and purple and orange, a visual promise of adventure that always lifted my heart without needing to be fulfilled. Autumn promises what autumn never brings; but what of that?

The massive gray square of the abbey proper did not pretend to beauty. I had been there. I knew the pillars of the church rose in clusters of stone palm leaves to a ceiling painted with gold stars, and that the nuns strolled and prayed along a delicately-pillared cloister at the heart of the square. With them lived their women servants. A well that rose into the floor of the kitchen (should defenders have to retreat to the building itself) also fed a fishpond stocked with carp, and on either side of this the Sisters tilled vegetables and raised herbs.

For this house was rich but not corrupt. Sisters and novices worked with their hands, their attention turned inward, with a skill I had learned to value, on the perfect performance of their task. Mère Agnès called it active prayer. "Body and soul together make a human being," she remarked to me once, after her agreement to let me sew. "Even when we go from here, Claire, we shall still be bodies inhabited by an experiencing intellect. Train the body, therefore, to obey, persistently and gently; train the mind to accept the body's discipline by focusing on work; and when one requires these capacities—of patience, persistence, attention—one will find one has been working to develop them all the time. Daily work is a means, and a means that lies so near it comes within the reach of every Christian person."

"I will try," I said, looking at the pincushion, thread, and array of fine steel needles that now formed part of my equipment.

She shook her head. "No. A musician knows all this, Claire; it is my Sisters who need to learn. *Your* discipline is to spare your eyes, to enact God's love for you by knowing when to stop, and to play for us when we ask. Have you time to start Sister Hélène's daughter on the lute?"

I did, of course, and found it an exercise in patience indifferently achieved. I was young enough myself not to like the young, and I find elementary lessons boring. But when I focused on the teaching, on the child, I sometimes forgot myself in an act of service that functioned, to my surprise, as smoothly as Gérard Lalemont's clock with its enamel and its golden balls. I do not suppose this was active prayer, but I began to work at it, understanding that, in my case, self-sparing rest formed part of the discipline. "It differs from woman to woman," remarked Mère Agnès. "It is a question of countering weakness, but always gently; and weaknesses are never simple. *Your* weakness is, of course, a temptation to work yourself to death."

My man, Gilbert Labourd, rode courier for me to Saint-Aurèle, delivering and bringing letters; got whatever I needed in the market there; scrubbed the stone floors, cut wood, and shot small game in the forests outside the walls. Between us the maid Josèphe and I did the cooking, and she carried back folded the mending I had done. I helped them both, but my work was to sew, to practice my music, to teach it sometimes, and to rest. Mère Agnès had forced the servants on me, and chosen two who would nurse me like a pair of mothers. Josèphe's bedroom opened into mine, and Gilbert's only into the common room where all doors and all inhabitants of my tiny household met.

Most nights I ate with them, afterward helping Josèphe with the washing-up; then sometimes I would play by candlelight to them, to the Mother Abbess or to those of the nuns and novices who longed for music. Mère Agnès considered music essential to the soul's composure, and was good enough to let me believe she regarded me as an important acquisition. Of course I never went to the hall where the pilgrims (whom the law entitled to one night's free food and lodging) ate; but I did sometimes dine with the Sisters. In good-natured silence we would listen as the lector read a chapter from works not invariably improving, though I disbelieved the rumor that Mère Agnès had prescribed Ovid for her flock during a dull winter. Their rosaries were silver, their habits of good cloth, and the Sister who governed the kitchen had a weakness, which Mère Agnès declined to correct, for serving us brandied peaches and *millefeuille* pastry dripping with honey and walnut flour. And every evening I bathed and washed my hair in the nuns' bathhouse.

They copied books: I have never anywhere seen better scribes than the Sisters who worked in their scriptorium. They taught children. They compounded herbal medicines; read books on surgery, mastering Arabic to do it; labored with their own hands; and worked in the hospital. During the Great Pestilence every nun had died there, a novice taking the place of each who fell, until only four remained in all the huge compound to bury the dead in convent and in hospital. When the mother house repopulated the abbey five years later, they lifted gently from the floor skeletons from which had vanished all infection, all offense.

I thought of this, sitting on my bench on the sunlight, as Mère Agnès rose from her morning visit—a privilege whose value, offered me by so busy a woman, so astonished me I had never even tried to thank her. I rose too. *"Ma mère,* may I take the vows?"

"What?" She had been, visibly, totting lists in her mind, and the abruptness of her returned attention hurt me. Then I saw the hurt had been delivered with calculation. "You, Claire? No. I have two ambitions for you. One, to hear Jean describe how you sang before all his Court. Two, to stand godmother to your child."

"And who shall be its father?" I inquired, gazing round in the stillness on a landscape whose orange, brown, and russet also rose above us on the hills.

She did not reply directly. "Claire, I do not mean to harrow you, and therefore I will not tell you again that you have a future."

"Where? And starting when?"

"I am not sure. But no woman should become a celibate through fear of men. If I take you into this convent, it will be when you are fifty and I am an ancient crone, and by then I expect you will be too busy to ask me: busy with your music, your grandchildren, and with printing the books Walter will leave to no other partner. And now compose yourself; here comes my brother."

He had bared his head and left his entourage to find their own entertainment. Now he grinned at me and, taking Agnès's hand, said, "Well, sister, what shall I kiss? Your cheek? Your ring? Your—"

"Cheek will do very nicely," replied his sister. "I have work to do. I just had to dissuade her from becoming our newest novice."

"What a waste," said Jean d'Aubry, and sank down beside me on the sun-hot bench. "Good morning, Claire. Here are letters. I've spared Gilbert the ride."

"Thank you, sir." I took them, scanned the handwriting: They came only from home. Elisabeth's letters cheered every week, and I tailored my pleasure to that sufficient gratitude.

Gradually the news had diffused in Saint-Aurèle that I was alive and expiating at the abbey an illness that excused my attempted suicide. Béatrice, Gérard, and the girls both wrote and visited, and I had become aunt to a small Claire; but whether the truth had reached Paris, or whether it roused any interest there, the letters never told me.

"What a waste," repeated the man who, with his sister's complicity, had removed me to this structured healing, taking me with as sure an authority as though I had been born his vassal. "Elisabeth wants you to choose some velvets: I had thought to invite you to the castle for our Christmas feast. Aliénor has asked to meet you."

Chin in my hand I watched him, and gently ventured, "How is it, sir, with you and Elisabeth?"

Jean d'Aubry smiled slightly. "One can last, while work and friendship make this so good a world. I am happy in having both. Perhaps I will marry someday. Some mistakes humble one so utterly that one ends by accepting them. Claire, the world will call you back."

"There is no world, sir, to miss me. I have watched my own death and seen it make little difference."

He raised his brows. "Have you?"

I cleared my throat. "When I was a child I imagined my life would matter, at least to me. Now I have discovered a humbling thing: there are many musicians, and every year brings hundreds of pretty little girls. I envy and covet them as if they were chestnuts glossy from the husk—so many children. Every lute-consort involves minds as loving, hands as skilled as mine. I have no particular value. My life has motion because I push it forward; and when I die, what value should any god perceive in these few, forgotten years? I have lived to learn that each of us is nothing. Mère Agnès knows I believe no God exists. But if one does, why should he value what I hate: my life?"

Like the last after-echo of a fever, this sorrow wrung my

mind, shuddered in me, and ceased. He knew I had considered each word and that I meant each one. Two winters ago he had helped to hold me when—a memory I still hardly dared touch—I had shrieked, "I am *nothing*; I am *nothing*; I am *nothing*": when I had screamed at him and at Walter obscenities that named the God who created men, and the parts and acts God approved in the only children he loved, his sons. I had described to them, hour after hour, anecdotes of rape assembled over a lifetime: tortures of women and of children, inflicted always by men, that had reduced Walter to weeping. I had tried to stab myself and been stopped; had tried to starve myself, and had pity on my body only when Mère Agnès seized my hands. "Look at them, Claire: *look* at them. A musician's hands. See their breadth, their strength, their flexibility. See the intelligence that lives in them. Can you kill them? Can you?" And I could not.

Now Jean d'Aubry said softly, "Claire, when was the last time you attempted violence against yourself?"

I bowed my head. "Last March. Gilbert stopped me: that's why he's there. It comes and goes, sir. I dread its coming. Some days now I feel happy; then in five minutes, with no warning, there comes a despair so deep—" He nodded. I said, "Sir, invalids are monsters of selfishness. They *take* like monsters. You, Mère Agnès, my parents, and all here, all have been so kind, and you ask of me nothing but hope. But I see no hope in a world where men can torture women for sport; where we live so briefly toward a death no generation understands. The pagans feared as we do and looked out on the same evils. If we live beyond our death, then surely that life must be as haunted by torture as our existence here. I believe death destroys us—I even hope it does; but if we survive it, I dread even Paradise. I pray to die in my sleep. Forgive my ingratitude."

"No one here thinks you ungrateful. You speak like this only to us; with the rest you are cheerful and useful, Claire. I have heard of this condition. Others, I gather, have endured it and recovered. I brought you some books this time. I found the Chaucer you wanted—and this, though in French translation."

He handed me a small book. I scanned it and glanced at the last leaf. And the voice that addressed me there sprang living from the page—a woman's voice, warm and sane, speaking an English idiom I must reconstitute by guess.

> This book was begun by the gift and grace of God. I do not think it is finished even yet . . . From the time it was shown to me, I desired often to know its meaning. But fifteen years passed before I was answered in inward understanding. Would you know the meaning in all this? Learn it well: Love was the meaning. Who showed it you? Love. What was shown you? Love. Why was it shown you? For love.
>
> Thus did I learn that love was the meaning.

For this evening interview Richard had prepared himself with care. He had already been for twenty-four hours within the abbey walls—resting, exploring, and cleansing himself in the bathhouse reserved for pilgrims: one for the women, one for the men. He had eaten in the refectory and had slept astonishingly well; and he knew now where she must be, for he had identified the peach-colored wall. Casual questions had informed him of the enclosure and its purpose.

He had deposited his sword with the captain of the abbess's guard, and had chosen a gray robe soberly belted, with red embroidery bordering its square throat and the wide cuffs of its sleeves. His shirt was fine voile bought in Italy, his shoes cleaned by the servant he had not yet turned off, his hair freshly cut. A smiling Sister showed him into a room where candlelight danced on whitewashed walls. He saw a prie-dieu, a desk with a chained book, another desk for working, one chair and several stools; and the beautiful woman he had known since he was a child.

As he entered she turned, all the strong perfect features vivid with intelligence and power. "*Ma mère*, you are still beautiful."

Her robes swept with her: the gray of the gown, the silk veil that concealed her hair. She smiled, her lips parting on white, unflawed teeth. "Richard. Thank God."

He came to her and knelt, and, when her hand had caressed his head in blessing, stood up to crush her in an embrace. "Oh, *ma mère*, how I've missed you all."

"Sit down." It was she who took a stool and drew another one for him close by. "Do you want wine?"

"Best without it, I think. I've been in Italy."

"So we heard."

"*Ma mère*, I understand you have Claire Tarleton here."

Agnès d'Aubry slowly straightened. "Yes, we do, since her accident. She was slow to convalesce, but this year she has done better."

"Tell me truly: If you let me see her, will I find the woman I knew? Is she"—he fought to speak it—"is she maimed? Or impaired in mind?"

"You will find her beautiful, though thin. She tried to starve herself, you see." He gave a soft moan and covered his face with one hand; that of Mère Agnès, accustomed to communicating comfort with authority, found his left hand and clasped it. "You may as well know the worst of that: there have been two other attempts, though none since spring. She seems to have no hope. God knows while she stays here she has no object to live for. I can give her work, but I cannot bring her events, and God refuses her those with a strange perseverance. She says no one will ever want her or call her back to the world, and the emptiness of her life here—though it has been a necessary reprieve—gives color to her despair. Her parents trained her for Florence. And in my opinion God made her for her husband's bed."

Richard gazed full at her. "Is she strong enough to bear

children? Did the shock make her sterile? Do her courses come?"

"She is normal, and needs to bear, to learn sensual skills, and to work. Both my doctor and I believe this."

"I should like to father those children," said Richard.

"Do you love her?" The rich voice revealed no surprise.

Richard shrugged. "I do not know. It does not matter. Two years ago, on a night whose circumstances you know, I bound Claire and threw her into the river to die. For that I owe her my body and my service, I think, for life."

Agnès d'Aubry rose; wandered to pinch a guttering candle; wandered back, her fists clenched together. "I know. I think you should be aware that my brother knows also. He found rope burns on her wrists. Claire has never told him. From the moment of her awakening she has protected you."

*"Why?"* whispered Richard. When she did not break the silence he said, "I will go to my lord."

"And find yourself Master of Works to Saint-Aurèle? Stay here instead and tell me why you came."

He had taken the two blows in stride, hardly noticing them, so concentrated was his urgency. "*Ma mère*, help me to atone to Claire. I told her long ago that I might help her. Since then I have had time to think what a pretentious boast it was. There is more here even than you know, some aberrations even when she was in Saint-Aurèle—and before that in Florence, according to an artist who knew her—that indicate some distress. Let me live near her; let me heal her if I can. I am no doctor, but I beg you, let me try."

Agnès d'Aubry leaned for support on the back of her chair, then found she had bowed over it, hands gripping the wood. "How?"

"I have heard you gave her a manservant. Dismiss him; let me take his place."

Her face, beautiful as that of a king's mistress, turned on him in anger. "Richard, you have forced yourself on her, I suspect, more than once." She paused, studying his crimson face. "Ah yes. I can probably shield you from the scandal of it; perhaps I can even persuade her father not to kill you when you tell him what I now know. But I will not help you to a final self-indulgence. I cannot in honor help you force yourself on Claire again. I lay on you this atonement: She must choose you freely."

"And if she does not?"

"Then go back to Saint-Aurèle and wait. Begin to write her letters. She will read them. Write her about Italy. Barthélémy Cottard died two months ago. Your title and your work await you." Slowly she left the chair and came to him. "Richard: He knows now he was wrong. *You may have it back.* Which now do you want?"

Without hesitation he replied, "To be with Claire."

She frowned. "Very well. You and your servant will lodge here tonight. It is late; I will not bring you to her by darkness. Sleep here, then. I call on her in the morning. Tomorrow when it is light, I will go to her and ask if she will see you."

Josèphe, slipping in from her own room, had kindled my fire to take off the night chill. I had bathed, frugally but decently, and combed out the hair still damp from last night's washing. Except for my infirmities of mind I was hardy and did not get colds, but when winter came I would have to sleep with my head coiled in a towel for warmth. Long hair, I reflected with regret, is perpetually damp if one keeps it very clean.

I had dressed in the dark blue of my ordinary costume. I had four such gowns, identical so I could wear a clean one every day; but though the rules forbade fashionable dress, I was not a novice, and Mère Agnès had forbidden me to wear gray ("A girl your age! Nonsense!"). Then I folded a white linen square around my head, since modesty required my hair to be hidden; and, having cleansed my mouth with myrrh and peppermint water, I went out to the breakfast for which I felt no appetite.

The whitewashed room refreshed me, as it always did, with its cool simplicity. We did not use rushes here, only soap and water on the flagstones, and we had only the furniture we needed: a settle, a chair and my mending things, the music cupboard, utensils for eating and washing-up. Both my servants had, like me, a bed, an armoire for clothing, a washstand with basin and ewer, and the indispensable fireplace. Each of us was free to use one of the nuns' excellent bathhouses, and other needs of nature we dealt with decently and at a distance. We lived close, but with reticence and an adult honesty, it worked well.

Josèphe fed me porridge with cream and honey, and a late orange. Then she went away to wash the plates in the stream. I had not seen Gilbert, now I thought of it, all morning. It was early, but I must make the most of daylight, since my fine work involved sewing white-on-white, which I could not do by candlelight. Therefore I settled in my chair, which stood in the full flood of sunlight, and pulled onto my lap a sheet I was mending. Mère Agnès would come soon; after that I supposed I would go for my walk.

And so it was, as Mère Agnès had intended, in the full, warm light of an October morning that I rose to greet her. She kissed my cheek. "Sit, child, and let me sit beside you. I can stay only a moment." She pulled up a stool. "Claire, you face (please don't waste on it either trouble or time) a brief inconvenience this morning. Someone has called to see you and has begged me to let him come in. He is waiting outside; I want you to talk to him privately, because with all his failures he does not lack wisdom, and I think he has always been your friend. Gilbert stands ten paces from the door. Only call him and your guest will leave immediately, by force if he will not obey your wish."

"Is it Thomas?" I said, guessing wide, already knowing.

"No." She shook her head. "Claire, it is Richard. Good-bye. We will talk this evening."

Another kiss and she was gone; and, as if they had choreographed it because they had, before I had time to rise—before I had time to reject the refuge and support of the great chair—a man six feet tall all but filled the doorway and moved quickly inward to avoid blocking the light. "Claire," Richard said quietly. "Good morning."

I simply stared at him, from the brown robe to the mature austerity of the face. He had aged: he must be, what now? thirty? I have seen men stare so at a beauty, and have seen the looks they exchanged with each other after she had passed. As though his presence had been food after starvation, water after thirst I stared at him—at the cleanliness, stature, and proportion that conveyed to all my senses that he was a man: at the long nose, the strong chin, and fine, high-molded cheeks; at the lips whose warmth was all of them I could remember, and the cool Norman-English eyes, vivid now with intelligent friendship. I suppose worship stood stark in my eyes. "Richard," I said; and rose; and fell forward into his embrace.

"Aren't you going to wish me good day?" his voice said into my shoulder, as his arms pressed me in a controlled grip that steadied but did not crush.

"Good day," I said, in the descent of a cold, sudden calm; and, shaking, found my chair.

He took the stool and lifted, with too careful a courtesy, the ripped sheet. "Is this the work you do?"

"Yes. I enjoy it."

"And your instruments, where are they?"

"There." I indicated the marquetry cabinet.

"Ah." He studied it, and seemed to decide my instruments were worthily housed. "In a way," he said, "Luca della Robbia sent me back. He sends you his love and his demand that he see you again. You for your own sake, not your parents'."

"He is not angry with them?" I had dreamed last night someone was pounding at the door.

"No, not at all," said Richard. "Which, of the many wrongs that stand between us, is the matter at this moment?"

And, because to trust him was the one risk I had never tried, I said, "Fear." For after the first shock of achieved longing I was beginning to recover memory.

"My quick solutions." The words were wry, his face gentle and somber. "I have never beaten a horse or a dog. In all my life, Claire, you are the only creature I desired that seemed to move in me—it was my fault, certainly not yours—the need to hunt, to strike."

"Then you say I am less than your horses and your dogs."

"I say you moved me to a complexity I have worked for two years to understand. And I sought the answers not in what you are or what you did, but in what you revealed me to be. Claire, beyond the wrong I did you lay other hurts. I was only beginning to divine that when all the reasons I must not plead—sickness, dread, protective love, self-seeking, rage, and impulse—tore it from our hands. Mère Agnès has told me everything Gilbert knows from his two years living with you, and also a great deal you have said to His Grace."

"Then she has betrayed my trust."

"Nonsense. Claire, no one would blame you for breaking an arm. But if no apothecary here can heal you, let me try."

I did not know whether it was by instinct or by calculation that he had reduced my longing to the dignity of anger; and I was now too angry to care. With him, some force had come into the room—some force he knowingly embodied, but that shimmered beyond him, charging the air and hazing his silhouette like a mist. I mustered my exhaustion to fight it. "Do not feed the dry well, Richard. It will suck you empty and leave us both parched—both nothing. Invalids are monsters who reduce their nurses. I cannot get well for them here. I cannot get well for you."

"Claire," exclaimed Richard, "I never yet knew you for a fool, but it seems you are one."

"Shall I make him go, Mistress?" demanded Gilbert from the doorway.

"Not yet, Gilbert; thank you." My servant withdrew. "Richard, I am dying, if I am dying, of life as I have found it to be. This is not your fault, whatever you did to me; and you cannot heal it."

"I can try." From roaming the room he had sunk back on the stool, his arms crossed on his chest.

I shrugged. "How?"

"As living with you gives me means. I am taking Gilbert's place as your manservant."

It silenced me. At last I said, "Why?"

"To rescue our friendship. To rebegin it and, this time, to found it truly."

"Friendship," I whispered. No heat here of desire or love: only a tonic coolness. *Friendship.* "I have already too many friends who have made themselves my servants, and I cannot pay them with recovered hope. If I ceased to breathe in my sleep I would be only grateful. Save yourself, while it is still possible to do so, from watching yourself fail. I tell you: *You may fail.*"

"I am listening." His voice was level.

"I do not want to condemn you to that, nor can I bear your—" I gestured, in a sudden tired hopelessness, at his hands, which closed loosely into fists. "I would fear your hands. I detest in myself what wants to use you for the pain that is in you—what wants to say: 'Beat me until I sink into sleep—until all I can feel is pain. Let torture absolve me of consciousness, for torture is respite from terror, despair, and loss.'"

He had risen again and now stood, one long hand, fine and strong, clenched against the door post. "Poor little Claire," he said softly. "Do you know, I understand, to my surprise. Perhaps to receive pain and to inflict it both tempt us because they limit us—and that is a despicable and pitiable mercy."

Since I offered no further resistance, he took the stool again and extended his hands without touching me. He still, I saw, wore the flawed ruby. "These are for your service. I can hunt, chop wood, scour pots and floors, mend things. Make use of so stubborn an object, for I will not go away. Gilbert will continue to run your errands in the town. I am not, I admit, quite ready yet for Saint-Aurèle."

"Have you been there?" I asked.

He shook his head. "They will all come to me here."

We spoke quietly of Italy; and around noon I went out to Gilbert. "Gilbert, I am sorry, but the Mother Abbess will give you other work to do. Master Linacre wishes to take your place."

Gilbert grinned down at me. "I know, Mistress," he said. "The Reverend Mother warned me first thing this morning."

# 14

And so we began together the long, slow climb up the days.

Days that would turn the rust-and-orange haze on the hills above us to the ice and silver and charcoal of winter. Days that were to melt into a delicate almost invisible green, which gathered richness and lay heavy on the hills. Days that would turn the fields from brown to green to wheat-gold in the year we lived together.

I never felt shy of him: the naturalness of our coming together locked into place and was accepted, no more a bondage than the inevitable functioning of a machine. Neither of us blamed the other for it. I wondered, at first, what he wanted of me, but he did not speak of it. I never asked him explicitly—and, in retrospect, divine in his silence a simple human uncertainty, combined with the stubborn intelligence that, lacking opportunity, could only wait. Therefore I never asked his help, and exclaimed in embarrassment when I found him scrubbing the floors, and thanked him for the hares and pheasants that appeared, gutted and ready for the pot, when he returned from his long walks alone.

His coming had reprieved me from my wish to die. We both knew the reprieve was a temporary one, but we both knew it existed.

Certainly our women's household was not enough for him: he walked, rode out, and, until the cold came, swam also at a lake two hours' ride away. Then, his body relieved, he would come back, bringing Josèphe and me his company and his service. Many weeks passed before I asked him his thoughts, but he always made clear that some work of his own preoccupied him, thus delicately sparing my parallel life from the pressure of his nearness. That he waited—and waited for something to happen in me or (worse) to me—I always knew, and the awareness that I could not satisfy him at first disturbed me. Nothing was ever going to happen to me again. Eventually, I told myself, he would realize this and go. The thought caused me a pang of loss and of angry eagerness to be finished with him.

When I laid my head on my pillow at night I could feel his thought take hold of me, not in lust but in contemplation; could sometimes even feel the moment when his thoughts turned to other things. At my first stir of waking I would realize there was something I had to remember, and then recall with happiness that Richard was here.

The purpose in his patience had altered our atmosphere, so that I moved (I mean it physically) almost through a different climate when I moved within the house. I knew he wrote to Paris. One day he told me he had informed Thomas I was alive. A letter came for him in return; he did not share it with me.

I thought of Thomas on the beach with its fossil pebbles and the crumpling crackle of its green-ridged waves; saw again his skin, rosy with the wind, and the virile half-question in his lips and eyes. He had not come; it was years since I had seen him. I had failed even in Florence, failed even as a child in growing too haggard, too angry, too different. Why had I imagined I was special? Love and mortality—these I had; and the ephemeral, illusory future for which my parents had trained me, filling with their own purpose the inertia of my ungifted emptiness.

I passionately approved the course they had chosen for me:

that of model, musician, and scholar. Now I perceived my prettiness faded, my music commonplace, my scholarship a matter for exhaustion. What failure, obscurely laid within me, had led me northward to this hiding at Sainte-Bertrande? How had I failed—when I could, scanning all my life, identify no single moment when I had not tried my hardest? Why had life not given me, in return for work, the reward of happiness? Fierce as a child I added and subtracted these sums.

Thomas had not written, had not come. This hurt me appallingly—a fact I was late in recognizing, having judged it ungenerous. The future had welcomed him—as, despite my labor, it had as mysteriously refused me and collapsed beneath my weight.

A night came when, with a fierce and simple agony, I endured my envy of Thomas. I am not proud to record it, nor any of the other distorted circles drawn by suffering. Perhaps I sound what I then thought myself to be: a monster of self-absorption. Let me make clear that I showed these feelings in no act. I spared absolutely everyone around me. I had mastered cheerfulness; I practiced it, together with industry and silence. But that night I wept for hours, stifling in my pillow a grief in which my soul spoke to the darkness that had created it. Trained to be beautiful and to give delight, expecting therefore simply (I now realized) to receive happiness in return, I had not dreamed of failure and agony of spirit. The future had revealed itself, exposing at once my weakness, my unpreparedness, my ludicrous astonishment.

Hoarse with the weeping I had striven to keep silent, I rolled onto my back. *Thank God there are other people in the house,* said the part of me that knew I must live, would live. Then I felt the agony gather itself to convulse my mind again; and as it did so, beating over me like a tide, I thought: *I will stop my heart. Heart, you are mine. I command you, stop.*

By then I was making no sound. The door opened silently. I lay inert as Richard's weight and warmth informed me of his nearness. Cool as a doctor's his hands inspected me—felt for pulse and breath, checked the coldness of my hands; then wiped my face and laid on my forehead a cloth steeped in cool water. It grew quickly warm. As he took it away he said, "No, you have no fever."

The secret was mine and God's, but humanity is kinder than divinity, and I desperately longed to speak to someone I could see. I whispered, "I tried to stop my heart."

"Do not turn flesh against flesh, Claire," said his soft voice in the darkness. "Your poor little heart, what harm has it done you, except to break? What Claire did you try to be, that you had to shatter her to escape? Perhaps, after the womb, air scalds the newborn child; perhaps that is why they cry. You are becoming Claire, and this is the agony of birth."

"*This* is the truth of me?" Appalled, I lost control of my voice, which ended ludicrously in a croak.

"Not yet. I think you told yourself, not wittingly, a lie about what you are. In India, you know, they have different gods. I have heard of one called Shiva the Destroyer. They say this god is part of God himself: that part which destroys all that is false in us, which seems to have no pity, so that the truth may grow. Has it occurred to you that, instead of becoming less, you are perhaps becoming something more?" Practical as a brother's, his palm smoothed my shoulder, then my arm, making sure I had not chosen to sleep naked.

"How can *more* be born from this?" Seeking the sleep I was too exhausted to find, I turned my head on the pillow.

"How," his voice replied, "can a baby be born from its mother's agony? Does she know? Surely at moments she must forget everything but the pain; yet it will end." Josèphe called softly, and was as softly sent away. In the darkness near my cheek his gentle voice resumed. "If some truth is striving to be born of you, then this agony is its sign and its necessity, and you will learn its meaning when the pain is gone. Pain destroys judgment. But the suffering goes, does it not?"

Tiredly I nodded. "Yes, completely; to come back like this."

His hand brushed back my hair from my forehead. "Claire, I am here to make sure you do not harm yourself."

"I am too weak," I said.

"I hope you are. Here, come here." He wrapped me, passive, in blankets, then swung his legs onto the bed beside me; he was wearing, I think, a thick wool day gown. "Come and be warm. I must stay here till morning. I'll not get under the covers, I promise."

"Then you'll be cold."

"No, I'll do well enough."

As he held me I murmured, "He never wrote."

"Who?"

"Thomas. He never wrote nor came after you told him I was alive."

"Good God, is that what started this?" His matter-of-fact embrace tightened, cool and strong, around me. "He wanted to, but I wrote and told him no. When you are well, then he may come, I said."

I nodded, murmured something, and kindness merciful as death plunged me into unconsciousness.

*My dear parents,* I wrote, *I hope it will please you to learn that Richard Linacre, our friend, has returned from Italy. It may surprise you to find him living at Sainte-Bertrande. . . .*

My letter did not bring Walter any sooner than his regular day. I knew this hesitation did not spring from indifference, and I understood and approved of the decision that brought me neither hasty rider nor reply.

On the day my father chose, Richard had in any case gone hunting, taking one of the two horses he kept in the convent stables. Swimming weather had gone till May, and outside the walls swineherds shook down acorns from the orange-leaved oaks as food for their lean, coarse-coated pigs. Here and there an oak blazed on the hill, but the branches around it had dimmed to a smoky haze, their leaves fallen into drifts as acid-fragrant in their way as flowers.

Walter arrived at noon, kissed Josèphe, and gave her, from Elisabeth, a small present. In these two years both his hair and his new beard, sleek in the French style, had gone gray, and the lines had deepened around his eyes. I was setting a collar and had begun to work a delicate whipstitch around the raw inside facing. Walter sat beside me, talking of friends, of the Parisian scholars who had stayed overnight, of servants I knew, and the small affairs of Elisabeth's stillroom. He had delivered a closely packed parcel of books, too large, I thought, to be meant for myself alone; but he did not mention Richard.

The sun had dimmed and Josèphe moved to light the candles when Richard—refreshed, I knew, from a bath at the pilgrims' hostel—came in, carrying a brace of skinned rabbits. "Claire, can you use these? Oh. Good evening, sir."

"I'll make a stew," I said, as my father rose to confront the man he had not seen since the night that had destroyed what all of us were still laboring to re-create. "We've got the herbs, and I'll use the vegetables Father brought. Sir, here he is. You remember Richard."

"I do, of course. Welcome back." Walter extended his hand. Richard took it and quickly stood away; his face showed how startlingly he found my father changed.

"Thank you, sir, but I cannot in honesty take your hand until we have talked together. Claire, will you excuse us?"

"Of course." If they fight, I thought, dreading it, it is their affair. Knife in hand, I began to deal with the rabbit.

They walked some way out into the dusk. Then Richard turned, fingers clasping his upper arms against the cold. Before he could speak Walter's open hand cracked him hard across the cheek. Richard bore it without staggering, his arms still locked in a signal of neutrality.

"That," said my father, "is for the rope burns on her wrists."

"Who knows that at Saint-Aurèle?"

"None but the Count, the Mother Abbess, and my wife."

Richard nodded, his face calm. "Then add a blow for the day I found her seeking the clerestory entrance, and beat her."

My father did.

Richard steadied himself, the flesh flaming where the bruise would come purple across the cheekbone. "And one for the night Thomas deserted her and me on our way to the Standing Stones, and I . . ."

His description was coarse, concise, and true. Walter struck him twice again.

Above them November had drawn a brilliant blue twilight flawed with plum-colored clouds. It was growing cold. In the light that streamed from the cottage windows, each man could see the other's face. Richard said, "Forgive me, sir, if sickness and longing and terror have ever made you, as they made me that night, half mad."

"I always understood that. I am sorry for Thomas's sake. Is he well?"

"Paris and study both suit him excellently, but he will come back to Saint-Aurèle. He'll make a good squire. He writes to Antoine Lalemont far oftener than to me."

"That marriage would please us all," said Walter. "And you, Richard? How many times have you gone out into the world, and every time been drawn back?"

The man before him, controlling the shuddering of shock and chill, shrugged. "When I went to school in Paris, then soldiering after: count that as once, perhaps. Then Kraków: twice. Now this third time in Italy. I do not mean to become a villager, but I'll remain all my life a man of Saint-Aurèle."

"Do. The town needs you, as this country of Normandy needs gifted nobles to govern her."

"I am not a nobleman, sir."

"You will be, when—" my father nodded toward the

candlelight—"when this service ends. Are you my daughter's lover?"

"No."

Walter drew a long, harsh sigh. "Perhaps there is a cause, or what might pass for a cause. Elisabeth and I did wrong, I now think, in our ambition for Claire. I have discovered failure can be complex and can arise from love. But if behind it all you find a reason for the breaking within her, does it not still go on back into the dark? Must we not at some point accept that we can understand no more? *Can* the past yield understanding? I think, not much. Turn her away from the past if you can."

"Tell me about the press."

"I brought books for you. Plotinus, Latin and French translation in parallel columns . . ."

And so, talking, they reentered the warmth where diced vegetables and herbs had begun to fall into the broth, and I noted Richard's bruises and said nothing.

A fortnight later it was Elisabeth who came: pretty, slender, and now visibly aging, and cloaked in elegant blue-green. Richard had been chopping wood, sweat staining his shirt in spite of the cool air. I saw him wipe his forehead with his sleeve and grimace with resignation as he identified a fastidious guest. I watched Elisabeth approach him; saw her say a word; and then saw her fall, weeping and smiling, into his embrace.

I did not go to the castle for the Christmas feast, nor to my family. On Christmas Eve I exchanged presents with my parents, and through them sent more to their hosts, Gérard and Béatrice. His Grace's courier brought me a kind letter. The Count's visits to me had stopped with precision when Richard arrived; but no letter had come from him to Richard, nor did this one mention him. I spent Christmas supper with my own small household and the nuns.

After the gray-white dusk the refectory was a cavern of

honey-colored light. Mère Agnès welcomed Richard and me to her left side at the high table and presented, on her right, the gentle visiting bishop stranded among us by a cold, whose misery he tried to deny in his courteous determination to enjoy the feast.

Not only the rule of silence had been relaxed; the rules of frugality had gone as well, and eleven courses after the roast goose in cherry-sauce we broke apart a marzipan Sainte-Bertrande whose sparkling battlements, complete with sugar hospital, stables, and latrines, had stood five feet high before we attacked it with our hands. I even identified, on a lawn of green nut-paste beneath trees of confectioner's sugar, my own cottage, made of blanched almonds. Richard, scooping, secured it for me. I gave him the roof.

At last we sat, drugged with the Abbey's own apple brandy, in the odors of meat-juice, of pickling-spice, of hot sweet vinegar and pounded almonds; and into this innocent satiety the Sister Lector read the ancient story, which drew some tears. Beneath the table Richard's hand found mine, clasped it with a seeming lazy spontaneity, and slid away.

"Claire, will you sing for us?" said Mère Agnès.

"More than gladly, Reverend Mother." Josèphe, her curd-white skin flushed pink with food and wine, smiled as she brought me my lute.

And because they were my friends, and their gentleness surrounding me put me in mind of all the human goodness that had enfolded me since this place received me, I said softly into the hush: "How many listeners have we, Sisters, that we cannot see?" The silence deepened, acquired a relaxed intentness. I had been tuning the lute, and now sounded it, each note brushing the stillness like a tight-drawn golden thread. "Yet sometimes—who knows why?—these guests let themselves appear. I saw one years ago: a child visible only to one other friend—a child who stood listening, as you do now, to a Christmas song. I do not know where she has gone, or whether she can hear me. Perhaps the air enfolds her and hides her from my vision, or perhaps she cannot travel beyond the house in which she died. But I sing once more for her, in thanks that one night, through her, the unseen became visible."

They only half-understood, but it sufficed. And in the voice trained in Florence, the voice pride had forbidden me to neglect, I sang:

> Joseph est bien marié
> à la fille de Jessé.
> C'est une chose bien nouvelle
> d'être femme et pucelle:
> Dieu y avait opéré:
> Joseph est bien marié.

"Joseph is well matched with the daughter of Jesse. It is a new thing to be both virgin and mother: surely this is God's work."

And last—to the man whose hands had beaten me, had balanced a sword against my throat, had gentled me rolled in blankets, and then, an hour ago, had so delicately caressed me—I turned and spoke directly. "This tune is one of the most beautiful ever written; and no wonder, for angels composed it in Heaven and sang it a hundred years ago to a holy man as he lay sleeping under the stars. The music moved him to dance with the angels; and afterward he wrote it down. This is a true story, my lords and Sisters. Listen."

> *In dulci jubilo*
> Let us our joy now show:
> He for whom we pinèd
>   Lies *in praesepio,*
> And like the sun he shineth
>   *Matris in gremio.*
> *Alpha est et O.*

> *O Jesu parvule,*
> With thee I long to stay:
> We were all forsaken
> > *Per nostra crimina:*
> In us thou didst awaken
> > *Coelorum gaudia.*
> *Alpha est et O.*

The song ended. I drew them, clapping the rhythm, into the cadences of *Ríu ríu chíu: God kept the wolf from our holy Lamb.* Soon after that we walked homeward through the dark; and two years passed before Josèphe told me how Richard sat all that night awake before the fire.

And now, as the short white daylight faded through gray to cobalt and indigo, I would watch frost crystals advance upon the panes. First at each pane's base grew a tumble of translucent roses; then the flowers would shoot out spears, the spears would clash, and along each spike the roses would cluster and climb. By dusk a border no jeweler could have copied fretted my windowpane, refracting every nuance of light, from primrose to sparks of cherry and violet to a brilliant, strange lime-green.

The hours too grew dense and gathered weight. Exercise had become, if exhilarating, more difficult. The three of us kept warm before the fire—I with my needlework, Richard with his book, Josèphe with housework or cooking. She was a freckled girl with gentle gray eyes, and Richard treated her kindly.

Sometimes we would talk, or one of us women would sing, or we would all sink into the deep silence of our house. Richard had gathered basketsful of pinecones, which he set to dry by the fireplace before casting them into the flames. They crackled, spitting yellow coals of resin, and their perfumed smoke made us sneeze. And then I would doze, to be carried once or twice to bed by hands that never undressed me and never lingered.

I was greedy of sleep that winter—as stupid as a pregnant woman or a sucking baby. I would drowsily apologize to Richard for the company, to receive a laugh and a joke in reply. I do not know whether the quiet of our house oppressed him. Certainly, having made sure that Josèphe or Gilbert would keep me within their sight, he would vanish for hours about the riding and walking he needed.

One afternoon, curled half-asleep on the settle, I stretched out my hand to him. He took it, his expression quizzical. Recently his face had grown thinner, almost gaunt. Since the first day I met him he had touched me as often as he in decency could—something about me drew him to touch, to caress, to strike. Recently he had touched me seldom, and with confidence. Now I said, "Am I boring you?"

"Why should a perpetually dozing woman bore me?"

"Thank you. For a moment I doubted." I sighed. "Don't go away. Wait till spring: I'll uncurl like a hedgehog." He laughed and said something I do not remember, except that it was not flirtatious. We flirted only with protective sarcasm. Both of us knew that if we kissed, then desire itself, not healing or friendship, would once again tear from us all choice. I opened my eyes. "Richard?"

"Yes?" His finger marked the Plotinus, in which he never troubled to glance at the French translation.

I said, "I do not know whether friendship or—or the proximity in which we live require you to use continence. Perhaps it is vanity to wonder."

It was a mistake, for he spoke, as he often did, to the core of the thought. "You are only twenty-two, Claire."

I nodded. "I meant no sidelong question. I wanted to say, what I should not say, that I am grateful."

He found his page in the Plotinus and inquired gently, "Is this thanks, and in what fashion should I receive it?"

"I'm sorry I spoke. I meant no quarrel either, and *now*," I said indignantly, "I'm too distressed to sleep."

"You sleep, in any case, like a sow with a bellyful of piglets. Oh, damn it." He snapped the book shut, glanced around for Josèphe, and said with precision, "Of course living here requires continence, and other practices a man may use." I opened one unastonished eye. "Unlike you, I have never been fool enough to consider sanctity at the price of celibacy."

"Then why," I inquired, "are you unmarried at thirty?"

Dark against the flaring orange of the fire I could see his profile: the nose unexpectedly sharp, the arrogant rounding of the chin, and the mouth that sometimes moved me to a shock of surprise by its firm maturity. "Since you ask, and since it occurs to me that no one now living remembers, when I was nineteen I fell in love, with a girl a year older. She married elsewhere. Young people who suffer deeply, and all young people suffer deeply, imagine the woman intended to inflict what in fact was somehow one's own self-enthralled creation. Indifference inflicts such misery. What a pity we cannot validly blame someone for it."

"You were angry?" Startled, I eased myself upright.

He nodded. "Anger intoxicated me for perhaps six years. With every second thought I hated her. I am confessing to a gross fault, I know. How long it takes us to learn that women are not goddesses: that they are poor stumbling children in some ways like ourselves, who inflict without understanding."

"I think," I said, "many of us are humble, and do not believe our actions could matter enough to cause suffering. It is hard, Richard, to know how another human being feels things. One inflicts, perhaps, some unintended pain. And you are proud."

"Yes. And you are gullible, Claire, since you seem never to ascribe to me simple human reasons. I think I lost the kind of confidence that never broke, for example, in Thomas. And since, as you imply, I know the worth of my intellect and my skills, it has made me cautious. I never meant to say this to you. If I can find Josèphe, will you do without me for an hour?"

"Of course. She's in the next room."

"I'll knock." He laid down the book and, in two motions, summoned Josèphe and plunged into his bedroom for his cloak. Then he let himself out, shutting the door with a crisp gentleness that sounded little different from a slam.

We never spoke of this conversation again, for even the inner events of our household were enough to carry us beyond it. Next day Richard was again, to whatever degree he chose, at my disposal; and, innocently selfish, I sank back into the sleep of nurturance in which, like a suckling baby, I was still too tired to recognize the first shadow-structures of healing.

Each evening at eight, after the Sisters had finished, he lit me, along the path he had helped the Abbey's servants to clear, to the nuns' bathhouse. This was necessary. Transient men, most of them armed (it is not fair to disarm a pilgrim; the world through which they travel is too dangerous) moved continually throughout the compound. For such a man, said Mère Agnès when she asked Richard to accompany me with sword and lantern, a rape in the snow is a simple and practical affair.

Richard frowned. "Is it?"

Mère Agnès frowned also at this suggestion of experiment. "I assure you. And, Richard, it would seem unkind to send you down afterward to the men's hostel, with the snow so heavy on the ground. I'll make Sister Jeanne curtain off a tub for you, and you may bathe there too."

And so when I arrived, escorted, at the bathing room we found it empty—gloomy and serene with its sconces set with candles. Sister Jeanne would unlock the door to us, in her hand a book that resembled Walter's pocket edition of Ovid. The steam shocked us pleasantly after the outside air, and the flagstones, which smelled of soap and scrubbing sand, were warm under the feet, heated by the Roman method of hot-water pipes beneath the floor. Before us stood the dozen big hooped casks that served as tubs. One would be filled for me; for Richard, another that gave him the privacy of one wall, and also of a curtain on a rod. He could change there too. The nuns had seen to it that the space included table and chair.

Chatting to Sister Jeanne, I would strip and sink breast-deep in the hot water, and the scents of my rosemary-wash and of Elisabeth's lavender soap soon perfumed the steam. From behind the curtain would come lazy sloppings of water, and, in answer to Sister Jeanne, the occasional ribaldry.

"*You* be quiet," she said one night. I giggled. Dried and wrapped, I was sitting before her on a stool, having my hair untangled with a thick-toothed ivory comb. "It's indecent enough that we let you in at all."

"If it's indecency you ask, Sister—" A threatening arm pulled aside the curtain.

Sister Jeanne groaned. *"Put that back!"* Arm and curtain returned to their proper modesty.

I suppose he enjoyed the women's admiration: any man would have done so, and they were frank and gentle, and not virgins. But he managed them not only with discretion but with compassion. I believe he had thought about the sacrifice a woman makes in choosing an empty bed. When he emerged, dried, robed, and cloaked, from the bath place, it was only (despite his threats) to smile at Sister Jeanne. The great charm I knew he could summon he never used to torment the vulnerable among them (that some were vulnerable he and I both knew); and he avoided with skill all the potential for jealousy that gives a mischief-maker power among women. I found him, with the Sisters, witty, gentle, and kind; they enjoyed him.

"Poor old creature," I said one night when we had closed the door on Sister Jeanne. I did not mean it cruelly.

"Why? This way." His hand on my elbow guided me, and the lantern swung an arc of light across the snow.

I shrugged. "I should not like to die a virgin."

"They will not. They have, like many widows, at least the memory of something that fulfilled itself and ended in its time. I pity the truly virgin nuns more; that breeds unwholesomeness, I think. But here . . . protected within a world where no one is safe; given leisure to cultivate their herbs, their scholarship, their cooking even; spared the dangers of a last late childbirth; sheltered, educated, fed—"

"They give themselves to all who ask," I said.

"That is luxury. Leisure for prayer and charity: that is luxury, Claire. Christ may make an unfruitful spouse, but I do not pity them."

I thought of the silver wedding ring each Sister wore. "Hush," I said, stopping under the brilliant blue-white stars. "You should not have said that here. Mockery is ungrateful."

We had entered the black shelter of the compound. Ahead of us flat crystals glittered from the snowbanks. And around us, above us, enclosing us lay the rich peace of a great religious House. "I did not mean to mock," said Richard. "But you are right: I should not have said that here."

And as he drew me onward I prayed, "May these Houses always stand: to shelter scholarship; to feed the poor; to nurture the arts of peace, the beauty built with such labor that soldiers so casually destroy. For if a world comes in which the great abbeys, stripped and shattered, lie open to the sky, then in that world I do not wish to live."


And so we bore, in a kind of drugged and stoic peace, the passage into March.

On the twelfth of that month I went (escorted as always, since the wisdom that guarded me knew the cheerful, healing patient is most to be mistrusted) to give a lesson to Sister

Hélène's daughter. The child was bright, plainspoken, and courteous, and I had grown fond of her. Behind us in the cottage Josèphe and I left only Richard.

When we had gone he stirred up the fire, whose spitting yellow with its tongues of blue cheered him. Then he moved my table into the light of the window, and, after mixing water with ink-powder and sharpening a quill, began on a letter to Thomas. When he paused he seemed to hear the kissing against the panes of clotted flakes that fell, trickled, and dissolved into rain. A gust of wind threw a spattering against the glass, like a hand tossing a fistful of needles.

> Mr dear Thomas,
>
> I am glad Monsieur Villon bores you. A wonderful poet, yes, but these undergraduate mischief-makers have short careers, and unwittingly repeat a type. I saw them in my time too: the dark, dangerous observer, attractive to women, who studies us all from the back of the lecture hall, proves witty at our expense with his disciples, and seems to court an early death rather than bear obscurity among equally gifted adult men. Fascinating, brilliant, and moving—especially when they achieve that early death, which canonizes them and haunts the rest of their generation ("I have grown old, but he—what would he have said? What might he have become?" Fortunate survivors who need not know the answers.)
>
> But after all, it is a type of swaggering child. And how many undergraduate mischief-makers show François Villon's streak of viciousness? I suppose most of us have killed in self-defense, but those I talk to call his exploit murder. Keep clear of a man who woos the executioner as this one seems to. And comfort yourself that he will be reincarnate like a Hindu in the dark, dangerous young poets, attractive to women, who study our descendants from the back of lecture halls a hundred years hence.

Claire speaks of you often, and sends that love which I, unlike most people, will not forget to convey. I think she is well; more, I believe she is glad of my company. You can imagine she seldom confides in me, and I in my embarrassment have been so sharp with her when she tried that the poor girl has retreated to her sewing. She is still a fine musician. When we first met her she had a quality of freshness. That has gone, leaving austerity, gentleness, and honesty, and an adult face so like and so unlike the girl you remember that it shocks me sometimes. She is never physically ill, and that hardihood combined with her profound deceptiveness (I do not mean deceitfulness: Claire could deceive, I think, only by keeping silent) make me despair of knowing her. She is all depth and no surface, a reserve so innate I think she long since despaired of becoming intimate with any human being. I am glad to have lived so near her, otherwise I should not understand her at all.

A time may come when I will tell you the true reason for my coming here. Just now—forgive me—I am not ready. And I would need, I think, Claire's permission, since that matter touches her privacy.

We have received information that the brigand Sir John Challoner has outfitted a pirate fleet and means to attack the coast this summer, stealing what he can and killing for amusement. These mercenaries pick us clean of our women, our crops, our works of fine craft, stealing wholesale, and firing wantonly what it has taken other men lifetimes to build. How long must we endure this from England? King Henry in one of his fits of sanity might stop it, but for the government of England we must look to Queen Margaret, or to the eventual usurper.

Have you seen King Charles, even in procession? I never came across him when I was in Paris, but then the Court travels constantly, and Paris has a traditional loathing for the king, as I am sure you have discovered. We never *see* the powers that dispose of our lives. Good training, perhaps, for Heaven."

"Richard," said a voice he knew. For an instant he sat still; then rose.

Behind him, the hood of his cloak thrown back, stood Jean d'Aubry de Saint-Aurèle. Richard knelt. "My dear lord."

"My beloved child." His shoulders were taken in a hard embrace; then an arm, lighter than his but as strong, compelled him. "Rise. May I sit down? My sister knows I am here and told me I should find you alone."

Richard took his chair and smoothed the letter with a hand whose shaking the Count openly, though briefly, remarked. "I just wrote to Thomas, sir, that we never see the powers that dispose of us, and that no doubt this is training for Heaven."

Jean d'Aubry smiled. "Where God will also be little in evidence? And meanwhile Agnès disposes of us all. She loves you and Claire. Can you induce Claire to marry you?"

"Induce her? Yes. But I should like her to marry me out of love."

"Ah." The vulpine intelligent face, so little changed, regarded him. "Richard, I had two choices toward a man tainted with concealment of treason. First, to withdraw from him my public endorsement, though not my trust in him as a friend. Second, to give him my public trust, and by my example to direct my people. I now know I chose wrongly. I beg your forgiveness."

Richard's eyes were steady. "When I can."

"Come back to Saint-Aurèle. We need you. Take back your title of Master of Works and build us new fortifications."

Richard rose, his arms crossed in the posture that both shielded and restrained. "And whom shall I find there? Walter and Elisabeth Tarleton, newly arrived—intelligent strangers who have a right to our kindness? Thomas, unmarked by the scars he will carry on his back all his life? Or Claire, not yet wasted by my cruelty? And by yours, sir; and by yours."

"You will find," said the Count, "that no remorse can force Time backward, and that we exhaust ourselves in trying. Come out of your childhood and see that Claire is better broken out of her parents' grip, even by force; that I have lost Elisabeth; that Thomas writes to me often and is fulfilling our best hopes; and that you may have to live without ever understanding, until the Judgment exhibits you naked to yourself, why you both love Claire and have destroyed her. Have you lain with her?"

"No."

"Bed her," said the Count. "In her bed, if anywhere, you will evoke the lust of cruelty you think contaminates your love; and there, to her delight and yours, you can study it. But understand this: a vice need not contaminate us. It can stand apart, isolated and used—even drawn upon, the vitality we gave it taken back again and transformed into creation. Come out of your self-contemplation. I have no time for it: I need you."

Slowly Richard took his chair again. "I cannot until she is ready."

"I understand. We are building walls, I assure you: even if I spare you till spring, Challoner will not find us unprepared. By the way, did you meet in Florence my old friend Cosimo de Medici?"

"I saw him at a public banquet once. The Medici hold themselves high, but they are not princes, are they? Only merchant bankers."

"The greatest of merchant bankers, and friends with all the others. No, they are not princes, any more than Augustus was *princeps* of the Rome he conquered: he too, if you remember, insisted on styling himself First Citizen."

"—Not needing to be King in name, since power sufficed him. I did not know you had met Cosimo."

"More than met him. We still write. I stayed five months with him in Florence eleven years ago, and at his country villa—when was it? Six years ago already? Before my capture by the English."

"I think I was at Kraków, sir."

"No doubt." The Count rose. "You broke an arm, I remember, when you were ten."

Richard smiled, rising also. "The left one, thank God. How my mother harried me to keep it *in* the sling."

The Count drew up the hood of his snow-drenched cloak. "I suppose it knit, and it does its work well enough. Richard, none of us makes mistakes like a mathematician, in a void of pure numbers. Our mistakes damage those we love. Forgiveness, I think, is not a feeling, but a willingness to go on, in dignity and with confidence in our own fundamental goodness. Come to me by summer; and bring Claire with you as your wife."

We never bored each other. At first, when I accepted his service, I felt embarrassed by the monotony of the life I could offer him. But one gift Elisabeth had encouraged in me—and one to which my nature was very apt—was to enjoy the treasures of everyday life. I found small tasks, small routines full of dignity and interest. Richard shared this capacity; and also he sought out the physical exercise that I did not want, yet, to share with him. I could no longer plead fragility, and, as the first ghostly green descended like a veil over the trees and the last rotten snow crumbled into the brook, I found myself eliminating the word "illness" from my private self-understanding. At this time I was deeply in love with quiet.

I wonder whether it surprised him, as it did me, to discover we could spend hours together about quiet tasks, feeling no weariness of each other. I knew him to be proud and often impatient of others. But I ceased to dread his temper as he applied, month after month, to the small affairs of our household a patience that never lacked grace and never contributed an unwholesome heat. I think Josèphe fell a little in love with him, for which I was sorry. (She married Gilbert soon after.) Meanwhile Richard and I seemed to draw from each other's presence a nourishment that sought no expression.

The time came when I found bluebells and lily-of-the-valley in the woods, springing out of the dense brown cake of last year's leaves. Now we lit our fire only for cooking, and on the warmest days a pot of green fern filled the hearth. Richard cut fresh boughs for me every day, filling my bedroom with the fragrance of leaves, by whose subtle odors my abnormally acute sense of smell could distinguish among oak or elm or chestnut.

About this time he again began to take the four-hour ride to and from the lake where he swam. I longed to go with him, but neither wanted to see him naked nor to hamper him with a loincloth I knew he did not use. What desire we felt the opener atmosphere of spring had perhaps dispelled; but there remained, I told myself, courtesy. Sighing, I resigned myself to his absences, which I had begun to dislike though never to oppose; and to a life within the abbey walls that had begun to chafe me almost imperceptibly.

Spring grew hot—gathered tones of honey and oat-gold and dense rich green; and summer passed. I sewed; helped Josèphe; taught and prayed with the Sisters—the abbey always offered me as much company as I wanted; and sat, often with Elisabeth and Walter as well as Richard, on my front step discussing war, politics, printing presses, the wisdom of writing poetry in the vernacular, and the purity of transmission in surviving texts of ancient authors.

One evening Elisabeth had gone to her lodging in the abbey's guest house, Richard had vanished inside to find a book and settle some playful quarrel between them, and I sat on alone, gazing at a fresh pale sunset. The last amber light had faded from the heights of the ramparts, and above the forest a streak of primrose blended upward into jade, and then into a blue behind which day still seemed to shine like sunlight through stained glass.

Now in the zenith blue had darkened to the colorless density of night, and the stars came out. Once in Florence a jeweler my father knew had scattered a handful of aquamarines over a scrap of velvet to show us how some dealer had cheated him: inferior jewels. I remembered them now: softer in their light than diamonds, their color ranging from ice-blue to the dull transparency of water.

And suddenly I knew I wanted my life to begin again.

I think I moaned softly, but aloud. Where could I go? To Paris? As what—a solitary buyer for my father? A friend of Thomas, forbidden because of my sex to hear lectures at the university? Go back to Saint-Aurèle: back to being my parents' child and working in the shop, hoping for someone to marry me?

If I had let the panic subside naturally, I would have recognized I must consult two people: Mère Agnès and His Grace. Neither would have let me fall back into a childhood I had escaped; both would have offered sensible advice, and opportunities lay in the gift of both if I could humble myself to accept a patron. But the world of fighters and male scholars offered a woman little beyond the cloister or marriage.

"Claire?" said Richard's voice. "What is it? I heard you make a sound."

In my distress I could, unjustly, have struck him. I wanted no patron, no charity. He, both a fighter and a scholar, could not help the limits Nature placed on me: I would not like a beggar seek his consolation. "Claire?" he said again. Smooth motion in the dark, he sat beside me. "How can I help if you will not tell me?"

"If I tell you," I said, willing my voice to be steady, "I might place you under obligation."

"And therefore be damned to me? Risk it."

"I've finished here. I want to leave."

For a long time he was silent. Then he said, his silence

having noted, summed up, and dismissed all my difficulties, "Come to Paris with me."

"How," I said, "*can* I come to Paris with you? In two ways, of which the first is to be your mistress."

"And the second, which you refuse to name, is to be my wife."

"I do not take charity, Richard."

"I do not give it."

The coolness in his voice shocked me. "I'm sorry," I said.

"Claire, do you fear childbirth?"

"No. I know I will survive it."

"Good, because if you married me I could not promise you continence."

"I would never ask it. I could not be so cruel, or," I admitted softly, "so cold."

"I know you have few choices." Still he gave me no clue, by voice or touch, what he was feeling. "But not so few as you believe. Use what you cannot change. I cannot promise you freedom from childbearing. I *can* promise you my friendship; my comradeship in your work; and good people to lighten the burden of children so that you may work."

His next word, delivered with quiet savagery, was a curse. For on the gloom of the path I saw coming toward us two figures we recognized.

I spoke quickly. "Richard, I'll call Josèphe and go to Evening Mass; I need time to think."

"You'll be late for Mass."

"It can still serve as my excuse. Can you deal with them?" He nodded. "Josèphe!"

She followed me. I beckoned to her and, hurrying forward, contrived a running curtsy. "Evening Mass, Reverend Mother—my lord."

"But you'll be—" called Mère Agnès—credibly, I hoped, too late to make herself heard.

As I fled along the path, poor Josèphe expostulating beside

me, Richard rose. "Please sit down." He gestured. "Just a moment, we have cushions and a stool."

"I'll trouble you for both," admitted Mère Agnès. "I've begun to feel the rheumatism. In summer, imagine, how disgusting."

When they were settled, His Grace said, "I was visiting my sister and came down to say good-bye. I have to take an embassy to Florence about a financial matter. King Charles informs me that his niece, Queen Margaret of England, is seeking a loan of a million florins from the House of Medici and its affiliates. Of course she means to use the money to make war. While this might divert England from us for the present, His Majesty judges that his niece, married to an imbecile, cannot win the war. Should the next king be Richard of York or his able eldest son, we wish to deprive England of this pretext, at least, for renewing war on France."

"But why choose you, sir?" asked Richard.

"Because of all his nobles I am closest to Cosimo. For myself I detest making use of a friendship; but I cannot, of course, refuse His Majesty's order. So I came to say good-bye. We leave in three days."

"Sir," said Richard, "tonight Claire told me she has finished here and wishes to leave."

A silence fell. Richard could feel the tired man before him gathering his strength into attention.

Mère Agnès said, "How?"

"Sir, I too dislike using a friendship."

Jean d'Aubry shrugged. "Which of the saints was it who said, 'Ask with an open hand'? Ask."

Suddenly his sister leaned forward and ran her fingertip across his forehead, bringing it away greased with sweat. "Jean, what is wrong?"

"A low fever. I always run one at this time of year. What a sickly pair we make. Ask, Richard."

"Sir, if you have to deal with an English delegation, will you meet them face to face?"

"I am not sure. Not necessarily. Cosimo may choose to hear the two embassies separately—England pleading for the loan, France arguing against it."

"I beg you, pretend not to know you may in fact have little to do with the English delegates. Appoint to your staff two English secretaries: Claire and myself. We might be of real use."

"Obviously, though I presume Cosimo's translators are honest as well as fluent."

"Still, it might be as well if Your Grace employed someone to listen to the English delegation without intermediaries. If you want a first and second secretary, I suggest Claire for first. English is my third language after French and Latin, but her father is a native, and they often speak English at home."

"I see. Excellent." Jean d'Aubry stood and cautiously stretched his arms. "I agree. Yes, Agnès, I'll see the Sister Infirmarer, and yes, I'll stay the night. Richard, at first light tomorrow I'll consult Elisabeth and dispatch her back home. It will be a hard two days' work for her, but such a task as women enjoy. Claire will need trunks packed with all those gowns her mother has gone on sewing for her."

"And we'll send to Verneuil for your provisions." Mère Agnès hesitated, then said, "I am glad of this, Richard. What do you think waits for her in Florence?"

"I do not know. But certainly," he replied, "a man named Luca della Robbia."

He got my consent, of course, laconically asked, and given without any evidence of jubilation. I did not sleep that night, but lay in bed trying to control the pulse that made the darkness shimmer. And we were on the road before some chance cue recalled to me—what I quickly dismissed—that, sometime in the half-sleep that blended so restlessly with thought, I had glimpsed a woman's body rolled from breaker to breaker on the beach.

# 15

The next day—the first of September—came in with floods of warm gray rain. Elisabeth and His Grace must, I supposed, have got soaked on their way back into Saint-Aurèle. I began to say my good-byes and to give what presents my means afforded: books for Sister Jeanne; money for Gilbert, who was to accompany us as Richard's body servant; for Josèphe a kiss and two of my blue dresses, as well as the shawl I had been saving for her Christmas present; for Mères Agnès, my lute. ("In Florence," said Richard, "I'll buy you another.") And all through the thirty-six hours of my farewells the rain continued—a rustling sheet that obliterated the yellow of autumn and sobered my jubilation.

Dressed in a brown velvet traveling gown and an oiled leather cloak, and mounted on the sidesaddle I never used except when, as now, appearances were important, I made the half-day's ride with Richard and our entourage into Saint-Aurèle. And there too my arrival held no excitement of welcome. In a rain-silvered mist the castle raised its gigantic assemblage of curtain walls, cylinders, and rounded pyramids.

Walter met us at the town gate. "You are to come at once to the castle. Something has happened."

"What, sir?" demanded Richard.

"I may not tell you: my orders from my lord Martin de Brissac. Nothing that will keep you from Florence, Richard; quite the contrary. Claire, remind me, I have a packet of letters for you to deliver."

"Yes, sir," I said. Walter spurred ahead of us, embarrassed, I thought, by a silence enforced on him by a superior he disliked and by Richard's frown of speculation.

No one greeted me from the nearly deserted streets. Instead, blurring the gables, there enfolded me a steam-white mist that only we who have lived on the shore love for its cries of gulls and its pungency of fish. *My home,* I thought with sudden finality. "Richard, I have just understood something."

His head turned in the wet oval of his yellow leather hood. Rain curled his hair in tendrils against the dripping planes of his face. From his hands, once, I had fallen in a streak of shattered stars. "Understood what?"

"That I will never see England."

He glanced ahead; a gate had opened to receive us. "Not while their war lasts, Claire; and it will last into the second generation."

"That is not what I meant. I meant that I need never go beyond the border. For some people a border joins two whole things. For others, I think, it is their habitation."

"I have heard His Grace say precisely that." We passed the gateway. "That some of us are born to exist *between.* Have you not noticed how many borders, Claire, meet here in Saint-Aurèle? Not France and England only. Lust and love"—a fall from the warmth of his hands that should have cradled me—a fall into a depth that had never ended. "Lust and love, peace and war, earth and ocean—daily life and the power that hallows the Standing Stones."

And now we were dismounting, I into my father's arms, in a courtyard from which the chill and our urgency drove out all memory of three years ago.

There had been time since then for Aliénor's first child,

Jacquette's as well, to be conceived and born; and at the head of the staircase stood Martin de Brissac.

As I copied Richard's composed and rapid ascent toward him, I thought, He is not wearing mourning. A dark blue robe and flat cap had replaced the red velvet of the wedding night, but the heavy, intelligent, scornful face was the same, and the deep voice in which he said, "Monsieur Linacre, thank you for your promptitude. You are needed more than you know, as I shall explain."

"His Grace, my lord?" demanded Richard, straightening from his obeisance.

Martin de Brissac bowed from the shoulders in reply. "He may live, but is extremely ill. You will please come with me to my brother-in-law's study, you and Mademoiselle Tarleton." Actually he pronounced both our names in French. He glanced at me—I curtsied—and then at my father. "Monsieur Tarleton, please go to your wife, she has been asking for you."

"In His Grace's chamber, my lord?" said Walter.

"Yes. Monsieur, Mademoiselle, come this way."

*He may live.* So, with the rapidity of extreme distress, I saw pass before me the suite of rooms I remembered only in the dark, and found myself seated in the chamber where the fire cast a silvery coldness over the foil of the ceiling and over the painted comets on the walls.

Martin de Brissac settled at the Count's desk. "You will go to Florence, Monsieur Linacre, as His Majesty's ambassador, with Mademoiselle Tarleton as your English secretary—a peculiar but not unreasonable whim of my brother's. Here are your letters of commission; here is His Majesty's letter to Cosimo; and here is a brief I sat up all night preparing."

Richard did not touch the ivory casket, banded and padlocked, that the other man pushed across to him. "My lord, before I protest this promotion, tell me what has happened to His Grace, who knows Cosimo and who alone is fit for this embassy."

Martin de Brissac shrugged; the innate gloom of his face concealed, I thought, a real concern. "A fever at the time he saw you—a drenching on his way home—an insistence, until one o'clock this morning, that he *must* go. Elisabeth Tarleton is with him, and I think Saint-Aurèle could offer no better nurse. The symptoms are a high fever, difficulty in breathing, and an intense pain in the side. A pleurisy, the doctor says. I gather he must keep still, as any movement could rupture the lung. As to your promotion: no, *I* should be the obvious deputy, except that my brother may die, and Sir John Challoner is at sea. All who can fight are needed here. His Majesty King Charles has taken the Court eastward. We cannot spend ten days finding him and ten more receiving his reply. Cosimo intends to meet the two delegations in Florence on October first. If we are late I fear he may simply hear the English and grant the loan."

"Therefore," said Richard, "an embassy leaves from here today if France is to put its case to Cosimo at all."

"We might reach our agents in Florence, but they lack diplomatic credit: Cosimo tolerates them merely. Even if we could instruct them in time, to employ one of our client-nobles or merchant gatherers-of-information would insult Cosimo and concede the case by default to this English representative, whoever he may be."

Richard nodded. Martin's dark eyes, heavy with sleeplessness and with burdens that had, I reminded myself, descended as well on this man I disliked, regarded him with a certain kindness. "Monsieur Linacre, I remember the night of your disgrace."

"I remember your presence there, my lord," said Richard gently.

"I did my duty. If you fear it made me your enemy, recall that I am not the heir: the heir is Philippe, the eldest son of Agnès. My brother thinks you his ablest servant. I hope he is right. If he dies, you will hear it first from me; and I guarantee you that the heir, or I as his deputy, will ratify your credentials. If you return successful, I will take care His Majesty hears of it. I surprise you? Of course you dislike me. But I am no thief of another man's credit. Do your best for us in Florence, and if Challoner comes, I will defend Saint-Aurèle. " He rose.

"I will do my best," said Richard. "I thank your lordship."

Martin de Brissac nodded. "You must set out today, but before you do, take an hour for the hot meal and dry clothes my servants have prepared. If you *all* go down with the pleurisy I shall, I think, simply make Sir John a present of the town."

Richard, after apologizing to me for his silence, read his brief during our hour of reprieve. My chill had subsided with the drying of my skin and hair. Richard had uttered only one protest: I could not tell whether his promotion had shaken him. "Are you afraid?" I said as, with a crisp rustle, he refolded the sheets.

"Afraid?" His profile, with its sharp long nose and firm mouth, did not turn to me. "I know I can speak well—I am not shy—and God knows there is a case here an intelligent man can make. In a way I am glad His Grace has been spared this prostitution of his friendship, which he so dreaded. It is an exercise, Claire: probably Cosimo has already made up his mind. I wish we could send a man of higher rank, though. To send a disgraced gentleman, who had done no work for his lord these three years, as His Majesty's ambassador— The intelligent man in me can speak our case, but my rank being so low may seem a subtle mockery. And Cosimo would despise nothing more than my pleading a last-minute substitution. We cannot *plead*, though I will inform him of His Grace's illness."

"Cosimo prizes intelligence, so they say."

"Yes, but he knows what is due him. I am a clerk, Claire; but we must not say so. Between here and Florence I must contrive to become, in my own mind, His Grace's ablest servant: the best man, the obvious choice. My coming must be made to flatter Cosimo; and if you can tell me how to achieve *that*—"

"I said Cosimo prizes intelligence," I replied. "He will listen to you, whatever your rank. Speak well, after telling him why you were chosen. Surely, if our arguments are strong ones, he is not so vain as to change his mind because a gentleman, not a noble, presents them to him."

"I suspect," said Richard, relocking the cabinet, "that this embassy is truly an exercise. Poor English commissioner who has come so much farther than I, if the decision has already gone against him. Cosimo already knows all the arguments both of us could present, and such decisions are not made in the open. Well, we will buy you your lute, at any rate."

When our train stood ready in the courtyard we went, as apparently the Count had requested, to say good-bye to him. He lay in his bed, his face white, his breathing shallow. "Richard," he whispered, "this thing hurts damnably when I breathe, but I do not mean to *stop* breathing on that account. Kneel down." Richard knelt. A hand, guided by Elisabeth's, rested in blessing on the crown of his head. "Tell Cosimo I chose you from among all my friends. You can trust Martin, and also Philippe, Agnès's son, who will be your lord if God takes me."

"Christ help me." Richard crossed himself, then kissed the Count's hand. "May God receive you, sir, or better, spare you to us."

"I will perforce hear *his* arguments." The Count smiled and motioned to me. "Claire, come here."

The hand, limp and hot, rested on my hair. "Leave Sainte-Bertrande. First stone; then earth; then blood. Be just, Claire. God's blood redeems our blood."

I stammered, "I—I thought, sir, that God's blood redeems us from sin."

His head moved on the pillow. "No; from abandonment. You are whole in body, Claire. Remember that when you rise up through earth again."

Weeping, I kissed him; then embraced Elisabeth.

In the courtyard I accepted Walter's packet of letters. "What did His Grace say to you? I was too far away to hear."

"Only nonsense; he had begun to wander. Sir, what do you know of my lord Philippe, the heir?"

"What you do: that Thomas has met him at the Sorbonne and has become his devoted follower in pranks of the usual kind. There could be worse bonds between vassal and lord. I hear Philippe has a gift for mathematics. He will make us a good master, if it comes to it."

"Then good-bye, sir."

"God have you in his hand," said Walter, and stood waving us farewell as our embassy turned through the rain toward Italy.

# 16

That summer there died of plague in Florence the whole family of Andrea del Castagno, and eleven days later my old friend himself, Andrea of the Hanged Men, aged thirty-four. But a merciful early frost had ended the deaths, which in any case had been declining for some weeks by the time we halted and looked down on the city I had left—a child, I now felt—only four years before.

In autumn Florence lies hazed with crumbling leaves and clustered cypresses, the only dark among the pink and yellow, rust and gray. The river lay brown beneath a delicate bleached sky. Jewelers' shops still propped themselves in a jumble on the span of the bridge, reducing it to a street like other streets, only narrower, busier, and more dangerous. The pink-and-green façades of churches still rose to unfinished ribs of yellow brick, studded where masons would screw on the marble panels. Watchtowers built by the old warring families still lifted their stubs above streets of rust-red tiles. Here and there in a hidden piazza flowers wilted before an ancient Madonna, her paint flaking to reveal the terracotta underneath; and from its hill Fiesole, destroyed, watched the prosperity of its rival from the stillness in which defeat in the war between the cities had arrested it.

Cosimo had given the French embassy a house: a fortified square, its walls featureless except for the windows the architect (an expert on the angle of crossbow-fire and the reach of ladders) had risked on the top floor. Within this square we found a courtyard with stables and latrines, and on the opposite side certain bedroom windows opened on a humid, yellowing garden.

In between lay the three-tiered hollow quadrangle of the house. A ground-floor loggia, surmounted by two rows of windows, looked down on cobbles and a fountain. The great front door could be barred, and it let out onto storerooms, muniment rooms, kitchens, and servants' quarters. A staircase swept up to the public rooms—studies, solars, and a paneled gallery, fit for winter exercise or for dancing.

On the highest story a simpler gallery floored with brown tile ringed the quadrangle and served as a corridor from which opened the bedrooms. Richard disposed of these, and assigned me the room next to his own. The nearness of our servants and colleagues would, I hoped, preclude gossip as much as possible. Even so we were few enough that several of the bedrooms remained uninhabited. Unlike many women of my rank when they must sleep alone, I never took a favorite maid to share my solitude. I wondered what warning Mère Agnès had given Richard about keeping close to me.

I glimpsed his room, with its hangings of brown velvet and its cabinet with *trompe l'œil* designs in ivory and contrasting woods, one day through the open door. My own I loved. It was immense, its floor patterned with tiles in beige and cream color that shone when the servants scrubbed them. A veined marble fireplace presented this carven reminder: SIC TRANSIT GLORIA MUNDI (*Thus, like these ashes, vanishes the glory of this world*). A woman, I thought, must have decorated the room, for the walls were a delicate eggshell-yellow, and the bed—reached by a step that ran all round it—had bolster-thick pillows in linen cases, and a mattress stuffed with goosedown. It had no canopy, but around its square frame rattled curtains on wooden rings, curtains of yellow gauze embroidered with small pink roses. Off the bedroom opened a linen closet and a garderobe, cleanly kept, but no quarters for my maid, whom I sent to sleep at a distance.

Only twenty-four hours now remained before the meeting Cosimo had set. We had heard the English commissioners were already in the town. That morning we despatched to the Palazzo Medici the gifts King Charles had chosen: among many other things, a pendant—a baroque pearl the size of a thumb joint, set in diamonds, and upheld by mermaids in gold and white enamel. I laughed over this hideous object, especially at the diamonds, which bored me.

"You dislike diamonds?" inquired Richard. "Frugality, or an artist's objection?"

"The latter," I replied. "Don't you find them ugly? All that cold sparkle."

"What do you like, then?"

I thought. I possessed little jewelry—no rings, and a few necklaces that Elisabeth had had, when I still performed in public, to remind me to wear. "Softly colored jewels. Topaz, amber, garnet, amethyst, tourmaline, pink and green crystal."

"All semiprecious."

"I suppose so. There are so few precious jewels, and all of them hard and sparkling. Oh, and violet jade. Once I saw a piece Maffeo Polo smuggled out of China."

"Pastels and the gold and fire colors, then," said Richard. "Yes, there is a greater range of semiprecious gems, and the colors are softer and more various."

He said no more, but at the noon meal laid beside my plate a case that came, I thought, from the tiered booths of the Ponte Vecchio. Inside I found an exquisitely delicate necklace: alternate beads of rose quartz and peridot, pink and green, each a shining globe of color.

"From King Charles," said Richard, his color heightened. "In thanks for your soon-to-prove indispensable services."

I wore it that night for our supper with Luca della Robbia. Since I was still a maiden, I left my hair loose over a gown of gray velvet figured with silver. We found Master Luca in the supper room where, an age ago, the death of the Byzantine emperor had caused us a moment's pity before we forgot that he had existed.

"My whole household is at the villa," said Master Luca, "so you find me alone. I sent them away for safety. We have had no deaths, thank God. Claire, my dear, welcome."

He took both my hands and stood studying me. The eyes, shrewd and gentle, seemed to say *Do not fear my judgment.* He kissed me. "Richard, what a delight to see you the servant of the king and escort to so beautiful a lady. Come, sit down to supper."

I was quiet that evening. I had expected if not Florence, then Master Luca to give me some sense of completion, of self-understanding. But like all who demand completion, I had come too soon; and in my emptiness I ought to have recognized that Florence now meant as little to the woman I had become as if it had been a map laid on a table.

Both men noticed my silence, but covered it with grace. "What can you tell me of Cosimo?" asked Richard over the nuts and wine.

Master Luca cracked an almond shell. "Probably nothing new. He is sixty-eight years old; a gardener; a Latinist; uxorious and a lover of his grandchildren. He is probably the richest man in Europe. He is banker to the Pope. His people call him *pater patriae,* though he holds no civic title. When he began to build his palace, it looked so princely the Signoria charged him with seeking to rise above his station as a citizen and exiled him to Venice. There he read the classics, rigged the next election, and accepted the invitation of his new, bought

Signoria to return home. The family live in the palace; you will not see the unfinished parts."

"All three generations?"

Master Luca nodded, splitting, with precision, another almond with the silver nutcracker. "Cosimo; his sons Giovanni and Piero; his sons' wives, of whom I recommend to your attention Lucrezia, patroness of our friend Sandro. You will not see Giovanni, the heir, who has gone to Milan on some commission for his father. Likely you *will* see Piero, the invalid. And the grandchildren—Lorenzo, Giuliano, Maria, and the rest."

"They sound a close family."

"They are. Cosimo, mindful of his soul, has taken a cell at the convent of San Marco; he retreats there to rest and pray. He will like your pretty secretary." Luca bowed to me; I grimaced. "He collects jewels, cameos, antique *objects d'art*. His library, over which his invalid son presides, contains original manuscripts by Tacitus and Cicero, the only ancient copy of Sophocles, the *Pandects* of Justinian, and the *Codex Amiatinus*. He has bought every alum mine in Christendom and throttled all lesser competitors, which means he controls the cloth industry in Florence."

"And is he likely to favor the French crown?"

"I should think him *un*likely," replied Master Luca, "to feel a pang of chivalry for a vindictive and desperate princess wedded to a half-wit. Claire, will you sit to me again?"

I started. "For what, Maestro?"

"For a Mater Dolorosa."

"Good God, is it *that* bad?" I had meant to sound droll; Richard's glance told me how poorly I had succeeded.

"Not at all. I had already been commissioned to sculpt a Mater Dolorosa and have been looking for a model. A freestanding bust, I think, to be done first in clay, then cast from the mold and glazed."

"Your colors are too bright. It would not," I objected, "be sufficiently *dolorosa*, unless, of course, my presence—"

"Be quiet, Claire," said Richard gently.

Master Luca poured wine. "I have succeeded in refining my colors somewhat, and sculpture interests me increasingly. The very brilliance you object to can, I hope, create an astonishingly lifelike impression. Please sit to me, Claire."

I shrugged. "I am, as ever, your pupil, sir."

Which is how—in between meetings of the embassies concerned with a loan to the English Crown—I came to model again for Luca della Robbia.

At three o'clock on October first, Cosimo de Medici sent his guard of honor to escort us to his house. Armed men cleared a way for us across the square of the Mercato Vecchio. Controlling my horse ( a woman who rides sidesaddle must, I believe, be a better rider than a man who is free to control the beast with his thighs), I barely glanced aside at the doctors' graphic signs, a chamberpot or a bone or a syringe to indicate a speciality; at the booths selling flax, whole woven cloth, and drugs; at the old-clothes stalls and the games of chance and the sides of pork that gave off a wholesome, disturbing odor of new-killed flesh.

The light had grown rich, and the shadows black and long. Shadow spiked every stone, alternating with grains of purest light that gave an unreal distinctness to every brick of every wall. Fans of black and ocher surmounted every arch. Feral cats moved from patch to patch of the retreating warmth, and one alleyway—the den of a family whom sixty years of blood feud had warred into nothingness—lay already bathed in blue. Blue, as well, the milk-pale ancient windows of bridges that spanned the streets from house to house.

And then the huge ugly edifice whose rusticity had seemed so princely as to send the builder into exile.

A steward and his staff met and bowed to us. We followed him upstairs, then along a corridor of columns, at whose end the steward said to Richard, "My lord, my master understands that you have already met the English ambassador. He thought, therefore, that a short private interview would spare you any unpleasantness of surprise. Please take a cup of wine with your friend, and my master will then summon you both."

"He is extremely kind," said Richard. His voice betrayed no surprise. He must, I suppose, have guessed already. The door opened on a little paneled cabinet and, standing at one window, a man who turned to greet us.

"Richard! Welcome."

"Have they ennobled you, Sir Edward?" inquired Richard with cruel lightness. "They have not me, but then they trouble little with sham embassies. Perhaps you do not know: His Grace had my brother Thomas flogged over delivering your letter. Mistress Tarleton, allow me to present our recent military governor. Sir Edward Palmer, Mistress Claire Tarleton, English secretary to this legation."

"Fluent enough to discover my dishonesty?" We had been speaking Italian. "I hope, then, I shall give her little trouble. Mistress Tarleton, your servant."

The man to whom I curtsied stood only an inch taller than myself, and might have been forty-five years old. Assessing him as a woman will, I judged his body to be good—well proportioned and strong despite his shocking smallness. And his face was handsome: square-chinned and blond, the lips full, the eyes of a deep, light, brilliant blue. At that moment his skin was scarlet. "Richard, I had not known. I left no record. Did our people at Bordeaux—?" Richard nodded. "How many masters can one obey?" demanded the English ambassador. "I forwarded it as my duty required. I am most deeply sorry. How is Thomas, and where is he?"

Richard told him; then Edward Palmer turned to me.

"Mistress Tarleton, are you the daughter of Walter Tarleton and Elisabeth du Pléssis?"

"I am, Sir Edward."

"I knew them in London long ago. Richard, after this business is finished, may I speak to you in private?"

"Yes, of course."

"Gentlemen, madame," said the steward's voice, "my lord will receive you now."

The room into which they led us had a floor intricately tiled in red and white stone, and walls half-paneled in some shining wood. Above this paneling rose sheets of malachite, its dark brilliance swirled with patterns in paler green, each five-foot panel unobtrusively jointed with gold. I saw a table set ready with chairs; and, in chairs apart, an old man in a red robe who stood to greet us and a younger one who did not rise.

"My lords, you are welcome," said Cosimo de Medici.

I watched, drawn back as my rank required, while he dealt with Sir Edward Palmer. I had chosen to wear a green gown brocaded with brown roses, and a veil, crisp and soft, wholly covered my hair. I knew I looked well, and felt Cosimo's attention glance across me without visible scrutiny.

Then it was Richard's turn. "Master Linacre, you are most welcome, but I had expected your master, my old friend. Have you any news of him?"

"Sir, no courier has reached us yet from Saint-Aurèle. From that I pray he is still alive. If Sir John Challoner has attacked the coast, they may be too busy to spare a messenger. When I have news of him I will send to you at once."

"Do so. And the lady Claire Tarleton: Come forward." I did, and made a deep curtsy.

*For seeking to rise above his estate as a private citizen*, I thought, and smiled into the shrewdest eyes in Europe. Cosimo said, "Of course I know your parents. I have sent north for a copy of your father's Bible to set beside Herr Gutenberg's in our library. Piero and I do not disdain printed books. In time the printers will stop trying to copy the scribes. You know, I think that is a mistake. And this is my son Piero."

"Please forgive me, I cannot rise." The voice had the warm confidence of power; the broad bones of his face and the size of the immobilized body made me think that, uncrippled, he might have been an athlete. "My lord my father agrees with me, mistress, that the aesthetic possibility of printed books is innate and different, and needs to be explored. I am saying it unclearly, but I think men like your father need not produce a machine imitation of the scribe's work. The type, the presentation, the binding of a machine-made book have, I feel certain, a potential excellence of their own."

"Sir, I will tell my father what you say." I curtsied again, less deeply than to Cosimo.

"Please do so," said Piero de Medici. He had bred, I knew, five children out of a beautiful and learned wife. His voice discounted without apparent effort the pain he must have been controlling at that moment—the disease that was expected to shorten his life. "We look to see your parents when next they return to Florence."

Cosimo's eyes assessed the company.

"Put your case to me today, gentlemen. We will sit here, if you please. After that I should like a few more days to consider, and then perhaps we can discuss the matter informally. As you see"—servants were moving back chairs too heavy to lift without unseemly effort; others had entered, carrying laden trays—"you need not go thirsty as we work. Very well, let us begin."

Cosimo took his place at the head of the table; servants gently rolled Piero's chair—I noticed it moved on wheels—to a position at his right. On the farther side sat Sir Edward Palmer, his two secretaries, and the translator with whom

Cosimo had supplied him; to Piero's right, Richard, another colleague, and myself.

Sir Edward Palmer began. He could employ an intelligent, workmanlike Italian, but he had, I think wisely, chosen to speak in his native tongue, relying on its lilt and on his air of composed intensity. He spoke without pathos of Queen Margaret: of her isolation, her need for support and counsel; of the danger to the nation if she could not end the war by winning it, steady her afflicted husband, and raise to manhood the son who must survive and rule before he could restore peace. For all these reasons the party of York must be put down; but to do that she needed help and, with dignity, begged for it.

Richard spoke next, without intermediary. The suffering of France, depopulation and famine, invasion justified by a manufactured claim to the French throne, had now lasted four hundred years. If Cosimo considered the instability of Queen Margaret's character, her husband's incapacity for ruling, the unlikelihood of her son's surviving to manhood; if he then compared the ability of Richard Duke of York and also of Edward his son, demonstrated in the field; if he further remembered that the Duke had been Queen Margaret's friend until her hatred had forced him to defend himself. . . .

And all the time I watched Cosimo.

Of course one had seen the pictures: the body wiry almost to emaciation; the short-clipped, monkish hair; the long ugly nose one saw also in Piero, whose line I was to suspect too in the young features of Lorenzo; the hollowness and down-drawn line of cheeks and mouth; the hands twisted between repose and temper. I had not expected the deep crimson robe. I had not expected to like him; but I did.

I thought, You are old. Who will succeed you? Against all expectation, the dying Piero? Giovanni? Lorenzo, whose minority would pose such a temptation for murder to the families who hate you? You have endowed many churches as you prepare to negotiate salvation with your Creator. And meanwhile—waiting with resignation for the death of a beloved son and colleague—you train the children in case power should fall on them too early. For Florence, like Rome, has become the shell of a republic; and your grandchildren must rule not only her—they must provide our Popes, our kings—they must beget the kings of centuries to come. Given prudence and daring—and you have both—it may be possible to compound both with God and with posterity. I wish you luck. You will need luck.

He had felt my thought, and directed to me a long, grave stare, which I met. Richard had finished and now sat, like Sir Edward, hands peacefully folded on the pages of his notes. Cosimo rose. "Gentlemen, we thank you, my son and I. Please stay to share our supper: the ladies, of course, are anxious to meet you. Mistress Claire, my grandson Lorenzo pleases his teacher, I am proud to say, with his progress on the lute. Perhaps you could play for him."

I felt myself go hot. "Oh, no, my lord, please!" Cosimo raised his brows. As a servant spared me the indignity of struggling out of my chair, the heavy thing sliding away from me, I rose. "Sir, you can command the best in Italy, which is to say the world. I will not play for you—not for shame."

"What a pity," said Piero, "when at our interval for wine I sent a man to choose the best lute the house of Salviati has in stock."

"While I," said Sir Edward Palmer," also heard the house of Salviati makes the best musical instruments in Florence. I wonder how they will deal with the same order twice."

"—To be delivered to the same lady at the same house," said Piero.

"Please," said Cosimo, "I will not embarrass you tonight, Mistress Claire. Tonight share our supper. I should like to consider your arguments for a week, then meet with you all a second time to talk informally. It may then still be several days before I give my judgment. When I have done so, we will have a party—just yourselves and my family, the children included—and you shall try your two lutes for us, Mistress Claire. We are not merciless judges." In his voice I heard a real gentleness. "Sing for us and give us pleasure; that is all."

On the way home I asked Richard, "What did Sir Edward Palmer say to you when he drew you aside?"

Richard hesitated. "He asked me whether you know you are adopted."

For a moment we jogged, the lanterns of our escort dazzling out the dark. "Did you tell him?"

Another hesitation. "Yes. I hope I did no harm."

"I do not see what harm the truth *can* do," I replied, and felt a pang of fear.

During the days we waited for the second, less formal meeting with Cosimo, I sat to Luca della Robbia in the studio where once I had knelt before him. There kissed and greeted me colleagues I remembered. Some apprentices had served their seven years' term and moved away; others Master Luca had taken into partnership; and I met four boys and one closely guarded girl who were new apprentices. I arranged myself in the simple pose required of me; Master Luca with his delicate tools, his fingers lightly crusted with clay slip, took his place before the gray mass that gradually assumed the shape of a woman's veiled head and shoulders. And on the wall behind me glowed my own young face, whose serenity would never gather laughter lines or crease like my own forehead with anger or fatigue. I feel, I thought, as though she were my daughter. Child of mine, set free into Eternity, you must last into a world where neither you nor I will have a name. I no longer envy you.

He wanted of me only that I sit, knees parted, my hands hanging down—a posture of weariness but not (to my surprise, considering the subject) one of grief. And he asked—like Jean-Marie Tavella so long ago—nothing of my face. "Claire, hold your chin level and look down at your lap—thus, with your eyes half-closed: excellent. No, no expression: just let the weight of your lower jaw drag your mouth a little open. So. Sustain it."

Thus I sat, a living statue, passive as he studied me. In the intervals wine was brought; and then the friends who had heard of my return came to embrace me and to gossip. I introduced Richard to them all, and he enjoyed them with an unaffected delight. I had never before been able to offer him so real a gift as the company of Alessio Baldovinetti; of Benozzo Gozzoli; of Paolo Uccello, Piero della Francesca, Domenico Veneziano, and the great Donatello, come home to spend his last years in Florence. Once or twice also there visited us the humanist scholar Marsilio Ficino, tutor to the child Lorenzo, who was, he informed me, progressing excellently with Ovid.

All these came to greet me; to embrace me; to talk of my parents, of shared memories, of Andrea whom we had lost. But when Luca worked and I went back to my strange expressionless pose I lost my shyness; for all conversation ceased into the compassionate silence of those who understood my work.

They welcomed Richard for his own sake. Only once, when Sandro Botticelli said to me something ribald, did I catch between them an instant that almost shook my dolorous composure. Merely a masculine glance, too explicit to require words, accompanied on Richard's part by a small, crisp salute. Sandro moved away from me.

Six days passed before we went for the second time to the Palazzo Medici. This time our party proved smaller: Cosimo and Piero, alone, received the two ambassadors and me in a room of which I had heard talk in the city. Glancing around me at the marble shelves, at the thin drawers five feet long and at the cupboards enticingly closed, I could see why, and longed to touch the precious things displayed about me. I remember Piero's saying "Sir Edward, would you like the service of an interpreter? We have, of course, no objection."

"I think my Italian will suffice me, sir. Perhaps Master Linacre or Mistress Claire will help if I find myself in difficulty."

"I'll help, of course," said Richard, grinning. "But I wouldn't count on Claire. Not here."

I sat and listened as the men talked of Queen Margaret's eight-years-delayed childbirth, of the baby's health and rumored paternity, of the remissions in King Henry's madness, of the Battle of Saint Albans. They passed to England's inability or unwillingness to control such brigands as John Challoner, to the new taxes levied by King Charles, and to the rebuilding of Saint-Aurèle, in which Palmer took a warm interest. "Remember who hired you," he said to Richard.

"You did. His Grace has reinstated me after my travels in Italy, and I will, I promise, take up the work again when I get home." *Travels in Italy.* That elided a year of his life. The silence delicately acknowledged an omission.

Then Cosimo said, "Mistress Claire, I cannot endure your fidgeting any longer." I blushed and laughed. "Go touch them. They are there to be touched, at least by my friends."

Some people reverence saints' corpses and slivers of bone and True Crosses of dubious, though Roman, origin. Perhaps, by the precedent of reverence alone, relics are indeed holy, even the false ones. But the things I now touched had been truly hallowed by that desert of oblivion to which the centuries destine each one of us. A red-and-black vase some boy ages ago had won in a foot-race at Olympia. A statue of the Muse Plymnia posed as a girl leaning on a wall, her body wound in a robe so fragile, so delicately creased that stone seemed to pleat like gauze. A double-handled wine vessel of silver so ancient and so polished that its brightness shocked the senses. A brown-and-gold agate bowl that had belonged to Octavia, the wife of Mark Antony. And last a wreath of strawberry leaves—a crown of leaf and blossom in beaten foil, its gold sprays shivering as I touched them.

"It came," said Cosimo softly, "from the tomb of Alexander."

Because tears were streaming down my face, I did not turn to him. "Conquerors, sir, are God's vengeance on us. I hate them."

"They vanish," said the gentle voice, which was also that of a cruel and shrewd old man; a lover of women also, and a judge of human souls. "Do you know the epigram on the death of Heraclitus? *Death destroys all things; but these he cannot destroy.*" His hand, swarthy and knotted as a laborer's, softly touched the wreath. "Alexander lies beaten into dust. But what life would you have us live? God wakens us here, to use the gifts and the love and the hatred that are in us; and so we learn to know our own souls. What can we be but what we are? He was not wrong to use his genius, although it hurt so many."

"Any conqueror is a monster." The strawberry leaves trembled as I withdrew my hand.

"Perhaps," said Cosimo. "But Redemption, subsisting in Eternity, reaches backward in Time as well as forward; for how could Time contain it?"

"Father, enough," said Piero.

I heard Cosimo turn away; and when I faced them again, saw Sir Edward Palmer's look of intelligent speculation remove itself, with courtesy, from my face. Piero's eyes lingered a moment longer, with an expression of friendship.

"My lord, we should go." Richard rose.

Cosimo nodded. "Come to me in another week. Then I will be able to tell you whether my House can grant this loan. And whatever my decision, I expect you to honor us on that night at a family gathering."

Five of the seven days had passed, and I was sitting reading in the solar, when a maid came up to ask me if I would receive Sir Edward Palmer.

# 17

His robe was blue, severe but made of excellent cloth; he wore a cap, which he swept off as he entered the room. I wondered with a pang of sympathy at what age he had had to accept his height. An abnormal smallness of stature makes some men bellicose; but it had been my experience that more seem to build upon it, as if in compensation, intense energy and charm. I remembered when I was ten, and such things held mystery as well as fascination, my nurse's remarking that small men are extremely virile. "Sir Edward, good morning. May I call for wine?"

"Please, Mistress Tarleton: white and dry, if possible. I should prefer water, but—" He grimaced, and took the chair opposite my settle by the fire.

I nodded. "I know. We boil ours when we must use it for cooking—distill *and* boil it, then flavor it with limes and lemons. My mother taught me the latter trick, but I suppose small ale is really best. Alcohol seems to cleanse water most effectively."

"So one finds by experience. In England—you would not know—we brew a very weak beer even for the children. It is safer than water." He laid his cap beside him and crossed his legs. No intensity here, only good looks and a grave, relaxed charm. "Odd: I somehow should not have expected Elisabeth Tarleton's daughter to be learned in stillroom skills."

"Then you do not know my mother very well. Or," I said, "my father?"

Sir Edward shook his head and accepted, with thanks, a red glass goblet from a tray. I also took one; I might want something to occupy my hands. "No, they were acquaintances only, not friends. Mistress Tarleton, I have something to offer you. It involves, so far as I know, no price, but I offer it with hesitation. Unless you return to England and search out your antecedents, which I should not advise, I am perhaps the only man you will ever meet who has known *all* your parents: the Carvers and the Tarletons."

A sting of pain informed me I had bitten my lower lip. "You knew Anne and David Carver? In what capacity?"

"I knew David: again, only slightly. I once employed him."

He did not hurry the silence, but sipped his wine and watched me. I remembered Richard's telling me that Palmer was a hero—some action fought outside Valenciennes, and another defending the Pale around Calais to which, with Boulogne and Guines, we had reduced the Plantagenet empire in France.

*We.*

"What is it?" said Sir Edward softly.

"I was remembering what Richard has told me of your service in war." He nodded, without blushing as Richard would have done. "I thought of the French, and found myself saying *we*—counting myself one of them."

"Why not? It is happening to the family Linacre. Poor Thomas; I'm damned sorry about that, Mistress Claire. Perhaps, if I owe your father's daughter any service, I am seeking to help Thomas through you. Forgive me if it is so."

"Readily. Tell me, what does Queen Margaret look like? I've seen a picture that made her appear like a German madonna, flaxen and bland."

Apparently he recognized the change of subject for the brake it was. "Then the chronicler had not seen her. Her Grace is dark, with brown eyes and good but uneven teeth. She has a snub nose, a low-pitched voice, and a laugh that fascinates. Women dislike her; many men are powerfully attracted."

"And you?"

"I," said Sir Edward, "am not attracted."

"Have you a wife, sir? And children?"

"A wife, Jane—my second—two daughters, and three boys."

"Why," I said, "should you owe David Carver a debt?"

The handsome face with its bright, subtle eyes considered me. "Understand, Mistress Claire, I did not know him well. When the plague struck I took my family north to our estate, as far as possible from London and from those who fled the city, carrying pestilence with them."

"And your family—?"

"Survived. Please understand, Mistress: *I did not know.* And when I returned and learned . . . Are you aware—?"

"How I starved in the house? Yes."

"Who told you?"

"Walter, after twenty years of hesitation."

"Why did he take so long?"

"I was incapable of speech when my parents found me. This much Elisabeth told me when I was about nine. Whatever that house hides, I chose at that moment to forget it. My parents did not insist. I think, indeed, they felt relieved."

Sir Edward frowned. "What I have to say may cause you some distress. By the time I learned roundabout what had happened to David and Anne and you, it was too late to help: the Tarletons had adopted you and taken you abroad."

I sipped the wine, glad of its dry coolness, though the glass was growing hot between my palms. "Sir Edward, if you had been informed—that my parents were dead in the house, and that I lay abandoned, waiting to die—knowing that you risked almost certain death—would you have come to help me?"

With absolute steadiness he replied, "No, Mistress Claire."

"And," I whispered, "do you happen to know the name under which I was baptized?"

"Yes. It was Anne, like your mother."

"Anne," I said softly. "Anne. Anne-Claire."

Again he seemed to wait, plumbing the silence. And when at last he spoke, it was to divine the single correct question. "Do you remember being called by the name?"

"Yes." Until he spoke it I had not known the shape of a certain emptiness. "Thank you. Yes. I was Anne."

I had begun to shake. Seeing it, he crossed quickly to the settle and took me by the shoulders. "Oh, my dear. Hush, be still." Hands, expert and hard, gripped me until the shuddering stilled; but he did not move away from my side. Gently he said, "Your father was a painter, did you know?"

"Walter told me. A portraitist at Court." With courtesy I moved away from him a few inches.

He nodded. "When my first wife Dorothy was nursing our son, I commissioned him to paint this." From inside his shirt he pulled a large square locket and, unclasping its silver case, laid it in my palm.

A lady drawn in the fashion of early in the century: her hairline plucked, her white pointed face stylized to the kind of prettiness one sees in illuminated manuscripts. Orange-blonde hair; arched brows, also plucked; a long nose and little red mouth; heavy-lidded eyes of an undeterminable color. The lady Dorothy Palmer had been pretty, but I doubted I should have recognized the living woman from this portrait. Behind her curled the fronds of a tree with red and gold leaves, and, above her head, the stork that symbolizes fertility. And, because she was nursing her first child, she had unlaced her bodice, which fell in a crisp V of black fabric and white laces. Through the age-cracked paint I saw, tears in my eyes, the fresh young whiteness of her breasts.

"She's pretty," I said.

"She was." Sir Edward nodded. "The boy is twenty-five now."

"I'm glad. What did he look like, my father? Do you remember?"

"Actually you put me in mind of him: your coloring, and he was slight, like you. Your eyes are his, your brows different, I think. He had a widow's peak. An agile, quick-tempered man."

"And a failure," I said. "Forgive me. I know you treasure this, but he was not a very good painter."

"Never mind." The locket clicked shut. "This, Mistress Claire, is for you. You have nothing else of him. Here: take it."

"But . . ." I let him press it into my hands, then sat for a long time thinking. At last I said, "Sir Edward, I thank you. But all I need of my father—all I can truly have of him—is the flesh he begot and whatever of my character depends on it. I will not accept this. I suspect you have no other portrait of Dorothy."

"The young do not expect death," he said with serenity. "They do not prepare against it; and how dreary if they did, instead of living, which is their business. No, I have no other."

"I will accept that lute and play it for you. Keep the portrait." I kissed his cheek.

Recognizing it for dismissal, he rose. "Mistress Claire, if what I have told you causes you any distress—if a friend can help—I still presume to consider myself your father's proxy."

"I will remember. Good day, Sir Edward."

In the vestibule he met Richard, just come in smiling from some parting with a friend. Richard started forward, his hand outstretched. "Sir Edward! How can I serve you?"

"I have been calling on Claire," replied the English ambassador. "I have misjudged something—I fear seriously. Have you a moment, Richard? I think you had better know what I just said to Claire Tarleton."

That evening at supper I dealt cheerfully with Richard and our colleagues. In the solar also, chatting or reading until ten o'clock, I felt well and found them pleasant company. But on Richard had settled that quality of waiting that neither sought communication nor invited it. He did not watch me, and spoke to me seldom. At ten o'clock I excused myself and, carrying my chamber candle, lit myself to my room where my bath waited by the fire.

Later, swathed in velvet, with my hair drying combed before the fire, I watched as my woman and a manservant emptied and removed the tub. I thanked them and wished them good night.

Most of our friends had now retired. I glanced into the corridor, whose tiles were too cold to tempt my feet, and saw a line of light beneath Richard's door. Bright light: I guessed, correctly, that he was writing letters, and closed my own door.

He heard the sound. He had stripped to shirt and hose and put on a loose, sleeveless robe. The letters were genuine enough. The heavily spiced wine he had ordered was intended to keep him awake till four o'clock.

I cleansed my mouth and wandered back to sit before the fire. Only one day remained before our final meeting with Cosimo. Between then and now we had no engagements.

The first sounds began at one o'clock. Richard, who had been waiting for them, sanded a letter and slid his stool noiselessly back into its place. His slippers made no sound as he moved to my door, beneath which firelight still showed, and laid his ear against the wood. Then, running, he moved three doors down and waked Gilbert. "Gilbert, Mistress Claire is in difficulty, as the Mother Abbess warned us might happen. Wake quietly the man next door and also the one a wall away from Claire's bedroom. Make some plea of sickness, urgent but not desperate on Claire's part, and move them to the unused bedchambers. Tell them she will be perfectly well when I have dealt with the matter. I want the corridor emptied and a pikeman at either end; and I want no noise."

"At once, sir." Gilbert rolled out of bed, snatching his daygown. In five minutes Richard would have with me the best seclusion of all—that of public acknowledgment.

Then, ignoring the figures that moved behind him in the cold of the corridor, he returned to my door and tried the lock. "Claire, it is Richard. Unbolt the door, or Gilbert and I will break it down."

The sounds stopped. After a moment he heard the bolt slip, and I opened to him.

He entered and slid the bolt to, and said quietly, "I heard you cry out."

"Why have you come?" My voice came thick against the pangs that wrung my torso and threatened to master my speech. "To witness this?"

"Sometimes it is best," said Richard, "not to be alone."

He went to the bed and sat there—relaxed, alert. And I, because the childbirth in me was an anguish to be cherished in dignity, found my way to a chair that faced the fire. I think I clutched my belly as I went. Seeing this, Richard stirred sharply, considered me, subsided.

The chair, boards and straw-stuffed cushion, creaked as I settled in it. My fingers gripped its arms; I laid my head back. I remember hearing my own shallow sigh; and then for a long time the complexities of silence—sifting of ash in the grate; the rustling collapse of embers; stirrings from the bed, though these came seldom, and I felt his attention like a solid presence behind me.

A group of young men, straggling homeward, called to each other in the street below, their drunken voices fading into the night. A dog barked. Both these sounds had to me (I remember) a quality of sadness. Like voices from another century, I thought, and leaned forward. The embers blooming incandescent looked almost soft—gently crumbling cubes of gold and coral, so feathery I could have pushed them with my fingertip.

Without a sound they fried, rustled, simmered—drew me nearer, drew me deep: became gigantic, till gold and coral spun into beads of light.

But the light was starlight now. Those who boarded up the front door had gone away hours ago, but they had not noticed the open shutter through which the light now streamed. It fell like blue-white fire across flagstones grown cold as river ice. For a long time I watched the starlight. I had dragged my special blanket around my shoulders, and put my thumb in my mouth to stop the shuddering. With my other hand I caressed the soft length of ribbon my mother had sewn to the blanket's hem.

I was very thirsty, but my sucking brought some saliva. It was many hours since I had moved from the flagstone I had chosen out as safe. Long ago, I did not know how long, I had been sitting on this flagstone playing a game with my doll, on a summer day while my mother and my aunt had baked the bread. Therefore it was this exact place on the floor I chose. From here, if I willed it hard enough, I might see sunlight fold out of the air—might smell the yeast in the warm dough and hear the voices of the women. I will make it be, I thought, thumb in my mouth, and did not glance at the sprawled darkness where my father lay.

It was very quiet. My hunger pangs had died; but boredom, exhausted and alert, tricked me into listening to the silence. It lay thick—depth upon depth. I began to whimper with fear of dark and silence.

At first I had seen phantoms: a man with ruby eyes, his head crowned with the horns of a bull, had seemed to stand in the shadows; and the shape that had sprung up and vanished near the roof had a lion's body and an eagle's wings. For a while too a woman had sung in the darkness, though I could not distinguish her words; and for an instant I had heard a baby crying. These things had interested me, but it was some time since they had stopped.

The starlight was beautiful. I sat cowled in my blanket and watched it flow like blue glass across the stones, and my nostrils caught, from somewhere in the shadows, a faint sweet fetor that all my senses knew.

I listened passively, my eyes alert, to the first drunken singing. Ragged with laughter, it drifted up the street—men's singing. Suddenly understanding, I lurched toward it with a cry. But the window was too high for me. The voices faded.

I cried out again, collapsing to my knees; and my baby proportions, the belly and short legs, assumed their ancient attitude of comfort. I lay in a fetal posture on the stones and cried with a barking animal anguish I have never heard in any other human mouth.

I began to crawl along the floor, toward the bed where my mother lay. Her right hand hung down, its knuckles folded against the floor; I did not touch it. I hauled myself up and laid my head against her breast, and her hair was soft although her breast was cold. I laid my cheek against her skin.

And thus, crooning and dozing, I heard a sound. It was very brief and was immediately subsumed, as I shall tell, by something else; and I cannot describe it exactly. It was as if someone had opened the door—I heard the crisp, sharp *click*—to let in the winter wind. Wind howled and moaned with voices that resembled human sounds; then another *click* sealed the wind away, and, still dozing—traveling vertically—I sank downward into soft black dark. Through the flags (I smelled their stone-damp fragrance); through earth—I felt its grainy moisture: noted, as I slipped past them, pebbles and the leached curve of an old bone. Another layer and water trickled, redolent of earth; and then it was sun.

White sun that dazzled me, and the working of the executioners' hands. The smell was blood, its intimation of the body's contents a shock against the senses. Someone had lost a great deal of blood. I turned my head; felt blood-slimed hair against my cheek; saw blood on the grain of new-sawn birch planks. Sun glittered in the grain, and I thought there must be mica crystals in the wood to make it sparkle so. The blood, spread thin, shone with an oily sheen, but the gathered drops trembled like rubies in the sun dazzle.

How beautiful the world was. I could no longer speak. What the executioners' knives had taken of me I may name before the Judgment seat, but I cannot speak it here. I felt great love for my flesh, the naked legs and the little hands, and the hair of which I had been proud. Intimate as giant gods the men's faces shone over me, passing in and out of the sun. Perhaps they had severed the nerves; or perhaps pain had become complete extremity, all sensation lost in the soul's astonishment of presence. It had been going on for a very long time. *I am beautiful and good: touch me kindly. That God shall be all in all. For what do the Elect over the dead, if the dead rise not at all?*

I had begun to sing—they could not hear me—and singing, rose into the sun, into the white dazzle. The sun blazed at me with a low billowing humming sound. I squinted at it; beads of sweat blinded my eyes. *That God be all in all.* Singing, I denied them, escaped them. One with the sunlight, I shone upon them; and the sun went on and on.

"Child?"

I screamed. But the voice was the gentle voice of Walter Tarleton bending over me. "Child, can you understand me?" And jarring through it Richard Linacre's cry: "Claire! *Claire!*"

Time collapsed. I screamed again, and found myself lying limp between Richard's hands. His eyes, blazing with shock, stared into mine. With great gentleness he laid me down on the floor and said, "When was it? And where?"

"I do not know," I whispered. "The boards were new-cut, and the sun shone hot."

"It must," he said softly, "have been a summer's day."

Because I could not move I lay there, staring at the ceiling. What could not be, ceased to be—depth after depth sealing shut within me, as my mind reached avidly for the light and for my weak, but whole and living body. Richard did not move. Then he crossed himself and, slipping an arm beneath my shoulders, dragged me into a sitting posture. "Let it go, Claire. You are with me. It was over long ago."

I nodded, my head lolling slightly. He brushed my hair away from my brow. Then he carried me to the bed, where I lay in the passivity of exhaustion. Before he moved away he leaned over me and kissed my cheek, and said—threading, as they came to him, beloved words we both knew: "Consider and hear me, O Lord my God: Lighten mine eyes, that I sleep not in death. From my youth up, Thy terrors have I suffered with a troubled mind. Thou hast proved and visited mine heart in the night season; Thou hast tried me, and shalt find no weakness in me. Therefore I will lay me down in peace and take my rest; for it is Thou Lord only that makest me dwell in safety. For with Thee is the well of life; and in Thy light shall we see light."

He left me. The embers had faded. Their light now pulsated coral and orange within cubes of ash. From the other side of the room came sounds of preparation. One log scraped across another: he was building up the fire.

He found the linen closet; set wine to heat, and water in another pot; found clean warm towels. "Come now," said his voice. I did not resist as he lifted me and laid me on a towel, then stripped off my single garment. "I am going to wash you. Lie still."

I lay luxuriating in the skill of his hands—a skill whose gentleness precluded all insult, as it precluded shame. A warm sponge, not too wet, cleaned my face of tears and sweat, then glided over my shoulders, armpits, and breasts. "Open your thighs," said his voice. I obeyed lazily. The sponge cleansed me, then moved down my thighs to the hot soles of my feet. "And now turn over."

I did, flipped with a competence so gentle it did not jar even my exhausted nerves. He brushed my hair aside and cleansed the nape of my neck; then shoulders, buttocks, legs, and folded arms. At last a towel, briskly used, left me to feel the prickles of damp on my skin as I dried; and, shawling me in another towel, he put a cup of wine into my hand. "Drink this, you need it."

The liquor was hot. He had set another cup for himself, I saw, on the hob. And as I watched he went to the second basin of water he had heated and began to take off his clothes.

Without shame, without hurry he stripped off every garment that the sweat of the last two hours had soiled, and began to prepare himself for my bed. From time to time he bent to drink the hot wine; for the rest he stayed turned toward the fire, and I watched its shadows mold the proportions of his shoulders and back, the beautiful functional tension of buttocks and legs.

He washed, and at one point hunkered down to investigate the pot of rinse water heating over the fire. It displeased him. I saw him shrug and, stretching, place another log on the flames. I studied the beauty of proportion where his shoulders rose to the muscular neck, and wondered at the degree of confidence that could reveal him to me in a posture so lacking in vanity. Then he straightened, moving relaxedly, and rinsed and dried. From time to time the firelight exposed, by some chance motion, the burden of the scrotum between his legs.

I set the wine cup softly down and slid out of the towel into the bedclothes. Richard cleansed his mouth with myrrh and water, and came to me.

He was, I saw, half ready for it. Beside me I heard him groan; and softly he laughed. "I should court you, Claire, but I've been courting you these four years. Do you mind if I teach you a workmanlike lesson?" By now—his body warmer than mine, and sweet of skin and breath—he was over me, sparing me his weight.

Then an embrace of arms and thighs, as tender as it was competent, lifted my pelvis; and with a single motion he entered me to the depths of my body.

I cried out, with surprise, not with pain. Gently he stopped my mouth; then he lay still, letting me feel the pressure that distended me. And then he began to move, firmly and with care.

It lasted longer than I had expected. At last he cried out, and filled me with a thick, hot liquid whose separate pulses I could feel.

For a long time we lay in a fatigue so healing it consumed the horror that had led to it, as the fire, cherry-red, was consuming from inside the still-subsisting structure of the log. Then he drew away, and gently touched, and tasted with his tongue, the blood that covered my thighs; and cleaned me with a cloth he burned.

After that there seemed no hurry. Presently he began to explore my breasts. "By God," he said softly, "I'll work to fill you with a child." And this time he dealt with me so tenderly I only felt the pulsing at the end.

Much later I said, "Richard, would you take me to Fiesole today?"

"To Fiesole?" He leaned over me, smoothing back my hair. "Of course. Why?"

"It would pass the day, and spare us gossip, at least a little. And I want suddenly to see Florence from the outside," I said, "I think, in a way to say farewell." For tiny among the crowds of a distant Florence there might by some magic linger the girl that I had been, going on to the future I had longed for. I must salute her before I turned away.

# 18

Last night had brought the first hard frost, and with it the end of plague. Now, outside the windows of the malachite room, autumn rain was hurling chestnut leaves that stuck against the panes. Wind had begun to strip the yellow trees. Our journey homeward, I thought, would be difficult and slow.

For today we had gathered to hear Cosimo's judgment. For this occasion the two entire legations stood ranked before Cosimo and Piero, as candlelight shone like oil in the green stone panels.

My eyes lowered, I stood well back from Richard. It embarrassed me, necessary though the costume was, to stand here dressed for the family feast Cosimo had promised, in dark orange velvet with a shimmering stripe of gold. Officially—except in the bright, speculative glances of our household—I was a virgin still, and I had allowed myself the luxury of wearing my hair brushed loose. Along each cheek fell a braid twined with river pearls—the gems that I had as a little girl called "bitten pearls" because they looked like a child's milk teeth. No jeweler would deal in such trifles, so I did not know by what enterprise Richard had produced for me, on our return from Fiesole, a necklace—three ropes of braided river pearls, each misshapen jewel a delicate shining pink. He had had no time. Whom had he commissioned, and at what price in gossip? As I thanked him, not daring to kiss him because I was shy, I met the smile, triumphant in its tenderness, that he must not let touch his mouth.

I felt him resist the pull to turn to me. But Cosimo had finished his first courtesies. The room stilled; a gust drove against the glass; and Piero, unable to rise, signaled alert respect throughout his unmoving body.

"My lords," said Cosimo de Medici, " I have heard you, and have taken counsel with my dear son and with such wisdom as I have. We have for many years assisted the kings of France. We have heard the arguments of Queen Margaret's representative; but I regret that, as a man of affairs, I must require a reasonable certainty of recovering my loan. Her Grace's courage alone is not sufficient surety. With her husband sick, her son ungrown, her realm unstable, her enemies so remarkable for their ability, and herself so ill advised, she would benefit by this loan far more than would my House. Yes, she can make war; but she may not win. And if the Crown of England defaults on its debt, I deprive my sons and grandsons of the patrimony I have built for them."

And as an autumn wind crisps the grass stalks with a delicate rustle, so I felt a sparkle of motion pass over the company: I heard the catching and cautious release of our collective breath. Richard shivered and straightened. So delicately, in such silence does the inception of an event go forth to the millions it will influence: go forward into the future, into lives unborn. Cosimo waited, gathering that silence into his hands. Piero, his hands linked, bowed his head; and so brazen a posture of humility almost mocked us with the answer his father had not spoken. Cosimo has decided to finance the Duke of York, I thought. Here in this room, however many years it may take to ratify the choice, we declare Henry of Lancaster a dead man. The Medici have chosen a new king for England.

Cosimo stirred; the instant snapped. "Sir Edward, the prince who drags his nation into civil war may lack the stability to rule it afterward. And England will not, in any case, forgive this French queen. On the night before the Battle of Actium, the troops of Mark Antony heard ghostly pipes and drums withdrawing into the distance. As a Christian man I cannot endorse the ancient opinion, that the god Mars deserted Antony at that moment. But Antony was a brave, impetuous, unstable man; and what god upholds such a general?" Sir Edward's face was flushed, but his courtesy seemed otherwise impeccable, and Cosimo's eyes, considering him, appeared innocent of mockery. "Remember that Caesar begot a son on the Egyptian queen. The boy's name was Caesarion, and although he was young his birth was most noble, and his character ambitious. And when Augustus had destroyed the other rebels—Cleopatra and Antony chief among them—he thought it best to kill this child."

Piero's face suddenly resembled, in its preoccupation, the bust of him that stood in his father's study. Cosimo spread his hands. "Sir Edward, England is little; France is great. I deal with the great who can pay me; I do not deal in courage and poverty. Let Queen Margaret drag her mad king from hill fort to hill fort as Richard of York pursues them. I pity her. But I am a banker, guilty already of the sin of usury. That guilt I have accepted. I will not help England to chaos." He turned to us all. "And now I have a meal prepared, and gifts for everyone, and two lutes for Mistress Claire, and five grandchildren, of whom I admit I am very proud. Let us not keep them waiting any longer."

The room to which they brought us had a floor of warm parquet, walls paneled in sheets of different-colored marbles, and a gold ceiling raised and bossed. Here a table stood ready, and stools and cushions lay scattered about the floor; and Madonna Lucrezia, Piero's wife whom I had already met, came forward to greet us. Her mother-in-law was feeling the weather, she said. Did my mother not know some remedies? And so, chatting about aching joints, I was drawn toward the children. Behind me I heard, with a shock of relief, Richard say something, and Sir Edward Palmer laugh.

Well, Sandro has drawn them all, and anyone can see the picture: the *Madonna of the Magnificat*. Admittedly the painting dates from three years later, when there existed a fat baby grandson to crush beneath his fist the pomegranate, symbol of Pride. Nannina and Bianca suspend a crown above the head of their pretty mother, who looks like herself and yet, oddly, like every other Madonna or Venus Sandro has ever drawn. I can attest the richly curving face was real, the plucked brows and red, sweet mouth, and the braids of heavy hair. And above the boys—her hair tangled, her face exquisitely young—bends Maria, most beautiful of the girls.

But the boys, I think, are badly drawn—absorbed in concord as Giuliano offers the book and Lorenzo the ink pot in which their mother dips her pen to write *Magnificat*: two perfect brothers.

Not that either boy was unpleasant in actuality. Giuliano at seven was the more beautiful, his red-blond hair already darkening, his bones as strong as his father's beneath the immature flesh, and his hard stare innocent of offense. But Lorenzo's voice was too deep for a boy of nine; and he had the dark skin Italians disprize, a flat shallow nose, and brilliant intelligent eyes. In some children one can see, reduced to an appearance of childishness for a few years, a soul already adult. And this, I thought, was true of Lorenzo and Giuliano.

The chaplain said Grace. We washed our hands; and it pleased me, as we settled at table, to see that the fingers dipping into the bowl we shared belonged to Sir Edward Palmer. The knife with which I diced my meat, the more neatly to roll each morsel in a fragment of bread, was not, thank God, made of gold; the platter was. As I sliced I said, "Sir Edward, I am sorry."

"Are you?" His hands, disposing deftly of food, appeared to engage his whole attention. "Why? You cannot, surely, feel like an Englishwoman."

"I don't. My family has been my country, I suppose." He nodded. "I don't know whether I shall ever feel like a native of any place. Florence is dear to me, but—but homes change."

"For some of us they do. Some of us are rooted; some seek a home. A very few seem happiest always to drift, never affiliating themselves. Will you have some of this?" I shook my head and let the boat-shaped object of parcel gilt pass down to someone who wanted it. "It seems to me, from what little I know of you, that Elisabeth and Walter created a country that was a condition of the spirit. A self-sustaining strength, but in some ways a lonely one. Does no place draw you? Normandy? The sea?"

"The sea, to my surprise," I said. "But the sea puts us in mind of our destination, and will eventually carry us there."

He had stopped eating. "How sad a thought for so young a woman," he said at last with light gentleness.

"Why?" At his nod of acceptance I handed him a dish of relish, noting with regret that the spoon to serve it with was gold. "Why does every—"

"Old person," he suggested.

"—Grown person imagine the young are happy and blind? I have," I said softly, "always lived on the shore, poised to go. Normandy has taught me to know it: that is all."

"Then I make a prediction. Life will hold you as the stone gripped Arthur's sword, which no man could withdraw before its time."

"Do you like beautiful nuns?" I inquired.

"Why? Can you offer me one?"

"If you dare to visit your fief again." He grinned. "Mère Agnès of Sainte-Bertrande would agree with you. I have found life holds us hard."

"Of course I know of Mère Agnès, but, having had no

occasion to invade her, have not encountered her. If she taught you that, I should like to meet her. As for revisiting Saint-Aurèle, I think I left there as good a reputation as a military governor can, but I do not expect a civic banquet. And," he added with sobriety, "there is always the man hurt whom one does not know about, and the arrow in the night. It was war we were making, Mistress Claire. They do not love me in Saint-Aurèle, but I left them no atrocity to remember: none that I saw and could prevent. I should like to know you better."

"How, if you go back to England? Will Queen Margaret harm you?"

"No, she is not that unjust. However, I think I may remove my family from England, and Florence attracts me. If I bring Jenny and the children, shall I find you here from time to time?"

Someone offered me warm water cut with lemon juice; I used it and the proffered towel. "I believe so. I belong to no one, Sir Edward, and I do not know what forms my life will find hereafter. I have no work after Florence, and my home is with my parents, or with the nuns at Sainte-Bertrande."

"Or with Richard Linacre."

"He has not asked me." Richard sensed, though he could not have heard, our speaking of his name; grave and startled, he looked up at me.

Sir Edward continued, "I'm sorry. Since I have been grossly impolite, I will go on blundering until I have said what I think you need to hear. I never yet knew Richard to dishonor a love, or to give it less form of courtesy than was its due. Many men take and walk away; he will not. When he asks you, accept. Yes, he will bind you to a future you cannot see. But I tell you it is there: I can feel its shape, if you cannot. What happened that night after I left you?"

I accepted a goblet of dessert wine. "A time may come when

I remember them as a living couple. But until I can imagine them *living*, I want not to talk of them again."

"I will remember," replied Sir Edward. And that confidence, I knew and he knew, Richard would never share with anyone.

The last platters were disappearing, sweet wine, custards, and marzipan fruits replacing them. Cosimo rose and clapped his hands for quiet. "Our friends have traveled far; each deserves our thanks. We have a gift for each."

I heard friendly laughter and a scraping-back of benches as the parcels, every one wrapped in silver cloth with ribbons of red velvet, were brought in. Sir Edward unwrapped an illuminated book. For Richard there was a sword of Damascus steel. As he slid it from its sheath, I glimpsed the watered shine of its blade, which proclaimed an Arab swordsmith had cold-hammered it fold upon fold, calling down the Grace of God upon each blow.

For me, so far, there had been nothing. "But Mistress Claire's gift is so large," said Cosimo, "that we must ask her to rise and sit there." He pointed to a cushioned stool set in isolation. "Surely my grandchildren will keep her company."

Maria, who seemed to like me, was already rising, bringing with her Nannina and Lorenzo. In the babble of speculation—some of it gently ribald—I caught, for the last time, Sir Edward Palmer's gaze. "Claire," he said softly. "Look around you. Others too have labored. Others too love honor, kindness, perseverance. Christ redeemed both man and woman. Do not thrust us away. If you will not trust us, we cannot help you."

I stared at him. Then the girls in their plain, rich gowns were around me, bearing me in convoy to the seat where the whole room could watch me. There, laughing, they spread their skirts on cushions at my feet, dragging their little brothers with them.

"She shall not know which is the giver," declared Piero. "She must judge each without prejudice."

They had not wrapped either one, but each came laid on a

cushion of blue velvet, and each was a jewel of its kind. The makers had not hollowed either out of the solid wood, as used to be the fashion; instead they had made each lute the new way, bubble-light from strips of wood. From the short neck and sharply angled frets there swelled a body that resembled a sliced pear, as weightless almost as the parchment rose set beneath the strings. One instrument was dark, with pale jewels inset around a rosette of carved balsa wood. The other—alternate stripes of pale and dark, its neck chequered with dicing in ivory and jet—had beneath its strings a parchment flower as intricate as a snowflake seen through an alchemist's lens.

Laughing, my face (I knew) carnation color with excitement and embarrassment, I tuned each instrument, listening to the tone. Their difference was exquisite and subtle, like the wine from grapes pressed in August and ice wine from grapes of the same hillside pressed after the first frost. Now I had them tuned.

"You must sing something," said Giuliano.

I cleared my throat; looked vague, since I knew the sort of refinement they would expect; then grinned at Giuliano and, striking a hard chord, silenced the room with the bright virile dance-tune children love:

*Pase l'agua, O Giulietta, l'agua—*
*Pase l'agua, vénitez-vous à moy!*

**Cross the water, Juliet, come to me!**

It went on and on, the children beating time, the adults singing; and when I finished I saw that even those—Richard among them—who had remained at the table rather than gathering round us had turned to watch me.

The panes had darkened. Servants bringing candles lingered to listen. Then, pitching my voice as Elisabeth had taught me,

to master and to hold them, I gave them what they did expect:
Dufay and Binchois, the great Burgundians:

> *Pastourelle en un vergier*
> *ouï complaindre et gémir.*
> *Disant, las! en quel danger*
> *me fait Amour maintenir.*
> *Plus ne veux ainsi languir:*
> *je me rends du tout à luy.*
> *Au besoin voit-on l'amy.*

Alas, how love endangers me: I will no longer suffer so: I will surrender to him utterly.

Richard sat leaning forward, his face as beautiful as every human face when one surprises it in perfect self-oblivion. I said into the stillness, "My lords and ladies, do you remember Francesco Landini? He was born in Florence a hundred years ago. A blind man, but the greatest musician of this city in his time. Perhaps you have seen his tombstone, where those who loved him wrote this for us who live after: 'Francesco, born blind, but skilled in music, whom Music has exalted above all others, has left his ashes here: his soul, beyond the stars.'"

And so I sang them *Giunta vaga bilta*, *De dinmi tu*, and *La bionda treccia*—songs they loved no less because they had known them all their lives. Around me the children sat still, in their eyes that mixture of alertness and reserve that so strangely resembles the innocent, cruel hauteur of an animal. Intelligent children, breathing with the music.

> *J'ai pris Amour à ma devise*
> *pour conquérir joyeuseté.*
> *Heureux seray en cet été*
> *si puis venir à mon emprise.*

I said, "Both lutes are exquisite. I will be greedy and keep them both."

Cosimo smiled. "Of course."

"This is the last," I said.

> *Très doux amy, tout ce que promis t'ay*
> *est tout certain, ne t'en iray faillant.*
> *Mais sans fusser entièrement tendray,*
> *très doux amy, tout ce que promis t'ay.*

> Dear friend, all that I promised you
> is firm, I will not fail you.
> I will honor every promise,
> gentle lover, that I made you.

Palmer was too kind and too adroit to register expression, though I felt his alertness focused on us both. Nor did Richard turn to me; but his averted face had gone a deep brick-red.

That night he came to my bed again.

The great atelier was empty and filled with cool gray autumn sunlight when Master Luca led Richard and me toward the finished statue beneath its shroud of sacking.

"Stop." We were ten feet away from the life-size presence: a woman's body from the upper breasts, the dimensions reproducing a sight more foreign to me than any other—my own body as it appeared in space. The Mother mourning the death of her Son—an ancient subject of Christian art. "She requires to be seen from a distance," said Master Luca, and pulled away the sacking.

I think I gasped aloud. Rising solidly from its oval marble base the presence of a woman, daunting in its brilliance, challenged and ignored us. Her gown was a dark bright pink, but over head and shoulders fell a thickly textured veil of a brilliant pastel blue. The flesh color was exact—there Master Luca had indeed achieved naturalness; and down either cheek, escaping the veil, fell a ripple of dark hair.

He had caught every irregularity of my face. I had not known the eyebrows, which I had never plucked, had that unevenness in their line, or that my nose was less than perfect. He had caught every divergence from the ideal, using the very qualities artists like Sandro had rejected.

The face was too young to belong to the Madonna of the Crucifixion, and yet it was not young. I had not known my jaw was so steep, or that my chin had one asymmetrically placed dimple, or that my throat was so muscular and strong. I saw the oval of the lid sheathing each eye: the bruises of exhaustion caught with a delicacy that moved me as though I had spied upon a private suffering.

And indeed she was too exhausted, this woman, to express grief anymore. If she grieved, it was against the inertia of the flesh; for exhaustion had pulled down her eyes at the outer corners, had slightly puffed the lower lids, had drawn the darkly glittering eyes into a contemplation so private she would never raise them to look at us. The mouth, stained dark as wine, drooped more deeply at the left corner than at the right; and it too, dragged slightly open, had the quality of something exhausted beyond speech. One will sometimes catch a woman so, in the single instant before she composes her features.

In her majesty and her self-containment she confronted us: caught off guard as though—the comforting friends escaped—she had just let herself slump against the door.

Richard crossed himself. "Some people will dislike it, Luca."
"I know."
"She is beautiful, but I find her shocking," I said. "What of me is there?"

"The working of Time and life," replied Master Luca, "upon that face." All three of us looked at the purity unmarked that glowed within the cobalt-blue medallion. "Accept it, Claire. In Paradise you may have *that* beauty again"—he gestured to the child Virgin bent over her prayerbook—"if you want it. But I think in Paradise you will carry all the marks."

"Then we'll all be scarred like old tilting shields."

"Of course. A child has a right to her simplicity. But if we ask a woman's face to bear no mark of experience, have we not deeply mistaken our idea of what is spiritually good, and therefore beautiful? Freshness has beauty, Claire, but in a sense it is potential, for the soul's experience has not yet transformed it." He gestured toward the face of sorrow: so brilliant, so commanding. "This is what a virgin freshness must become. Rejoice in what must be."

"You have set me a hard lesson," I said, "but I will try to learn it. I still long for my child's face, which seemed to have all possibilities. This is only what I have become."

"We have to choose," said Luca della Robbia, "The Madonna, by the way, is for Cosimo's private chapel. Look on the truth, Claire, at least as I have power to show it to you."

"It only hurts."

"I know. But what does Redemption mean, unless our way lies somehow through all the processes of humanity, including suffering, loss and death?"

"Suffering has no value," I said. "It destroys in us far more than it creates." Richard looked down at me with troubled eyes.

Gently Master Luca raised the statue's covering. "Yes, it destroys. But who knows how different, perhaps how much less, you might have been without it? If healing comes—and I know it does not always come—then we will have also the courage that endured, for we will have needed it . God himself went into extremity for us. It is no dishonor to follow him there."

"And beyond extremity?" The daylight had sunk; the shadows were turning indigo.

"I do not know," said Master Luca. "Do you truly value your virgin childhood more than the wisdom you have fairly won, and by such labor? For with the Fall we descended not only into labor, but into wisdom of our own. Do not mistake, Claire, you do not want the past."

"What then do I want?"

His hand on my shoulder turned me to go. "To be made whole," said Luca della Robbia.


"I have news for you," said Sir Edward Palmer, come to bid us good-bye. "An autumn storm has destroyed Sir John Challoner's fleet with great loss of life. They say Sir John's body was washed up and identified near Dieppe."

"A loss to neither side," said Richard.

"So I think. Richard, I have a request to make of you."

"Ask it."

"When you see your brother Thomas, I entreat you to do this"—he sank down before us on one knee—"and say: 'I ought never to have accepted your letter, whatever the penalty to myself. I did not know of your punishment. Forgive me; or if you cannot, know that I still remain your friend.'"

"I will tell him," said Richard.

Sir Edward rose. "That eases my conscience a little. You will have a filthy journey north in this weather."

"We mean to go slowly," I said.

He nodded. "My Jenny will soon see Florence. Life at home has become too dangerous; one's children risk perils enough. Well, the time has come to say good-bye."

"I thought when I returned here," I said, "that I was coming to old friends. I never expected the joy of finding a new one."

He hugged me, then opened his arms to Richard. For a moment we stood so, linked all three in a triple embrace.

# 19

In this manner did the things I had despaired of come back to me—in life's time, not in my own, and on life's terms. During the few nights that remained to us in our Florentine house, and during the weeks northward on horseback through mud and rain, I thought often how the power that guided me possessed an intricacy and a cruelty more profound than any evil.

We were leaving Florence; our farewells were made. In a side chapel at Santa Croce I lit a candle for our safe return. For a long time I knelt on the altar step. Today I must finish what Florence had given me: for life, which once had abandoned me, would now endure no resistance of mine to its renewal.

Only a few days had passed since Richard had sheltered me in his arms and had confided, with simplicity, his acceptance of my memory that was not a memory: the place of blood and new-sawn boards, discontinuous with any other recollection I possessed. I lifted my hand; spread the fingers, gazing at flesh formed in my mother's womb. Hands skilled for music from my birth. Might such gifts encode knowledge otherwise discarded by the mind? Plato said that before their birth some souls drink the water of forgetfulness, but other souls drink less of Lethe. Had I—child of the Church, God-created, ardently longing to find communion with my fellows—still drunk too little of the mercy that spares us memory?

Was the memory even mine? I thought. Had starvation, had loneliness given me access to someone else's pain, suffered long ago? But no. The memory had left with me a relief as physically arduous as the aftermath of a beating or of violent weeping; and it had left—however broken, however enigmatic—the accuracy that is kin to joy.

Yet the story is broken, is lost, I thought. It would vanish, like the lace of foam that evanesces down a beach, leaving nothing to connect it with my days. I dropped my hand and softly folded my fist against my brocaded skirt. It was time to rise. And as I stood I thought suddenly: The stealing, of course, was hunger. A last gift, gracious and gentle, of the receding wave.

I left my candle burning in its cup of ruby glass, and turned my back on Santa Croce.

I remember the struggle northward, traveling—cursing, mired down, and threatened by thieves as soaked with cold rain as ourselves—at the worst time of the year. We made slow progress, and left one or two of our colleagues with friends, to follow us in the spring. But as an embassy we could command clean inns with suppers of wine punch, cheese, roast meat, and hot bread; baths; and beds from which our major-domo insisted on stripping the sheets, to replace them with our own. And in the larger centers Cosimo's letters got us a house owned by the bank, each well staffed and furnished, and reserved for the convenience of the firm's agents. We never slept under canvas that I remember.

Christmas drew nearer. Ice crystals cross-hatched the puddles, and snow fell melting into the ruts on the road. But no one sang a carol in honor of the season. Both lutes lay wrapped for traveling in one of the huge chests suspended on poles between two mules. Like Richard, I continued in good physical health; but I spoke to him seldom, and all my thoughts were inward.

A gray frame, then—rain and stinging wind—around a jewel of amber: the night hours when he came to me, in room after room, all (thank God) decently clean, after bathing away the day's sweat. Once or twice he delicately excused himself, and once only, a woman's normal pain had given me such a day of agony that I told him, making a joke of it, I wished to sleep alone. I did not sleep. I lay till dawn and cried because I felt him, two rooms away, closed in the temporary indifference of sleep.

We were not brazen, and by day we preserved discretion. But we were both of us enthralled, and did not delude ourselves it could remain unseen. I had seen other fools, regarded by the sane with indulgent pity, who imagined their fascination was invisible. It does not reveal itself by any simple clue. A couple on whom it has settled cease—often with skill—all flirtation, all obvious preoccupation with each other, as I had seen Richard do with Marianne. What a pity that such skill should go to waste; for between them there incandesces a fascination so primitive that every human being in the room perceives it and watches nothing else.

By day we were friends. And our manner made clear that neither of us would tolerate speculation to our faces, or jesting. Therefore the others left us alone; and, satisfied in the one thing we required of them, we turned back to our unceasing contemplation of each other.

I did not conceive during those weeks. That, looking back, also surprises me.

On the first night I had been too exhausted—perhaps shocked too cold by the novelty of the encounter—to desire him; I had, rather, accepted and enjoyed him. I do not know in what beds he had acquired the skill he showed; but I delighted in my own lack of it, even to the point of shamming coldness. *I would fear even your hands,* I had told him, not knowing it then for what it was, an entreaty; and also: *Let me serve you.* If that disposition shaded into darkness, he led me toward it gradually, as—sometimes with courtship, sometimes without—he taught me to desire him.

Some nights we hardly touched, but lay naked between the sheets, talking softly—I flat on the pillow, Richard propped on his elbow, shifting with a genial curse whenever his arm went numb. The pine logs in the fireplace would send up a spitting of yellow sparks. Often, these times, he caressed me, teaching me his touch, gliding over my shyness with a hand so gentle it seemed a confidence we shared in perfect intimacy. Then I would go rigid, not with modesty but with the resistance I wanted him to overcome—and my eyes, open, passively challenging, would dare him to draw from me a sound or motion. Sometimes he simply continued his exploration of my body: discovering the texture of belly, breasts, and thighs, comparing aloud the scent and texture of each. "It's softest and finest-grained on your inner thigh—finer even than on your breasts or below your collarbone. Did you know your body is bloomed all over with tiny silver hairs?"

"Like the Queen of Sheba," I murmured, remembering Solomon's odd delusion that the lady would mistake a mirror for a pool, and lift her skirts to cross it.

Richard grinned. "No, not at all. They're so fine I can scarcely see them, like the bloom on an apricot."

In retrospect I understand with what kind cleverness he handled me, pushing my endurance but not my shame. Despite my eagerness, shame did exist, and he could have forced on me things for which I was not ready. He never at this time inflicted on me the deepest and most animal pang of all, though his fingers sought the place and then moved on in a caress.

He knew my coldness was a game. Sometimes he chose to play it with mock anger; and then—in spite of his patience and a calculation that I suspect he seldom ceased to practice—I did not find him gentle. And I, who did not know what appetites moved his mind, would find my breasts and mouth crushed, my lips forced open and my tongue explored to the limits of modesty and beyond. That he enjoyed this was evident; I enjoyed, with shame, the fear it inspired. And then he would open what his gentleness had kept sealed, and satisfy himself so roughly that he had—twice as I remember—to close my mouth against weeping.

I never wept for long or with deep cause; and when he had filled me, his shoulder, mouth, and hands were all again to shelter me, easing me back from the darkness that linked us in a shared complicity.

The beauty of his hands continued to fascinate me. In quiet moments I would examine them joint by joint, flexing them, turning them. Once I tried to kiss them: he recoiled with a humility so spontaneous I dared not try again.

Sometimes he visited me, so he let it seem, only for my body, and took me as straightforwardly as he might take a prostitute; or sometimes with the simplicity of a man breaking bread and satisfying a necessary hunger. Then he would scarcely speak to me, and I, always his pupil, would lie still as he used my body with skill to satisfy himself. All that was necessary would be done, with kisses, suckings, kneadings so casual that the deep pleasure they gave me would seem no part of his intention, but an accident he left me to enjoy in solitude.

I had no choice, those nights, whether, laid on my belly, I would feel him part my buttocks and fill me, crushing my breasts with his palms as he cried, wept, swore his ecstasy against my shoulder; or whether, laid on my back, I felt his hands cup my haunches and tutor them most precisely to serve his need. Twice, three times he would satisfy himself; lie still with an arm flung across his face; then, having searched his desire not mine, choose again how I should serve it. And I, open-eyed, enthralled—making sounds, though I did not hear them—would watch him: the sweat, the dark lowered lashes, the intelligent beauty of a face suspended in contemplation.

And then he would collapse upon me, his mouth and eyes half open, and I would catch that ecstasy still reflected, fading, in his exhaustion.

I learned a good deal about myself during these nights. I decided that of all the saints I would most like to be Mary Magdalene, because (I think) she loved Christ bodily; and how more truly can God be rendered incarnate to a woman than in the body and virile functions of a man, all of which I found beautiful?

I said to him one night, "I am the nymph Evadne, who lay under the god Apollo."

"What?" He had been lying resting, smiling at me, his head on his crossed arms. The muscles of his back and buttocks so displayed to me were beautiful in their latent tension.

"I mean," I said, "that I now see the ancient priestesses were right to worship the god with their bodies. The girls were right who went to give their virginity in the temple as the property of the temple, because the act is holy and pertains to the true Temple. And the priestess was luckiest of all who lay hallowed, waiting not for his human representative but for the god himself."

He stirred and gazed down at me with a strange seriousness. "Do you think he came?"

"I know he came, and she bore children to him."

Richard's mouth sought my breast; his tone was a warning. "All this is nonsense."

"Of course," I agreed, mindful that we are children of the Church.

Richard said, "Claire, are you with child?"

"Despite your labors in the vineyard," I answered softly, "I am not."

That fact was proven three days after; and then, with gentle, implacable insistence, he drank the blood from between my thighs.

\* \* \*

On a day early in December it had rained with such cold violence we had traveled only six miles. Nevertheless this sufficed to bring us to the next important town, and to one of those houses the Medici Bank provided for the use of its guests. The staff, undismayed by our condition, made us efficiently comfortable; and if I thanked Piero for the lute (I had checked it only yesterday, to find it safe inside its padding), I thanked his father even more as I watched servants carry away the bath and handed them my day clothes to be cleaned and dried.

The room, dark wood and blue cloth bed hangings, bore no feel of being lived in; but the floorboards smelled of new wax, and the sheets of lavender. Beneath the pillow I found a sprig of rosemary to make me sleep.

I lay in bed and watched the fire. It was one of those canopied beds so broad that they look shallow, though the depth of this one was a good seven feet. Rain made rivers against the small, thick panes. Lost in fatigue and well-being, I drowsed in the huge bed.

When I woke Richard was sitting beside me, wearing the brown day gown he sometimes used as a robe. I stirred. "Have you been here long?"

"About ten minutes. I mulled some wine in the kitchen and have kept it hot for you. It may taste of cinders from the poker, but I think I got it upstairs unobserved. Will you have some?"

"Yes, please." I sat up. He handed me a pottery mug. I said, "Richard?"

"Yes?"

"What is the matter?"

"I was thinking of Simone."

I had never heard the name before, but guessed, with a start, whom he meant. He did not elaborate, but added after a moment, "And of my mother."

"How old were you when she died?"

"Eleven." He set his mug down and pulled the robe off over his head. "When does grieving stop, Claire? You would think twenty years would be enough."

Peacefully he laid his head against my breast; peacefully I held him, sinking back onto the pillows. He had not uttered the word "anger"; but after a long moment I spoke the name that lay always unspoken. "And Thomas, Richard?"

Remembering his face, I do not know even now how I dared it. I said, "It was Thomas who betrayed your trust and destroyed your name: Thomas whom you cannot beat or hate or touch. Thomas, not I, Richard. For which you destroyed me."

Richard sat up. Then he drew breath and said, "No, Claire, I can feel no hate for Thomas."

I spoke softly. "You are the servant, are you not? And Thomas—"

"Is the cherished prodigal?" He shrugged. "Do not force him into comparison with me. If the burden of service kills the elder brother, comparison may kill the younger. How harsh he must have found me. I do not know, Claire, what age I was when I first began to understand that I am a child of war. To defend my home has always been heartbreaking work. Perhaps it will, all my life, remain impossible. You have met Edward Palmer. He is one of the better of our conquerors, but he, like me, must know that only another hundred years of history can unmake this war. We live submerged in it; we are lost in it. Yet even the lost must work until God releases them."

All tension had left the moment. Richard gently touched my eyes, which were wet with tears, and bent over me. "Do you love me, Claire?"

"Yes." It came with the simplicity, almost the bleakness of a child answering a catechism question. "I would die for you."

"I know," he answered. "Why then does this love give you no joy?"

I closed my eyes on tears, only to open them as Richard's fingers gripped my chin. "Claire, we cannot go on like this without your becoming pregnant. Am I planting seed in my wife, or driving you to turn away? No woman I make pregnant shall kill herself while I can stop her."

"Why should I kill myself because of a baby?"

"I do not know. I only know that while, with other lovers, some god blesses them in theory then keeps his distance, in my bed I have a rival: whatever power you commune with when you shut me out."

"I cannot help it, Richard. I long to trust whatever has led us here, but I hate it and despise it."

"Why? For making so bad a world?"

"For children who starve without the mercy of death. For Thomas flogged. For you weeping in the rain. For a drowned woman rolled from wave to wave. For Elisabeth's sister Catherine, dead without any comfort of understanding to those who loved her. For Madame Marie, whose portion of Eternity was thirty-seven years. For my father's endurance of the knowledge that he comes second. For Andrea del Castagno and his wife and children. For—"

He stopped my mouth. "And so on and on and on. Claire, the mystery to which we go requires of us *experience*. We are here to learn; in what service I do not know."

"It makes no sense."

"It never will; sense is not what it makes. Look deeper." He brushed back my hair. "Understand me: It is *you* I value, more than any child I may plant in you. And I will not let you escape me, or—" I scarcely heard him as his mouth covered mine, though I remembered after: "I will not let you escape me or abandon me."

*Abandon me*. After that I had no strength to wonder what moved him, that night, to a calculated savagery that stopped short precisely of doing me harm. Once when I could speak I exclaimed, "If I were pregnant this would kill the child."

"If you were pregnant," replied his voice close to my ear, "I should not be doing this. In a moment you will not remember where you are; and that, I have found, is a kind of respite. Accept it. I can give it to you."

So I accepted; and in a tide of endurance graduated and controlled by another will, I indeed forgot everything but my body.

I surfaced weeping with shame, my head against his shoulder. *"Why?* Why do I let you?"

"I don't know, Claire. You will marry me and live your span, and I will teach you trust. I think I can. And perhaps then hope will come." He sighed and was quiet, cradling me gently.

At noon on a day when the sky was gray with flowing cloud, and the bare trees lay like charcoal smoke upon the hills, we came to the Abbey of Sainte-Bertrande.

# 20

Desolation filled the great court. I had never seen it, if not so empty, then so silent. Around us the dead light reduced the walls to the color of chalk. The sergeant of the guard came pelting toward us. "My lord Ambassador!"

He brought us at a run to the chambers of the Mother Abbess. "Captain Jenner took a fall from the parapet yesterday; his back is broken. He is in the infirmary, and dying."

"God help him," said Richard. "Has all you can been done to comfort him?"

"We gave him opium for the pain, and he has confessed. I think he is prepared. In here, sir."

"Thank you, Roger."

"Richard!" Mère Agnès had, as usual, been pacing. A black shawl covered her from head to feet; she halted, her eyes brilliant in the swirl of white and black. "Claire, my dear, welcome. Richard, I need a captain."

"So I hear. Why not Roger Belot?" Behind us the man stirred at the mention of his name, and I saw a glance pass between him and the Abbess.

"Because," said Mère Agnès, "I need a soldier accredited by my brother and, through him, by the King."

Richard demanded, "What has happened? Is His Grace alive?"

"He made a long recovery and is weak, but he will live." Her big hands, the emerald of her office glistening on one forefinger, clenched in front of her. "Do you know Elisabeth's manor of La Pipardière? It lies an hour's ride from here, in my immediate suzerainty."

Richard's "no" was interrupted by my cry: "*I* know it, of course! Reverend Mother, what has happened there?"

"Nothing we can now prevent. You heard the rumor that Sir John Challoner had been killed?"

"Yes."

"It was false. The body, closely examined, proved to be that of his brother. A week ago intelligence reached His Grace the Count that Challoner, with two of the ship's boats, had in fact succeeded in making landfall down the coast and had vanished with perhaps twenty men into the forest. There, we think, they have lived quietly, healing themselves as best they could in this weather—building shelters and hunting for their food. They were not strong enough to raid, and contented themselves with evading notice. My brother has had scouts and then men out after them, starting a week ago. Perhaps that is what drove them out of the forest before they were ready."

"*Ready?*" exclaimed Richard. "Twenty men? Ready for what? The whole countryside hates them. They can look for no help."

"I know. They know it too. Perhaps at best they hoped—may still hope—to fight or bargain their way to the coast, to get a ship somehow. Last night a party of about their number stormed and took La Pipardière. They are safe there for a few days, but they cannot get out."

"Are you certain of their identity?"

"Not yet."

"Then they have not declared themselves to the extent of holding the family to ransom—say, for safe passage to the coast."

"There is no family to hold. Claire, sit down." I did. "This morning at dawn they threw outside the farm walls the body of Blaise Mercier's son, together with the bodies of his wife and the two girl-children. All had been murdered. The family were alone and undefended in the house; the fieldhands had gone home to the village. The attackers waited until they left at dusk."

Richard's palm gently rasped his cheeks, hiding his mouth. "Murdered, how?" Mère Agnès turned to the window.

Richard shouted, *"How?"*

She turned back to us. "Inside the farm they will have provisions, but we do not know how many arrows they have found, how many they can afford to waste. Few, probably. In any case they did not shoot the village priest and the brave men who went to give the bodies burial. The midwife laid out the women, Richard. Each, including the youngest girl, had been raped, she guessed, about thirty times. Neither child survived it. Even so they had to stab the mother."

"Suzanne was twelve years old," I whispered.

"And Isabelle," said Mère Agnès, "was eight."

"And Monsieur Mercier?" I demanded.

"They spiked his head on the gate."

It was Richard who moved first. "Claire, describe this place to me."

I thought; I have seen it only once. "Steep wooded hills, as I remember; trees come right up to the walls. An old building, moated, of timber and thatch with some brick."

"And the walls? Why does Mère Agnès say they are safe?"

"The walls are a solid key shape—masonry five feet thick. They encircle the whole complex and open only at one point, a tunneled gate."

"How high are the walls?"

I shrugged. "Ten feet—twelve."

Richard gestured me thanks and silence. *"Ma mère,* have you pioneers on your staff here—masons who could undermine the walls?"

"I have masons, yes."

"Is there a tunnel or passage that leads out of the house—a secret exit?"

"Not," I replied, "unless they are digging one."

"They are not, if they spent the night—at a guess—drinking, eating like the doomed men they know they are, and raping the women. Whoever they are, they have thrown away their chance to ransom the family, and that means they know they have no hope."

"And nothing to fear," said Mère Agnès.

"You could *scale* the walls," I said. "The trees come right up, or did when I saw the place four years ago. Unless Elisabeth ordered Mercier to cut them back."

"They'll be leafless," said Richard, "and will offer no cover. These men know we will come against them. They are saving their crossbow bolts."

"Then wait till dark," I said, "and *fire the thatch.*"

"Fire arrows," whispered Richard. "And they'll have only one way out. Roger, go prepare a party and supplies."

"Thirty minutes, my lord."

"I'll give you an hour; we want to arrive in the last light. I must parley with them first, if I can. Ma mère, I take it you have set guards around the house?"

"Yes, to contain them while we await my brother's orders; but you are experienced, and he has already accredited you. They'll not get out unless they rush that single gate."

"Unlikely."

"Yes; and if they try to go over the walls they must see that my men will pick them off one by one. I have sent to my brother. If it is John Challoner, the King's Majesty may want him alive."

"If it is Challoner, then he knows that and would prefer to die. They have come to the end. Only a man seeking death would have sacrificed the family, assuming he retains any control over his men. *Ma mère,* will you ride with us? You are suzerain of this place under your brother. His Grace should be represented."

"I will, of course."

"And I," I said.

To my surprise he did not demur. "Then you'll find out how heavy ring mail and a helmet really are. We want no women's hair betraying you as marks. Send me your chaplain. I want to confess and take the Sacrament."

"I'll call Père Christophe." She moved quickly to the door.

"So we have come this far," said Richard, "only to have me shot fifteen miles from home, with some English brigand's last crossbow bolt. Oh, my darling, come here." I came to him, to be lifted in an embrace that crushed me. "My darling, *ma bien-aimée,* my well beloved."

When his kiss released me I said, "Richard, live. Live and let me live with you, every day that God requires of me."

"It may be too late."

"I do not think so," said a voice.

We started apart. In the doorway stood a little plump man with an ironic mouth and intelligent eyes. "I am Père Christophe, confessor to the Sisters here. You wished, my lord Ambassador, to receive the Sacrament?"


We took about fifty men, including the most skilled archers not only from the garrison, but from among the pilgrim-volunteers. Every man in the compound wanted to destroy the child-killers who had captured La Pipardière. With us too rode Mère Agnès, cloaked over light armor, and Père Christophe.

"Richard." I drew abreast of him. My helmet, whose weight and discomfort astonished me despite its cushioning leather skullcap, bumped inverted like a bucket at my saddle bow. For the rest I wore a cloak and a boy's ring-mail shirt over boy's clothes someone had found for me. "You seem to know nothing about La Pipardière."

"There is more to tell?" The sky had begun to offer us one of a winter day's few beauties, a long sapphire twilight.

"There may be. Elisabeth has told me some evil influence pervades the house, though it has killed only one person—her sister. And there is a haunted room. I have felt the cold there, and it is not natural."

Richard swore, giving me his attention. "Claire, if we do not destroy these men or preserve them for the Count's justice, the country people here will kill them more cruelly even than they deserve. Probably they have lost two men in five to exposure and starvation during their weeks in hiding. They are half starved, filthy, and in despair: perhaps half mad. I pity them. For beggars not choosers, they happened on a rich find for their last week of life: a fortified farmhouse that offered them food—the first full belly in weeks; women; and the wine they must long for, if only to numb pain and fear. They are going to die, and I am going to kill them. They feel me coming, or someone like me. Tell me this story exactly."

I did. When I had finished he glanced back. "Père Christophe!"

"My lord?"

"Father, do you know how Elisabeth's sister Catherine died?"

"I do. So does the Reverend Mother."

"Whether or not I survive this night, La Pipardière must be cleansed with fire. I want you to perform a service of exorcism and to sow the ground with salt."

"I'll see it done, my lord." Père Christophe fell back; I heard him murmur, "The Reverend Mother will be *most* pleased."

There was still enough light that I could see Richard glance at me. "I have done as you wish?"

"Yes."

"Why do you think it important? I have told you all the human reasons for what has happened in that house. This among other things, Claire, is the gift England brings to Normandy."

"England's gifts to Normandy," I said, "include yourself and me. I think it important because Catherine did die. I know human evil has manifested at La Pipardière. But do not leave any truth out of your reckoning, Richard." Around us wind stirred the dark trees. "I say only that the place is evil too, and that the house should be destroyed."

Of my only other visit to La Pipardière I retained an impression of greenness; the blue roof of the church; the dappled cattle and the chalk ruts in the road. But by the time our cavalcade reached the farmstead, all these impressions had sunk forever into the indigo that spread above us. La Pipardière became, and in my memory will always remain, starlight remote from us, wind swaying whole hillsides of winter branches, and torch-light in the dark.

Mère Agnès had left a large garrison of watchers, and they had ringed with torches the old walls where grass grew between the blocks of stone. I could see no lights in the house beyond. A man rode forward and called quietly, "Who approaches?"

"They know my voice, not yours," said Mère Agnès to Richard. She called, "The man you will obey, because he represents my lord the Count: Richard Linacre de Verneuil, returned from Florence."

"My lord, you are welcome." If the man thought this disgraced Master of Works, so hastily reinstated, an odd or an unworthy choice, he gave no sign of it.

"Has anything happened," said Richard, "since they let the villagers take away the bodies?"

"Nothing, my lord. The house might be empty for all we see or hear."

"We'll soon know. Keep your party in a ring around the wall.

Roger, draw up our men out of bow-shot just beyond the torchlight. I must ride out where they can see me; you are commander if they kill me. Madame l'Abbesse, have you a scarf?"

"Here." She pulled off her helmet and unwound the veiling from her hair.

Richard unsheathed his sword and tied the white rag to its point. "Will two men light me, a torch on either side? Thank you; good. Claire, draw well back with Mère Agnès, and keep your head covered. If I am killed, obey Roger as you would me."

"I will. God speed you." Since I could do no more I spoke what might be my last words to him and drew back into the darkness. There I sat, numb with submission to the knowledge that I could not now protect him, and watched.

Out of the dark he called—in English, in French, in English again, "A parley! A parley!"

We had a long moment in which to study the play of torchlight on stone. My eyes wandered onto the yellowing object, wizened as a winter apple, stuck on a pike above the gate. Its face was human, though it was not recognizably the face of Blaise Mercier.

I leaned leftward and vomited. The hand of Mère Agnès, strong from her work in garden and in hospital, slipped around my waist, steadying me in the saddle. I vomited bile and sat shuddering.

"Let it come. You will not fall," she said softly.

At that moment a man's voice called from behind the gates—a voice too strained to have any inflection or any individual quality. "Come into the light. We will hear you." In English, hoarse with exhaustion, each word lilting artificially upward, the sound jarred into an echo against the encircling trees. "Who is it that speaks our tongue?"

I saw Richard, the white token raised, guide his horse down a little slope between his torchmen, into arrow range of the walls. "A Frenchman: Richard Linacre de Verneuil, ambassador to Florence by the appointment of His Majesty King Charles." He continued, like his unseen respondent, to speak English, but his name as he had sounded it was pure French.

Another silence. "How does such a man come here?" demanded the man we could not see.

"By accident, and was asked by the Mother Abbess who rules these lands to treat with you. How many crossbows have you?"

The sobbing sound might have been a laugh. "Enough to kill you, Master Ambassador."

"Then you kill the one man who will ask His Majesty's officers to ransom you. You will hang from the trees here if you come out to any other; and if you stay inside the walls you will starve. You cannot wait; we can. Are you an Englishman?"

"I am John Challoner." Echoing, uninflected, the voice sounded from the devastated house to where the boles of trees danced in our torchlight.

Richard's horse sidled; he controlled it. "Then, John Challoner, I require you to answer for the murder of this family. Come out with your men and you will purchase what mercy I can get for you. I swear I will try. There is a chance of ransom." Richard's voice was a controlled shout, and in the dark all around us, seen and unseen, I felt men listening. At this instant fourteen of them, their faces, hands, and naked feet smeared with earth, would be climbing trees by feel in the blackness. A single crack—a single broken branch—would destroy the distraction Richard was creating: the focus on himself. "There is a chance of ransom," he resumed, "and death can be swift or slow. I promise you shriving, and some mercy."

A bolt shot his horse from under him. His torchbearers moved so swiftly I almost missed it. They scooped him from the falling horse and threw their torches in front of them to dazzle the archer's aim. All three withdrew into the dark. Then, at the knee of Roger Belot, Richard said, "Now."

The whistle might have been one boy calling to another in

the woods. But the bolts that shot from the darkness carried pale yellow fire. From every angle they buried themselves in wood, in seventy-year-old thatch. Inside the walls we heard shouting; and all around me men moved to surround the gate.

The house caught as if wood and ancient straw had been waiting to drink flame. Among the screaming and milling I could, if I had chosen, have seen the capture and search of the men as they ran out; but what I watched was the roof as it took the flames.

*Catherine, go free; and free Elisabeth, who loves you. I, almost her child, stand here for her. Go to the blessed souls.*

Flame ran with precision along the pattern of beams. Latticework stood black against it, its charred shell preserving for an instant the shape of a window; then it fell into the yellow blaze of the rooms. Something exploded in the cellar. Coals spat; fired ash came fluttering to be stamped out. One of our men doubled over weeping curses, clutching at his eye.

And then the fire's delicate play with timberwork, with lattice—its shadowing of rooms—ended. All fires coalesced, and with a crackle and roar there bloomed into the sky a monstrous crocus of flame. We fell back before its heat and could no longer see the stars.

"God send it doesn't catch the trees." Richard, remounted, watched his men surround the prisoners. "Roger, how many?"

"Twenty-two, my lord, very ragged and starved. We've taken every weapon off them we could find."

"Poor bastards," said Richard. "What shall I do, Roger? Shall I hang them here?"

"The crowd may force you to, sir."

"And you?"

"If the Count's Grace wants them, I will save them for him if I can. But get them away quickly back to Sainte-Bertrande."

"Very well. Take them there"—Richard pointed to a clear area in deep darkness on our left—"and rank them, bound, by fives. All except John Challoner; bring him to me. I intend to create something for the men to watch, and as I do so I want the back five drawn off into the forest, guarded by men who may manhandle but not kill them. Draw them off line by line; all should be gone by the time I finish. When they reach Sainte-Bertrande I want them fed a hot meal and their wounds dressed. I will visit them myself to see these things were done, and to count them. Twenty-two leave this place under your care. If I find twenty-one, or nineteen, in the abbey's dungeons, I will flog every soldier who killed a man."

"I will do what I can. Here comes your prisoner."

The man they dragged to Richard had obviously gone hungry for many weeks. Even so his handsomeness and his youth astonished me. Thinness makes anyone look younger, and the light was changeful and gentle; but I guessed Challoner to be perhaps twenty-five. He was tall too and had been strong, with a slender grace, though the bones of his wrists showed big as the joints of a starved colt. His hair and beard were auburn.

Richard had ranged the torches around him, creating a bright stage; and even I hardly noticed the quiet work of organization beyond the light. The square of fives that was to save them began to form, blending back into the dark. Then I forgot to watch.

Richard dismounted. "John Challoner?"

"I am he." The young face regarded him with that primitive dignity that sometimes settles on a man in the immediate presence of death. With a crumpling sound the flames caught a tree on the hill. Richard glanced at it but did not hurry. All around him the men had closed in—men who had known Blaise Mercier and both the slaughtered children.

"Do you admit the murder of the family Mercier?"

"I admit we killed the people of this farm."

"You will die for it," said Richard.

"I know," John Challoner replied.

Two files of five had gone into the dark.

Richard gestured to the gate with its watcher. "Who raped to death the eight-year-old child?"

Another tree burst into flame. In its light I felt the two men, locked together, rest for an instant on each other like fighters preparing to reengage. I saw Richard's stance of unconscious exhaustion, passing even as I glimpsed it into a reassumed self-mastery. Challoner's young haggard face incandesced with acknowledgment of a presence we could not see.

Whatever our shock or lust had expected of that moment, it fell among us with great gentleness. *Who raped to death the eight-year-old child?* John Challoner gasped, gathered breath, and said, "I did."

We sighed with the knowledge that it could not be true, though Challoner hanged for it two weeks later in the market square at Saint-Aurèle; and suddenly the pity that had appalled us was succeeded by an anger we did, with relief, recognize. The moment, with its glimpse of private prices and private reckonings, vanished, snapped off. The third file of prisoners had gone; the fourth was going; and Richard, with a breath I could hear, gave them the only thing that would hold their attention on him. He said, "Free his arms."

At least he gave that to a man who, tottering with strain, had no chance at all. He did not fight, nor did he make more than involuntary sounds as Richard's fists and knees doubled him, staggering; as blow after blow, absorbed in silence and upright, at last reduced him to the ground, his eyes glazed open. Shuddering, Richard stopped. "Is he dead?"

Someone laid two fingers on the prisoner's throat. "No, my lord. He'll live to hang."

"Make him a stretcher. And as I served him, so I will serve any man who tells me he died between here and Sainte-Bertrande."

On the windward side the hill was burning. As our people formed for marching, the same man said, "My lord, where are the other English?"

Richard gathered up his reins and looked down at him with the arrogance of exhaustion. "Removed to prison at Sainte-Bertrande, of course."

As we rode away, Mère Agnès said, "Claire, forgive him when you can. It was necessary; and if he found release in it, so did they in watching. A crude revenge for the children; but did you notice he prevented any other? They will die, yes; but they did not hang for the flames to torture them. That was Richard's work."

I watched the shoulders, still forced upright, whose nakedness I had found beautiful. "He enjoys inflicting pain," I said.

Her quick glance comprehended a good deal. "Are you afraid for yourself?"

"I am afraid for his self-respect."

Mère Agnès frowned. "Yes, to inflict pain gives him relief, and that frightens him. Set that truth beside another: that he is gentle and deeply kind. There is no contradiction. What would you say, Claire, is Richard's greatest virtue?"

I considered for a second. "Love of truth."

"Odd: I should have said it was his loyalty. Yet do you know any man in Saint-Aurèle whose loyalty has been so outraged? Was Thomas worth his loyalty? Were my brother and Saint-Aurèle—both so quick to use his service, so woundingly quick also to discard him? On the night you chose Elisabeth over Thomas, did you seem worth his trust? And beyond these things lie antagonists too intangible to reach: the border which is indefensible; the war that never ends."

"Does he think us worthless, then?" I asked.

"No. But he knows he has never yet encountered a loyalty equal to his own." Her horse stumbled slightly; she overrode the motion with grace. "You do not know it, Claire, but he has marked you, without conscious arrogance, for his equal. Consider well what he offers you, and do not despise your place among this living generation. The sea will claim you soon enough. Richard loves you; so do I; so do your parents and all our friends in Saint-Aurèle. Love us; make music for us; make books our children shall take joy in reading. For God who made you and we who love you have not given you leave to go."


At the abbey they gave me one of the guest rooms. I now knew I would not even ask to see the cottage in which I had lived for three years. I had heard them lodge Richard down the corridor, but I had not spoken to him since our return. I bathed and collapsed into bed, and fell at once into a hungry sleep.

Sometime in the night his voice wakened me. "Claire."

I stirred. "Yes?"

"I had nightmares. May I come into your bed and be warm?"

"Of course." Naked, half asleep, I received him; and, curled in the shelter of his body, began a conversation in which Mère Agnès seemed to be answering, until in a last flare of consciousness I heard his assuaged and gentle breathing.


We woke to a knocking on the door. "Claire," called the voice of Mère Agnès. "May I come in?"

I exchanged glances with Richard. "Mother, I am not—"

"I know. Please let me come in."

With a comic shrug Richard called in an exaggerated baritone: "Good morning, *ma mère*."

"Good morning, my dears." She was dressed for the day, her hair swathed in a new white veil.

Richard, naked in my bed, lay propped on his elbows. "*Ma mère*, don't be hasty. Doesn't Pelagius talk about virgin marriages? I haven't touched her. We resisted temptation with a heroism worthy of the dullest Fathers of the Church. *It isn't what it looks.*"

Mère Agnès laughed. "Every man I've ever heard say that was lying, thank God. Richard, I came to tell you they're heating your bath, and your servant will come in a few minutes to make up the fire. Get back to your room at once."

Richard, reaching for his gown, inquired, "Was it Pelagius?"

"No," replied the Mother Superior. "All I remember is that Saint Cyprian objected. So, I think, did the Council of Nicaea. One can understand, of course."

He wriggled into the gown and glanced at me. "I'll see *you* later."

"Oh, get out," said Mère Agnès.

That morning an advance courier arrived to tell us that the Count had dispatched one hundred men to deal with (as he still believed) the emergency at La Pipardière. Mère Agnès explained the night's events to him, and said to Richard and me, "They'll arrive this afternoon. I think I can safely consign the prisoners to their captain, to do with them as my brother wishes."

She rode with us part of the way home. A rainstorm while we slept had stopped the forest fire; but as Richard and I, Mère Agnès and Père Christophe approached the cracked stones of La Pipardière, the heat made us sweat inside our clothes. Embers smoldered coral and orange on the hill, and their gold shimmered with dangerous softness beneath the ash, the tangle of beams and flagstones and incinerated brick. The head no longer guarded the gate. We stopped, unable to go farther because of the heat. The collapsed structure would in any case have made it too dangerous.

With Richard swinging the censer, which added its smoke of frankincense to the stench of burning, Père Christophe spoke the ceremony of exorcism. At last he turned to us and said, "Holy Mother, this matter concerns your friends; Mistress Claire, this matter concerns your family. Approach therefore with blessed water and blessed salt, and cast them into the ashes, with prayer; and may the Holy Spirit guide you."

Mère Agnès cast the salt and said aloud, "May this ash turn to flowers in centuries we shall not see; and in this place, many years from now, may there rise another house. Let barrenness be cast out: may this earth bloom, and may this place be cleansed of all remembrance."

I came next and sprinkled water on the ruins. Aloud I said, "And when that house is built, may it prove famous for its gardens; and may children be gently nurtured here. Especially may the daughters be happy; and may many children be here conceived in love."

Richard said to Mère Agnès, "Let the walls be torn down."

She nodded. "And we will sow the foundations with salt." And so we turned away forever from the manor of La Pipardière.

In the road we knelt, both to Père Christophe and to Mère Agnès. She said, "Well, my children, it seems I shall not see you for some weeks. Greet my brother for me. And remember, Claire, that my son Philippe also has his father's lands."

# 21

All along our route our friends took leave of us and departed to their own homes, so that our cavalcade with its men-at-arms was a small one by the time we came within five miles of Saint-Aurèle. It had begun to snow, and out of a delicate gray sky, stars, each frosted and intricately spiked, fell melting onto the palms of my riding gauntlets. We picked our way among the frozen ruts of the road, then found a stretch of Roman paving. Taking advantage of the smoother traveling, I raised my voice to honor the season.

> Now spring up flowers from the root—
>   Revert you upward naturally,
> In honor of the blessed fruit
>   That rose up from the Rose Mary.
> Lay out your leavës lustily—
> From death take life now at the lest,
>   In worship of that Prince worthy
> *Qui nobis Puer natus est.*

Our guards smiled at me and a few called soft *bravos*. At that moment a rider came galloping toward us. He wore a blue cloak: a burly, handsome man with a sleek brown beard and a likable air of energy. Some messenger, to judge by his evident recognition of us; but I could not remember having seen him before.

He drew rein, and Richard and I exclaimed together: "Thomas!"

He grinned. "His Grace the Count greets you and requests that you pass this night at his villa outside the walls. Tomorrow afternoon he will call you into audience. We all, to our grief, know about La Pipardière."

He wavered between us, then flung himself into Richard's arms. A moment later he caught me in an embrace that lifted me from the saddle. He set me back with a surehanded gentleness; his eyes, intelligent and kind, smiled at me. "I would have come, Claire, but I didn't know what to do for the best, so I let Richard instruct me."

"It's all right," I said, "I understand." Never again, I guessed, would his blood kinship to Richard be obvious. The two men had matured too differently. The beard gave him an air of elegance and vivid handsomeness, and the bulk, as far as I could judge, was hard bone and muscle.

"All's well, then?" he said softly.

"As well as it can be on this sad day," I replied.

Richard added, "Elisabeth has lost the immediate use of the property."

"Claire would know better than I, but I should guess that won't matter much. Walter's income from London is so large now the war is over, and the press has become famous and is returning a profit. And Elisabeth has the three other farms."

Richard nodded. "And she knows about the family?"

"Yes, the news reached the town this morning. You won't see her do her grieving, but I think she blames herself for not having left some kind of garrison with them."

"Someone once said to me," I remarked, "that this war would die long and viciously."

We turned to ride. "We are not to go to our own homes, then?" I asked.

Thomas shook his head. "No. His Grace wants to welcome you formally. He'll walk with a stick for a while, but we won't lose him this year, or next."

The little stone manor house with its red tiles and its patterns of ornamental cobbles was waiting to receive us. The staff greeted and housed us all, but I ate alone with the two brothers. I could not look sufficiently at Thomas. All that his boyhood had promised seemed realized here, warm and solid and shockingly unexpected. Richard grinned at me. "Yes, I *know* he's turned into a beauty, but don't touch him."

"She may if she wants," said Thomas, noting my blush and laughter.

"Don't let her." Richard poured wine. "Or I shall have to knock you down."

Thomas kissed my hand and then, most gently, my cheek. "You may as well know the other news. His Grace is to marry Antoine Lalemont."

For a moment we could find no response. Then Richard said, "Does she desire it?"

"She tells me she does so warmly and truly, though with obedience. You know Gérard and Béatrice: they would never force her, nor would His Grace. He loves her and can, I think, teach her to love him. And now he will have children."

"I suspect he will make her extremely happy," said Richard.

I said gently, "Had you asked her, Thomas?"

"No, damn me, not yet. I'll go serve my lord Philippe, I think. He's asked me."

"Then you'll be nearby."

"Yes. Richard, go to bed; I want to talk privately with this lady."

"I will; but first, Thomas, I have a message for you from Sir Edward Palmer."

He delivered it on his knees. For a long while Thomas gazed

333

at him. Finally he said, "I have several weaknesses, and it is no one's business how, these last years, I've thought about them and labored to correct them. Poor man. Tell him, if you see him before I do, that I never blamed him for doing his duty."

"I will. Good night." Richard smiled at me—a smile of curious gentleness—and left us to the fire and candlelight.

Thomas's huge hand folded around mine. "Here, come to the settle. Have you any objection to embracing your brother-in-law?"

"None at all." We sat down before the fire, his arm around me.

"Are you married, Claire?"

"Not yet."

"I see. My dear, Sir Edward's decency shames me, for I owe the deepest apology of all. I beg your forgiveness for my confession on the beach. Had I had the manhood to endure that burden alone, I wonder how much of this would never have happened."

"And your English cousin Alison?" I ventured it hesitantly, seeing across the years a stone embossed with a fossil snailshell sinking beneath the waves. "Might you marry her now, Thomas?"

"Alison?" For an instant his face betrayed a surprise almost brutal in its purity. "Who—? Ah." He blushed scarlet. "I remember I carried a letter. But my dear, as you can see, for a moment I had forgotten who Alison was."

I leaned back against his shoulder. "Tell me one thing if you can. Did you see Elisabeth today?"

"I spoke with her this morning, before I rode to meet you."

"Would you know if His Grace told her *himself* about his decision to marry?"

He hugged me; his chin settled comfortably against my hair. "She asked me to tell you specially. His Grace came to her and talked with her for a long time."

\* \* \*

For our audience I chose my dark green velvet gown, and braided my hair with silver ribbons. Richard wore gray and Thomas blue; both, as formality required, went girt with sword and dagger. A snow-filled winter dusk showed blue beyond the panes. Up staircase after staircase candles cast their wavering yellow light; and to my astonishment, the audience room outside His Grace's study was full.

As we proceeded through the crowd, women came forward to kiss Richard, and men stepped out to take his hand. "Richard, you are welcome back. The couriers came in yesterday with news of your work at La Pipardière. Welcome home; we need you."

Candles whose beeswax smelled of honey turned the foil ceiling to orange and made the comets sparkle on the walls of the room where His Grace rose to meet us. He looked handsome and happy. I saw Elisabeth, whose thinness caused me a pang as I returned her smile; and Walter; and Béatrice; and the sprightly little figure of Gérard; and Antoine, dressed modestly. I noted—then realized with compunction how often such calculation must have studied her recently—that her broad shoulders and full breasts promised children. She had always been the plain one beside the enchanting Jacquette, and bore it as cheerfully as her good nature and her love for her sister taught her to do. She had brushed her hair loose over her shoulders; her skin in its clarity reminded me of the white flesh of an apple.

"My dear children, welcome home." The Count discarded his stick and approached us; we knelt. "Richard, Cosimo sends me good word of you; I fear King Charles must hear of it as well. And they tell me Cosimo's chapel has a new Madonna." I smiled at him. The experienced eyes scanned me for whatever changes a man senses in a woman another man has enjoyed. "Rise, all of you, and forgive me for sitting down." It was Antoine who moved to pull out his chair; he clasped her hand where it rested on his shoulder.

The leaves of the door opened on the crowd; yet, enclosed here, we had a kind of privacy. I looked at my parents, standing handfast. Elisabeth's profile was pretty and composed. I thought, Someday it will be me, watching as a younger girl shines with the light no woman can keep. Then I met Walter's gaze. Gently he clasped Elisabeth's shoulders, and his eyes reassured me.

"A banquet waits below, and the cooks will riot if we let the food grow cold." Jean d'Aubry leaned forward, his hands clasped on the desk; and his voice, soft and carrying, reached no farther than this group of his friends. "My dear children, what shall I say to finish this story we have lived together? For we must end it; another story is beginning. We have given all we have of compassion, of forgiveness, of endurance, of understanding. Even God, so we are told, asks of us only the best our humanity can give. We have done our best, and lack only one conclusion. Claire and Richard, kneel."

We did so. I was shaking violently and longed to cry; Richard took my hand, clasping it firmly. The Count came to stand before us. "Richard, Claire, your lives have lain together from the moment you met. That bond has involved us all, has touched this whole town, has created the story all of us have lived. For that you owe us atonement, which you will now give. You will find the chapel furnished for a wedding. I decree that your futures lie together. Come, therefore; for the banquet is a wedding feast, and it is for you."

With His Grace preceding us, Richard led me back through

the crowd. I remember nothing of the vows that married us, except that, when I had spoken the words Father Paul told me to, His Grace produced a thick gold ring and Richard slipped it on my hand. Then people called for the country custom, and he took me in his arms and kissed me, and I could not stop weeping and no one rebuked me. Then Elisabeth hugged me and whispered in my ear, "Weep, then, and be joyful. I am, believe me."

The women took me aside to wash my face, and led me to the banquet where I sat between the Count and my husband.

At ten o'clock a procession formed, and they brought us to a low gray manor that had risen in what once was known as the Burnt Ground. Around it in the torchlight I saw a pillared colonnade, more Florentine than Norman, with pots hanging for flowers in summer and ridged slopes of red tile. In the foyer a staff of servants, men and women, greeted us smiling; and some of them I knew.

The Count said, "This house is yours. We will leave you. They have, I think, prepared baths and a place to rest. Thomas, attend your brother; and Claire, God forbid I should keep you from *your* attendants: your mother, Béatrice, and Antoine. Good night. Sow a child for us tonight, and sleep deeply, and wake refreshed."

He kissed us both and was gone, leaving us with a tiny group of friends. Together we drank a marriage cup, then were briskly separated: I to be stripped by the women and plunged into an herb-scented bath. As we passed through the rooms, I saw piece after piece of furniture from my cottage and from my room at home: my music cabinet; the writing table; the settle with red cushions; the millefiori bowl owned long ago by a girl named Fannia Redempta. But much of the furniture was new: Elisabeth and Béatrice, I gathered, had been embroidering the hangings for months; and they gently dried me with new towels. Somewhere, I supposed, Richard was being similarly dealt with by my father, Gérard, and Thomas and the other men.

And I had never before seen the bed to which they led me, in a room where frankincense perfumed the fire and hangings of fawn-colored cloth embroidered pink and green had been looped back out of the way. Snow was falling, but no wind penetrated the latticework of lead and glass. Elisabeth ran a warming pan over the sheets, and they laid me in the bed.

I was too tired for embarrassment by the time Richard—robed, it touched me to notice, in his cherished brown day gown—entered with his friends. "Damn it," he said mildly, "I *won't* climb in with her until we are quite *alone*."

"Very well, we're going." Gérard laughed. Walter's private salute to me was discreet and gentle. Thomas blew me a kiss; and then they left us.

"Do you feel," inquired Richard, "as though someone just struck you a blow on the head with a hammer?"

"Do *you*?" I asked, lazily insulted.

He grinned. "Well, something just happened very quickly. I gather there's been a conspiracy for months, if not for years. The whole town dismissed Thomas as leading candidate within six weeks."

I stretched out my hand to him; our fingers interlaced. Then he said softly, "My dear, let us hallow this house as it deserves. I know you are tired. You need do nothing but, with body and with heart, accept me."

He stripped naked, and I lay beneath him for an act more ritual than personal. Desire, I knew, would come, with rest and the wearing-off of shyness. Gently we descended into the darkness of the senses; and as my husband filled me with his child I saw suddenly, small and clear, the Standing Stones and a rose withering in fire.

And I knew I had always misunderstood the magic I had

worked, for the lovers' bodies are the rose and the fire. A bare simple act; yet the power that transfixed me was life forcing itself from the source of Life. Grain, crocus, apple tree, and woman's flesh—life forces itself into these vessels; and so all created things burst forth from Eternity.

# NOTE

I have made free with the age, appearance, and family circumstances of Luca della Robbia, but otherwise the history depicted in this book is generally accurate, except for the existence of the fictional comté de Saint-Aurèle. There seems increasing archaeological evidence that Basque fishermen had been working off the coasts of Newfoundland and Labrador for several centuries before Christopher Columbus "discovered" the New World (to which, in any case, Irish pioneers like Saint Brendan, as well as the Vikings, may have been making infrequent voyages since late Roman times). I have assumed, without evidence, that names applied to these places in John Cabot's time were already current informally among mariners a century earlier.

I wish to thank the staff of the William Lyon Mackenzie Homestead (Toronto, Canada) for allowing me to examine the nineteenth-century hand press in their possession, different though this is from the press Walter used. The quotation on page 216 comes from *Revelations of Divine Love* by the fifteenth-century English mystic Julian of Norwich; I am aware that my use involves a slight anachronism.

R.N.